What they're saying about
L. j. Charles novels...

A TOUCH OF BETRAYAL

"A combustible concoction of intrigue, betrayal, and murder. Everly's latest adventure has a 'touch' of everything.

~ *Andris Bear, author of the Deadly Sins series*

THE CALLING

"L.J. Charles has a distinctive voice, a fast paced plot and draws the reader into The Calling with both."

~*Teresa J. Reasor, author of The SEAL Team Heartbreaker Series*

"The sexual tension in The Calling is crazy good. Plus, it's a fun cat and mouse game as the hero and heroine try to outsmart each other."

~ *Adrienne Giordano, author of the Private Protector series*

L. j. Charles

Also by L. j. Charles

The Everly Gray Adventures

a Touch of Ice
a Touch of TNT
To Touch a Thief (An Everly Gray
Novella)
a Touch of the Past
a Touch of Betrayal

The Gemini women trilogy

the KNOWING
the CALLING
the HEALING

L. j. Charles

THE CALLING

The Gemini Women ~ Book 2 ~ Whitney's Story

L. j. Charles

White Hibiscus for Immortality

L. j. Charles

The Calling

Cover Design by Lucie Charles

Editor: Faith Freewoman

For more information: lucie.charles@ymail.com

Voices. Terrorists. Abducton.

And a partner who claims her heart.

The dead talk to her. Some might call it a gift. She's a retired police detective, and he's a by-the-book FBI agent with a leak in his department. Connected by a terrorist and a murder victim, they partner up—strictly business—until her Grandmamma is abducted and she's forced to deal with the truth about her past.

For my readers.

I appreciate each and every one of you.

L. j. Charles

Chapter 1

THE sultry song of the bayou played with my mind and left equal measures of icy panic and hot pleasure in its wake. I wove through shadows and listened to the plants breathe while I kept an eye on the Pitre brothers' cabin. The scent of moist earth, lush vegetation, and yesterday's garbage lingered in the air. My nose itched.

Snatches of the brothers' discussion drifted through the trees, and crackles of electricity flickered under my skin. Tonight was it. Finally. I'd gather the proof to incarcerate them for the rest of their natural lives. Now, if they blathered on just a bit longer—*crack*. The brothers' conversation stopped cold. Blast and damn. I glanced at the broken limb beneath my boot, and pressed the heels of my hands against trembling quads.

An eternity and the mother of all muscle cramps later, the Pitres got on with their chat. I eased from my crouch and edged closer to the window, vigilantly making sure I didn't step on any more buried branches.

Perfect. They were sniping at each other about whether they should move Avril's body, what they were going to do with the money they stole from beneath her floorboards, and the best place to relocate so as not to get caught. Their voices floated on the air and blended into the quiet of the night, but were distinct enough that I didn't miss a thing. Nor did my recorder.

I'd been chasing the brothers for eight nights running. Ever since Avril Dupré's very dead, very demanding voice took up residence in my head, I'd been slinking through the Bayou trying to gather proof of her murder. I couldn't argue with her ghostly contention that they'd buried her not ten feet from where I stood, especially since the brothers had angled an old wooden picnic table to cover the freshly turned earth. It was hardly a fitting gravestone for Avril Dupré—at least not according to her.

The conversation in the cabin was replaced with the sound of silverware scraping against tin plates. I backed away, paused briefly behind a renegade banana plant to tuck the recorder in my pocket, and then faded into the shadows.

Avril objected to my retreat. She wanted me to dig her up—right now—and move her remains to consecrated ground. And she intended to chatter in my head until I remedied the situation.

The amazing thing? This was absolutely normal. Had been for thirty days, seven hours, and sixteen minutes. I fidgeted with the new diamond stud in my left earlobe. Grandmamma Boulay's engagement diamond had been a thirty-fifth birthday gift to me, to celebrate the awakening of my calling.

She'd made a ceremony of adding a second piercing to my lobe, and then positioned the sparkling gemstone just so while she explained its meaning. It was a symbol of courage that intensified the qualities of the wearer. Both positive and negative. My guess was she'd stressed the last part to keep me on the right side of the Universe. What with murder victims prattling on about how they wanted me to rectify the circumstances surrounding their deaths, I suddenly had to fudge the law when necessary. A muscle ticked in my jaw. As a former police detective, it hadn't come easy, solving crimes without benefit of proper procedure.

I rubbed the faceted surface of the stone. Courage. That'd be good. I was learning to cope with the dead, hearing their voices, separating their thoughts from mine, and blocking their emotions, but not as successfully as I'd like.

Fifty feet from the Pitres' cabin, I stretched into a run, hoping it would quiet Avril down. It didn't help. I shook my head, and pressed my fingers into my temples, but her voice still raged in my brain. Grandmamma Boulay hadn't been able to offer any sage advice about how to silence the homicide victims once they started nattering. I was still miffed that her only suggestion had been, "Do what they say, child. Just do what they say."

I jumped in my car, eased it onto the road, and zipped toward Grandmamma's cabin. Avril nagged me every minute of the half-hour trip, so I turned up the radio—a futile attempt to drown her out.

Grandmamma waited on the porch, the click of her knitting needles keeping time with her rocking chair. The spicy smell of a traditional Monday supper, red beans and rice, chased away the musky scent of the Bayou and made my stomach rumble.

I parked, then took my time walking up the steps to bend and kiss her papery cheek. The peppery aroma of our dinner mixed with the sweetness of the baby powder that surrounded her in a fragrant halo. "The Pitre brothers killed Avril."

"Yes, 'n tha's what she's a' been sayin' to you."

"And continues to nag me incessantly about it." I dropped to the top step of the stoop, pulled the elastic out of my hair, and scrubbed it loose. "Tomorrow I'll post a note to the sheriff telling him where to dig, and send along the recording of the Pitres' conversation. They admitted they'd murdered her and stole money from under her floorboards."

"Avril will stop talking then, ché."

"If she's like the first three, yes, she will. Grandmamma?"

"What's a'troubling you, Whitney, child?"

"Why is *this* my calling? Why couldn't it be, oh, shape shifting? Something more interesting."

"Oooh, now. We haven't had a shape shifter in as far back as forever. Don't know as I've heard of one 'cept as legends. Why you askin' 'bout that, child?"

I rolled my shoulders to ease the muscles that cramped whenever I thought about my calling. "Nia mentioned something about it when we…last month."

The rocking chair came to an abrupt stop. "You told her? About the calling and this being your thirty-fifth birthday?"

"Absolutely not." I'd met and become sister-close to Nia during one of my Honolulu Police Department cases, but I hadn't shared my calling with anyone.

"It's the way of the women in our family and naught to be ashamed of."

"I'm not ashamed of it. It's just a damn nuisance."

Grandmamma tisked. "Language, child. Bein' schooled in England is'n no excuse."

"Um. No, it was rather a lot of other things, but not an excuse."

I stretched across the wooden porch to pat her bare feet, warm and rough with calluses. "Nia had enough to think about, what with saving her parents' lives and falling in love—"

"She's stayin' in your home with your friend, the attorney, yes?"

"Trace Coburn. They'll be at my place while they oversee

the work on his condo." A jolt of pain stabbed the back of my skull when Avril decided to give me a piece of her mind. I gave my head a hard shake, hoping to dislodge her.

"Avril's a'talking at you?"

"She is." The bottle of ibuprophen sitting on the bathroom counter called to me.

"Grandmamma?"

"Um-hmm. What is it, ché?"

"About my calling. Why isn't it clairvoyance like you, or seeing mathematical patterns like Mum?"

She tisked again. "So many questions tonight, child. Not always comfortable, clairvoyance. Oh, not like havin' dead people a'talking at you, but it's not an easy thing to see the future. 'Specially the bad things. Your mama had an easier time of it. Took to a'working for that government think tank like 'gators take to marshmallows."

Not much point chatting about my mum, as she'd left me with Grandmamma when I was fifteen—the year she turned thirty-five and became so adept at seeing numerical patterns, she could crack the most complex code. Mum did a lot of work in cryptography back then. It was anyone's guess what she was doing now.

Over the years I'd come to accept she didn't have a choice about leaving me. It was like that with the calling. We either embraced it completely, or went absolutely nutters trying to run from the responsibility that came with it. Insanity didn't appeal to me, which was why I planned to become accustomed to the voices in record time.

I stood, brushed off the seat of my jeans. "I'll post the letter tonight so the sheriff will get it first thing tomorrow. Then Avril will leave me alone so I can get some sleep."

Grandmamma's gaze was steady. "Anonymous, yes? Tha's

not the quickest way, child."

A chill snaked along my spine. "Quite. I could ring him up, but I'm not ready."

Arielle Boulay pushed herself up from the rocker. "Not'a gonna get any easier, accepting who you are."

I swallowed a sigh. "I know, but it's all a bit much. I scarcely get any peace from the newly dead, and if I tell anyone, word will get around, and then the living will start going on at me just like the dead. Wanting to know about their loved ones who've passed. Only it would be worse because I'd have to be polite to the living."

Grandmamma looped her arm through mine. I helped her up, handed her the basket of lush, purple yarn, and held the screen door while we made our way inside.

SUNLIGHT danced on the worn kitchen table in crazy, happy patterns that aggravated the throbbing in my temples. Grandmamma slid a steaming mug of café au lait in front of me.

I rested my forehead on the edge of the table. "Blast and damn." I cut a quick glance at Grandmamma through the space between the tabletop and the underside of my arm. "I'm claiming temporary insanity and lack of sleep," I muttered. Then I lifted my head, stuck my nose over the mug, and inhaled all the way to my toes. The rich scent, heavy with chicory, wove through my throbbing temples, and calmed the pounding. I took a sip, paused for the bite of herb and the mellow flavor of the cream to blend on my tongue before I swallowed, and then waited for the caffeine to shock my nerve endings awake. Bayou coffee, a blessing when I was over the edge of sanity and well into a bottle of ibuprophen.

Grandmamma's hand curled around my shoulder. "More

voices?"

I nodded. "A new death. Someone I knew about. Through work, actually."

She met my gaze, her warm, caramel eyes brimming with too much knowledge. There was no mistaking what *that* look meant.

"You had a vision about her, then?" I asked.

"Yes, 'n you'll be a'leaving me today, ché."

I dipped my chin in acknowledgement, and then blew across the mug to cool the fragrant brew. "In a few hours. What did you see?"

She settled into a chair and cradled a mug between her hands. "Jus' that you'd be a'leaving and the man you're a'going to see—"

"Evans. Blake Evans. He's an FBI agent on temporary assignment at the Minneapolis airport." I dropped my forehead back to the table when his image popped into my mind, clear enough to send a rush of heat twisting in my chest. There couldn't be a man in my life. Not with the demands of the calling. And especially not Blake Evans. It had only been the one kiss. It shouldn't have affected me at all.

"Whitney, child?"

Damn, I'd been quiet too long. I sat up and took a quick swallow of the café.

Arielle Boulay's mouth curled into a mischievous grin. "He's, what do they say nowadays? A hunk?"

I sputtered. "Not so."

The grin became a belly laugh. "Ah, yes'n he is. What is it you young'uns say? A bad boy? In my time we girls would'a been a'buzzing all 'round him."

Goosebumps prickled against my light cotton shirt. Bad.

"Where did that come from? Why did you call him a bad boy?"

"Why, child. I can see him plain as day. My eyesight may be a'going, but my *sight* is just fiiine." She'd closed her eyes when she drawled out the *fine*, and a blissful smile settled on her face.

I rapped her hand. Harder than I should. "He's too—"

One of Grandmamma's eyes snapped open and I knew I'd been had. "Perfect is the word you're a'looking for, child."

I shivered. "Nia called him bad. Threw me to hear you say the same. And I don't fancy him."

"Un-huh, an' you can keep a'telling yourself that."

I took another sip of café. It was a waste of time to argue with the woman because she *always* won. Likely a manifestation of her clairvoyance.

"Time has a way of changin' things. There's a tangle 'round what this new woman is a'telling you 'bout her death. Layers an' secrets an' lies."

I ran my tongue over my lips, savoring the lingering nip of chicory. "This new victim, she disappeared a while ago. It was in all the papers. Both here and in the UK. She's from Hampshire. Was from Hampshire."

Grandmamma reached for the pot and topped our mugs off, then added a stream of warm cream. "They still seem alive, telling you their stories like they do, yes?"

"Quite." I scooted my chair back, stood. "I'd best get packed, as the flight leaves just after noon."

"Will you be a'going to visit your father, then?"

The café spun in my stomach and threatened the back of my throat. "No. It's time for me to go home. I've been away from Honolulu for too long."

Genteel. Eloquent. Demanding. There were no words to

accurately describe Arielle Boulay's eyebrows when they asked a question—and demanded an answer.

"I'll give Agent Evans a report on what happened to her and let him deal with it. He's not one to understand the calling, so I'll just drop my report on his desk while I'm between flights. Mala Sen," I said, bending to give Grandmamma a hug. "The dead woman's name is Mala Sen."

"Uh-huh. But tha's not what's important, child. All the time you've spent here a'talking to me, always with the accent of your father. Not once slippin' into the rhythm of the Bayou. Now tha's important. Closer to bein' a Brit than you'd like, I'm thinkin'."

"No. Definitely not. It's because Cajun words flow with mysticism, and my calling is eerie enough, what with the dead crowding into my head. In my father's world there's no room for magic, no room for anything but crisp, clean logic. It's safe. Predictable."

I scooped my mug off the table and headed for the bedroom before Grandmamma could say another word. I wasn't running from her. I just had to finish packing, and make some notes on Mala's abduction and murder to drop on Agent Evans's desk and run…before the lure of his perfect body, lopsided, sexy smile, and warm brown eyes made my hormones spin.

In spite of what Grandmamma thought, a lot of the Cajun had seeped into my bones, and I needed to pull the British half of my ancestry firmly into its proper place. More than a month in the Bayou had softened my stiff upper lip, to say nothing of the mess the dead had made of my otherwise orderly mind. It had nothing to do with my father. Not a single, blasted thing.

By the time I finished packing, Grandmamma was settled on the porch, knitting needles flying. A ray of sunlight caught the skeins of gold lamé yarn in her basket. "I'm off." I reached down and ran my fingers over the spun gold. "This is really quite lovely. For something special?"

Delight played along Arielle Boulay's lips and sparkled in her eyes. "For your weddin', child. For your weddin'."

Chapter 2

THE plane touched down in Minneapolis with a series of bounces that sent the knots in my stomach into an unfortunate tangle. I wasn't at all fond of flying. Not only had I inherited the long, lean Boulay body, a frame that doesn't fit well in commercial airline seats, but floating above the ground simply wasn't my thing. And there were two more bloody legs to go.

I stretched out the kinks, shouldered my backpack, and licked the dry from my lips. I could almost taste Blake Evan's spicy, dark flavor. The gobsmack of a kiss we'd shared after our last *friendly* dinner with Trace Coburn had left me lusting. Nia would say I had the hots for Evans, and she'd be right. But the timing was off. Had been since before The Kiss.

Back then, my thirty-fifth birthday loomed, and combined with the uncertainty of what my calling would be…well, I'd never been a one-night-stand woman. Honesty forced me to acknowledge the pleasurable anticipation that zipped through me when I pictured his broad-shouldered, slim-hipped body. The one with the sexiest denim-clad ass I'd ever had the good fortune to fondle. And those eighty-percent-pure cacao eyes? They'd haunted me for three years, since the day Coburn introduced us.

The sudden bite of tears burned my eyes. I sucked in a

breath and tamped down the sadness. Not allowed, not now. Relationships had to be a thing of the past. What moderately sane man would accept a woman who listened to the dead, and worse, did their bidding? Not Special Agent Blake Evans. I'd understood and agreed with his by-the-book approach to law enforcement—before the calling. Now that the dead told me exactly who'd killed them and how, I had no choice but to develop a broader view of justice.

I stopped at a kiosk for a couple bottles of water, gulped one down, and then did another tongue-across-lips taste test. No way around it, I could still taste him. Entertaining fantasies about Special Agent Evans was one thing, acting on them was something else entirely.

I had a long think on it as I strode toward his office. Rather than just drop the file and run, why waste our delicious chemistry? Why not use it to my advantage and get him to help me find Mala's killer? Now *that* was a plan. A crazy, possibly lust-induced plan. One more kiss—a memory to warm cold nights. Whyever not? I could call it a late birthday present.

And then I'd put him out of my mind, and focus on more important things. He would do the same. Had done on several occasions when he'd shared dinner with me and Coburn, discussing his thinly-disguised cases to get our take, to help him wrap up loose ends when he couldn't find the right string to pull. Other than our single kiss, Evans hadn't indicated he wanted a...anything from me. He'd used our friendship to his advantage. Now it was my turn.

His office loomed in front of me. I tossed my empty water bottle in a recycle container, and drew in a fortifying breath. A mistake. Along with hearing the dead, I'd been noticing a change in my other senses. Vision, taste, smell, and touch had become a shade keener. I fiddled with the diamond stud in my earlobe. *Intensifies the qualities of the wearer.* Perhaps Grandmamma was right, and that was why I picked up the heady scent of Evans that clung to the air outside his office.

My heart responded with an unwelcome lurch. The new me, the one with both a calling *and* a plan, shouldn't indulge in heart-lurching moments.

I inhaled his scent again, and then backed away as heat flooded my body, settled low in my torso. Damn and blast. I should just run. Forget the whole thing.

Mala objected with sharp stab of pain to my temples.

No running away, then. And no denying I wanted to explore every possible nuance of touching Blake Evans. Breathe in. Breathe out. I adjusted to the scent of him, and since his door was open in irresistible invitation, scooted close enough to prop myself against the wooden frame.

"Whitney Boulay. Get lost, did you?" His gaze fastened on my feet, and then his mouth curved into a lazy smile as his eyes caressed my body with tangible interest. He leaned back in his chair, locked his fingers behind his head, and met my cool stare. Well, what I hoped was a cool stare.

"Absolutely. No other reason for me to be in Minneapolis, now is there?" My traitorous libido wouldn't let go of the memory of our last encounter, and of its own volition my tongue slipped out to wet my lips. I dropped my shoulder, let the backpack slide to the floor, and leaned toward him.

It took two seconds and two strides for him to shove the office door closed and cradle my face in his gentle hands. The warmth of his palm against my cheek both soothed and excited every damn nerve ending in me. It took forever before his lips touched mine—a brush of skin, the taste of mint, and heat. Oh damn, the heat.

I ran my hands across his shoulders, the crisp cotton of his shirt cool to my touch. That wouldn't do. I hooked my leg around his delectable backside—a comfortable fit, as Evans was only a scant inch taller. I planned to make our final kiss the best damn lip-lock possible. His spicy essence flooded my senses, and pressure built in all the appropriate places. I rubbed against him, nipped at the fullness of his lower lip, and then explored his mouth with delicate persistence. I wanted to remember every detail, every possible sensation. He trembled. His need a mirror image of my own.

"Incredible legs." His palm skimmed over my hip, down the length of my leg and back. Big, slow hands. My breath caught. His fingers found, and toyed with, the seam that ran along my inner thigh. Need exploded in my core.

"And this...freckle makes me crazy." The tip of his tongue touched the edge of my lip, caressed it. I pressed my back tightly against the wall to keep from slipping to the floor. Blake Evans didn't devour my mouth. He cherished the curve of my lips, the fullness of my sensitized skin, and I forgot to breathe.

My head dropped back. He found the vulnerable spot under my ear, the one with a direct connection to my center. And then his tongue circled the diamond stud in my ear.

Fear rocked through me.

"Nice," he whispered. "New. Not regulation dress code."

He backed away, confusion clouding his eyes. Then he ran the pad of his thumb over my lower lip. "Fascinating mouth. I can't keep from touching it, even when I know it'll get me nothing but a quick trip to hell."

Hell. Oh, yes. My calling. I found some words. "Comparing me to hell, are you?"

"Fire and ice, Whitney. A hellish combination in a woman."

The phone on his belt buzzed, shattering the sensual cloud that had obliterated my common sense. I unwrapped my leg from his hip, planted both feet on the floor, and fought to control my surging hormones. He shook his head and took a full step back to check the number on the phone, then shut it off and leaned toward me.

Reality cashed through my libidinous haze. No relationships. Not now. Not ever. I planted my palm against his chest. "We could do with less touchy-feely and more chatting—about your time in the Special Jurisdiction Unit, actually."

His jaw tightened.

Cold crept into my bones, chasing the heat away. I absolutely had to stop touching him before I suggested a tumble on his government-issue desk. Agent Evans would never accept the dead taking over my life, a nonnegotiable requirement before any tumbling could take place. I gave it a firm mental shrug. But damn if the loneliness didn't creep back in.

Evans stepped back, leaned against his desk, and then folded his arms tight across his chest. "What about it?"

Anxiety snaked along my nerves. It wouldn't do to let him catch even a whiff of it, so I went on the offense, hooked my thumbs in the front pockets of my jeans, and rolled my shoulders back. "Rumor has it you chose to leave. Something went awry with pirates and a cruise ship."

His mouth flattened. "Mala Sen. Twenty-two. Her first job out of college. Went missing. My watch."

Flawless skin stretched taut across his angular cheekbones, a pale contrast to his double-espresso-with-a-single-shot-of-cream complexion. I recognized the trace of Native American in his features, because when I looked in the mirror I saw the same bone structure. Only difference—my skin was single espresso with double cream. Made sense, as Grandmamma Boulay's family came up heavy on the Native American component of Cajun ancestry.

"You profiled the scene."

He nodded.

"It's been almost a year with no trace of her. What's your

take on it?" My voice held firm.

"Classified. It's an open case and I've been out of it for nine months." He scratched his nose, a sure sign he was lying.

Blake Evans knew about tells, and it made no sense that he'd make the mistake of showing one. Later. I'd figure it out later. "Wrong. You've been working it. Under the cover of playing airport security liaison."

He sat on his desk, draping a leg over the edge, and then flicked the phantom itch on his nose for the second time. "Your imagination is on overtime, Whitney. I requested this assignment. Needed a break."

"Absolutely. I heard Amar Barat is the responsible party. Nice work on the profile."

His fingers did an almost imperceptible rat-a-tat on the desk. "Coburn been talking?"

"Not this time. Your best bud has been occupied with falling in love, so there hasn't been much time for lengthy gossip sessions."

He shrugged. "Yeah, I hear about Nia all the damn time."

"And? Barat?"

"Okay, yeah. I profiled Barat. Ugly bastard."

I inhaled a slow breath, let it curl through my mind and settle across my shoulders. Evans was one of the best in the business, and I had his complete attention. "I hear the cruise ship escaped, outran the pirate ship."

He pushed off the desk, circled it, dropped into his chair, and opened a file.

I'd been dismissed.

Not bloody likely. I took his place, propping my butt on the desk. Warmth from his body seeped through my jeans. "Mala Sen went missing at their next port of call."

He flipped the folder closed with a snap of his index finger. "What do you want, Boulay?"

I leaned forward, flattened my palms on the folder. "I want to know how you're going to stop him, what you've been doing to track him since you holed up in this office, and when you're going to step out from behind that desk and get back into the thick of it."

"You're way off base." A low growl threaded his words.

"Nope, I'm not. The evil in Barat contaminates and destroys. It's not just weapons and cargo he's after. He's stealing people, selling them."

Evans slammed back from his desk, the chair leaving a dent where it bounced off the wall. "Mala Sen is British. Pirates, especially Barat, target third world populations where the paperwork on a missing female falls into a black hole, forgotten. Besides, his country of choice is India, not Britain."

A husky feminine voice sounded from outside the door, followed by a staccato rap. "Agent Evans?" she asked, poking her curly blonde head into the office. "Everything all right? I heard loud voices and a crash."

He shooed the young woman away with a flick of his wrist, but not before a glimmer of macho interest sparked in his eyes. "Fine. No problem."

An irritated huff strained the buttons of her dark blue shirt with what had to be surgically enhanced feminine assets. She scurried off, but not before sizing me up, her claim on Evans unmistakable.

I don't sing. Not ever. But I went for it. "She likes you. She really likes you."

He leveled a glare at the door, then swung to face me.

Best to nip off the singing, then. "True, India is Barat's native country, but he has strong ties to the UK. It's a nasty way to treat your allies."

"There's a task force in place, but from the way you blew in here, I figure you already know that." Evans jabbed his index finger at me. "It's their call," jabbed his thumb at his chest. "I'm out of it," If you have questions, go through channels."

I swung my leg just enough to call attention to my ass. His eyes caught the movement, and I suppressed a grin when his pupils dilated. "Absolutely brilliant plan. I'm sure they'll be pleased to fax the particulars to me ASAP. This is *personal,* Evans. I'm here *because* it's personal."

He shook his head. "Can't be. It's way out of your ballpark. The Honolulu PD doesn't touch pirating. We're talking off the coast of Arabia and Somalia. The other side of goddamn Africa, Whitney, not Hawaii."

I nodded. Best to be agreeable whenever possible. "I resigned almost three months ago."

He stilled. "Want to run that by me again?"

I lifted my shoulders in a delicate shrug, the plan being to accentuate my feminine attributes. Hey, if it worked for Miss TSA, why not? "It was time," I said.

He turned away from me, then abruptly spun back. "No, it wasn't goddamn time. What the hell is going on here?"

"Nia needed my support, what with falling in love and being a homicide witness. As an HPD detective, I had a conflict of interest."

His eyes sparked, and he flapped his hand in an impatient come-on gesture.

"Then I went to the Bayou to spend some time with Grandmamma Boulay."

"Huh-uh. Nope. Not buying it. You don't quit your career mid-stream to babysit and visit family."

"You did."

He leaned into my space. "What the hell?"

I opened my arms to encompass his office, and raised my eyebrows.

He pointed at the floor. "Working here. This *is* my job."

"*This* is a unconscionable waste of a talented profiler." I hopped off his desk, propped my hands on my hips.

He nodded toward the door. "I'm sure you can find someone else to chew up and spit out."

I waited until he dropped back in his chair, opened the file, and pretended to read.

"Mala Sen is dead."

Chapter 3

BLAKE Evans placed his palms flat on his desk and stood, his actions deliberate. "Mala Sen is *not* dead."

The air crackled. I backed against the wall, pressed tightly into it, and sucked in a grounding breath. I expected anger, maybe an outburst of entertaining language, anything but the wild, crazy static arcing between us.

The vehemence of his tone triggered Mala's anger, and her yammering filled my head, turning into a full-blown tirade. "*How dare he not believe me? I'm stuck here. My body covered in dirt. Bugs crawling all over, feasting on me. What does he mean I'm not dead? Of course I am. So, I'm not actually in my body anymore. A mere detail. What does he know about it? Standing there all alive and handsome as sin, he doesn't know—*"

I blocked her tirade as best I could, managed to smother it some, but the pain hung on. I slid down the wall, planted my ass on the floor, and rummaged in my backpack for a bottle of ibuprophen, all the while sending a fervent prayer into the ethers to control the headache, at least until I could escape Evans's office.

He leaned over his desk. "What the hell is wrong with you, Boulay?"

I dug my fingers into my temples, and tossed him a brief

glance before closing my eyes to shut out the light. "Not a thing. Why do you ask?" I grappled with the lid on the plastic bottle with my eyes closed, an unsuccessful endeavor. "Damn all childproof lids to perdition."

He rolled his chair back, then his shoes slapped against the tile, the sounds a salt-in-wound accompaniment to Mala's tirade. I eased my left eye open a smidge to see if he was holding a gun on me. Evans in a snit is not something to mess with.

He stood in front of me, grim plastered on his face. "You're sick. Brain tumor? Some kind of breakdown? Damn it, Boulay, what the hell is wrong with you?"

I blindly pushed the bottle toward him. "I could do with some help, if you don't mind."

He took it from my hand, his fingers barely touching me, like he was afraid I would break. Irritation itched under my skin. I could only handle one irate person at a time, so I focused on Mala's tirade. "*It's* my *murder. Tell him to do it my way. I want Barat killed, and there's no time to waste. I'm rotting in my grave. Tell him that. Tell him about the bugs and my family. They need to give me a proper funeral. I was only twenty-two. Much too young to die. He needs to get his ass moving. Why aren't you telling him?*"

"How many do you want?" The smooth cadence of Evans's words clashed with Mala's brittle rant.

I held out one hand, and rummaged in my backpack for a bottle of water with the other. "Three."

"Overdosing on this stuff isn't good for your kidneys." He sounded unsure.

My eyes popped open. Bright light. I squeezed my lids shut against the streaks of pain shot through my brain. The groan hanging in the air must have come from me. Embarrassing. I popped the tablets and swallowed half a bottle of water. "The pain isn't good for my psyche, so my kidneys will have to cope," I said.

"Wanna tell me what in the goddamn hell is going on?"

I used my index finger to pry my eyelid open a few millimeters, and noted Evans's expression: a volatile mix of anger, confusion and impatience. And his fingers were doing a rat-a-tat on the weapon in his shoulder holster. Not that he'd use it on me. Surely not.

I braced myself, and then did a mental scream in Mala's direction to shut up and listen. The quiet in my mind was sudden and complete. Well, damn. It was the first time *that* had worked. The contrast between Mala screaming and total quiet left me wobbly, so I downed the rest of the water and took a few deep breaths.

Evans gave my foot a light kick. A kind of guy hug, maybe. "Any time, Boulay."

"You'd best sit down."

He crossed his arms and angled his chin in my direction, all manly and tough. And then dropped the pose, forced out a sigh, and offered his hand to help me up.

It messed with my pride, but I took it, gathered my legs under me, and stood. "There's a thing with the women in the Boulay family."

"A thing? You're talking insanity, right?"

I started to shake my head, thought better of it. "Some would say so, yes. It happens on our thirty-fifth birthday."

"Some sort of Cajun ritual to keep from aging? I never pictured you as the type to fall for that crap." He eyed me up and down, and his lips twitched in something close to a smile.

I braced myself against the wall. "Aging isn't our issue, no. We come into our...heritage."

He dropped into the chair behind his desk and leaned

back. "Uh-huh. Heritage. You're talking some kind of crazy behavior, right? It happens in the best of families. My paternal grandmother used to do some sort of chanting, and herbal thing when one of us got sick. Didn't cause any harm, and she was normal the rest of the time. Died peacefully a few years back. In her sleep."

"Normal the rest of the time? Quite straightforward, is it?" Anger sizzled, and I pushed away from the wall. "There's nothing wrong with me. The calling is a gift. A privilege."

He chuckled. "Um-hmm. Right. A calling. Most women who have a calling join the convent." He paused. Time stretched.

"Not funny. Not funny at all."

"So you're telling me…no, nope, not buying it. No way are you doing the religious, cloistered, habit-wearing deal. Doesn't compute, and it sure as hell isn't why you're in my office acting—"

I gave him my best innocent smile.

His shook his head. "Look, Whitney, why don't you grab a cup of tea? Better yet, I'll treat, and then walk you to your gate."

"How about you stop talking at me and listen?"

He ran his hand over his mouth and nodded, but his eyes shot sparks.

I took a breath to settle my anger. No point in sounding like the lunatic he'd labeled me. "The women in my family receive the calling on their thirty-fifth birthday. It's different for each of us, a heightened sense of one sort or another, like ESP. Arielle Boulay is clairvoyant. My mum has an unusual affinity for numbers, and I—"

"Yes, Whitney, what about you?" Evans's upper lip curled slightly.

This was worse than I'd imagined. "Dead people talk to me."

He pushed back his chair, doubled over, and snorted a bark of laughter. The sound slammed into my stomach with the precision of a sledgehammer. I dropped my backpack on his desk. "Splendid. No reason to tell you about Mala Sen, then, is there?"

He swiped at the tears rolling down his face, and struggled to contain the snorts. "You almost got me on that one. What'd you do? Watch a rerun of that movie last night and decide to screw with me? What was it called? *Sixth Sense* or something like that, right?"

I glared. Speechless.

He composed himself. "So, what about Mala Sen? I'd know if something changed with her status."

"Thought you were off the case. Didn't know anything about it."

He shrugged, a fluid movement that warred with the tension around his eyes. "I hear things."

"Um-hmm, quite. No need to bother with me, then." Mala started to nag at me again, and a shaft of lightning-swift pain shot into my temples. I offered her silent reassurance while I sorted through the notes I'd prepared for Evans. I didn't want to help the arrogant bastard, but I had to give him the information about Amar Barat.

He snagged the papers from my fingers. "Whatcha got?"

"Nothing you'd be interested in. A bit of info on when, where, and how Mala was killed." I zipped my backpack and shouldered it.

He rustled through the papers, pinned me with a look. "Goddamn it, Boulay. Where'd you get this?"

"Mala told me."

"Sure she did." He leaned back, rested his ankle on his knee. "Level with me. And don't feed me any of that paranormal crap."

I backed toward the door, and gave him a perfect Valley Girl finger wave. "I'm off. Plane to catch."

He bolted from his chair. "I'll—"

"Threats, Evans?" I eased out the door, turned, and winked. "Nice kiss."

A few feet from his office the pain in my chest crawled into my throat and latched on. Unexpected. I thought I'd prepared for this. Knew it would be messy trying to tell Blake Evans about the calling, and his response wasn't that far from my prediction. But I didn't account for the emotional hit. Somewhere along the way I'd nourished the hope he'd understand, accept my gift and…me.

I shook off the melancholy. I didn't fancy him. Couldn't. Wouldn't.

Chapter 4

IT was good to be home. I shook out my ponytail on the way to the passenger pickup area, and the soft Hawaiian breeze ruffled through my hair. Nia's jaw dropped when she spotted me. She elbowed Coburn hard enough to make her dark, spiral curls bounce, and then she pulled me into a hug, and dropped a lei around my neck. The heady scent of tuberose filled the air. I instinctively buried my nose in the fragrant flowers.

Nia grabbed my arm. "Stop with the sniffing and pay attention. Your hair's down. What's wrong with you? You're different. What happened to you in the Bayou? You *always* have a slicked-back ponytail. Well, except for that time on the beach—"

"Looking loose." Coburn interrupted Nia, and gave my hair a tug. "Lost some of the Brit in the Bayou, did you?"

I fingered the hair band in my pocket. "Definitely not. I'm quite as British as I've always been. Actually."

He nodded toward baggage claim, his eyes sparkling. "Luggage?"

I shook my head. Nia elbowed him again. "Remember that box we got a few days ago? That was her luggage."

"Um-hmm. Weighed a ton." He wrapped his arms around

Nia, pulling her close. "You don't stop with the elbow, I'm gonna cuff you."

Nia grinned and planted a noisy, sloppy kiss against his neck. "Cuffs are at home, safe on the nightstand."

I glared. "A bit too much information."

Coburn's face turned an interesting shade of red. He hid behind Nia, turning her to face me. "The cuffs were her idea."

An unfamiliar pain knotted in my chest. Could that last kiss with Evans have left me lonely? No, impossible. I'd conquered loneliness by my eighth birthday. "Splendid. And when, exactly, are you leaving for North Dakota?"

Nia tilted her head to look at Coburn. "'Bout a week, I think."

We ambled toward the car, settled in, and were immersed in the traffic flow within minutes. Nia leaned over the front seat to face me. "So, want to tell me about the earring?"

Damn, but she didn't miss a thing. "A birthday gift from Grandmamma. Her engagement diamond."

"Um-hmm. Chloe called. Said stuff."

Chloe Channing, the third soul sister in our Gemini triad, had suffered severe burns when her herb shop burned to the ground a few months earlier. She was now counted among those who'd had a near-death experience. Twice. I'd visited her during my layover en route to Honolulu.

"She told you about Dominic Justice, did she?" I asked.

Coburn met my gaze in the rearview mirror, his eyes reflecting concern. "I hear he's a world-class thief. Works for the highest bidder. Chloe's not serious about him, is she?"

"She is. Fancies herself in love, and thinks that blasted Romany can be trusted." I shivered. "I convinced her to return to Honolulu. Soon."

Nia wrinkled her nose. "Her version: you badgered her until she agreed."

"Not nearly enough, as she's still in Seattle, supposedly winding things up with her doctors, and spending a few quality days with her sister." I adjusted my seat belt to keep it from crushing the lei.

Quiet filled the front seat. Too much quiet, considering Nia's normal talkative and bubbly personality. "Is there something you're not telling me, then?"

Nia shook her head, sending her curls into a tumble. Coburn eyed me in the rear-view mirror, and then his gaze skittered away. Guilty as sin. Both of them.

When we pulled into my driveway, Coburn cleared his throat. "Um, we're going out for a while. Let you get settled in."

A yawn sandbagged me as I climbed out of the car. "Quite. I'll be making an early night of it."

Nia was fiddling with her skirt, pleating the fabric. "See you later...uh, tomorrow probably. We have dinner reservations tonight..." Her voice trailed off.

I nodded and barely managed to slam the car door before Coburn peeled out of the driveway. I chalked it up to the handcuffs on the nightstand, and with some relief strolled up the walkway to my house. My only stop was to pluck a pink hibiscus blossom and tuck it behind my ear. It was good to be home. Alone. Nia and Coburn were absolutely correct. I did need time to think, relax, and sleep.

I unlocked the door, pushed it open, dropped my backpack on the kitchen table, and then rummaged for the bag of trail mix I'd been snacking on during the flight.

A movement caught the edge of my vision. I whirled, heart in my throat.

Blake Evans stood in the dining room.

My dining room.

Chills rooted me to the floor. "Made use of some connections, did you Evans? Called in a favor, grabbed a government flight to beat me here?"

He took a step toward me. Two more. Slow. Measured. Totally ignoring my anger, he slid the hibiscus from behind my ear. "Nice. You belong in Hawaii. Lush. Tropical. Not an English rose at all." His voice was soft, seductive…and irritating.

I swung my leg out, caught him behind the knee, and dropped him to the floor. Not hard, a soft, barely-there drop because I snagged his shoulder in time to break the fall. An attention-getter with no permanent damage intended.

Immediate regret slammed into me. Would I ever outgrow the need to fight my way out of overwhelming emotions?

"Not an English rose. No." I backed away. "More of a Cajun street fighter."

He stood, tossed the mangled blossom on the kitchen table, and stuffed his hands in his back pockets. The movement strained the fabric of his slacks, outlining the interesting bits of his masculinity. My gaze moved up to catch the *gotcha* smile playing in his eyes.

Score one for him.

"Blasted male ego," I muttered. We were so damn much alike, Blake and me.

His lips curved into a blatant grin.

The only thing for it was to change the subject. "I can see Coburn letting you stay in my house because he's a hopeless romantic. But Nia? She still hasn't forgiven you for that rather unpleasant incident with her pink knickers."

The muscles in his jaw twitched. Not so calm, then. I ran my finger along the chiseled edge, and was rewarded with a most excellent glare.

Score one for me.

"Trace Coburn and I have a history, one you're well aware of. You knew he'd make me welcome, his home or not."

I turned my back on Evans and made tracks for the teakettle. Time to balance my Cajun heat with some British cool. No point arguing with the power of male bonding. Like Nia, Chloe, and me, the two of them were...soul brothers. Was there such a thing? Probably not. It was more a Special Air Service or Navy SEAL sort of thing. I filled the kettle and set it on the burner. "And exactly why are you here?"

"Mala Sen."

I scooped a measure of orchid oolong tea into a pot and turned to place a couple mugs on the table. "You know she's dead, then?"

He curled his hands around the back of a kitchen chair, squeezed until his knuckles turned pale, and then splayed his fingers. "Missing. Not dead. Her location was known, but she hasn't been spotted for two days."

Mala started a tap dance in my head. I rushed to fill the silence before she started to chatter. "Mala would like you to know that she's been dead for a bit longer than two days. She was there. Attended her own death, so to speak."

"Uh-huh. What say we focus on her current location?"

I shot him a look, and heat pooled deep in my body. I breathed in his clean, salty scent. Hormones. Damn and blast. I did a quick mental shake to get my mind back on track. "The location of her grave was in my notes."

"An estate in Hampshire, England isn't what I'd call precise."

"All the same, it is a place. She's buried there. Has been for months." I poured boiling water into the teapot, covered it with a cozy, and set it on the table.

Evans slammed his chair back, then straddled the seat. "An address, Whitney. Give me an address."

I checked the cupboard for biscuits, and located an unopened bag of double chocolate crème Oreos. Should sweeten Evans up some. I considered putting them on a plate, then tossed the bag on the table. "If I had an address I'd've included it, wouldn't I?" But there was something nagging at me.

Ahimsa jumped down from the refrigerator with feline grace, and landed next to me with a thud. He'd put on a good bit of weight under Nia's care. I scooped him onto my lap. "And what have you been up to? Eating extra treats? Dusting the refrigerator with your tail?"

"You're talking to a cat, Whitney."

"Absolutely. Chloe's cat. Not the same as an ordinary cat at all."

"Uh-huh. Back to Mala Sen's address. *Would* you have included it? Or are you jerking me around?"

I sat, tore open the Oreos, and shoved the bag toward him. "Coburn's been after the grocery shopping."

"Yeah, I figured. We always had a case of these around the apartment during exam week in law school. Never got the ones with chocolate filling, though." He grabbed one, split it apart.

"I don't know anything else. The calling doesn't work that way for me. Not yet, anyway, or maybe I just haven't got the hang of asking dead people questions."

"Uh-huh."

"The dead aren't…um, they talk *at* me more than chat *with* me, actually." I waved my hand back and forth between us.

"It's not like this."

Ahimsa grabbed my hand between his paws, and licked my fingers. "Hasn't anyone been playing with you?" I rubbed my cheek against his face.

"Cats don't speak English. Not even Chloe's cat." Evans's...tongue shot out, licking the chocolate filling from the Oreo. Spirals of heat coursed through me, doubling my heart rate. I reached across the table, yanked the biscuit out of his hand, and nipped off a bite. "Enough with the licking."

He leaned back, winked. "You like my tongue."

A sheen of sweat whispered over my skin. I wanted—needed—to plant my mouth on his and explore the possibilities of exactly what his tongue could do.

I set Ahimsa on the floor, wrapped my hands around the warm mug, and inhaled the scent of orchid oolong. The light, flowery fragrance filled my nostrils, and I considered offering Evans another Oreo, decided against it. Grandmamma had warned me it was best not to taunt a man's fire.

"All the same, I'll be staying on my side of the table." I popped the rest of the biscuit in my mouth. It was rich with the sweetness of chocolate and a touch of Blake.

He reached across the space between us, and brushed his thumb over my bottom lip. "Just a bit of chocolate...right there."

Heat ripped through me. He licked the chocolate off his thumb. I crossed my legs to stop the throbbing at the apex of my thighs. It had been too long since I'd invited a man to my bed. Two bracing gulps of tea later, I managed some words. "Let's get back on topic then, shall we?"

With a grin, Evans snagged another Oreo from the bag.

"I'm not comfortable with all the bits and bothers of my gift." Exhaustion dragged my shoulders down. Not the message I wanted to send, but I didn't have the energy to put on a facade. "Don't know exactly how to use it as yet."

"Not a problem. I'm looking for Detective Whitney Boulay, not some wacky Cajun. I figure you saw something, talked with someone, read something. Whatever. It got stirred up in your head and you believe Mala Sen is talking to you. Fine with me, long as I can access that information."

Talented tongue or not, the man was an absolute idiot. "I've told you everything Mala said." I shoved my chair back, stomped to the kitchen door, and flung it open. "Out."

He shook his head. "No can do. The boss man says I'm your new best friend."

I slammed the door. Ahimsa hissed. "Run that by me again."

"The Special Agent In Charge says I'm supposed to keep my baby browns on you until we locate Sen."

Was that a smirk twitching at the corner of his mouth? I fought the urge to break his nose. Preferably with my foot. Unfortunately, neither of us would come out the winner in that sort of tussle. He wasn't going to budge on this. Not with direct orders to keep me under surveillance. "I'll have a go at it. But getting Mala to do anything is—"

"You do that. Meanwhile, we'll be heading for Hampshire tomorrow."

Panic clawed at me. "No, *we* absolutely will not be going to Hampshire. No one could possibly have spotted Mala, not wandering about. She's buried. In the ground. Without a marker. No reason to go digging up bodies, especially as we don't have an exact location." Or did we? That awful nagging feeling chewed at me every time a Hampshire estate was mentioned.

Evans grabbed another Oreo, slid it apart. "It's not looking good for you, having this info about Sen. Bogus or not. You'll want to clear up any confusion about your part in her disappearance."

I topped off my tea. "All the same, I won't be going to the UK." It looked bad. I knew that when I wrote the report, and wouldn't have done it if I could've stopped the headaches any other way. Mala had a way with her ranting.

Evans flicked the entire top of the Oreo into his mouth, then tried to talk around it. "Iss urrr ome."

"Was. Hasn't been for a long time."

He swallowed. "It'll give you a chance to catch up on things with Lord Chilton."

"He'll be off somewhere. Always is." Stress had tightened my throat, but my voice sounded solid. Not a shaky syllable to be found.

"He's in residence."

I lifted a shoulder, let it drop.

"Sen was last seen on your father's estate."

Chapter 5

SILENCE rattled through the kitchen, and a spike of panic chased up my spine. I oh-so-carefully set my mug on the table, and made a triangle with my fingers around the mug. A balanced geometric form. Not that it did a blasted thing for my shaky psyche.

An eternity later I met Evan's gaze. "Impossible. She's been in my head for days. She's dead. Very, very dead, and definitely not capable of wandering around."

He stood, shoved his hands in his pockets. Implacable.

I tried the words out on my tongue. "You're saying Mala Sen is alive? That my father knows her?"

Evans rocked on his heels. "Looks that way."

I moistened my lips, fought through my confusion and jet lag for a reason, any reason, that someone who looked like Mala Sen would be on my father's estate. She was beautiful. Exotic. Classically elegant and thirteen years my junior— exactly the right age to interest Lord Chilton. Suspicion lodged front and center in my mind. It took a bit of deep breathing before I could voice it. "You think, then, that my father purchased Mala Sen, and that Amar Barat sold her to Chilton like he sells children into slavery? You think my father killed her?"

Evans shuffled his foot against the terra cotta floor, and then focused those delicious brown eyes on me. "Do you?"

Confusion coiled in my gut. "It's rumored that my father often has a companion, sometimes more than one. And he has a long and sordid history of purchasing anything he wants, but a person? No, too messy. There would be too many loose ends for him to bother about in that sort of arrangement. And if he spent the money to purchase her, he wouldn't kill her." I had to force the words out as they were laden with childhood memories. Doubt niggled at the threadbare remnants of our father-daughter bond. I couldn't completely trust any assessment I made of Chilton, but I could trust Mala. Surely ghosts couldn't lie.

Evans rounded the table, stood behind me. "You're sure?"

According to Mala, my father wasn't her killer. Still, it was rather a shock to be faced with the possibility, especially from a man I respected and knew to be a highly trained and intuitive law enforcement professional. Evans had to know that Chilton didn't traipse about engaging in mad killing sprees. He was testing me, rummaging for answers.

I turned to face him—the special agent, not the man who made my body and soul hum with longing. "Quite sure. Lord Chilton has tried to control me with money since I was born. But violence? No. That's not his style. I'm the only offspring he has to account for, illegitimacy notwithstanding, and if he were prone to killing, I wouldn't still be here."

Evans gaped at me. "Hold up. You're saying your father *bought* you?"

"Not at all, as his attempts have been unsuccessful. But he tried to bribe me. He was adamantly opposed to me pursuing a career in law enforcement, and still dumps money into my trust fund when the mood strikes." I pushed my chair back, forcing Blake to back away, then stood and faced him. "We never really got on."

"Yeah. I get that." Evans ran his hands over his head.

I recognized the movement, grabbed a bottle of ibuprophen from the counter, and tossed it to him. "And?"

"I've seen the financials. We know your father can afford to purchase a woman. Probably a dozen."

"True. All the same, he can have any woman he wants with a wink, a crook of his finger, and a flash of cash. Why buy one from someone like Barat?"

Evans filled a glass from the tap and chugged two tablets. "Exactly my point."

"Mala Sen is dead." There was a touch of doubt in my tone. I pulled the elastic band out of my pocket and secured my hair in a tight knot at the base of my neck. "She *couldn't* have been on my father's estate."

"You're kidding, right? I've seen the photographs, Boulay." He popped the tablets and chugged the water.

I paced the length of the kitchen. "Not kidding, no. You're obviously mistaken. Barat, or probably his minions, kept her on a boat for a long time. Months. Barat made a mistake, then. Couldn't sell her, what with all the pirating publicity. Delivered her body to Hampshire." That sounded better. My conviction was solidly back into place.

Mala chose that moment to kick up a temper tantrum that had me reaching for the bottle of ibuprophen. "Sorry, not a mistake. Ms. Sen insists she was a threat to Barat, if I'm hearing her correctly."

Evans reached out and grabbed my shoulders. "Damn it, Whitney. Stop with the hearing voices crap. I need you to function. Here. In the real world."

I twisted from his grasp, put some much-needed distance between us. "This *is* my world, and it's more than real enough. Painful enough."

"Yeah, well, we've been watching her, waiting to see if the bastard would tag her, maybe kill her. She disappeared off our radar two days ago."

"Can't have been her. Mala has been dead for…she says forever, but I think she's just miffed that I can't get you to listen to her." I filled his discarded glass and downed the blessed white pills. "How are you involved in this? You don't have jurisdiction on British soil."

He threw his hands up. "Consulting with Scotland Yard. It happens occasionally, and this case is unusual enough…forget it. Mala Sen was not dead as of two days ago. I saw the photographs. Held them in my hands. She. Was. There."

I contemplated a third pain killer. "Well, then. That proves I've gone nutters, doesn't it? I'm off to bed."

His voice cut through the silence before I made it halfway to the bedroom. "See you in the morning."

I whirled to face him. "In the morning? Ah, you've taken over Coburn's room, then?"

"Yeah. He moved his stuff into Nia's room." Evans took a few steps in my direction. "Said he slept there every night anyway."

I tilted my head, looked him up and down. "Keep your baby browns out of my room. I don't need looking after."

"Got that. But, just so you know, I'm a light sleeper."

"Splendid." I didn't bother to stop the grin. "Bet that makes Coburn and Nia a bit twitchy, what with the cuffs and all."

He glanced down the hall toward their bedrooms. "Cuffs? You're talking handcuffs? No way. Coburn found a lady who—?"

I held my hand up. "I wouldn't care to speculate about that, nor would I go wandering about at night."

"Uh-huh. Gotcha. Maybe I'll, um, crash on the sofa in the sunroom." He expression drooped, like someone had just stolen his favorite teddy bear.

I shut my bedroom door with a firm click and grinned at my reflection in the mirror. Got him. Not a chance he'd be able to sleep wondering about Coburn and Nia. I muffled a yawn, gave a moment's thought to feeling guilty, and then tumbled into bed. Guilt could wait until morning.

Or not.

A perfunctory rap on the door roused me, and Nia poked her head in. "You asleep?"

"Um-hmm. Asleep." I reached for my cell, checked the time. I'd been asleep for about an hour. Nia bounced into my room, closed the door behind her, and leaned against it. "The light's on. You're completely dressed and lying on top of the bed. That's not asleep. It doesn't count if you're not under-the-covers asleep."

I opened one eye, squinting at her. "It bloody well does count."

She pushed my legs out of the way and sat. "Nope. Doesn't. Besides, I want to know what's going on. Dish."

I groaned.

"If you don't start talking I'll break up the guy fest, tell them you're in trouble and need help. Better yet, I'll scream."

She meant it. Her voice held that obnoxious tone that crept behind my eyes, forcing them to open. I slammed a fist into my pillow, bunched it against the headboard, and sat up. "Splendid. You didn't wake me without bringing along a glass of wine, did you?"

"Better." Nia reached in her pocket, pulled out a handful of dark chocolate truffles, and dropped them in my lap.

I unwrapped the green foil and popped one in my mouth.

The rich flavor melted on my tongue, and the crisp taste of mint exploded on my palate. "Most excellent."

"Enough with the stalling. Every time you phoned from Grandmamma Boulay's, you sounded like you were having a demonic nightmare. Something's going on."

I steepled my fingers against my mouth. "What exactly does a demonic nightmare sound like?"

"Bad." Nia tucked her legs into a crossed position on the bed. "Hounds of Hell bad."

I plucked a truffle from the stash on my lap, held it out to her. "I'll share if you go away."

She shook her head, her curls bouncing around her face. "Not a chance. I gobbled down six of them before I came in here. I'm armed, dangerous, and cannot be swayed by bribery. Now what in the holy hell is going on?"

I considered the truffle, turning it over in my fingers. It was bothersome, trying to explain the calling. Best to just spit it out. "There's a thing about the women in my family, happens on our thirty-fifth birthday."

"Huh. It can't be any worse than what happened to me on my thirty-fifth." She shuddered hard enough to shake the bed. "Unless you have a psycho family member."

I patted her knee. "Absolutely not. No murderers in the family. And the thing is, you didn't kill Marcellin. The sharks did."

"Doesn't matter, I'm the one who pushed him over the cliff." She snatched the candy wrappers from my lap and busied her fingers shredding them. "I'll carry the memory forever, Whitney. The worst part is living with the guilt. I'm glad he's dead. Trace is still talking me through at least one nightmare every time I fall asleep."

There wasn't a blasted thing I could say to help Nia deal

with the guilt, so I focused on the good. "Well, he would, then, wouldn't he? That's Coburn to the core."

Nia bobbed her head, love shining through her smile. "Yeah. I haven't figured out how he can be such a badass in court and such a perfect lover at home. Guess I should just appreciate him."

She pointed at the pile of truffles. "Have another one and then start talking. What's with the big birthday deal?"

I twiddled a piece of candy, unwrapping it. "Dead people talk to me."

"Holy hell. Whitney, I'm so sorry. Is it like my visions? Do you see them being killed? In real time? I definitely know what that's like."

"No, it's not like your visions. They tell me who the killer was and some details about how it was done. Useful information for proving who's to blame. Not a bad calling except for the headaches."

"Calling? It has a name, this thing that happens in your family? Kind of cool. Surely Grandmamma Boulay knows what to do about the headaches. She helped me with the whole vision thing. Told me to accept...oh, I see the problem."

"Your lips are going to develop a permanent tic if you don't just go ahead and laugh. I agree that *accepting* isn't my strongest trait." I tucked my hair behind my ears. "Still, I would like to dispense with the headaches. Maybe I should give her a call, see if she's come up with any advice about it."

Nia leaned in, touched my earring with the pad of her index finger. "I'm thinking it's probably because you're so stubborn that you have the headaches."

I started to protest, but Nia held up her hand. "You *are* stubborn. Don't try to deny it. Any time Blake Evans has to show up on your doorstep to get you to cooperate, it's a safe bet that you're being obstinate. Especially when the appropriate response would be to melt at his feet."

"Absolutely. Just like you did with Coburn, then."

"Ah, totally different circumstances. He was defending a cold-blooded killer, not trying to catch one." Nia pointed at my ear. "And the birthday bling?"

"To remind me to stay pure and faithful to my calling."

"Perfect. How does your special agent like it? He has the hots for you, and it would be a terrible waste not to sample the merchandise."

I choked.

Nia's pupils dilated. "You have. You've sampled him. Way to go. How was it?"

"No tasting to speak of, actually—"

"You lie." She crossed her arms. "If you don't spill right this second, I'll have Trace ask him tomorrow. They talk about everything, you know, just like a couple of old biddies. So?"

She had me. They did gossip a bit. "Two kisses. That's it. Nothing to speak of."

"Uh-huh. Right. Your eyes go all sparkly, and you get pink when you talk about him. So I'm guessing those had to be curl-your-toes, knock-your-socks-off kisses."

"Well, then. Not that it matters. Blake Evans and I never really got on, and what with the calling, there's no room for a man in my life."

Nia snagged a truffle out of the pile, hauled back and tossed it at me. "That's stupid. And you're not...well, most of the time you're not stupid. In this case, maybe so. Take Trace, for example. He loved me even though I had visions of murder. Didn't once accuse me of being nuts."

"Um-hmm." My mouth was full of truffle so it was the most articulate comment I could make. Besides, Nia was right.

Coburn didn't question her sanity. Time for me to end the comparison between Evans and Coburn. "There's something else. Chloe thinks I should telepathically ring up the body from her stoop, the one that introduced us."

Nia grabbed another truffle. "You, ah, know how to do that? Is that part of the calling?"

Her question stopped me, and an unfamiliar twinge raced over my skin. "It's bad enough, them taking up residence in my head without me trying to—"

"But you'd have control. If *you* contact *them*, you'd get to choose the time and place. Surely that would be better than having the dead drop in whenever they please."

"That's what Chloe said."

"And?"

"She said it wouldn't be *my* calling if I couldn't figure out how to manage it." Cool shadows fluttered in my chest. "She said there's more to the calling than I know."

"Not my area of expertise, but I trust Chloe."

Time for another change the subject. "All the same, I need sleep. Now. And just so you don't fret, Grandmamma says I'll be sleeping a lot for the next seven days. Something about processing the calling. It seems we work with it for a month, and then take a week to do a mental reconfiguration of what we've learned. Or something."

Nia uncurled her legs and stood, hands on hips. "We're not done with this conversation, but since you look like hell, I'll back off until tomorrow. Or until you wake up."

I made shooing motions. "We'd do well to forget this discussion. Toddle off now, before I have a go at you."

She scooped up the last few truffles in one hand and wagged her fingers at me. "Going."

I shut off the light, pulled the pillow over my head, and fell into a deep sleep.

The first grey streaks of daylight peeked through the shutters on my bedroom window and bored into my head with the tenacity of a jackhammer. Time to face another day. And Blake Evans was living in my house. Planning to take me home to Daddy. He was all wrong about that. I started to get out of bed, but tumbled back.

I couldn't stay awake.

Chapter 6

ON the morning of the eighth day, I struggled to consciousness, pried one eyelid open, and focused on the bedside clock. Six fifteen. Dawn inched through the dark with a slow, muted stretch. For the past week I'd only been awake for short snatches of time—to eat, shower, and use the loo.

My body ached from lack of use and my mind craved caffeine. I'd expected to be ready for some strenuous exercise, and maybe some complex problem-solving by now. Turned out sleeping for seven days had all the backlash of a bad hangover.

I fumbled to my feet, did a short yoga routine, and then slipped into a robe and headed for the kitchen to press a pot of coffee.

The house was quiet. No yammering voices, no lovey-dovey couples, and no macho men. Maybe waking up wasn't so bad after all. The edge of the sun climbed from behind the mountains, and chased away the gray shades of dawn. The thing to do was put the day on hold and take my favorite mug of the brew back to bed. A brilliant plan, that. Especially if Mala stayed quiet for a few more hours.

I set the timer for the French press, then wandered back to the bathroom. Maybe a splash of cold water would chase away the groggies. When I pushed the door open, a cross draft whooshed in and flipped a piece of paper that had been taped to the bathroom mirror. Nia must have come in the night before and left a note. Odd, that. She'd be more likely to bounce on the bed so as to share in my grand awakening.

I tore the note loose.

An eerie mix of magazine cutout and plain block letters came into focus.

So pREtTY WheN yOU sLEep.

A chill touched my nape.

Not Nia, then.

A rap on the bedroom door sent my heart pounding, and I whipped around to find Evans lounging against the doorframe.

The soft skin around his eyes tightened. "What's going on? You look like hell."

There were no words rumbling about in my head, so I pushed by him, my movements slow and stilted.

Evans tailed me to the kitchen, watched while I fumbled for a baggie, slid the note inside, and then zipped it closed. I handed it to him just as the timer for the French press dinged.

"Damn it, Whitney. Where did this come from?" His voice spiked through my shaky muscles.

"Bathroom mirror." I pressed the coffee, poured a mug, and carried it to the back door. The alarm wasn't set. Well, then. Instinctively, I breathed in the comforting scent of the coffee and took my first swallow. Kona beans weren't a bit like Bayou chicory, but they'd do to wake a person up.

Not that the note hadn't already jolted me into the day. I pointed to the baggie in Evans's hand. "What do you make of it?"

He huffed, impatient, then tossed the baggie on the table, and snagged a mug from the cupboard. "Doesn't make any sense. At least not in relation to Barat and Mala Sen. What else are you into?"

I shrugged my shoulders to ease the nagging ache that had settled in my upper back. "Nothing to warrant a nighttime visit. The dead *talk* at me. They do *not* leave notes lying about."

The clear, sparkly sound of Nia's laughter rang through the kitchen as she ran in, scarcely dressed in ratty khaki shorts and a threadbare tee, her bare feet slapping the tile floor. She had a white polo shirt clutched in her fist. Coburn was hot on her heels and shirtless. She skidded to a stop in front of Evans, shoved the polo in his hands, and barreled out the back door.

Coburn nipped the mug out of my hands. "She's nuts." He grinned, then downed the rest of *my* coffee.

I reached for a fresh mug, filled it, then pointed to his chest. "You've some shaving foam just there."

Evans thrust the polo shirt at Coburn. "You set the alarm last night?"

"No. Nia usually does. She's still touchy about things, likes to do it herself. Something wrong?" He mopped up the shaving foam, pulled the shirt over his head, and worked his arms through the sleeves.

I glanced outside. Nia jogged down the driveway, probably on her way to collect the morning Advertiser. I handed the baggie to Coburn. "Perhaps we'd best decide how to tell her about this."

He blanched at the words on the note. "Where'd this come from? Not in the house? Nia always sets the alarm, usually checks it twice."

Evans glared. "Yeah, well, not last night. The note was taped to Whitney's bathroom mirror this morning. Some goddamn pervert was in her bedroom, watching her sleep." His voice inched up a decibel with each word.

"Where were *you*?" Coburn's jaw was set in a hard angle. "I thought you were supposed to be on guard duty."

Tension crackled between them, male posturing at its best.

"I need someone to look after me, then?"

They gave me identical you've-got-to-be-kidding expressions. I would have taken a moment to put them both on the floor, but my body wasn't quite ready for it.

Nia bounced into the kitchen, tossed the newspaper on the counter, and cuddled Ahimsa against her chest. "What're you all twisted up about, Blake?"

He hadn't stopped glaring. Scuttlebutt was that that particular glare had frozen hardened criminals in the act of a crime. Or a lie. Nia shrugged it off with a delicate hitch of her right shoulder. "I could hear the pissed-off in your voice all the way down the driveway."

He bit down on his lip, didn't say a word. Coburn slid the bagged note under the newspaper while Nia fussed with Ahimsa, then put him down to pour a cup of coffee. She stare at us, one at a time, hands on hips. "What? You all have that look like there's hellhounds loose in the house. What'd I miss?"

Evans cleared his throat, took a swallow of coffee. Not smooth.

Coburn hitched himself in front of the counter blocking Nia's view of the newspaper.

Absolutely amazing. Two hunks (to quote Arielle Boulay) scared to face one tiny Haitian woman. I would've rather bypassed the issue, myself, but she knew something was amiss, and knowing Nia, she wouldn't let it go until she had the details.

She shook her head, reached behind Coburn, yanked the paper out from behind him, and started a freaky slow-motion time warp in motion.

The note drifted to the floor at Nia's feet. Coburn tracked its descent with dilated pupils, then flicked his gaze up to meet hers. Her chin hardened in a decided angle. Coburn bent to grab the baggie and Nia set the newspaper down, swept her palm over it with agonizing precision as she smoothed out invisible wrinkles. And then she held out her hand. "Gimme."

A crook of her fingers later, he placed the baggie on her palm.

The mug slipped out of her other hand and crashed against the tile floor.

"Marcellin. Dear God, no."

Coburn settled his hands under her arms, lifted her out of the mess, and sat her on the counter. I bounced a roll of paper towels against his arm with a solid thwack. "Wrap the broken bits so they don't cut through the trash bag."

I sidled around Coburn and grabbed Nia's hand. "The note was for me, Nia, not you. We scared you, and I'm sorry. This isn't Marcellin. He wrote notes longhand, and this one is cut-out letters. Your nemesis is dead, and the dead don't leave notes. They chatter all the damn time, but believe me, I'd have piles of paper stacked up by now if they were into the paper and pencil gig."

Her eyes were huge and bright with fear. "No body. They've never found his body."

Evans had the good sense to keep quiet. A first.

Coburn threw the wet paper towels and pottery shards into the trash, then set about pouring Nia a fresh cup of coffee before elbowing me out of the way and wrapping her in his arms.

I left them to it, hustled to my room for a quick shower, slipped into a short, nondescript beige dress that showed my legs to advantage, and then slicked my hair back, securing it with a clip. When I unzipped my makeup bag, a neatly folded slip of yellow paper tumbled out. It was the same ugly yellow as the note that had been attached to my bathroom mirror. Damn and blast. My stomach clenched as I plucked my tweezers from a container on the counter and lifted the note from the bag.

TwO pm NEImAN maRCUs. ALONE. i'Ll FinD yOU.

My stomach clenched. Gray threatened my vision.

Inhale. Exhale.

Looked like I had a date with a psycho. Probably best not to mention it. I wasn't concerned about meeting whoever left the notes, because Neiman Marcus was a public, well-populated store in the middle of the Ala Moana mall. Nevertheless, I strapped a knife to my thigh. No reason to gamble with my longevity.

By the time I returned to the kitchen, Evans had made pancakes, the scent of sweet butter, maple syrup, and a hot griddle filled the air, and everyone sat around the table discussing what to do about the situation. Nia's cheeks were flushed with healthy color, and she'd made headway with her stack of pancakes.

My stomach rumbled with anticipation. I grabbed a seat, and flicked a napkin open on my lap.

Coburn handed me the cafetière with freshly made coffee. "What's your plan?"

"A quick call to the HPD." I filled my mug. "Turn over the note and then—"

Evans set a plate of pancakes on the table in front of me, his eyes alive with heat. Anger? Lust? A bit of a mix? I licked a drop of coffee from my upper lip and his gaze followed my tongue. My stomach flip-flopped. Lust, then. He turned away and thunked his forehead against a kitchen cabinet. He spun to face me, determination in his gaze. "I'll be taking the note, and there's no need to call in the HPD. A team from the Bureau will go over the house."

I wrapped my hand around his wrist, and heat zinged up my arm. I was absolutely *not* attracted to anger. I swallowed the thought, grappling for words. "That will complicate things, and this probably isn't about Mala Sen. The note is a minor nuisance—"

"Since you're not involved in another case, it has to be connected." Blake shook his arm free.

Nia ran her fingers through her hair, then pressed her hands tight to her scalp. "I'm going to open the door in my mind. It's Marcellin. Has to be. He always left notes, although…"

I took a bite of pancake, stalling while I organized my thoughts. "Did you set the alarm last night?"

Her mouth dropped open. "I *always* set the alarm. But, no. Ohmygod. No. I was in such a hurry to talk with Maman and Papa, and then finalize our plane reservations for Minot—"

"And then I distracted her." Coburn interlaced his fingers with Nia's. "My fault."

I nodded. "So, it could have been anyone, actually, and not necessarily related to any of us specifically. My windows were open and I had the ceiling fan running on high. There was too much white noise for me to hear anything."

Nia pushed her plate away. "Wait. If your windows were open, the entry alarm wouldn't have set anyway, only the perimeter alarm."

I forked a bite of pancakes, savoring the buttery taste. "Quite. And if I know Evans, he's made a circuit of the house and didn't find anything."

He nodded. "I did a double-check while you were in the shower. And yeah, nothing looked out of place."

I finished my last swallow of coffee, carried my dishes to the sink, and swished them with soapy water. "I'll make a copy of the note for the HPD. This is their jurisdiction and I'd rather not—"

"No, Whitney. This needs to stay within the agency since it could be connected to Barat."

Best not to argue with Evans when he pulled out his special agent persona. A flash of sunlight on metal caught my attention, and I glanced out the kitchen window. "We have company. An unmarked white van and a plain grey sedan."

Evans stood and jogged out the back door and down the steps to meet the FBI team. I snatched the note off the counter, hurried to my office, made a copy, returned the note, and then slipped out the sunroom door. I had nothing to discuss with the FBI. Not one blasted thing.

I hurried down the block, out of sight of the agents swarming my house. City buses stopped at the end of the street every fifteen minutes, so I wouldn't have long to wait. My car had been totaled while I was helping Nia last month—a minor problem with cut brake lines—so I needed to purchase a vehicle. Today. But first a quick stop to deliver the note to my former captain at the HPD.

Twenty minutes later, the officer in charge of reception waved me on to the security checkpoint, and a few minutes later I stood opposite Captain Harte's desk.

"Boulay? Last I heard you were off-island." The hearty bass notes in his voice rumbled through the room and he motioned to a chair. But sitting wasn't on my agenda.

"Yes, sir. I got back last week, actually, and seem to be in a bit of a situation." I handed him the note. "Woke to find this taped on my bathroom mirror."

He took the copy, raised his eyebrows.

I wiggled my toes in the three-inch heels that matched my dress. I'd chosen them knowing I'd appreciate the extra height when facing the captain. "The FBI is hovering about, as they think I'm connected to one of their open cases."

He flicked the note with his index finger. "Are you? Do they have the original?"

"No, and yes, they have the original. But this is your turf, sir, and I don't think the note has anything to do with their investigation."

"Who do I talk to?" Harte reached for his phone.

"Special Agent Blake Evans." I handed him one of Blake's cards. "Nia De'brie thinks it's Marcellin. Any word on his remains?"

"No. Didn't think there would be. The sharks don't leave much, and the tides take the rest." He squinted at me. "Can't be Marcellin. What aren't you telling me?"

I held up my hands and backed away. "Not a thing, sir. Enjoying my retirement. I'll catch you up if anything else happens."

The captain's grunt of disbelief echoed behind me as I hustled down the hall.

Time to focus on my new car. I pulled out my cell, rang up a taxi, and settled to wait on one of the wooden benches that lined the veranda outside the HPD. Several hours, a test drive, and a bank draft later, I was the owner of a sparkly new John Cooper Clubman—small enough to fit in Honolulu parking spaces, and roomy enough to accommodate tall human bodies.

I drove it off the lot just in time for my rendezvous with

the psycho. I couldn't control when or how he would appear, but I could choose to place myself in the busiest location within Neiman Marcus, the Mariposa restaurant. Great view. Excellent food. I took my time over lunch.

He didn't show.

I wandered through the accessories department on the main floor searching for a much-needed backpack.

He didn't show.

I'd lingered over lunch and shopping to give my stalker several hours and plenty of opportunity to locate me, and was busy transferring things from the canvas tote to my new Prada backpack when my mobile rang.

My watch read three-fifty. Caller ID read *restricted*. It could be the FBI wanting to question me about the note. But since crazy psycho person missed our scheduled meeting, it could also be him.

A ripple of unease caught under my breastbone.

And Mala, agitated, nudged my mind with more than her usual persistence.

I pressed the green answer bar, and a distorted electronic voice rasped in my ear. "Your grandmother, Arielle Boulay, will stay safe only if you do exactly as I say. Wait for the next call."

Chapter 7

MY heart slammed into my throat. Grandmamma Boulay? A threat against the woman who didn't believe in modern conveniences and didn't have a phone.

I rubbed my fingers against the diamond in my earlobe, finding it cool and hard to my touch, and then jabbed wildly at my cell, fumbling the numbers, trying to reach the information operator in Grandmamma's parish. When he finally connected me with the sheriff's department, rivulets of sweat had dampened my skin, and fear was churning sour in my stomach.

"Sheriff Dugas." His voice held the melody of the Bayou. It wasn't comforting. I drew in a breath, tried to still my panic. Dugas's reputation was good. I could trust him.

"Whitney Boulay, here. I just received a threatening call about Grandmamma and need you to go 'round and check her cabin, see that she's all right."

"Arielle? Nobody the heck better be messin' with Grandmamma. I'll get right out there, Miz Boulay. Give you a call back soon's I know what's what. You'll be at this number?"

"Yes."

"Anything else you can tell me? Any idea who did the callin'? What sorta trouble am I ambling into?"

"No idea who'd be after Grandmamma. The caller used an electronic distorter and said she'd stay safe if I did exactly what they wanted. No particulars."

I disconnected the call and punched in Blake's number. Damn, but I'd done it again. Evans, Evans, Evans. Not Blake. I had to keep my distance. I disconnected the call. Best to tell the group of them together. Tidier. Less fuss. And it gave me more time to collect myself.

I merged into traffic, but a construction project had turned King Street into a car park, so it took forever to inch my way through downtown Honolulu. The pace was slow enough that I focused on the emotions chewing me to bits, wrestled them under control, and armored myself with "cop mode." Then I began to sift through the odds and ends leading to Grandmamma's capture.

Crazy, psycho person skipped our face-to-face, so why leave the note? *To get me out of the house?* Surely not. Still, I reached for my mobile to ring Nia, but traffic started moving, so I didn't place the call. There were enough FBI types swarming the property to stop the most persistent criminal. She was safe.

But the possibility that Barat could have Grandmamma pressed thick and heavy on my heart.

I screeched to a stop in my driveway, ran up the walkway, and absently kicked my shoes off before entering the kitchen. Silent. Not an FBI agent in sight. Nia was loading the dishwasher and spun to face me. "Where have you been? I must've left three messages. And did you bother to call back? Let me know you were okay?"

"I didn't check in, no. Where are Evans and Coburn?"

"Trace is on the sun porch working 'cause he just got a new client, and Blake is pacing around the back yard. Last I saw, he was having a heated discussion with someone on his cell." She sent me a piercing glare. "*They* haven't gone missing."

"No one is missing except, perhaps, Grandmamma Boulay." I sunk into a chair, pressed my fingers into my temples to stop the throbbing.

Nia set a glass of water and two white tablets on the table in front of me. "These headaches are happening way too often, and I'm thinking you need to see a doctor. Now tell me. What have you been doing, and why did you leave me alone with a slew of FBI agents? Also, there's some leftover supper if you're hungry."

I popped the tablets and chugged the water. "Not hungry, thanks. I need to talk to all of you."

I levered to my feet, but Nia grabbed my arm. "Not so fast. What were you saying about Grandmamma Boulay?"

I shook my head. The tears I'd been holding at bay threatened. I needed to get into the shower where no one could hear me while I fell apart.

Nia tugged on my arm. "That cell phone has either been in your hand or in front of you on the table since you walked through the door. You didn't answer *my* calls, so I can only guess that whatever is going on is more serious than scaring the life out of me."

I patted her hand, and then pried her fingers off my arm. "I'll fill you in after I shower. Round everyone up, will you?"

I took off for the privacy of my room, mobile clutched in my fingers. Ever so carefully, I set the phone on the bed. Damned inconvenient that free hands were necessary to strip out of clothes. Clutching the phone to my chest, I carried it into the bathroom, and set it on the commode, within easy reach of the shower. They'd call again. Surely, they'd call again.

By the time I stepped under the spray, tears were streaming down my cheeks. They mixed with the warm water, and then slid down the drain without leaving a trace. The lump in my throat hardened into a rock, turning my breathing to a rasping ache. I clung to the slippery tile walls with the tips of my fingers while water sluiced over me. Sobs broke free and wracked my body.

Grandmamma was smart, cagey. Was probably fine.

Someone pounded on the bathroom door, and a shadow tracked across the shower curtain. "Whitney? What the hell?"

Evans. A tremor crashed through me. Not yet. I wasn't ready. I sucked in a breath, talked myself into a parody of calm, and then peeked around the curtain. "Out. Now."

He yanked the heavy fabric from my hand. Time froze. My stomach fluttered with anticipation, and my thighs clenched when Blake's gaze inched over my body, devouring every detail.

A naked confrontation crossed the line from business into…something. My heart did a flip-flop.

A light sheen of sweat beaded Blake's forehead. The tip of his index finger touched my chest, sending a shaft of heat to my core. He followed a drop of water trickling between my breasts. "Beautiful. I'd take advantage, but the timing is wrong. You're hyped on adrenaline, and I want more than that."

And then he backed away, disappearing into the shadows.

I popped out of the shower and chill bumps spread over my skin, a combination of arousal and cool air on wet skin. Adrenaline, huh? My body screamed lust, but Blake was right about the timing being all wrong. I checked my mobile and then popped back under the spray for another quick lather and rinse. To wash away his touch.

By the time I dried off, slathered on some citrus-verbena lotion, and slipped into white shorts and my favorite Riding the Wave tee shirt, I'd pulled myself together enough to go looking for my housemates.

Cradling the cell phone in my palm, I headed for the

kitchen. Empty. I grabbed a bottle of water and followed the voices echoing from the sun porch. Worry tightened their words, and confused tension hung in the air. I allowed myself two deep breaths before I rounded the corner and settled in an overstuffed armchair.

The questions started before I could get the cap off my water. I didn't respond. Couldn't. They fell silent and Nia crouched in front of me, her eyes shadowed with worry. "What in the holy hell is going on? First with all the sleeping, and now this creepy behavior."

When I tried to speak the fear came back, tearing into my throat. "Grandmamma." I'd put some force behind it. Wanted to sound capable, in control, but my voice was so faint it barely stirred the air.

Evans crowded Nia aside, grabbed my shoulders, and gave me a shake. "Damn it, Whitney. Talk."

He jarred the words loose. "Phone call. Electronic distortion. Voice said Grandmamma will stay safe if I do what they say. The sheriff from her Parish is checking the cabin for—"

The shrill sound of my mobile invaded the room. My stomach clutched with panic, and the phone slipped from my fingers. I grabbed for it, noted the caller's number, and then flipped it open, cutting off the harsh sound of the second ring.

"Did you find her?"

"Empty cabin, Miz Boulay. No signs of struggle. Everything's in its place. I put the word out to see if she's tending the sick. There's a couple women 'bout to birth, but I'd a heard if it was anything else."

"Quite. No one noticed strangers, then?" My nerves quivered, and I swallowed bile.

"No, ma'am. Not specifically. Possibility of a pirogue bein' seen on the stretch of water heading up Arielle's way, but, like I said, nothing was disturbed 'round the cabin. We'd all know if strangers were askin' questions."

He was right. Very little got by Bayou residents. "Find her, sheriff. Please. If you could ring me up as soon as you know anything? Keep me posted, actually, whether there's news or not?"

"Will do, Miz Boulay."

I thanked him, snapped the phone closed, and glanced up. "They haven't found her. There was another note this morning in my makeup bag telling me to be at Neiman Marcus by two this afternoon. No one showed. It was almost four when I received the call."

"You didn't tell me?" Blake's tone was a frightening combination of blazing anger and icy control. He jerked his head at Coburn. "Get it."

"It's still in the red makeup bag on my bathroom counter, and, no, I didn't show it to you because you were busy with FBI bureaucracy, and I needed to take care of it." I looked directly at him. "Do I go to the Bayou, then?" Odd how I turned to him for confirmation. Did I trust him? Or was I looking for his dissent as my confirmation?

Nia interrupted my musing. "What call?" Her arms went akimbo and she paced, her steps jerky, agitated. "I repeat, what in the holy hell is going on? What are you involved in?" She stopped, rounded on Blake. "What message?"

He lifted his hand in a plea for time and silence, and then slammed outside, disappearing into the dusk, while he punched numbers into his phone.

Nia turned to me. "Why?" She spit the question out.

I slumped into the soft comfort of the chair. "Someone rang me up with the message—"

She flapped her hands in my direction. "Got that part. My

question is why?"

"That is the question, then, isn't it?" I mumbled.

Her nose flared with an unladylike huff. "You think you can just sit there and tell me you don't know? You can't be serious."

I tipped my head back and rummaged for some words. "One of the dead who's been chatting me up, Mala Sen, is connected to an FBI case. It's international, and Evans did the profile that led them to a suspected arms trafficker who's also brokering in slave trade."

Nia dropped into a chair. "International? Arms *and* people? Why you?"

Evans snapped on a table lamp when he came inside, and the warm glow softened the harsh lines in his face. "Anything?" He nodded toward my mobile.

"No. This is wonky. No one could possibly know I'm involved in this. I'm not, actually, so why the threat against Grandmamma Boulay?"

Nia flicked her index finger back and forth between us. "I'm not getting it. Blake's case, dead woman talks to Whitney, and somehow someone connects the two and is using Grandmamma...to what? Threaten Whitney? What does this dead woman know, anyway?"

"Now there's a rather inconvenient question." I rubbed the ache between my eyes, and then directed my attention to Evans. "Who knows about the report I gave you?"

"The team. Higher-ups, possibly." He tucked his hands in his back pockets. "There wasn't a damn thing in the information you gave me that would send anyone looking for Grandmamma Boulay. You know that."

"I...Mala might know something." I rested my elbows on my knees, and searched my mind for any sign of her. Quiet.

Incredibly annoying. "Naturally when I need her, she shuts up."

Nia shot me a tight grin. "I know all about that from having Marcellin in my head. Always crept in when I wanted to hide stuff from him, but totally disappeared when I wanted to track him down."

Blake's mobile rang again, and he headed outside, disappearing into the dark that had closed around us.

Coburn had been suspiciously quiet, but when he spoke it was exactly what I needed to hear. "You want me to make a trip to the Bayou for you?"

Nia rocked back and eyed him, a quick up and down. "Say what? You'd know how to find Grandmamma?"

He wrapped his arm around her, tucking her against his chest. "Made the trip with Whitney years ago."

The color bled from Nia's face. "You and Whitney—?"

I fought the laugh, lost. "Not hardly. We'd both had a bad week at work, and I brought him to Grandmamma for a bit of healing."

Coburn dropped a kiss on Nia's nose. "Whitney and I…we'd kill each other. Fight like—"

"Siblings." Nia smiled. "Got it. I've seen you in action. Just threw me for a minute, thinking there might have been something else, you know, when you first met."

I pushed a loose strand of hair off my face. They were trying to distract me. I decided to go with it, as the waiting was tearing strips from my soul. "Quite. Our first encounter was a bit of a free-for-all, actually. I'd worked for months, finally arrested this despicable chap, and Coburn gets him off with a that-was-naughty suspended sentence. Two days later the guy shoots a pregnant woman in a convenience store robbery and—"

Coburn grinned. "And while I'm innocently waiting for the elevator in the HPD, she flipped me on my back with an interesting move I hadn't seen before. Caught my attention."

"It was an excellent adrenaline moment. The woman and her child survived, the shooter was killed a few months later when he tried to escape from jail, and Coburn and I became—"

"Siblings," Nia said. "I defined your relationship as siblings and that's where it stays."

Coburn shuffled his weight. "I joined Whitney's dojo to learn all her Hakkoryu jujutsu tricks."

"Right." Nia jabbed her finger in my general direction. "You said something about that when Marcellin was after Trace, but you didn't tell me you'd introduced him to martial arts. And isn't it a federal offense or something, to deck an attorney?"

"No one was around, and Coburn wasn't likely to report it. Too embarrassed."

Coburn grinned, a sneaky quirk of his lips. "Not exactly. I hadn't liked defending the bastard, and figured Whitney had one punch coming. Besides, look at her."

All eyes focused on me.

"Yeah. I get it," Nia said. "She's all elegant and graceful. Last thing you'd expect is for her to come out swinging."

Blake interrupted us, disconnecting from yet another call. "Unless you've been on the receiving end of her temper. Then you'd know first-hand how beauty and elegance can pack one hell of a wallop."

It was the second time in less than an hour Evans had described me as beautiful. I wasn't ugly…but beautiful? The tight skin around his lips pushed the warm fuzzies to the back of my mind. "You learned something, then?"

Blake frowned, tossed the phone in the air and caught it. "No. I'm getting the runaround. And orders to get you to Hampshire ASAP."

A sliver of panic lodged in my chest. "Not an option. And as I'm not under arrest, I won't be—"

My mobile rang. I checked the incoming number and answered. "Yes, Sheriff Dugas."

"Grandmamma was in the pirogue. You know, the ones the tourists rent from that shack just down the way, Old Michael's place? A deputy working out at Avril Dupré's cabin spotted her as it went by. Funny thing though—she didn't give him a word."

"Was she hurt, then?"

"No, ma'am. Looked just fine. The deputy didn't recognize the man with her, but said she didn't look scared, wasn't tied up, had her knitting basket on her lap."

"Find that pirogue, sheriff. It's not like Grandmamma to pass by someone without a word."

"I'm pulling into the rental place now. It's way past closing but I'll pry Michael away from the TV. Gonna ask questions until I get the right answers."

"Thanks. Ring me as soon as you have the particulars." I disconnected and nodded toward Coburn's laptop. "See if you can get me on a flight to New Orleans, will you?"

Blake shook his head. "Bad idea. You don't have enough information. Arielle Boulay could be anywhere by the time you get there, *and* we need you in Hampshire."

I shuddered. "Well, then. That's helpful, isn't it?"

Nia touched my arm, glanced at Coburn. "We'll go with you. We can change our flight from Minot to New Orleans."

The phone rang again. "Yes, Sheriff?"

"We found the pirogue 'bout a half mile from here. No one on board. Man who rented it, name's Justice. Dominic Justice."

Chapter 8

"**DOMINIC** Justice?" Sheriff Dugas was mistaken. My hand clenched around the phone. He had to be wrong. "Are you quite sure about that?"

Blake, Nia, Coburn. All eyes on me. All movement stopped.

It wasn't possible. Justice was in Seattle. With Chloe. I mumbled some sort of acknowledgement, disconnected, and immediately punched in Chloe's speed-dial number, impatience thrumming along my nerves while I waited for her to answer. "Dominic Justice? Is he there, then?"

Silence. Emptiness. Not at all like Chloe who bustled with positive energy. The silence, yes. She could do silence with the best of them, but the empty? No. A single shiver flicked between my shoulder blades. "Justice? Is he with you?"

She breathed a sleepy sigh over the line. "No. Not here. Why would you think he's here?"

What the hell time was it on the mainland? Evening here. Night there. Not that it mattered. I'd have yanked her out of a sound sleep no matter what time it was. "Looks after you, doesn't he? Ought to be hovering about, practicing those Romany spells and such."

"Sarcasm is beneath you, Whitney." Her words held a whisper of righteous kindness that scraped against my raw despair.

I clamped my mouth shut, struggling to stop from saying anything I'd regret. "I need a quick word with him. When did he last darken your door?"

A rustling sound carried over the phone that went on forever, and spun my fear out of control. Taking a swipe at Chloe wouldn't help me find Justice. Blake's hand on my shoulder calmed me. And annoyed me.

"It's been a week since I've seen Dominic. I've been staying with Jessi, seeing the doctors, getting ready to move back to Honolulu. You know that." Hurt sounded in Chloe's words. Damn. It was like I'd slapped a kitten. I didn't know any other way to deal with fear, but to smother it in anger, and I'd been doing it so long…since the year Id been shuffled off to live at Chilton Manor.

I closed my eyes and attempted a calming breath. Chloe was right. We'd talked a few days ago, and she'd mentioned about staying with Jessi. The words blurted out before I could stop them. "Grandmamma Boulay is missing—"

"Missing? How? When?" Chloe's disbelief was tangible enough to cross the vast expanse of the Pacific Ocean without losing a bit of its impact. She caught me dead to rights when she questioned me, and then calmly pointed out that I hadn't described Dominic as a kidnapper, but rather as a thief. *A scummy, lousy thief.*

My temper flared again. "Not much of a difference, actually. He's one of the few people capable of stealing Grandmamma. And until I have her back safely, he's guilty."

"You do have a point. Technically. But Dominic wouldn't—"

"Now isn't a good time to bring up Justice's sterling

qualities. When do you expect him?"

"Expect him? He said he'd see me before I left, but I just got back to the cabin a few hours ago, and it's late."

I didn't care about late. "Find him. Have a go at getting him to confess, would you? Although, as he knows we're friends, maybe he won't talk to you either. How about you just ring me when you locate him?"

Another sigh, this one impatient and agitated. "The woods are dark and the trails are tangled with tree roots and undergrowth, plus I have no idea where to start looking. But as soon as it's light I'll scout around and see if I can find his house. He's always met me in the woods, though, so I'm guessing that if he doesn't want to be found... And Whitney, this works both ways. *You* can call *me* when you find Grandmamma Boulay. I want to know she's okay."

Chloe's words hit me with a painful lurch. It was a casual request...innocent, but she was infatuated with Justice. Blake's fingers kneaded my shoulder and his strength flowed into me, helping me find reassuring words. But I couldn't trust her, so I lied. Made the promise and ended the call.

Blake leaned in, his gaze intent. I skimmed a glance over the three of them, and then focused on the billowy clouds outside the window. "She'll lie to protect him. She hasn't, not yet, but it's coming. Chloe's never loved before, not like this. She'll protect Justice."

Nia rubbed her hands together, then reached for Coburn and threaded their fingers. "Chloe isn't like that. Lying isn't who she is. I doubt that she *can* lie. You know that. You know her. It would destroy her to lie to you, Whitney."

I strode to the window, and flattened my hand against glass. It still held the warmth from the sun, so incongruent with the malevolence lurking in the unknown. Nia was right about Chloe, but I just couldn't...didn't know how to trust...anyone. I spun to face Coburn. "What time is my flight to New Orleans?"

"Eight-ten tomorrow night. Found you a non-stop. You arrive in New Orleans a few minutes after eleven the next morning." He slid his hand from Nia's, and focused on the keyboard. "Want me to book it?"

Evans grumbled, a strangled sound. "Make reservations for two. We'll be heading in the general direction of the UK, and—"

"And you're just as worried about the situation as I am. Admit it." I watched his face closely. I needed to know he was on my side, and if his expression didn't match his words…

He scrubbed the back of his neck. "Yeah. Okay. I'm worried. Justice thrown into the mix changes things. He's a loose cannon. Lives by his own rules, and is unpredictable as hell."

A sigh of relief eased my muscles. I couldn't argue with Blake's assessment of Justice, so I glanced at my watch and focused on Coburn. "No way to leave tonight, then?"

"Not unless you teleport to Honolulu International. The flight's taking off in five minutes."

"Damn and blast." I paced the length of the room, rounded on Evans. "You have connections. Get us a flight to New Orleans tonight and I'll go to Hampshire with you. No questions asked."

The tired was beginning to show in his eyes and around his mouth. And it curled through his words. "I definitely don't have the connections to call in a chit for this."

My fingernails cut into my palms. "Grandmamma is part of your case now, your very important case. Why *not* call in a favor to help us find her?"

"Because I don't want them to know what we're doing. Taking the scenic route to Hampshire won't go over. At all.

On a commercial flight I can stall for time and maybe figure out what the hell is going on with all the damn quirks in this case."

I listened to his voice, ignored the words and focused on the tone. The tells. There was a bit of emotion there, tucked behind the party line. I dug my fingers into my shoulders, kneaded the knots, and fought for control. "You're worried about Grandmamma, and your intuition is on high alert about the...coincidences. Right?"

He fumbled with his phone. "It's simple. Gotta get you to Hampshire. Bayou's on the way. If I can rule out any connection between Grandmamma and Mala Sen in the process, it'll be worth the trip."

I considered his words, then leveled my gaze on him. Was I looking for truth? No. Trust. Evans was going to drop me into my British past. Uncomfortable, that, and I wanted no part of it. A shudder curled along my spine. But it was a beginning, trusting Blake. "Okay then. We'll leave tomorrow night."

He squeezed one eye shut, assessing. "I'm trusting you to cooperate, Boulay. When I say we leave for Hampshire, we leave."

That damn *trust* word. I shifted my eyes down and away, knowing it was a lie well before I nodded my agreement. But then so did Evans. He was an expert when it came to reading faces.

THE long minutes of night crept into hours, and what little sleep I got came in short naps. I harassed Sheriff Dugas with frequent texts and calls that left me, and probably the sheriff, exhausted and cranky.

The scent of coffee roused me from the restless tossing

and turning, and I opened my eyes to find Nia hovering in the doorway. She cradled a mug between her palms. Smart woman, Nia. "You said to get you up." Her words were soft, unsure. "That you wanted to run with Trace this morning."

She set the coffee on the nightstand and backed away. I must've looked on the shoddy side. Or dangerous. Not surprising, as the impotence and frustration of being stuck here, instead of personally on the scene searching for Grandmamma, was taking its toll with an unrelenting vengeance

"Thanks." I inhaled the pungent scent of chicory. Nia had made me Bayou coffee. "Trying to soothe the savage beast, are you?"

Nia focused on me with barely constrained worry. "I thought brewing New Orleans coffee might help you figure out where to focus your investigation. Crazy, I know. But they say smell is the strongest psychic sense—"

"You're brilliant. It could be just what I need to help me to find Grandmamma, see where she is, if she's safe."

Nia's chin jutted to an angle. "I've only met her on the phone, but you talk about her enough for me to know. She's safe. Holy hell, Whitney, it's Grandmamma. No one can make the best of a crazy situation as well as she does, and she simply wouldn't stand for playing the role of victim."

Nia made another excellent point. I savored the chicory, and allowed memories of the woman who'd nurtured me to surface, the richness of her laughter and the depth of her loving heart. Contentment settled around me. "She's all right, then, isn't she? You knew. Before you woke me, you knew?"

"Uh, well, no." Nia did the shuffle again. "I thought, maybe. Had a dream about her, and everything seemed so *right* that I thought it'd be good for you to touch her, you know, make use of all your new, heightened psychic, intuitive…whatever you want to call them…abilities."

I shuddered, then swung out of bed, barely controlling my temper. "Grandmamma isn't dead, Nia."

"That's not what I meant and you know it. Use the *other* psychic enhancements that came with your calling."

Maybe she had a point. Hadn't I noticed Blake's scent before I got to his office? Still, it was just too odd. "Absolutely. Make the best of being crazy." But the truth of what Nia said settled somewhere around my heart. Maybe my calling would be the key to learning how to be…normal.

Nia snorted. "Watch your mouth. You never accused me of being crazy when Marcellin played fast and loose with my mind. Looks to me like a little acceptance of who you are is in order here."

Acceptance. I really had to work on that. I made shooing motions in her direction, and focused on the smooth grain of the wood floor under my feet while I trudged to the bathroom.

"Leaving now," Nia said, backing toward the door. "Trace is sending an email to his new client and should be ready to leave in fifteen."

I dressed in running shorts and a sports bra, did a bit of time with a toothbrush to scrape the morning from my mouth, and went to meet Coburn. He didn't bother with a verbal greeting, just gave my ponytail a quick tug, and then jogged down the back steps.

For a solid hour there was nothing but my feet, the pavement, the healing scent of jasmine, and the sounds of Hawaii waking to the day. It was exactly what I'd needed to reset my objectivity from whacked out and emotional to clam and controlled. Not that it worked worth a damn.

The day stretched on, with everyone insisting we take the Clubman (and me) for a test drive around the island. They did their best to keep my body occupied and my thoughts from wandering into an abyss of useless worry. Good friends were like that. Bloody annoying.

When we returned from the motor trip, I jogged down the driveway to check the mailbox, agitation dogging my steps. I thumbed through a stack of flyers addressed to *occupant,* and a small manila envelope fluttered to the ground. My address was printed in plain block letters. No return address. I shivered, goose bumps popping out along my arms. "Evans," I yelled.

He stuck his head out the kitchen window. "What's up?"

"Bring some tweezers and an evidence bag." Panic quivered at the edge of my mind, and I anchored my hands behind my back to keep from scooping the envelope off the ground and ripping it open.

Evans, Nia, and Coburn exploded from the house and gathered around me. Too close. I waved them back, took the tweezers from Blake and shifted the envelope into the baggie.

Evans snagged the baggie and turned toward the door. "Let's get it inside, take a look."

We gathered around the kitchen table, and I grabbed a pair of gloves. My hands trembled, so I passed them to Blake. Blake, again. His given name kept popping into my head like a jack-in-the-box on crack. Why couldn't I distance him, keep him Evans?

He slit the envelope and eased a photograph out. Grandmamma. Smiling. Knitting.

"You recognize anything about the background?" Evans asked, punching numbers on his phone.

I studied the photo. No date. Front or back. "No. Nothing here to help us find her then, is there?"

Nia pushed her chair back, stepped behind me and peered over my shoulder. "No postmark. She looks good in the picture. Content and safe."

"All the same, we don't know, do we?" I clasped my

hands, an attempt to stop the tremors. "What do you make of it, Evans?"

"Don't know. Doesn't fit with the phone threat for them to send a photo like this. Someone from the local office will pick it up in a few."

I jabbed my hands into a pair of gloves, picked up the photo, and then headed for my office. I had to turn the photo over as evidence, but not before I made a copy.

By the time one of Blake's colleagues arrived to collect the picture, I was drained and in need of some alone time. I'd been thinking about Nia's theory that the calling had unlocked more potential psychic abilities than just chatting with the dead. So I locked myself in my bedroom, folded my legs into a lotus position, and placed Grandmamma's picture in front of me. Calm brushed against the raw edge of my thoughts, and my breathing deepened.

Until I heard footsteps outside my bedroom window.

Chapter 9

THE footsteps stopped just beyond my window. "So, you and Whitney?" Coburn's words caught on the breeze and drifted into my bedroom. They were pure Coburn, erudite accent with a hint of laughter.

"Me and Whitney, what?" Blake Evans's bourbon voice. "A more opinionated, stubborn woman—"

"You love her," Coburn said.

My breath caught. Grabbing a pillow, I jammed it tight to my abdomen and held on. What kind of guy-bonding ritual was I listening to? Nia was absolutely correct. These two gossiped like old biddies.

Blake's silence bellowed through the window. What nonsense. He didn't love me. The quiet grew heavy, and time spun out. Coburn's pronouncement must have been too inconsequential to mention, or even notice, actually. I found myself creeping along the bedroom floor toward the window.

"Hell, yeah, I love her."

I tamped down the rush of heat choking me. *Really? That was the best he could do?* Not that it mattered. We weren't suited, and there was absolutely no reason for the twinge of regret lodged in my chest. Not a single reason.

"So, what's the problem? You're sleeping on the sofa, and she's in her bedroom with the door closed." Coburn's voice held an undercurrent of disbelief that made me fidget. Evans, without doubt, lusted for my body in much the same way Ahimsa appreciates a good ear rub. My lips quivered with the memory of his lips, soft, full, responsive. A sliver of need flashed in my belly. We had a normal male-female connection, but he'd never pushed for more, never pressed to change our sleeping arrangements.

"Yeah," Blake said with a sigh.

Apparently, the man had been reduced to a one-word vocabulary.

I peeked over the windowsill. Coburn did a punch-shove move on Blake, one of those guy things that only mean something if you're born with a Y chromosome. I couldn't see their faces, but since I'd been watching them interact for years, I'd bet that Coburn was giving Evans a smartass, knowing grin. The one that said *gotcha*.

"You're gonna have to do better, or Nia will have me cuffed someplace other than our bed."

"Nia sent you out here?" Evans asked. A flock of sparrows fled from a nearby tree. Apparently the sound of panic transfers across species.

"Nope. She asked nicely if I'd have a talk with you before you drag Whitney to Hampshire."

"She's afraid I'll, what? Beat the crap out of Whitney for being stubborn, obstinate, and clinging to this crazy notion—"

"Don't go there." There was a warning growl in Coburn's voice. "Not with Whitney. Not with Nia. You know Nia struggles with nightmares since Marcellin, and Whitney's pain is obvious. They're not jerking you around, Evans."

"Whitney's—"

"Difficult, demanding, smarter than hell, and a pain in the ass. Yep. Those things I know. Frustrating as all get out. So's Nia. They're also the most loyal, honest, got-your-back women I've ever met. So, why aren't you moving on her?"

"Her choice. There's too many conflicting signals, and if I make a mistake—"

"She'll beat the crap out of you?" The laughter was back in Coburn's voice.

"*Try* to beat the crap out of me. I'd take her down, but damn if she wouldn't put me in the hospital right alongside her." Blake sucked in a raspy breath. "And she thinks dead people are talking to her. I can't get past that."

Shame. It hit me in the gut. Blake Evans was ashamed of my calling. Ashamed of *me*. I'd believed the calling was just an irritating bit of bother to him. Anger seeped into my blood, propelled me off the floor and into a squat. I edged my way under the window and peeked over the sill again. My plan: to take him with a flying tackle.

Coburn's back was to me, and I'd have to go through him to reach Blake. Couldn't do that to the guy defending me. Coburn squared off with Evans. "Dead people *are* talking to her."

"Absolutely," I whispered. "Well said, Coburn."

Evans cocked his head. "Come on man, you know that doesn't happen. What if she's sick? Brain tumor, maybe. Or, shit, I don't know. She slept for a solid week. What the hell?"

"You're an ass, Evans. There's nothing wrong with Whitney. Nia says she's having a hard time adjusting to the—"

"Insanity." It burst straight from Blake's mouth. "Go ahead, say it. I love her. You're right. Thought there might be a chance for us until she showed up in my office with this fucked-up story about a calling. I can't separate the impossibility of that from the..." He knuckled his forehead.

"Sometimes her expressions, the crap she says, it seems so real."

"Nia had Marcellin in her head for years. Showing her how he murdered." Coburn hunched his shoulders.

"Yeah, yeah. But Marcellin was real."

"No." Coburn shook his head. "Not easier. Worse. Think about it."

"You mean the connection between them?" Evans asked.

"Well, shit. You're not as stupid as you've been acting. Gives me chills." Not many people can paint their language with perfect disdain. I offered Coburn a virtual high-five.

"Cut the crap, Coburn. How do you live with it? With Nia seeing things she honest to God can't know?"

"I wouldn't want to live without her. It's that simple. I love her. Trust her. End of story."

"You really think there's something to this friggin' damn calling thing? Whitney's not just screwing with me? Trying to get rid of me?"

Screwing with him? Damn and blast. Like I'd asked to be born with this?

"Come on, Evans. We're talking Whitney. She may kill you, but she damn well won't jerk you around."

"Scares me." Blake barely whispered the words. If my hearing hadn't been enhanced by the calling I'd have never heard him.

"Like Nia doesn't scare the shit out of *me*. She doesn't think, acts like she's related to Wonder Woman, and tackles crazy bastards off the edge of cliffs."

Nia strolled into the back yard, her timing perfect. "I heard that."

The rustle of clothing caught my ear and experience told me Coburn had just wrapped Nia in his arms.

"Eavesdropping?" Coburn asked.

Panic rocked through me. Had they spotted me, then?

"No." Indignation enhanced Nia's denial. "That would be tacky. I'm here because the two of you are the best gossips ever, and I hate to be left out."

She paused long enough to draw in a deep breath. "Not that I listened in on your discussion, but Blake, fear happens when you love someone."

"You believe her? About the calling?" Blake's tone held a tinge of incredulity that set my teeth on edge.

I shifted my jaw to ease the stress, and then noticed the silence. Nia had a flair for speaking silence.

I inched up, peeked outside. Her toe was tapping. She held her hand up, palm out, then jabbed her fingers into Blake's rock-solid abdomen. Got him talking. "Yeah. Right. I know Whitney doesn't pull crap like this, but hearing dead people talk. How do I live with that?"

I ducked back down.

Silence. No birds chirping. No breeze rustling the leaves. No response.

It lasted long enough to have me popping back up. Spying was damn hard on the thighs.

Nia planted a kiss on Blake's cheek. "Try listening to her. Maybe even go so far as to believe in her. You have a choice, and can run from this if you want to. Whitney can't. She's in a much tougher place than you are."

"Doubtful. At least she knows what's going on in her head."

"Does she? I'm guessing Whitney's voices are a lot like the

images I saw through Marcellin. There was always a terrifying moment of revulsion when I realized he'd taken control. That I could only see what he showed me."

Blake's shoulders twitched. "Point taken. I'll listen, but I'm not making any promises. She annoys the hell out of me."

The tip of Nia's tongue toyed with her crooked front incisor. "Should be an interesting plane ride. Hours and hours together, with no escape."

My legs were cramping, so I collapsed back on the floor. I'd come close to leaning out the window to offer a comment or two, but thought better of it. It would be…prudent…to wait and see how we did with the forced intimacy of an overnight flight.

I bypassed the short dresses and strappy heels I typically wore and filled my new Prada backpack with serviceable items: blue jeans and t-shirts, a toothbrush and my lemon verbena lotion. I slipped the straps over my shoulder and headed out. "Time to go," I announced as I rounded the corner of the house.

Blake did his habitual watch check. "Right. I'll grab my bag."

Coburn trailed after him, but Nia caught my arm. "You remember that Trace and I are leaving the day after tomorrow. We have a meeting with the architect in North Dakota to start designing our Minot house."

Blake stuck his head out the door. "Hey, this cat is about to purr me to death. Didn't anybody feed him tonight?"

"Ahimsa. You and Coburn are leaving?" I didn't sound as coherent as I'd have liked.

Nia slid her sunglasses down her nose. "Um-hmm. Thought that might be an issue. I sent Chloe a text when I confirmed our reservations. Our flights will be crossing paths somewhere over the Pacific, so she'll be here to take care of him within hours after Trace and I have left. Also, I'm leaving her a key to the condo. I don't think she should stay here by herself, what with the cryptic notes on your bathroom mirror and creepiness happening all over the place."

"Absolutely," I agreed. "As the threats were directed at me, I should think she'll be safe, but...what the? She *talked* to you? I've nagged her all day with unanswered voicemail about the whereabouts of Justice, and she rang *you* up?"

Nia planted her feet and anchored her glasses on her nose. "Nope. Didn't talk to me. Sent a text with nothing but her arrival time."

My temper cooled a notch. "All the same. What do you make of her silence?"

"I think she hasn't found him, doesn't have a clue what to say to you, and is on her knees offering her firstborn to every god and goddess she knows."

"Now there's an image. Whyever would she do that?"

"Gratitude that you won't be here when she arrives."

Chapter 10

BLAKE and I were airborne two hours later, with no word from either Chloe or Dominic Justice, and Sheriff Dugas had nothing to report about Grandmamma. The paucity of information left my nerves brittle and my patience thin. Blake, in self defense, plied me with champagne, and I surrendered to deep, dreamless sleep until voices filled my head and images exploded against the back of my eyes, disrupting in their intensity, confusing for their lack of clarity.

In a burst of panic I startled awake into unfamiliar darkness. I dragged in a breath that was filled with the salty, fresh scent of Blake's skin.

His hand clamped over my mouth.

Terror ripped at me. Heart pounding, blood racing, I struggled to free myself, but Blake held on with the tenacity of duct tape. He whispered soothing, unintelligible words that were probably meant to chase the crazy from my behavior. Didn't work. I rammed him with a panic-induced jab to the stomach.

"Sweet Jesus, woman." He caught my elbow, tucked it tight between us, and stroked my hair, his touch gentle. I grabbed his hand and held on, giving my battered psyche time to settle.

"It was a dream, Whitney. A dream. You're okay."

Pressing my cheek tightly against his chest, I focused on his soft cotton shirt and the steady thud of his heart. Safe.

Not that I *needed* to lean on anyone. "Mala was reaching for me. Grabbing at me. She hasn't talked to me in days, and she was trying to pull me into the grave with her."

The soft rumble of his laughter gathered underneath my ear. "That wasn't Mala. It was me. I did the grabbing when you started to wail. Unholy sound. Scared the shit out of me."

My breathing steadied, and I pushed free of his arms. "I don't remember what she said, and now she's gone, not a single voice in my head. Grandmamma was there too. And Avril Dupré."

Blake winked. "Sounds like a nightmare with an overload of estrogen. No wonder you were screaming."

"Screaming?" I grabbed his arm, listening. No one stirred. An assortment of snores and sleepy snuffles punctuated the whining drone of the airplane engines. "You lie. Everyone would be awake, asking questions, if I'd been screaming."

Blake pried my fingers off his arm. "I covered your mouth, kept the gnashing and wailing from becoming a security issue."

"Quite." It was a perfunctory response as my mind still grappled with remnants of the dream. "Grandmamma was there. With Mala and Avril."

"Uh-huh. So you said." His calm-the-crazy-woman tone was…annoying.

"Mala and Avril are both dead."

Blake framed my face with his hands, touched my lips with his. Tender. Caring. It worked. Calm and a spiral of heat worked its way through me, diverting my attention.

"Arielle Boulay isn't dead," Blake whispered.

He got it. I hadn't explained the panic ripping at me, and he got it. I rearranged my categorization of his assets, adding a positive checkmark for ability to decipher my occasional bouts of crazy.

I touched the diamond in my earlobe. "Mala and Avril are."

"Avril I'll give you. Hard to argue with dead and buried. The jury's still out on Mala, but I'm trying to keep an open mind. And Grandmamma is much too tough to die. There's no connection between them, Whitney. It was a dream."

I rubbed my cheek against his chest. "You're wrong about Mala. But as I can't prove it until we get to Hampshire..."

He ran his thumb along my cheek. "Neither of us wears patience easily. How about we table this discussion until we're on British soil?"

I rested my forehead against his, closed my eyes, and relaxed into the moment. We were somewhere over the middle of the Pacific, my mobile was shut down, and my lips tingled with need. I knit my fingers through his close-cropped curls, and pulled his mouth toward mine. Close enough to taste him. Close enough to send a ribbon of heat spiraling through my belly. Blake's lips lingered against mine, demanding more from me.

Unrequited lust. Powerful. I jerked back, tucked my head under his chin. "We're on an airplane. Public."

He tipped my chin up, covering my mouth with his, insistent and demanding. Raw need raged out of control, and I matched him stroke for stroke. He slammed the armrest out of the way, yanking a blanket over us. His hand slid under my t-shirt, a flash of heat against my skin.

I sucked in a breath, leaning into his touch.

He teased the underside of my breast with his fingertips. "No bra. Beautiful."

I shifted, moving into his touch, wanting more.

He rewarded me with a wisp of his fingertips, barely there. A shiver of delight captured my breath in the back of my throat. "More." I breathed in the scent of male arousal. Beads of sweat broke out along my spine.

Blake palmed the fullness of my breast. I shook, my body taut with need.

Someone coughed. *Shit.* The whine of jet engines slapped at me.

I flattened my palm against Blake's chest. His heart pounded against his ribs, matching mine beat for beat. I clung to the edge of control. "Not here. Sex at thirty-five thousand feet is too…common."

"Not common. Comforting," he mumbled. "Keeps your mind from the dark. Stops the pain."

His words rubbed rough in my mind. "You've got your hands all over me as a distraction, then? To keep me from dropping off the deep end?"

His mouth covered mine in a hard kiss, then he eased back. "Not hardly. I have my hands all over you because I can't stop. Don't want to stop. You screw with my head, Whitney Boulay."

He rubbed at his forehead, looking a bit helpless. Naughty delight coursed through me. "Caught up in the romance, are you?"

He grinned. "You'd hate it if I was. Not your style." He separated my lips with his tongue, then dipped inside for a slow taste.

A flash of heat shot through me. "Amazing mouth," I said, nipping at the soft spot behind his ear.

He groaned. I weakened with the need for his touch. "You aggravate me 'til I'm set to have a go at you, then you plant those amazing lips on me."

"Umm. Good to know you're not immune to my charms." He angled in for another kiss, and I was lost in a heady mix of wild tingle and hypnotic pleasure, leaning into him, frantic to be closer, to rub against his bare chest. My fingers found the buttons on his shirt…

The plane hit an air pocket, and a shaft of fear rocked my nerves. I ducked my head, nestled into his chest, and hoped he hadn't noticed my sudden preoccupation with hiding from him. It was embarrassing, hating to fly.

Blake's muscles tightened. "I've got you." He blew out a sigh, shifted his weight, breaking our intimate connection. "I'm trying to wrap my head around it."

What was he talking about? If I hadn't been lost in the threat of the bouncing hunk of metal and the murk of my own mind, I'd have been paying attention. Heard the weary in his voice. And the wariness.

"Your gift. The whole talking to dead people—" A faint shudder ripped through his body.

"A damned nuisance, isn't it?" I didn't want him to be afraid of me.

"For me, oh yeah. For you?" Curiosity wove through his words.

Was it genuine? Was he beginning to believe in the calling? "It wasn't the gift I'd planned on."

"Planned?" He stiffened. "You can plan for this—"

I covered his mouth with my palm. "No. I tried. Didn't work. Thought I'd be like Grandmamma. Clairvoyant."

If I'd been less exhausted and a bit more comfortable with staggering through the air currents that were bouncing us around, I'd have paid more attention to the catch in his breathing. I dropped my forehead to his chest. "Human's weren't made to fly," I muttered into his shirt.

Blake stilled, his muscles giving a decent impression of granite. "Clairvoyance?"

The seat belt sign flashed on and the captain's voice broke into the dark. We were in for a bout of severe turbulence. Over the middle of the ocean.

"Damn it all to hell and back." I hadn't meant for the words to slip out.

Blake's fingers tightened on my arm. "Clairvoyance, Whitney?"

"Grandmamma's gift, not mine. The dead are my gift. I've been preparing for the calling all my life, and it still unnerves me to hear them in my head. You're probably well shut of me after this affair with Barat is over and done."

"Don't know if that's an option." He tucked me into the blanket, checking that I was buckled up, then dug a couple bottles of water out of his seat pocket and offered me one.

I shook my head, and clicked on the overhead light. I fumbled for my handbag, the seatbelt cutting into my abdomen. "There was something about the picture of Grandmamma," I said. It had been nagging at the back of my mind, and finally pushed its way to the surface.

Lowering the tray table, I centered the picture just so, and stared at it. The focused concentration shuffled the terror of the lurching airplane to the back of my mind.

Blake stretched one leg into the aisle and angled his chin toward the photo. "What?"

I pointed to the photo. "See here. She's knitting."

"Strategic move for her kidnappers," Blake said. "Usually they go with scare tactics, but this is downright homey. They're playing to your sensitivity."

"Right. It doesn't fit a typical pattern. And the piece she's working on is…large."

"You lost me."

I glanced at him. "It's the gold lamé. When I left her, she'd only just cast on."

Lightning flashed. I dug my fingers into Blake's arm. A wave of nausea rolled through my belly, and I held perfectly still so as not to affect the stability of the plane. Silly. But I wasn't rational about anything that happened thirty thousand feet in the air.

Blake levered my fingernails out of his skin and twined our fingers. "You've definitely lost me."

"Huh?" I dared a quick glance at the sky, solid black broken only when the lights from the wingtips cast fleeting shadows against the clouds. A shudder skipped across my shoulders.

Blake squeezed my hand and I turned to face him. His glazed eyes told me I wasn't making sense. "You begin a knitting project by casting on stitches. It's the foundation row."

"And?"

"This is a large piece." I pointed to the pile of worked yarn on Grandmamma's lap. "As quick as she is, it would take a fair bit of time to complete this much of the pattern."

Blake downed the rest of the water in his bottle. "Keep talking."

Hope quivered deep in my belly. "It has to be recent. It's eight, nine days since I left the Bayou?"

"Nine."

"It wouldn't take her that long to complete this much, but the sweater she's wearing…"

"Uh-huh. Purple. Long-sleeved. Buttons. Got it."

I elbowed him. "She was working with this yarn before I left, but only had the back finished, so she's had time to complete it, *and* make decent progress with the lamé."

He skimmed his thumb over my hand. "You're saying she was okay as of yesterday?"

"Best guess. Yeah. And I'm betting she made them take the photo while she had her knitting in her lap, and deliberately wore the sweater—she was sending me a message, Blake. Telling me she's okay."

"Whoa. That's a jump, Whitney."

"A bit. But, no. I'm positive about this. It's not a by-the-book conclusion, but I'm right."

Blake's grunt touched off a tremor of annoyance, and I tucked the picture away. "She's clairvoyant. You're probably not comfortable with that, but there it is. She knew I'd be getting this, knew I'd understand the message."

He shrugged. "What are we, supposed to do with clairvoyant information? It doesn't come with instructions, and the unsubs who abducted her haven't contacted you."

A sharp jolt of turbulence hit, and my stomach lurched in a nasty series of bumps and rolls. I locked my tray table, and slid my hands under my thighs, grabbing the seat. "You're right about the lack of communication from the unknown suspects. They're not following any sort of classic abduction pattern."

The plane lurched. Beads of sweat trailed down my back.

Blake caught my chin on his index finger, and tipped my head up. "You're white, which should be damned impossible considering that rich Cajun blood." He gathered me in his arms, and then reached down and ran his index finger along the back of my hand, the one gripping the seat, and brought my other hand to his mouth, and pressed a soft kiss against my palm. The threat of death-by-dropping-into-the-Pacific was replaced by the greater threat of losing my heart.

I slid my hand around Blake's neck. He rubbed against it, and explored the arch of my cheekbone with the tip of his tongue. Gentle. Loving. Narcotic pleasure hummed through my body. I skimmed my fingers over his rough cheek, enjoying the dusting of stubble. He pressed into my hand, not unlike Ahimsa when I found that special place at the base of his ears. My heart smiled.

Blake pulled the blanket over us again, slid his hand under my shirt, and stroked my back with single-minded dedication. Tender, kind, calm. Everything but sexy. "Tell me something about you, Whitney. Something I don't know."

His request whispered against my ear, tentative. My heart tumbled into love. Blast it all. *Play the game, Whitney. Just play the game.* "I don't have a middle name."

"Say what?"

I batted my eyelashes against his neck. "You expected a confession from the dark depths of my soul?"

"Uh, no," he said, sounding confused. "Is it unusual? Having only a first and last name?"

"In my world it ranks right up there with the calling."

He tipped his head back to meet my gaze. "You're serious."

"Quite. There wasn't one other student in my boarding school with fewer than four names. Made for considerable teasing and grade school angst."

"I can, ah, beat that. My, ah, middle name is…"

His garbled mumble didn't come close to being discernable. "Again."

"Abner."

I bit my lip to stop the grin. "As in Li'l Abner? The comic strip?"

The groan came from deep in his chest, and ended with a sharp nip to my earlobe.

"Well, aren't we just the pair," I said, ignoring the flash of heat that slammed into my core.

He smiled. "A perfect match. One for one in grade school angst."

BLAKE was still holding me when the captain announced our imminent arrival in New Orleans. Sunlight streamed through the window. Too bright. Too harsh. I shook free from the comfort of Blake's arms. I'd been dependent on him, let him hold me while I slept. In the middle of a personal crisis, and trapped in an airplane bouncing around in the nothingness of a bunch of clouds.

He grinned. "Morning." Amusement trickled through the single word, more threatening than a crash landing. The man was decidedly dangerous.

Blake wisely didn't utter another word. Not when the flight attendant offered us orange juice. Not when we deplaned. Not until he turned his phone on and checked for messages.

"Justice called."

Chapter 11

"**B**LOODY hell." I grabbed for Blake's phone.

He captured my wrist with a single, sharp move. "Hang on. Need to punch in my password."

Roaring filled my ears, but I backed off. Blake held the phone between us, angled so we could both hear. "Dominic Justice, here."

"That's it? That's the message?" I groped in my handbag, palmed my cell, and checked for messages. Nothing. "What's his number?"

I tapped in the numbers as Blake read them off, and then pressed Send with enough oomph to break a nail.

"Justice, here."

"You bastard," I yelled. "What the hell have you done with Grandmamma?"

Blake tapped my shoulder, motioning to the crowded baggage claim area. I moistened my lips, tried for a smile to keep innocent passengers from siccing TSA on me, gave up, and leaned against a support column for more privacy.

Dark silence sizzled over the phone line, and then the faint click of a broken connection pierced my bones.

"He hung up on me." It came out as a whisper. My rage had moved beyond wild ranting to lethal quiet. "That makes him an official suspect."

Blake backed two steps away from me before he answered. "Not without more evidence. Not surprising he hung up. I doubt he's big on either denial or confession."

I thunked my forehead on column, hoping to knock loose the red haze crowding my vision. Blake pried the cell from my clenched fist and hit redial. I worked to shake off my wild Cajun woman persona so I could slither into the calm, cool elegance I relied on to get me out of tight spots. I had to finesse this bastard, not alienate him. Not if I intended to find Grandmamma.

"I could murder him." I shuddered with the truth of my statement. "Dominic Justice could well be my first kill."

Blake twitched. "Not your best plan. He can't lead you to Arielle if he's six feet under."

"Quite. Didn't realize I'd said that out loud." I pointed at my cell.

"No answer." He handed it to me, pulled the band out of my hair, and wove his hands through my tangled curls. "Gotta get some space around your brain before you overheat. You ready to ditch this place?"

I plucked the hair band from his fingers, slipped it over my wrist. "More than."

There wasn't a line at the Hertz counter, so I had the keys to a sporty convertible jingling in my pocket in less than fifteen minutes. Heat rose from the pavement, shimmered in the still air, and left beads of moisture on my skin. I secured my hair into a tail so I could drive with the top down—not a typical choice in New Orleans. In July. At high noon.

Blake squinted at the open vehicle, then strapped himself into the passenger seat, all athletic movements and toned muscles. "I'm gonna catch a nap. Keep the speed legal, will you?"

A quiver of need thrummed between my thighs. I bit down on my cheek, hoping for a modicum of control. "Um-hmm. Absolutely."

"You lie." A nearly imperceptible grin twitched at the corner of his mouth.

I couldn't argue with that, as speed would help to work off my temper. The drone of wheels on pavement and the rush of air against my face had an hypnotic effect, giving me space to think.

A scant hour later I parked in front of Grandmamma's cabin, eased from behind the wheel, and stretched into a wide-angle forward bend to release the kinks in my lower back. "I can't get 'round the idea she isn't here," I said.

Blake snagged the bridge of his shades, gave a tug, and peered at my backside over the top of the frames. "How do you want to do this?"

A frisson of heat curled through my body in response to the double entendre. I tamped it down, barely, and focused on the reason we were here. I straightened, and listened to the cacophony of the Bayou, lapping water, rustling animals, birdsong, the wind as it wove through the trees. And then I listened to the quiet. The absolute absence of humanity. "She's not here. No one is."

Blake stretched his arms overhead, yawned, and, cool as you please, tapped his hand on my backside. "Nice," he said, and then headed toward the cabin like a 'gator on the prowl. Sleek, silent, and deadly. Every move casually lethal.

I let him take the lead, needing time to settle into the Bayou energy before I faced the emptiness of the cabin. Running my finger over the diamond in my ear, I offered a silent oath to find Grandmamma. Soon.

Shaking off my melancholy, I strode after Blake, caught up as he stepped onto the front porch. He flicked his finger at me. "You have a key?"

I rocked back on my heels, nodded toward the door. "You might want to take a closer look."

"Uh-huh." He turned the knob, pushed the door open and stood aside. "How about we get a lock installed before we leave? Less chance she'll turn up missing in the future."

"You'll be keeping your grubby fingers off Arielle Boulay's property. She'd feed you to the 'gators for suggesting such a thing, and since she chats them up on a regular basis, they'd be likely to nibble on you for days."

"Your grandmother talks to alligators?" The skin around Blake's eyes crinkled with his grin. "Crazy runs in your family, woman."

The flowers in Grandmamma's garden had grown tall, and vines were curling up the side of the cabin. I stepped over the threshold and inhaled the dull, stagnant scent of abandonment mixed with the heady fragrance of earth and vegetation. She'd only been gone a few days, and already Mother Nature was beginning to reclaim her space, the space Grandmamma borrowed and tended.

I kicked at the braided rug covering the wide plank floor. She was alive. Had to be alive. Baskets of colorful yarn filled several shelves behind her rocking chair. Books were scattered on tables and a shawl hung in elegant folds over the kitchen chair where she sat to peel potatoes.

"Anything feel off?" Blake asked.

His words bumped into the silence, and caught on the raw edge of my emotions. "Not a thing. It's as though she went to shop, or birth a baby, or tend to…Avril…"

He slipped a knuckle under my chin, tipped my head up. "What?"

"Avril. There's something about Avril Dupré, the woman the Pitre brothers killed just before I left the Bayou."

"And you know this how?" Blake asked.

I jerked the band out of my hair, slicked the loose curls back with my hands, and wove them, along with the hair band, into a twisted knot at the base of my neck. "She's whispering, pushing at my mind, but I can't make out the words."

He shrugged. "Okay. I'll leave you to it while I walk through the rest of the cabin."

I blinked at him, parsed his words to keep them separate from the background simmer of Avril's voice. "Mind the steps. The third one has a raised area that's easy to trip over."

He gave me a thumbs-up.

I wandered outside, and settled into Grandmamma's old pine rocker. Dapples of sunlight cut through the brilliant blue sky and glittered on the water. I let my thoughts drop away to make room for Avril. She'd been quiet since the full Cajun funeral mass that honored her passing. I kicked off my sneakers, and pushed against the rough boards of the porch with my toes.

Blake poked his head outside. "Nothing upstairs. Looked like your room."

"Um-hmm. Go away. I'm thinking." I followed the creak of the rocker, trailed it back into my mind, and brought up an image of Avril Dupré. Her words were desperate and garbled, as though she spoke to me from deep under water. The only word I could make out was *home*, and I wasn't positive about that. A biting chill settled at my nape. Chloe was right. I had to try to talk to her, to call her to me. How was I supposed to crawl into the mind of a dead woman?

The tu-wit call of a Ruff interrupted my quest for answers, only to provide the exact information I needed. It flew past me and landed on the water with a delicate splash. I stripped off clothes, making a dash for the cabin and Grandmamma's bathroom. I needed to be under water to hear her, but I sure as all hell wasn't going to jump into the swamp.

Blake grabbed my arm as I dashed for the back of the cabin. "Whoa. What the hell?"

My jeans were unzipped, my shirt untucked. "No worries. Be ready to leave soon, won't you?"

"Whit—"

I jerked free, tearing at clothes while I ran. I turned the shower on full blast and stepped under the spray, praying for a miracle. This had to work. It had to.

Nothing. Water sluiced over my body, but my mind remained completely free of Avril and any thoughts she might be trying to share.

Blake yanked the curtain aside, his gaze traveled down the length of my body. "What the hell are you doing?"

"Water. I need to be submerged in water to hear Avril."

"Uh-huh. Distracting as the view is, I gotta tell you that you're more under the water than submerged in it."

I stepped back from the spray, brushed the water from my eyes, and caught the gleam of pure lust in his baby browns, as well as the quick adjustment he made to his jeans. I wrenched the curtain into place before I could give in to my lust and drag him into the spray with me.

His laughter wrapped around me. "No way am I going to forget that view."

"Added a dash of flavor to your day, did it?"

"Umm. While you're ah, communing with Avril, I'm going to clean out the refrigerator. No reason for your grandmother to come home to spoiled food."

"An excellent use of your time." My words were gaspy,

little breaths that could only be accounted for by the way Blake had stroked my body with his gaze, like a feather caressing my skin. Damned inconvenient.

I snatched a scrubbie from the shelf and squirted a dollop of body wash into the net fibers. A good scrubbing would clear my mind and set me to focus on Avril Dupré, who didn't have a sexy bone in her body, nor a glimmer of lust in her very dead black eyes.

The scent of lemon filled the bathroom, and when I finished rinsing the suds off my body and out of my hair, I bent to stuff the stopper in the drain. The tub filled while I stood under the spray and let the hot water beat on my shoulders. After it filled, I turned the shower off and gradually immersed myself. And then popped out to do some deep breathing and center my mind on the image of Avril. The more prepared I was before submerging myself, the faster she could catch me up on recent events. An excellent plan, as I couldn't hold my breath for an indeterminate amount of time.

I sank down for a second time and her voice came through, garbled at first, and then a few words ricocheted through my mind so quickly I barely caught them.

My home.

Go there.

Chapter 12

"WE'RE going to Avril's place," I called through the bathroom door, tugging clothes over still-damp skin. I caught my hair in a towel, wrapped it turban style around my head, and hustled into the kitchen.

Blake came in from outside, passing me as I grabbed my handbag off the table. "Going somewhere?" he asked, holding the door open for me.

"Avril's place. Now."

"You have a towel on your head." He let the screen slam behind him, and I paused to watch him through the mesh grid. He moseyed over to the sink, ran water to wash his hands, and then stuck his head under the faucet for a long drink, came up for air and swiped his hand across his mouth. "We're going to Avril's house because?"

"She told me to go there. While I was under the water."

Blake followed me to the car. "Any clue as to why?" he asked, maneuvering into the passenger seat with enough hip movement to catch my attention.

I turned the key in the ignition and fastened my seat belt. "No. But the dead rarely tell me why they want me to do something. Apparently, dying skews our minds."

"I'm trying to understand, Whitney, but the idea that we still think after we die is just weird."

I backed out of the driveway, and took off. "Yes, well, we do. You really are doing quite well with all this, considering."

Blake's fingers trailed along my neck, over my shoulder. "You're tense. What's going on?"

My hormones twanged. No way could I keep this man at bay, at least not in the confined space of an automobile. I peeked at him around the edge of my sunglasses. "I'm fine. Thanks for asking."

He shot me a narrow-eyed stare. "It wasn't a throwaway question. Something's happening in that busy mind of yours, and I'd like at least a clue about what we're walking into."

"It's the next right. We'll both find out in under a minute." I swiped at the water seeping in rivulets from under my makeshift turban.

His sigh circled around the car, sharp enough to jab at me and release a twinge guilt. "I'd tell you if I could, but I just don't know."

The waterway came up fast in front of me, and I slammed on the brakes. The towel tumbled from around my head, covering my face. I peeled it away, tossing it over my shoulder.

There was no cabin.

I blinked. There were pieces of wood, and the cement outline of what had been a home, but definitely no cabin.

"Damn and blast. What happened to Avril's house?"

Blake stepped out of the car, looked around. "Doesn't look like fire. Nothing's charred, and there's no odor of burnt wood. Damage looks fresh."

I groped in the console for my mobile and punched in the number for Sheriff Dugas. He answered on the first ring.

"Whitney Boulay here, Sheriff. I'm at Avril Dupré's cabin, and it appears to have come out on the wrong end of some vandalism."

"You got that right, Miz Whitney. Don't rightly know what happened. Went to check on things during my regular patrol and found it like that. Must have been, oh…day before yesterday."

"The Pitres are still locked up, then?"

"In Baton Rouge. They were transferred shortly after their arrest. Anythin' I can help you with?"

Why wasn't he looking into this? "No, but I would like to take a look around. Would that suit?"

"Yezzum. There's no problem with that. Don't rightly know what the crime would be, since old Avril didn't have any interested family. All eight of her young'uns up and left, and the cabin wasn't worth much even before someone took it to pieces."

"Quite. I'll just take a quick look 'round and be on my way. And I'd like to question the owners of the establishment that rented the pirogue to Dominic Justice."

"Y'all are welcome to it. Hope you find some answers. It's a sore bit of bad luck to have Grandmamma missin'. We all need her here to tend the sick and whatnot."

I slipped the phone in my pocket, and then wandered toward the remains of Avril Dupré's cabin.

Blake stood hipshot, fingers hooked in his belt loops, shaking his head.

I circled the perimeter of the cabin and tried to open my mind to Avril. Dead quiet.

Blake came up behind me. "Not much we can do with this mess. K-9, maybe."

It threw me, hearing him essentially write off a potential crime scene. The man who left no page unturned in any procedure manual. Was he hiding something? No telltale nose scratch, so probably not. I gave up trying to figure it out and went with the obvious question. "Dogs?"

"The canine nose is a remarkable thing." His inflection was normal, no hint of malicious intent or devious manipulation.

"Um-hmm, but we're not looking for drugs, a missing person, or a specific accelerant. Are we?"

"What *are* we looking for?" There it was. The edge.

"If I knew, we would have found it by now. Your knickers appear to be in a bit of a twist."

Blake glanced down, adjusted his jeans. "Men don't wear knickers. My boxers are perfect. Tailored to fit. You, on the other hand, are pushing my buttons."

"It's the water. You haven't been able to find a way to account for my underwater chat with Avril. Forced both of us to face the wonky in me. Scared you."

He nodded. "Yeah. It did."

My heart stuttered. "Scared me, too. But it's who I am, Blake. The thing is, Avril isn't talking and I'm wandering about—"

"With no freakin' idea what to do next." The irritation slid from his stance, and a smile played behind his eyes.

Well, then. I ran my hand along one of the boards that had been loosened from the framework, thinking maybe it would link me to Avril, but she remained quiet.

Blake hovered. "How about you ask her?"

I whipped around, fisted his shirt in my hand. "If I knew how to do that I wouldn't be standing here without a clue as to what's going on, now would I?"

Blake shoved his hands in his pockets with an impatient twitch. "You're a *detective*. Figure it out."

Irritation temporarily hampered my ability to grasp the obvious. A detective. Absolutely. Before my calling, I sifted through evidence to solve crimes. Before the dead began *telling* me who committed murder and why, I absolutely figured it out on my own. Finally I stepped back and ran my palm down the front of his shirt to smooth out the wrinkles. "You're suggesting I fall back on my training and stop depending on dead people to do all the work."

He ran his tongue over his bottom lip. "Looks like someone was damn determined to find something. Question is: what were they looking for?"

"The Petrie brothers found the money, murdered Avril. The newspaper reported the homicide and her funeral arrangements, but…"

I snatched Blake's cell from the clip on his belt and phoned Sheriff Dugas. "Whitney Boulay, here. Whatever happened to the money the Pitre brothers stole from Avril?"

I listened, thanked him, then rang off, then returned the phone to Blake. "The Pitres spent a fair amount, lost some in a series of poker games, and they contend they don't know what happened to the rest. Not surprising as they're a bit to the left of center on the bell curve."

"How much money are we talking?" Blake asked.

"Twenty-five K."

He whistled. "Not likely they'd misplace that amount."

"There you are, then." I ran my fingers over the remains of Avril's front door. "An excellent reason to take the house apart."

Blake's eyebrows shot up. "You lost me. Why not take the Pitre house apart, since they were the last to have possession of the money?"

I headed in the direction of the waterway, pushed some Spanish Moss out of the way, and shock slammed into me. "Well, blast and damn." I did a double-take at the Pitre brothers' cabin, yanked my sunglasses off, and pointed.

Blake's gaze traced the path of my finger, and he blew out another soft whistle as he eyed the remains of the cabin. "Gives a new meaning to thorough, doesn't it?"

"It does. Took a bit of time and work to tear down two cabins that comprehensively. Doesn't leave us with a blasted thing to do here."

Blake's forehead furrowed. "Not a lot of potential witnesses in the area?"

I nodded. "None, actually. And with just the two cabins there wouldn't be any strangers wandering about. Avril was a dodgy old lady. Her children scattered across the country years ago to avoid her wicked temper. Not one of them wanted to live like this." I waved my hand in the direction of the cabin. "But then they didn't know about the money, did they?"

"It's out of place. The money doesn't fit. Your grandmother being kidnapped doesn't fit. You, on the other hand, fit. It's as if you have a target painted on you, a bull's-eye, right in the middle of that beautiful chest. You're the key."

I responded with an unladylike grunt. Blake was right. The whole blasted mess centered around me. I wandered through the pile of boards and trash, searching for Avril, straining to hear her words in my mind. My calling work was to find killers and bring them to justice. I'd done that with Avril. The Pitre brothers were tucked away and Avril was…

"Talk to me. What's going on?" Irritation. Impatience. Both colored Blake's demand.

I spun to face him. "Avril isn't the dead person I need to chat with. Mala is. And why the hell are Grandmamma's kidnappers so quiet? They should be contacting me, asking for whatever they want."

Blake scrubbed at the lines on his forehead. "Let's not have the conversation about Mala again. How about we check out the rental place, see what they say about Justice? As far as them not contacting you, they're criminals. Enough said." He turned on his heel and headed for the car.

I conceded the point and trailed after him, my mind absorbed with the need to reach Mala. I fingered my cell, randomly tracing the irregular surface and decided a chat with Nia would do as an excuse to avoid Chloe, and her prodding at me to contact the dead. At least for a bit longer.

"Heads up." I tossed Blake the car keys. "You drive. I need to ring Nia."

He caught the keys in mid-air and slid into the driver's seat. I typed the address of the pirogue rental place into the GPS, plugged in the charger on my phone, and punched in Nia's number. "Don't listen," I said, giving Blake a squinty-eyed glare.

His laugh caught on the wind and evaporated into the afternoon heat. A tide of happy curled around my heart, made me want to lean into him.

And then he shot me a heart-stopping grin. "Got it. Ears wide shut. Give me a tap when it's safe to join the party."

Nia answered on the sixth ring, breathless and laughing. "Hey. How are things in the Bayou? Did you find Grandmamma yet?"

An innocent question. Genuine. Nia cared. Still, her words smothered me with dread, and left a bitter taste in my mouth. "Not as yet, no. And there's something else. Chloe—"

"Talked to her a few minutes ago. She'd just landed and was on her way to your house. She sounded good, but tired from the flight."

"Quite. Chloe taught you how to reach Marcellin, to get into his mind."

Silence. Shuffling. "Yes."

Icy sweat coated my body. "Can you teach me?"

Nia stuttered through a series of incoherent words.

I took pity on her. "Should I take that as a no, then?"

"Chloe's the one who needs to teach you. She does something…odd…with the space. Makes it safe. And that tea stuff she brews, it smothers the fear. Call her."

"As she's an ocean and a fair portion of the country away, it would be a bit impossible for her to ply me with tea and whatever else she does—" Agitation had me reaching across the console for Blake, twining my fingers in his shirtsleeve, as though I had the right to trespass when I'd asked him to give me privacy. Nothing like sending the man mixed signals.

"You're making excuses." Nia put some oomph behind her words, bringing me back to our conversation. "You're avoiding this because you don't want to accept Chloe and Dominic as a couple. Get over it. You aren't going to find Grandmamma until you learn how to use your calling, and Chloe is the only one I know who can help you figure out how to do that."

When did Nia become a shrink? "Quite. However, his influence means she's unpredictable. She could say something, alert him. Even if it's an accident, Justice could…I have to protect Grandmamma."

Blake pried my fingers from his mangled shirt, and then pressed tender kisses along the back of my hand. I stopped listening to Nia, and turned toward Blake. He set my hand on his thigh. "Easy, Detective. This is a job first. Later you can wallow in the personal."

Anger flared at his insinuation, then abated. I turned the

phone in to my chest. "I absolutely hate when you're right."

Nia's voice came through, muffled. "Whitney? Are you listening? Chloe is the only one who can help you and she's in the throes of serious jet lag. It's a reprieve, but you can't put this off, no matter how valid your feelings."

Damned inconvenient, emotions. "I'll ring her up tomorrow. See how it goes."

I could feel her grin over the phone

"Don't gloat." I tried to put some bite in the words, but smiled instead.

"Not gloating." She laughed. "What's next?"

"We're pulling into the shop where Justice rented the pirogue. I'll fill you in later."

I disconnected. The seatbelt cut into my shoulder when Blake made a sharp U-turn into the drive-thru lane of a fast food restaurant. "What—"

"We've been going strong for hours and this place smells damn fine. What would you like?"

He had a point. I was starving. "Whatever and a Diet Coke."

Blake placed our order, paid, collected his change and our food.

And then Mike's Pirogue Rentals blew to smithereens.

Chapter 13

A surge of heat intensified the afternoon humidity and my ears echoed with the reverberation from the explosion. Mike's had been little more than a shack, but threw off enough ash to float leisurely on the damp air and settle around us in a slow-motion blanket of dust.

Blake mopped at the soda he'd slopped when the blast hit. "What the hell?" he yelled.

I leapt from the car, yanked the driver door open, grabbed the fast food bags out of his hands, and tossed them in the back seat. Overcome by a fit of coughing, Blake motioned for me to head for Mike's while he parked.

Nodding, coughing, I grabbed one of the sodas from him and sucked down a long swallow while I raced toward the waterway. I headed straight for an obviously stunned older gentleman who was wandering around the pirogues.

"Sir?" I reached for his arm, gave it a gentle shake. "Are you all right, then? We need to move you away from here, see to your safety."

No response.

Blake jogged up, phone in hand as he relayed the particulars to nine-one-one. He made his way past me, moving closer to the fire, and absentmindedly brushed his forearm over the splotch of Coke staining his shirt.

Blast it. What was he thinking? Flames licked at the dry wood, crackled and sputtered as they ate the remains of the shack. "Blake!" I grabbed his arm. "I shouldn't bother about that. You'll singe your eyebrows if you get much closer."

He shook his head, hard. And then back-stepped, tossed his empty cup in a rusted-out trash barrel, and moved to flank the old man. "What's your name, sir?"

"M-Michael. I'm Michael." A shudder racked his body. "My livelihood. My life." Tears pooled in his eyes and streamed down his weathered cheeks.

Sirens cut through the Bayou evening. I turned Michael over to the paramedics and tugged Blake away from the action. "I need to talk with Michael. Keep the sheriff busy, will you?"

"Uh-huh." His cell rang, he glanced at caller ID, and turned away from me with a flip of his hand. A premonition crawled over my skin. Something was seriously amiss with that phone call. Later. I'd have to deal with it later. I rolled my shoulders back, shook the sensation from my mind, and headed for Michael to have a go at gathering information about Grandmamma and Dominic Justice.

An hour later, Blake and I collapsed in the car. I opted for the passenger position, planted my feet on the dashboard, and dug eagerly into the white take-away bags for a cold, less-than-tasty hamburger. Night had covered the Bayou, burying the few remaining shadows of evening. It should have been peaceful.

Blake jerked his sunglasses off, tossed them on the console, and held out his hand. "Hamburger."

"In a bit of a snit, are you?" I asked.

"Ummph."

Might be best to let him eat before I got to asking

questions. "Michael described Dominic Justice. There's no doubt Chloe's new boy-toy was here and rented a pirogue. And as for the kidnappers, they're communicating with me. Telling me to back off. They're just using action instead of phone calls. I preferred the phone calls."

"Ummph." Blake swallowed, sucked down most of a bottle of tepid water, and then grinned at me. "Boy-toy? Last I noticed, Justice had streaks of grey at his temples and badass written across his butt."

I sniffed. Haughty. "Boy-toy suits. Can we get to the phone call?"

"No."

An odd mix of guilt and fury churned in my stomach. I fought to keep the hamburger down. I could account for the people who knew our whereabouts on one hand. "Nia and Coburn, Chloe, maybe Justice, are the only ones who know we're here. None of them blew up Michael's business or hired someone to do it for them. He lived there, you know, in that beaten-up shack." Tears blurred my vision. No time for emotion. Not now. I squeezed my eyes shut, and willed my heart to stop hurting. "I'll see to having it rebuilt for him. It's you, Blake. You're connected to this in some unholy, horrible way."

His sigh was heavy, and it settled around us with dogged stickiness. "Yeah. It's fucked up."

Well, he got that right at least. "Every time you ring up the blasted office something bad happens—"

"What the hell are you talking about?" Was that fear making his voice too rough, too loud?

I flipped up my index finger. "The note in my bathroom. Shortly after you turned it over to your *people*, Grandmamma Boulay turned up missing, and that note hasn't got a thing to do with Barat and Mala Sen."

Blake's fingers did a staccato tap on the steering wheel. "Sure it does. Has to. Unless you're mixed up in something else." He drilled me with a look. "What the hell aren't you telling me?"

I ignored the question, and flipped up my middle finger. "And then you rang them up before we left Honolulu. After you informed me there was absolutely no way you could arrange transport for us. Didn't have that kind of pull, no one owed you—"

"I have a job, Whitney. Finding Amar Barat is my job, not searching all over the damn place for your grandmother."

Pain ripped through me. I dragged in a lungful of air to blast him back to Minneapolis.

He glared. "Don't. Don't even think about laying into me about this. I'm here because I *want* to be, *not* because it's my damn job. I might not even *have* a job after this."

The red haze of my anger abated some, but not enough for me to be civil. "You're talking rubbish. Don't you get it? The FBI has taken Grandmamma, and I'm responsible for you being here. *You* followed me. *They* did it. Someone you work for has leaked the information to Barat. Whoever destroyed Michael's livelihood—the agent responsible for the leak or Barat himself—it doesn't matter a whit to me. It's quite straightforward. I will see the miserable excuse for a sentient being who hired Justice to steal Grandmamma from me is locked in a pigsty until they meet their demise." I paused to take a breath. "Possibly at my hands, as I wouldn't want to subject a pig to such garbage for a lengthy period of time."

If Chloe had looked at our auras right then, she would doubtless have seen streaks of energetic blood.

Blake choked down a mouthful of hamburger. "No. Not someone I work for."

How could he deny it? I wadded the empty take-away bag,

worked it into a tight ball. "You're the link. Justice chatted Michael up about renting a pirogue, and his description of the bastard was absolutely perfect."

Blake pulled to the side of the road, slammed on the brakes and skidded to a stop. "Can't be. Barat is high profile. Evil. Every one of us on the team wants him—"

"Locked up or preferably dead. Absolutely, I get that. But someone is cozied up nice and comfortable in Barat's pocket. Someone who stole an old man's livelihood with the flip of an incendiary device."

"Whitney—"

"Do not 'Whitney' me. It's bad enough that I need to watch my back around the FBI, but now I have them, the people I'm *supposed* to be able to trust, feeding Barat information. Doesn't that just add a nasty dash of flavor to the mix?"

Blake glared. "You done yet?"

"No. The question is: who's actually responsible? *Your* people or Barat? Mala Sen's death was absolutely a mistake, yes, but not a big enough mistake to warrant taking my life, putting my family in harm's way, or destroying Michael's home and livelihood."

Evans slammed his hand against the steering wheel, and then pulled back onto the road. "This conversation is over. I need a shower and sleep."

He was right about that. Other than napping on the plane, we hadn't slept in too many hours to count, and a film of dust covered our clothes and skin with mottled shades of gray. But the conversation was far from over. I ran my tongue between tight lips, tasted dust and stale hamburger, and struggled to keep from saying anything that would prove me to be a wonky bitch. Not that I wasn't. But acting either wonky or bitchy would give him fuel to make me wrong. And I wasn't wrong.

We didn't speak. Not when we parked at Grandmamma's cabin, not when we bumped into each other filling glasses of water at the sink, and not when we headed for separate rooms to shower and sleep. I needed a plan, and until I had one there was nothing to say.

The call of the neighborhood Ruff woke me as dawn spread hazy light through the bedroom window. The unmistakable scent of Grandmamma's coffee drifted into my room, and for a moment I forgot she was missing. The pain of her disappearance lodged sharp under my breastbone, and I pressed into it with my fist, tried to rub it away as I headed for the loo. I ignored the fragrant call of freshly brewed coffee and began a series of yoga Sun Salutations, then dropped to the floor in a comfortable cross-legged position to meditate. I needed to clear my mind and plan.

Fifteen minutes later I wandered downstairs and helped myself to coffee. Evans sat at the kitchen table in his boxers and a t-shirt, hands latched around a mug of the steaming brew, his gaze unfocused and drifting in the general direction of the water.

I blew across the top of the mug and took a tentative sip. Time for a truce. "You look a bit on the peaked side. Rough night, was it?"

He didn't move. "Our flight for Heathrow leaves in three hours. You might want to get dressed and wrap things up."

His arrogance twanged my last nerve, even though he'd played directly into my plans. I carefully set my coffee on the counter. "We're not done here. There are others to question, and I need to make arrangements for Michael, get him settled. Or have you forgotten about him?"

He still didn't move, not even a twitch. "You can take care of that by phone. Your grandmother isn't here. Justice isn't here. Be ready to leave in thirty."

Rage simmered deep in my belly, spilled into my words.

"Absolutely. Thirty."

The muscles in his jaw clenched. "I've kept my end of our bargain. Yours is to travel to Hampshire, no questions asked."

Pompous ass. "Only after we've collected a thorough account of Grandmamma's activities and traced the path Justice took. Not on your whim."

"My *whim* is based on solid investigation. Mala is in the UK. We're leaving in—" he glanced at his watch— "twenty-eight minutes."

I made an excellent show of stomping upstairs to do his bidding...and to put my plan into action.

I jerked on my jeans and a t-shirt, slung my backpack over my shoulder, and maneuvered from my bedroom window to the deck surrounding Grandmamma's cabin, then down to the waterway where she kept her pirogue. I fought my anger, crammed it down tight into my belly, and slipped silently into the boat, then edged away from the dock and down the waterway.

I checked my watch every few paddle strokes, sticking to my schedule. I'd used fifteen of the twenty-eight minutes Evans had *allotted,* and he'd be looking for me right about— now.

Unsure as to where he'd begin his search, I needed to stay away from the places he would think to look, so I quickly hid the pirogue in plain sight, tied into the line of boats at Michael's. It was the one place Evans would surely look for me, not that he'd recognize Grandmamma's pirogue, but it would work in my favor if he spent valuable time chasing after me.

I grabbed a cab to my attorney's office and made quick work of the financial arrangements to rebuild Michael's home and business. And then I wandered deep into the Vieux Carré in search of Grandmamma's oldest and dearest friend.

Madame Tatiana Leblanc lived in a little-known, difficult to find courtyard pied-à-terre that was tucked inconveniently off a back alley. An excellent place to spend some time while Evans chased his tail in pursuit of my whereabouts.

Madame was fussing about her garden when I knocked on the gate, didn't bother to turn and *see* who was about to invade her space, simply motioned me inside. Not surprising since she had the sight, just like Grandmamma.

"Bonjour, ma petite. I was expectin' you sooner." She stood, brushed the soil from her hands, and wrapped me in a hug. "Come along inside now an' share some *pain perdu* and café au lait while we have a petite tête-à-tête."

My stomach rumbled at the mention of the Cajun delicacy. It'd been a long morning, what with escaping from Blake and tending to Michael's situation, and a bit of the *lost bread* would be just the thing.

"You know why I'm here, then?" I asked.

"But of course. Come, sit. You need food before we speak of Arielle." She winked. "And that handsome young beau of yours."

I shivered. Whether it was from the fresh coolness of Madame's parlor or hearing Blake described as my beau, I didn't want to know. Madame Tatiana's home carried the scent of lavender and chamomile. So much like Chloe. And with that thought, another shiver skimmed over my skin.

The *pain perdu* was made from Madame's own bread, laced with sweet butter, fried, and topped with orange crème instead of the usual sugar or syrup. Melt-in-your-mouth delicious, and sure to add a kilo or two to my hips. A trip to the gymnasium loomed in the very near future.

Madame set our plates aside and took my hands. "Time to go to work, I think, ché."

"Oui. What have you seen of Grandmamma, then?"

"Healthy but not happy." She leaned closer to me, squeezed my hands. "Where she is, it's a confined space, and your Grandmamma, she likes to move."

"Can you see where she is, who's hiding her?" My heart raced with hope.

"Non. I can tell you she's not here, not near Louisiana." Madame's eyes went blank. I held my breath, not wanting anything to disturb her concentration. When she brought her attention back to me, it was with sadness. "Non. Nothing else to help you. How is it going with your calling, ma petite? This is all connected to your process, to your coming of age. *Adoptèrent*, Whitney. Embrace your gift. It is the only way."

I slid back in my chair. "I have. You know I led Sheriff Dugas to the Pitre brothers for old Avril Dupré, and the others—"

"Oui. But of course you did. Still, you are not yet one with the gift. *Adoptèrent*. You are not yet embracing the dead. You keep them at a distance, ché."

I freed my hands and stood. "Quite. You're saying I need to chat them up, deliberately open my mind to them."

"Yes. They're right there, but you are stubborn. Like the English, non?"

I dropped back into the chair. "Non. I'm not. Just a bit reluctant to have the dead take over my mind. They have quite nasty temperaments. It's annoying. They steal my life and fill it with their chatter. It's—"

"Frightening. Oui. As it is to see the future. But it is what we are, you and I, your maman, and your Grandmamma."

She was right. "May I stay with you for a bit? While I work on this? I'd rather not leave, not until I know where to look for Grandmamma."

"Hiding from your beau?"

I huffed. "Oui. But he is absolutely *not* my beau." The denial left a knot in my throat.

Madame tilted her head, deep brown eyes softening. "We shall see. First you must learn to share your mind with the dead. There's a teacher at home for you, yes?"

Home? "Do you mean in Honolulu?"

"Oui."

Chloe would be there by now. Bloody wonderful.

Chapter 14

I followed Madame Tatiana to a hidey-hole guest room on the first floor of her pied-à-terre, my mind reeling over how I'd approach Chloe. The tiny room was completely white—walls, painted wood floor, bedspread, and ladder back chair—except for huge bouquet of lavender centered on the chair seat. The fragrance washed over me, calming and hopeful. Madame had casually suggested I work with Chloe by phone rather than make the trip to Honolulu, but although I desperately wanted to avoid the flight, I was also nervous about trusting long-distance energy work. There were so many what-ifs, and this was Grandmamma's life.

Blake would be after me, but he wouldn't ask for help to find me. Not with the situation so dicey. He *would* trace me, maybe by late tomorrow—unless I rang him up before then. I'd toss some information at him, and give him something to think on while I learned about my calling.

A twitch nagged at the back of my mind. How was I going to ask Chloe to work with me, when I'd alienated her so completely? My threats to kill her lover *had* been a bit over the top. And nature sprites can pack a wallop of nasty when you set them off. Why couldn't I just accept being afraid and not lash out at myself and everyone around me? I could pinpoint a couple reasons. When Mum and Chilton ripped me away from Grandmamma to be educated in the UK, and then when I turned fifteen and Mum had disappeared into the think tank environment. Both times I'd hurt so damn bad. Knew it was me. That I wasn't good enough for anyone to love...except Grandmamma. I trusted her. Damn Dominic Justice for stealing her.

I stretched out on my temporary bed, and clouds of a sweet lavender scent drifted in the air.

Madame had a way with herbs. Like Chloe. Time to hone my groveling skills, ring her up, and apologize. I checked my watch. Ahimsa would be weaving between her feet in a persistent plea for breakfast. It was absolutely the right time to ring her up, but Dominic Justice hovered about like spoiled fish, and I hadn't the faintest glimmer of a plan how to... Unless I...yes. I'd text her. Safe. Distant. I typed in a message and sent it off.

A chill shot through me. How could I have screwed up so badly? It had been idiotic to use my phone. I'd have to... *oh, bloody hell*...dispose of it. Destroy it. My mind toyed with possibilities: lock it in a safe deposit box, mail it home. Either option would create a dead end for the FBI.

The phone was my only contact with the kidnappers, but that had become moot, what with the connection between the them and someone on Blake's team. The phone had to go.

I borrowed Madame's computer to print my contact list, grabbed my wallet, and tore out of the house. A branch of my bank was nearby, and then, just a few blocks down, there were several establishments that sold disposable phones. I'd require a fair bit of money since I had no idea where my work with Chloe would send me, and mobile phones...I needed lifelines. These would only work in the States. I'd have to replace them when I arrived in Hampshire. Wherever, disposable phones would be my only means of communication for the duration of this blasted nightmare.

Minutes ticked by. In fifteen the bank would close for their noon break. Each second that passed nudged my steps faster, ratcheted my breathing. I pushed into the bank lobby and confronted a teller, female, tight bun, blank eyes. "The manager, I'll need to speak with him immediately, please."

Her mind was elsewhere. I tapped her sleeve. Her pupils dilated, and her arm trembled under my touch.

I backed away. "Sorry. You're about to close for break, but I need to complete my business quite quickly." I slathered the words with as much innocent Brit as I could.

She nodded, a quick series of tiny chin dips. "Right there." She pointed to a corner office. "Sign in at the podium."

I pulled up a smile, minus the teeth. "Thanks, ever so."

What the hell was wrong with me? I did not fall apart. I planned, executed my plan with precision, did not rush about, and definitely did not panic. Not like this. I would have been killed years ago, as criminals are quick to spot panic in a cop. And take advantage of it. I drew in a long breath, and then moved across the lobby at a fast clip.

I wanted funds to see me through my search for Grandmamma, but not enough to alert the authorities, so I requested nine grand. Twelve K would have been better, but the bank would have to note it in their Currency Transaction Report. And I needed to fly under FBI radar.

Fifteen minutes later I was on my way to Café Du Monde, a six-pack of the latest in disposable phones tucked under my arm, each giving me sixty minutes' talk time, limited to outgoing calls, and then I could drop it in the trash. I elbowed my way through the lunch crowd, ordered café au lait, and opted to skip the beignets. My taste buds protested, but what with the *pain perdu* Madame had fed me for breakfast, my hips couldn't afford any more sweets. I was halfway through the life-giving mug of chicory-laced brew, ruminating on how I'd treated Chloe, when a flash of brilliance seeped into my cloudy brain.

I rummaged for one of my new phones and with a few key punches, reached Honolulu information. "I need the number for that flower kiosk on King, the one by University. Do you know it?"

"Do you have a name?" asked a tinny voice, obviously not Hawaiian.

"Not exactly, no. There's only one kiosk there. Excellent selection of flowers. Surely you know it."

"One moment please. I'll connect you with my supervisor."

Emptiness droned in my ear, broken shortly by a too-chipper voice. "You're trying to reach the flower kiosk on King Street, yah?"

"Yes, do you have the number, then?"

"My mother works there. They're not open quite yet, but I know she'll answer. I'll connect you."

Mom was delightful and helpful. I placed an order for a braided ti leaf and white orchid lei and read off my credit card number. After this, no more credit card. Too dangerous. Blake probably hadn't started a trace yet, but by this time tomorrow I had to be on the move.

I synchronized times with the flower kiosk so I could make my call to Chloe just after the lei was delivered. Timing was everything on this one. I wandered about, clock-watched, sipped my to-go beverage, and finally selected a park bench, sat, and made the call.

Chloe answered on the sixth ring. "Namasté, Whitney. The lei arrived and it's lovely, but…why?"

She sounded unsure, and maybe sad. The anger simmering in my chest turned inward, morphed into guilt.

"A peace offering." Tentative. I didn't sound like me at all. There was still too much unsaid between us, a world of pain and harsh words that needed to be forgiven.

I hadn't come up with a hint about how to explain...anything. Desperation blurred my mind, and words caught in my throat. The idea of apologizing kept knocking against the persistent anger I used for protection. Still, how could she fancy herself in love with the bastard who stole Grandmamma?

She broke the silence. "In traditional Hawaiian culture, ti leaves are used for protection against psychic evil. A good choice for a peace offering."

"Psychic evil, you say?" I could do this. "Well, damn. We could do with a whole lot of protection from that, considering the reason I'm calling."

"First, before you say anything. Let me. I need to tell you. You were right." Her breathing skipped a beat, sounded harsh in my ear. "About Dominic, you were right. He did abduct Grandmamma. Wouldn't tell me anything about it, didn't admit it, but I could tell."

Relief swept through me, followed closely by another dose of guilt. Much as I hated Justice, I wanted Chloe to be happy. "Quite." I swallowed, my mouth dry. "It's a bother, the Y chromosome. I've left Evans in a snit. He'll be tracing my whereabouts if I'm not careful about it."

"Okay, we're going to be all right now. We are, aren't we?" Her voice trembled.

"Absolutely."

"I know you didn't call because of Dominic or Blake. Nia said you were supposed to be on your way to Hampshire after you checked on Grandmamma's situation, and you wouldn't stop searching for her. Not without good reason. What is it? What's wrong?"

My mobile vibrated. The real one. Annoying. I ignored it. This was more important than Blake Evans wanting me to account for my whereabouts.

"Whitney?" Chloe sounded tentative.

"Um. I need your help."

Deep, hollow breathing came over the line. Made my skin itch, and I took a bracing swallow of my café.

"From the energy around you, from what I can tell at this distance, there's danger coming from two places. Here in Honolulu, and in Hampshire. It looks like you're the epicenter for whatever it is you're working on with Agent Evans. But I'm not sure. It's different for me, working at a distance. And this smattering of pseudo-clairvoyance that's been showing up since my deaths—I'm not comfortable with it. Have no idea how accurate it is. So, really, I can't be much help."

A beep from my mobile indicated that Evans had left a message. Blast and damn. "Danger, hmm. Sounds to me like your intuition is spot on. There is a bit of danger involved, what with the nasty mess surrounding Mala Sen and Barat, and not knowing how to account for Blake Evans's connection with them. Somehow it's all tied to Grandmamma. I have to find her, Chloe."

"Okay. I get that. Tell me exactly what you need from me."

A sliver of ice trickled down my spine. It had been suspiciously quiet in my head. No voices whatsoever. "I need you to help me reach Mala Sen, like you helped Nia. Remember—"

She cut in. "You're different, you and Nia. She feared for her life. A very strong motivator. You're much more controlled. And at this distance, unless you're planning to come home, I'm not sure what I can do."

I tapped into the churning in my stomach. Fear? Not likely. Rage? Yes, that fit rather nicely. Could that be blocking the dead, keeping them from reaching me? "I'm not feeling much in control of anything, actually. How about I call you back when I get…never mind. I'll give you a ring in a bit."

I fumbled for my mobile with shaking fingers. It would be the last time I punched in my voicemail password. Blake's tone was sharp, harsh with anger. I could almost see him running his hands over his head, his tight curls flattening under the onslaught. "Whitney? Answer the damn phone. We need to talk. You may be in danger. Don't fuck with me on this. Call me."

The need to reassure him came from nowhere. I squashed it, smashed it deeply into the depth of my unconscious mind. That sort of thing was *not* to be acknowledged. I couldn't trust him, couldn't trust anyone connected with the FBI.

It was time. Destroying my phone sent a dark shaft of uneasiness through my chest. I'd prepared for this, but still I fumbled with the phone, mentally juggling between keeping it or not, while I wandered through the park. I found an out-of-the-way spot, placed my mobile on the cement path, and smashed it with the heel of my boot. It splintered. And my heart shattered, the shards a painful testimony that I'd just eliminated my only connection with Grandmamma's abductors. But the bottom line? If destroying my phone would keep her safe while I tracked her whereabouts, so be it. I had my calling to help me, and Chloe would teach me how to reach Mala, and then Grandmamma. If I could reach the dead, surely I could reach a blood relative.

I dropped the phone pieces in the trash and hurried out of the park.

PANIC hammered me. After dinner with Madame, I'd rung Chloe again planning to set a time for us to work on my problem, but it didn't work out quite as I'd expected.

"We need to have a session." Chloe's voice was crisp in my

ear. "Right now, Whitney. I'm still not sure how this will work with the distance between us, but it's the perfect time to try."

"Not at all a good time. I absolutely have to sleep before you start poking around in my psyche."

"No. Oh, no you don't. If you're rested and have the energy to fight me, we'll never find a way to break through your wall."

Suddenly chilled, I tugged the blanket loose from the bed and wrapped it around me. "Absolutely. But, no. I need to be focused to do this, not all dodgy and woozy."

"You want my help, Whitney Boulay, you do it my way."

"All the same, a shower first would be just the thing. Back at Grandmamma's cabin, it helped with Avril. Nia probably told you, when I was under water I could hear Avril."

Water ran, and the familiar clink and rustle of Chloe making tea sounded in my ear. "Wrong. It wasn't the water. It was the distraction. You're stubborn, got bogged down in your mind, and you needed something to focus on so that you could hear her. She, being in spirit form, knew that and came up with a quick solution to your controlling personality."

"But—"

"Now! Sit on the damn floor! Probably a half lotus position would be good."

"Who has the controlling personality?"

She ignored me. "It's all about breathing. Even in yoga class, when I taught pranayama, you refused to participate. Why?"

"I sound ridiculous. Like a rhinoceros with a cold, and I've never fancied myself as a rhino."

"Okay. Time for some truth. You've been fighting your calling since your mum left to accept her psychic gift. You're all tough elegance, and have pretended since you were a teenager, to both yourself and Grandmamma, that you were proud to be born to it. But you hate it. Not the calling *per se*, but you hate not being in control."

"Blast. What I hate, actually, is when you're right. Absolutely loathe it. But we're going to need to skip over the analysis and go straightaway to chatting up the dead."

"You can't have one without the other, Whitney. You need to step out of your mind and into the depth of feeling in your heart. Listening to the dead, *hearing* them speak, isn't logical, but you're approaching it as though it's an alien phenomena. It's a part of you that comes from your gut and your heart. Your mind is just a place to store the information. The energy that comes from love is what opens your intuitive gifts."

"Precisely. I've heard that before, and it makes as little sense now as it did then."

"Breathe. Don't analyze it, just feel it."

"Breathe, is it? I'm not feeling much in control of anything, actually." Weariness had eaten all of my reserve energy and I collapsed onto the bed. Fragments of thought blended into a muddle, and I let my control slip away soundlessly, into the abyss of nothingness. The fragments began to coalesce into new meaning, new images…I gasped and pressed my fist hard against my mouth. *Loving images.* "Oh, bloody-freaking-hell. I love Blake Evans."

"Of course you do." Chloe's voice wobbled.

Was she freaking laughing?

Another muffled chuckle. "I wish I could see you. What's going on? Are you breathing?"

"Breathing?" Chloe had a point. I inhaled hard and long, blew the breath out with a whoosh. "Absolutely. Breathing."

"Um-hmm. Let me hear some steady, even breaths." She

paused to listen. "So, if I'm interpreting your wail correctly, you've accepted that you love Blake Evans."

"Love is…so—"

"Nope. You can't back out of it now. The words are out there in the ether. You've loved him since the day you first met him…what? Two, three years ago? More?"

Tremors raced through me, and Chloe's words turned to mush in my brain. "I can't possibly fancy him. It's simply not the thing. He's consorting with the enemy. Worse than me listening to the dead, he's conversing with some living bastard who's helping Barat, and might well be responsible for stealing Grandmamma. No. I absolutely could not possibly love him."

"Love isn't a decision."

I scooted up, braced my back against the headboard, and settled into a half lotus. "What with the situation, it is absolutely a decision. My decision."

"Just breathe and feel it. Don't analyze it and don't assign it to a person. You probably don't realize it, but you've just made a major breakthrough."

I gasped a last breath of sanity, and then the sensation, the energy poured over me. Thought disappeared and I drowned in wave after wave of heady emotion.

"Hang on. Your landline here is ringing."

I drifted into the corners of my mind, found Blake hiding there waiting for me, and surrendered into—

"Whitney. Thank God you're still—"

A freight train of fear crashed into my chest. "What is it, then?" I interrupted, my voice thready.

"Not Grandmamma, but it's bad."

I dragged in a breath.

"It was your attorney. He'd like you to call him later to talk about what's to be done."

"To be done? About what, then?"

"He wanted to let you know that Michael was murdered. In his hospital bed."

"Michael? Murdered?" I braced my elbows on the nightstand, and cradled my head against the overwhelming grief. "Did he say how?"

Chloe hesitated. "Stab wound. Directly into his heart. Died instantly. Who's Michael?"

I didn't try to control my grief and anger. "He's the unfortunate bloke who made the mistake of renting a pirogue to Dominic Justice."

"Oh. I'm, ah…I'm really so sorry about Michael. It looks like he transitioned smoothly to the other side. He'd seen a lot of life, Whitney, and was ready to go."

Sadness engulfed me and a suffocating ache rose in my chest. Michael. "If he's settled, does that mean I *can't* talk to him, do you think?" This was one person who'd passed over that I *wanted* to talk to. Wanted to apologize to, and just wanted to let him know how much I'd come to care about him. He was the soul of everything that's right in the world. Like Grandmamma. And losing him hurt.

"Umm. Hard to say. It's your gift. You know better than anyone how it works."

I fumed. Since my sixth birthday, I'd been hiding my pain behind anger. A skill that was dammed difficult to overcome.

Chloe kept talking. "If I had to guess, I'd say no, you won't be able to reach him. His energy is calm. It feels like he passed without seeing his killer, without even realizing he was dying until he'd transitioned to the other side. It was a brutal murder, but there wouldn't be an image of it in his conscious mind."

"All right, then. This escalation, the kidnappers acting out like that, it's bad. A twisted riddle that must somehow relate to Grandmamma." I gulped a breath, let my mind wander through Chloe's last comments, and then snapped my attention back to her. "How can you possibly know Michael was ready to go? None of the dead people who've talked at me have accepted their death."

"No, of course not. That's why they talk to you. Unfinished business. It doesn't feel like Michael left anything undone. I don't know how to describe the sensation I have when I look at his energy. Probably because it's a feeling, like liquid peace, rather than an image. He's completely transitioned, no lingering energy left behind."

"Quite. That makes sense."

"You need to call Blake."

"Absolutely not."

"Barat? Isn't that what you called him? If someone in Blake's organization is leaking information to him, you need to know about it."

"Evans either doesn't know the truth or isn't telling *me* the truth. Why would I want to listen to him?"

"Because if you don't, more innocent people may be killed. Oh, hang on. Your landline is ringing again."

Chloe's footsteps faded into the distance, and then there was rustling as she came back on the line. "I didn't catch the call, but I think Blake left a message. I'm going to play it back for you."

"Michael stabbed. Homicide. Barat knows your location. Watch your back, and fucking call me."

"Blast and damn. If Evans knows that Barat knows my location, there was definitely a leak in Evans's team."

Chapter 15

THE next day arrived early. Too early. When I opened my eyes it was dusky dark, the air draped with the smell of damp heat and sleep. The bedside clock read half five. I'd slept for twelve hours.

After talking with Chloe, I'd scraped together the mangled remnants of my sanity and made arrangements for Michael's funeral. It hurt, and I vowed I'd find whoever killed him and see that justice was done. And then I'd tried to reach Mala. She toyed with me, came close enough to whisper in my mind, but not close enough that I could understand her. Failing that, I tried to reach Grandmamma. The silence pressed against my mind, throbbing with loneliness and worry, until I'd dropped into a deep, dreamless sleep.

Now I swung my feet to the floor, made my way to the loo, then balanced on tiptoe in a tall, arms-overhead stretch. Before my heels came back to touch the floor, a wave of voices rattled about in the back of my mind and a rather unpleasant bit of pain angled through my skull. The dead were most assuredly back. Not talking yet, just leaving my head congested with the silent promise of a headache.

After I washed down two Ibuprophen with a glass of water, I pulled on shorts and a tank and crept out the back door of Madame's home. Humidity hung heavy in the air, thick enough to fill my throat and leave a musty taste in my mouth. A typical summer day in New Orleans. The cotton of my white tank was soaked by the time I finished my morning run. I cooled down with a stroll around the city. Hiding in plain sight. Like yesterday, when I indulged in café au lait at Du Monde. But I could feel Blake Evans pressing closer. Knew he'd catch up to me if I didn't leave Louisiana soon. But there had to be a trail here somewhere, a clue, something to lead me to Grandmamma.

I strolled through Madame's front door, and she handed me the phone. "It's Chloe Channing."

I'd left Madame's number with her just in case. I ignored the fear digging in my stomach, and put on my happy voice. "Chloe? I wasn't expecting—"

"There's been a…I really don't know how to tell you this. You're going to completely freak out."

Too late. I'd already passed the point of freaked out. "Spit it out. Your dithering has already knocked me askew."

"When I got home today, from ah—oh, damn. I don't know where to start."

I twisted the phone cord. "Talk. Now."

"I bought a house. In Ewa Beach. But we can talk about that later. When I got home from the closing there was a deadbodyonyourporch."

What the hell? "You bought a house? No one buys a house in a day."

"Forget the house, Whitney." Impatience slammed through her words. "It's the body you need to pay attention to."

"Body?" Slivers of alarm raced along my spine. "You were mumbling about a body?"

"Yes. I…found him when I went to pick up Ahimsa."

I tugged on the hem of my tank and wiped the sweat off my face. She sounded okay. "You're all right, then? Not hurt at all?"

"I'm fine. Shaky. It was the same as last year. He...ah... was laid out crucifixion style. Naked. Only difference, this one wasn't stabbed. He had a broken neck."

I thumbed through my memory for the photos of the first body. "You're thinking it's tied to you. That there's a connection. Where are you?"

"In my new house."

"Right, then. I'll catch a flight—"

"No! No, there's nothing you can do here. The good detective has been trying to reach you. I told him you'd check in, that your phone was destroyed, and that I'd have you get in touch with him."

"Frey. Well, damn. I'll ring him up, but I should come home. The John Doe—he is a John Doe? You don't know who—?"

"There was no identification. Do not come home. What you're doing, trying to find Grandmamma is critical. She's alive. This man is very, very dead and beyond your help."

Madame Tatiana handed me a towel and a tall glass of lemonade. I nodded my thanks, and then set about wiping up the sweat I'd dripped on her hardwood floors.

"I'll ring Frey up straightaway, then give you a call back. You're sure you're safe? Is there an alarm system in the new house?"

"I am and there is. Not the best, but it works. Could you hold off a few hours on the callback? I really need some sleep."

We rang off, and my body quivered with the need to act. Was the new John Doe a warning? Was there a connection between him and the notes that had been in my bathroom?

Maybe a connection with the body left at Soma Herbal? Nothing made sense, and the loose ends were wadded into a knot that had taken over my stomach.

A quick shower and two lemonades later, I reached Frey. "What the hell, Whitney? It's three in the damn morning."

"What happened?" I had no time for the niceties, not with Frey.

He huffed and sputtered, swallowed some liquid that gurgled over the phone line, and finally woke up enough to talk. "Your perimeter alarm went off. When you didn't answer your phone, a black and white checked it out. Homicide picked it up when they found the John Doe."

The alarm had worked. Thank God. "Particulars?"

"Mixed race male, brown and brown, broken neck. Looks like mid-twenties, could be drug-related. Shitload of tattoos, and the clothes we found fit the look, dirty t-shirt and homeboy shorts. Empty pockets. I have a call in to vice. See if they recognize him."

I did a mental comparison with Chloe's first dead body. "It has too much in common with the one from Soma Herbal last year. You might want to check my file from that case. And keep a watch on Chloe, would you? Keep her safe."

The string of coincidences was chilling. When Frey rang off, the empty hum of the phone line crept along my spine, whispering that I needed to contact Evans. This wasn't something I could keep from him since it would likely hit the FBI radar. They'd been to my home twice about a possible connection to Amar Barat, and weren't likely to overlook a dead body at the same address.

I flipped my mobile open to type in the message, but quickly realized that would be a bad move. If the situation were reversed, and he didn't talk to me, I'd be on the next plane—and I definitely did not want him chasing after Chloe.

Questioning her. The woman who couldn't lie worth a fig.

He answered on the first ring. "Damn it all to hell, Whitney, what the fuck is going on?"

I moved the phone away from my ear so as not to break an eardrum. "Dead body on my stoop. Frey has it under control."

"Whitney? Whitney, what's going on?" His shout reverberated against my collarbone.

I blew out the mother of all sighs and brought the phone back to my ear. "Nothing. Everything is excellent. Chloe bought a house in Ewa Beach. Gated community, and I'll arrange to have a new alarm system installed for her today."

"That's impossible. Nobody closes on a house in a couple of days. And what the *hell* is going on with a dead body?"

"Actually, it seems you can acquire a house quite easily if you have the cash on hand, and there have been no previous occupants. Very tidy, that."

"You're there? In Honolulu?"

I didn't deny it. Best if he didn't know my location. "Everything is well in hand, even if Frey is a bit of a prat."

"We need to talk—"

I snapped the phone shut, tucked it away in my handbag. "That's that, then."

It took all day to threaten, nag, and charm the security company to install an alarm in Chloe's new house before the next twenty-four hours had passed. And then there were the canine handlers to interview. I had to find the perfect dog for her.

It was after ten when I finally dropped into a light sleep, my mind wrestling with the juxtaposition of thinking like a fugitive who had a law enforcement resume. I couldn't continue my search for Grandmamma without direction, so I needed to know where to go next. And that meant another session with Chloe.

The phone jarred me awake. "Chloe?" I sounded all groggy and muddle-mouthed.

"We need to have a session." Crisp. Her words snapped through the phone line.

Had she been reading my mind? "How did you know?" I swallowed a yawn. "It's a bit after midnight here."

"Yes. Your defenses are down, and it's time to work. Wait. What did you mean how did I know?"

I stifled another yawn. "I decided before I fell asleep."

"We're on the same page. That's good. We need to get you up to speed on casual conversation skills with the dearly departed." She sounded quite sure of herself.

I snagged a bottle of water off the nightstand and downed a swallow. "You've had a rough few days between the dead body and the new house. Probably we both need a long lie-in before—"

"It's time for you to commune with the dead." There was steel in her voice. "I've been meditating, waiting for the right moment." Pause. "Your aura is clear, and there's some indigo, so now is a good time." I could almost see Chloe's sneaky bit of a smile, the one that barely curved her lips. The one that showed up when all hell was about to break loose.

I needed to shift our pending session into the right direction. "Not the dead. It's Grandmamma I need to reach. Can you teach me how?"

"Well, no. I mean, she's alive and telepathy isn't your calling, right? I'm one hundred percent positive that you're supposed to communicate with the dead, and that through your calling you're going to find Grandmamma."

I couldn't very well argue with her. The etheric was her business, not mine. Well, not until recently. And she had a point, my calling was mixed up in all this mess. Somehow. "I'm willing to try anything that will help me find her."

"We need to start by working with the dead. There's no way around that."

I dropped to the floor next to the bed and sighed, defeated. "Let's have a go at it, then."

"The timing is excellent, actually. Not that I'd wish harm to the John Doe, but since he died on your porch...think about it. You have a fresh body to work with. A man who was possibly connected to one or both of us in life, and definitely connected to both of us through death. It doesn't get any more personal than that... well, unless the body is a family member."

I shot up, a fresh bolt of panic toying with my sanity. "You want me to talk to the body that was on my stoop? Not Mala or Grandmamma?" I was accustomed to Mala. Knew what she *felt* like in my mind.

This new body was so fresh. So wrong. Possibly a threat to Chloe. Well, then. Maybe she had a point.

"You're resisting. Why?"

I sighed again. It was becoming a habit. "Mala has been nagging at me. No distinct words, just an irritating mumble in the back of my mind, so I thought we'd start there. See if I can't get through to her."

I wasn't making any sense, and worse, I knew it. Something was very wrong. I could feel it twisting around me, pushing at me. Nothing rational about it, and I had no words to explain. For a fleeting moment I longed for a normal life. Without a calling.

Chloe's breath rasped in my ear. "No. I'm sure we're supposed to start with the John Doe. I know it's ugly, but will you think of him, how he looked?"

Frey had emailed his report to Madame's computer, but only because I'd threatened him with dismemberment and a reminder that he owed me. It wasn't difficult to bring an image of the John Doe to my mind. I'd lived with those sorts of images, not of this particular one, but I clearly remembered all of my homicide victims. It was part of the job. A way for me to respect them, by remembering. "Absolutely, a clear picture, a rather unpleasant one, actually."

"Hold the image and breathe." Her tone was all business.

It wasn't easy. The cop in me couldn't stop analyzing the crime scene, replaying Frey's report as I searched for clues. And then I zeroed in on John Doe's eyes. Cloudy in death, blind to corporeal life. And I dropped into…emptiness. Deep. Black. Nothing. Velvet. Choking. Heavy. Sucking the life from me. I couldn't breathe. Tore at my neck and gasped for air.

Next thing I knew, Madame Tatiana held my wrists in a death grip, and was yelling at me. The sound of her voice penetrated the depth of the chasm I'd fallen into. "You need to come back, ma petite."

I focused on the compelling, controlled strength in her voice, on forcing my eyes open, but the dark called to me, dragged me back into oblivion. An abyss of blackness, a non-place. Such a relief from the bright light. I ignored Madame, pushed the light away, and sought the dark.

Cold sloshed over me.

I startled to an upright position. Drenched in ice water.

Madame stood over me holding a large, empty pot. And a towel.

I sloughed water from my face and arms, shot her a glare. "I could do with less water."

Her face was pale, bordering on parchment. "You wouldn't wake up, ma petite, and your Grandmamma would be most upset if I let you pass to the other side."

"Absolutely not my time to die." I plucked the wet tank top away from my skin. "Whatever made you think I was at death's door?"

She handed me the towel, then folded her arms around the stew pot. "When you stopped breathing, ché. I could feel your departure all the way in my bedroom."

I gave up trying to ease the discomfort of the wet fabric clinging to my skin and yanked the sopping tank over my head, wrapped the towel around me, then headed for... "Not my home."

"No. My pied-á-terre." She held out her hand for the dripping wad of material, dropped it in the pot. "Your room is just there, at the end of the hall. Bathroom's next door. There's more towels on the rack."

I sifted through the fragments of my memory, searching for stable ground. Madame Tatiana's house in New Orleans. Absolutely. Dead guy on my porch in Honolulu. I was trying to reach him. I whirled to face Madame. "Chloe?"

She scrabbled under a table, pulled the phone out and handed it to me.

I grabbed it, none too gently. "What in the bloody hell happened, Chloe? Are you all right?"

"Me? Am I all right? Other than you scaring thirty years off my life, I'm just peachy."

"Right, then. Maybe it wasn't such a good idea to chat up the dead? Um, where am I?"

Silence. Then, impatiently, "In New Orleans. At Madame Tatiana's."

"I *know* that. What I want to know is—" I fluttered my hands around my body as if she could see "—what my aura looks like. I still feel a bit wonky, can't seem to shake completely free of the black."

"Your aura is looking considerably better than it did a few minutes ago. And, yes, I know about the black. I've been there."

Madame scooted up behind me, handed me a dry tank. I nodded my thanks and turned my attention back to Chloe. "It was thick. Suffocating. But for all that, the most peaceful I've ever felt. It was like floating in nothingness but still supported by sweet, soft warmth."

"Sounds like death."

"Can't have been. There was no light at all. Those New Age books, they talk about how bright it is, how you follow the light when you die. This was black as the Bayou on a moonless night."

"Been there. And yes, the light is amazing. I've never wanted anything so much as to reach for it, become one with it. But after that—"

"After that? You weren't dead that long. I was there, remember? And although it seemed to take forever, they did resuscitate you within minutes."

"Remember? Hardly. And it wasn't all that quick the first time I died. I went beyond the light, not for long, but definitely beyond. Interesting that you were able to chase our John Doe to the other side."

Chloe's words caught my memories, brought them to the surface, and a sharp blast of panic ricocheted around my chest. I rubbed at the sensation. She was fine. Alive and talking to me. "That time in hospital with you, it's an upsetting memory." Why couldn't I just tell her it had ripped me apart? Anger thrummed, looking for a way to escape.

Ice chinked against glass in the kitchen, and seconds later Madame placed a frosty glass of mint lemonade in my free hand. The hot August night deposited an instantaneous layer of condensation on the glass. I drew patterns on the surface that quickly disappeared into the dewy background. A momentary mark. Here and gone. I needed to find Grandmamma. Now. Before she completely disappeared.

Chloe's words cut into my thoughts. "My deaths aren't the important thing here. This is about John Doe. Was there any hint of what happened? Why he was left on your porch?"

"Only black." I reached for the glass, cradled it as I tried to shore up some courage. "Should we try again, do you think?"

"Not in this lifetime. The thing is, your trip to the darkness might have opened some doors to other parts of your brain. Odd things keep happening to me, and it's been well over a month since I died."

The lemonade soothed my throat, and then I shivered. A head-to-toe tremor that left my knees weak. "Quite. Odd things. Perhaps we've both gone nutters. And the only thing that needs to happen immediately is that I have to move. Literally. Evans will be on my tail by now. I'll ring you up when I can, and let you know…whatever."

There was nothing left to do but exchange namastés.

LOOSE-LIMBED and quiet, Madame's nephew lived in a world of his own creation. She'd volunteered him to give me a lift into Baton Rouge, and he'd graciously accepted. For fifty bucks. The truck was old, lumpy, and not up to any sort of speed over forty miles an hour. It was destined to be a long ride, and as I had little to discuss with a spacy teenager, I wedged my backpack against the door and curled up for a short lie-in. Not that I intended to sleep. Not quite yet.

I needed time to think. To do a run-through of the conversation that had landed me in this truck heading for an off-the-radar airport, and a flight to the UK. After my encounter with the black abyss of death, I'd tried to reach

Mala...and succeeded. The first time I barged into her mind, she'd greeted me with the energetic equivalent of a pat on the head. "Nice work," she'd said. "I've been holding back, waiting to see if you could do it."

"What? You've been quiet for days, letting me fumble about on my own, pushing Chloe's patience to the breaking point."

She'd offered an energetic nod, and then dismissed my irritation. "We're going to embark on a journey, and my job is to keep you alive. So, you need to be able to reach me. Not a skill you would have bothered to learn if I kept appearing at random times in response to your stress."

A journey? "What journey? And things were working famously well with you drifting into my mind at will."

"True. But it's difficult for me to confine myself to your mind. Small as it is—"

"I do not have to take this from a ghost." If she weren't dead, I'd seriously consider offing her.

"You do if you want to find you grandmother." Mala had my complete attention.

"Quite. And why can't I reach her like I do you?" I'd asked her. "Seems all wrong to be limited to chatting with the dead."

"It has to do with your calling and how *limited* your experience has been so far."

My hand tightened into a fist. "Where is she and how do I get her back?"

"I'm not privy to that information. I do know that if you find Barat, you'll find her. So it's imperative that you find *him*. Now. Travel...carefully."

A tremor ran through me. "Where is he, then?"

"The UK. Go to your father."

Panic shot through me. "What the—? Is my father mixed up in this?"

She'd already faded from my mind. Dead clever, Mala.

MADAME Tatiana's nephew turned out to be good company. Silent for the entire ride. He tossed me a wave when he dropped me at the airport, and then rattled off in his dilapidated, once-upon-a-time-red truck. I slung my backpack over my shoulder, relieved we'd made it to Baton Rouge, and doubly so to step into my new anonymity.

I had a bit of illegal business to take care of before I left the country, so I nabbed a cab, had the driver drop me in a seedy area, and settled in at a nondescript motel, the sort where you can register without identification and pay by the day, or by the hour.

The motel was within walking distance to several strip malls. I strolled along the shop fronts, checking out my new neighborhood, and then headed back to the motel.

As I neared the motel, the scent of pizza filled the air, heavy with roasted tomato, fresh-baked bread, and the bite of basil, oregano, and garlic. I followed the aroma to a hole-in-the-wall bar at the far end of the block, tucked my hair under a ball cap, tugged it low over my forehead, and placed my order. I'd found the perfect place to lie low while I enjoyed a veggie lover's pie and an icy cold pint of beer.

Sleep came in snatches that night. The flashing neon sign from an all-night diner spilled an intermittent wash of dull red light into my room. Dark corners loomed where the light didn't reach, making the entire effect disorienting and disturbing.

My thoughts and dreams bled into a mélange of memories and images of Blake Evans, and how comfortable it was to be cuddled in his arms. I woke knackered, to the point I couldn't stop yawning. Not the condition I wanted to be in when I faced the forger creating my new ID. A pot of steaming hot coffee was at the top of my to-do list.

I hustled across the street to the diner, found a booth in the back, and ordered my brew. No breakfast. Not until after the meet. I'd spent my life enforcing the law, so breaking it didn't sit well. But I couldn't afford to alert anyone, law-abiding or not, to my presence in Hampshire.

With the forged ID tucked in my backpack, there was one last thing to do: send Special Agent Blake Evans a cryptic text that would keep him occupied while I disappeared into the British countryside. Something to throw him off my trail.

On way to HI. Staying with Chloe. Connection between Barat, Chloe's DB, and the John Doe on my stoop.

That would keep him up to his sexy backside in paperwork.

Chapter 16

MY journey to new york was deliberately hit and miss. I needed to stay under the radar, so traveled standby on whatever flight headed east. There was no discernable pattern, and I made sure none of the layover cities had personal meaning for me. I divided the down time between flights to either plan how I wanted to handle things in Hampshire, or to practice contacting Mala. I could reach her at will by the time I boarded the plane for Heathrow, but it was still damn inconvenient having a ghost for a partner.

According to Mala, everything was *just fine*, but the knot in my stomach didn't agree. I'd have laid money that my gut knew more about it than she did, and that all hell would break loose as soon as I set foot on English soil.

I slid my hand into my backpack, wrapped my fingers around the trusty bottle of melatonin, my new friend, but a poor replacement for Blake Evans's arms. I buried myself under a British Airways blanket and did some deep breathing until I fell asleep.

After we landed, I made a quick trip to the loo, purchased several British disposable phones to replace the US variety, and then caught a train to Waterloo Station. I'd decided to make Winchester my home base, and was lucky enough to find a vacancy at a quaint bed and breakfast. The layout was excellent, as I could come and go through a seldom-used side door with no one the wiser. And my ability to slip between British and Cajun accents allowed me plenty of trail-muddying anonymity.

A quick browse through the dailies put me in touch with a man selling his Vespa, and a scant hour later I was on the road, heading toward the Chilton estate on a rare Daring Plum GT200 Granturismo. The wind caught strands of hair from my slicked-back ponytail, and the joy of flying free temporarily buried my worries about Grandmamma, and about sneaking back into my paternal environment.

I parked the bike in the midst of a nearby copse and made my way along the bank of the river bordering my father's estate. Having spent a good part of my childhood setting off the Manor's perimeter alarms, I'd learned exactly how to avoid them. That the manor felt like home was more than a bit unsettling. I brushed the thought away, selected a favorite tree, hiked myself to a sturdy lower branch, and scanned the acreage behind the manor.

There wasn't much movement, no one working in the flowerbeds, trimming shrubbery, or dealing with the lawn. Anything can change in ten years, but this much quiet was all wrong. Chilton's land usually bustled with gardeners, maintenance people, deliveries. There had never been quiet. Not like this.

Icy fingers set to dancing along my spine as the back door from the kitchens opened.

And Mala stepped out.

"Mala!" The silent scream reverberated deep inside my skull, but fortunately emerged as a whisper that blended with the afternoon breeze.

Damn irritating ghost.

Or not?

She had to be a ghost…didn't she? My calling hadn't come with a handy option to visualize the dead. It was all about *verbal* communication and had nothing at all to do with ghosts wandering about or suddenly turning into corporeal bodies. Still, she appeared to be very much alive. Substantial. Like I could reach out and touch her. My palms itched with the need to try, to find out if she vaporized or if she was warm and breathing.

I inched down from the tree and made my way amongst the various landscaped plots, shrub by shrub. I had to get closer to this apparition. A sneeze threatened, and I wiggled my nose to mitigate the scent of summer flowers that permeated the air. Did ghosts hear sneezes? She couldn't be real. And where the hell was *my* Mala?

I rounded the last bit of shrubbery and crouched, spreading the foliage apart so I could get a better look at her. My father stuck his head out of the kitchen door. It scared the beejezus out of me, and I had to bite my lip to stifle a scream. His words floated into the garden. "Mala, my dear, would you come in please?"

Mala? His dear? My father? He'd never referred to anyone as *dear* in his life. She graced him with a sweet smile and sauntered toward the back door, her ankle length skirt swishing around her legs. Shapely. *My* Mala did not flounce. Ever. I did another silent scream in her ethereal direction and was met with complete silence, so I sent her an irritated huff.

I edged along the side of the house, fumbling for the key I'd tucked into my back pocket. Looked like I was going to have to brave the fortress that Chilton called home. My watch told me it was teatime, so the kitchen would be bustling with staff. Probably the very reason Chilton had called Fake Mala into the house. He didn't like household inhabitants to miss tea. Messed with his control issues.

I decided to sneak in through a side door that opened off the library, and ran my fingertip over Grandmamma's diamond for good luck. Tea was usually served in the parlor, and because the two rooms connected, I could crack the library door and listen to their conversation. Not a great plan, but it was the best I could do on short notice. I slipped the key into the lock and carefully turned the knob. Sweat prickled along my spine. Two Malas, my father's house, breaking and entering—even if I did have a key—a nightmare of a combination.

I cracked the door. No voices.

I pushed. It creaked. Loud enough to alert every dead body in the place, and to bring an immediate halt to my breathing.

Still no voices. No cry of alarm. No bells, no whistles.

What the hell? Where was everyone? Not that I wasn't grateful for the absence of living bodies, but still. I pushed the door open, scooted inside, and silently eased it shut it behind me. No creak. Whoever heard of a door that only screeched when it opened?

I'd almost shaken off the willies when footsteps and voices came drifting in through the library door. A flying leap behind the sofa left rug burns on my forearms, and a gold damask accent pillow overturned onto the floor. The rug burns weren't a problem, but the pillow was definitely noticeable.

I reached around the sofa to do a grab and replace maneuver at the exact instant the library door opened. It was a no-go on replacing the pillow, so I tucked it against my belly and stretched out behind the sofa.

"I'll put the trolley here where you can both reach it. Would you like me to pour?" Damn and blast. They were having tea in the library. The voice was feminine and respectful, ergo it had to be one of the staff. My father *never* had tea in the library. Why the change of plans today?

"No, Agnes, thank you. Mala will pour for us. We'll ring if

we need anything else." Footsteps, and then a door opened and closed. The delicate clinking of silverware and fine china skittered over my nerves.

"I appreciate you changing your routine to take tea in here. It's my favorite room in the manor." Fake Mala. It had to be. She sounded a lot like my Mala, and had excellent taste. The library had always been my favorite room, with its welcoming fireplace, huge windows that offered a view of the gardens, and rich, warm-toned furnishings.

Chilton cleared his throat. "You need to be cared for. How are the headaches, my dear?"

My dear. Again. Not at all like the Chilton I grew up with. They chatted about Mala's therapy, and the gist was that she'd had appeared in the Manor garden, her body badly bruised, and with a nasty concussion that left her with frequent headaches. I could relate to the headaches.

Their conversation faded into background noise, and my muscles cramped from holding still for so long. The spasms demanded my attention, painfully and insistently, and it would be a freaking miracle if I could move at all by the time DD and FM finished chit-chatting over tea and crumpets.

Chilton Manor had a fabulous cook, and the thought of dainty sandwiches, and crumpets with fresh jam and clotted cream caused my stomach to voice a not-so-silent request for sustenance. Damn. Not the time. I rammed the pillow tighter against my abdomen and willed the rumblings to stop. The fire crackled some, but not enough to mask any unusual sounds coming from my belly.

Chilton words grabbed my attention. "Would you like another log on the fire?"

No. Oh no, *not* a good idea. Even plastered against the back of the sofa, if he crossed the room to attend the fire, I'd be in his line of sight.

The clear, dulcet tones of Fake Mala's voice tightened around me, stealing my breath. "That would be wonderful, thanks. I thought I'd stay here and read for a while, and it's cozy with the fire. I'll ring Agnes to pick up the tea trolley later."

Damn and blast. Chilton strode toward the fireplace. I stopped breathing and sucked in my stomach, pressing so tight to the pillow I'd be wearing the rose pattern for days to come. I watched him bend and pick up a log, putting him at an angle that made me clearly visible in his peripheral vision.

My heart pounded, begging me to inhale. I opened my mouth to slowly and silently drag in some air. My father tossed the log on the fire, and poked at it.

Sparks flashed.

I concentrated on invisibility.

Chilton turned, pulled a pristine white handkerchief from his pocket, and wiped nonexistent soot from his hands while he strolled across the room. I silently chanted, *don't look up, don't look up,* please *don't look up.*

And then he was across the room, opening the library door. "I'll see you at dinner. Nap if you can, Mala. You know how important rest is to restoring your memory."

Restoring her memory? What the—?

The sound of the knob clicking into place pushed the breath from my lungs in a silent whoosh. Safe.

I shifted away from the sofa to ease my cramping muscles. My eyes darted upward when the afghan adorning the back of the sofa began to move. Fake Mala had to be settling in for the duration. Her sigh drifted down, the sound mixing with the rustle of paper, presumably from her book. Blast. Didn't this just add a dash of flavor to the mess I was in with Barat and Dead Mala?

After a few minutes of hearing nothing but the crackling fire and pages turning, I began stretching my legs. There was every possibility I'd need to run at a moment's notice, and it would be best if they were functional.

It wasn't too long before a gentle snore caught my attention. Fake Mala had fallen asleep? Did I dare make a run for it? Evening shadows created patterns along the walls and across the carpet that would help to cover my escape. Now or never. It would be several hours before someone collected Mala for dinner, and I did not want to spend them with nothing to do but admire the back of the sofa.

I eased to a squat, measured the distance to the door, and then remembered the creak. Not a viable escape route. I flicked a glance toward the hall door, then toward the parlor entrance. Did I dare stroll through the house? Whyever not? I opted for the hall door, because I knew it opened without any bothersome, telltale creaks.

Fake Mala's breathing was still deep, and much as I wanted to linger and see if I could spot the differences between her and my Mala, I didn't dare take the time. No point in tempting fate, so I wrapped myself in mental invisibility and headed toward the hall door with measured steps. Not too fast, not too slow. Invisible. Movement that allowed the airspace to close around me with each step, or at least that was my plan. After a quick listen at the door, I cautiously turned the knob, slipped into the front hallway, and flattened my body against the wall.

Quiet settled around me. There were several ways I could exit the manor, but all of them led past Chilton's study, one of them directly through it. Unfortunately, that particular exit was my best choice. The others opened into more public areas, the front entrance, the kitchen, and into the servant's wing. All busy at this time of day.

I skulked along the hallway, checking every door between the library and Chilton's study, listening at keyholes and peeking through cracked-open doors. Too peaceful. Nothing out of place. And through it all my Mala remained frustratingly quiet.

The scent of the manor, a mix of lemon furniture polish and ancient library stacks, brought back memories I'd hoped were forever lost. The double oak doors to Chilton's study stood heavy and imposing, a perfect fit for the man who conducted business behind them. There was no way to ascertain if the lord of the manor was ensconced behind his desk. That left me with one option: open the door and take my chances.

Footsteps slapped against the floor. Damn and blast. I had seconds, maybe less, before someone spotted me. I sprinted around the corner, into the sitting room, and behind the draperies.

The footsteps followed.

"Where's Ms. Sen, Chilton?" The words low, masculine, and held a touch of menace.

"Resting. No reason to disturb her."

I recognized my father's voice, but I'd never heard the other one. Not British, but with an accent I couldn't place. My nape twitched.

"She has information I need. And this business about not remembering what happened to her—rubbish. The woman knows something, and I want answers."

Clothing rustled. "Time is essential to her healing. If you don't back off, you may never get your answers."

"Twenty-four hours, Chilton. That's it."

Silence.

A door clicked. Open? Closed?

The stranger must have left, because the only sound in the

room was a drawn-out sigh, one I recognized. The locking mechanism clicked again, and I peeked around the curtain. The room was empty. I crept to the door, pressed my cheek against the cool wood. Voices had faded into the distance. Time to hustle.

I slipped out of the sitting room, breathed in another mental plea for invisibility, and without hesitation entered my father's study. I pulled the door shut behind me, and seconds later I'd made my way to the porch, hotfooted it to the Vespa, and was on the road.

Darkness closed around me, and the wind whipped through my jacket. I'd forgotten how black these roads got after sunset, and my stomach continued to remind me that I hadn't eaten. A hot meal, bed, and then I'd have a think about what to do next. The soft glow from the upstairs windows provided enough light for me to locate a shed at the back of the property and park the Vespa inside.

I shivered in the chill of the evening and— wait. Light. Back of the inn. My room.

Damn it all to bloody hell.

Someone was in my room.

Chapter 17

ADRENALINE surged, and then dissipated while I studied the situation. Perhaps the innkeeper did a turndown service. Not likely, but possible. Too bad, because I could do with a bedtime mint after tangling with the bastard waiting in my room.

Options flashed through my mind. Sneak up the fire escape? It angled underneath the window and would make a decent platform for peering into my room. Rusty, but solid, it wouldn't be a difficult climb, but my jeans would be covered with iron oxide that would most likely leave permanent stains. I only had two pair with me, and not a lot of time to fuss with laundry.

The wind picked up, scattered leaves along the ground, and raised chill bumps on my arms. I'd have to see about getting a heavier jacket. Later. Right now, I needed to evict whoever occupied my room before I froze to death. I shouldered my backpack and made my way to the front of the building. The hell with the fire escape. Whoever usurped my space was about to have an in-your-face confrontation with me coming out the winner.

I stepped through the oversized front door. Faded chintz, and the fragrance of a crackling fire cozied up the common room. Not only did the soft light take the chill from the summer evening, but it provided shadows for me to use as cover while I studied the other patrons. No one I recognized, or who looked like a threat. Excellent. I sidled up to the bar and caught the innkeeper's attention. "Anyone asking for me this evening?"

She shook her head with a decisive jerk. "No one since you checked in this afternoon."

I nodded my thanks and edged upstairs, sticking close to the wall, seeking the smooth treads to avoid squeaks and creaks from the aged wood. Odors from the kitchen followed me, teasing my stomach with the promise of dinner. I put thoughts of food on hold and did a quick mental check-in with Mala. "Anything you'd like to offer in the way of help?"

A light wisp of her energy floated through my head. No words. Not that I expected any as she hadn't seen fit to comment when faced with Fake Mala. There was no accounting for how a ghostly mind worked. None at all.

"Can you at least give me a hint about whether there are weapons trained on me?" I asked her.

A definite sensation of *no* brushed my mind. It could've meant she didn't have a clue, or that there were no weapons. I didn't bother to clarify. I mentally released the Infidel 3310 from my ankle holster, and then the Fairbairn Sykes tucked against my left wrist. Mental preparation for a potential confrontation was essential. I didn't palm either knife, however, because there was a good chance the intruder was a hotel employee, or someone who'd simply stumbled into the wrong room.

Still, it had been a smart move to purchase the knives while I waited for the insurance papers on the Vespa.

When I reached my room, I slowed my breathing and listened to the quiet.

To free my arms, I lowered my shoulder, let the backpack

slip to the floor, and then slowly turned the doorknob.

Locked.

Blast and damn. Someone hijacked my room and then had the nerve to lock me out. Irritation simmered, and I almost kicked the door in, but I didn't want to damage it. I hunkered down and retrieved the key from my backpack. No way could I make this a stealthy entry. The locks were old, and antique keys rattled by virtue of their age. Better to make it quick, then.

I turned the key and the knob at the same time, stormed through the door, did a graceful dive into the room, and then bounced to my feet—and into the arms of Blake Evans.

He caught me in a fierce bear hug, smashed my head against his chest and covered my mouth with his hand. "I'm gonna let you go. Do not even think of running." He stared at me, assessing. "Or beating me with those lethal fists of yours. Got it?"

The need to fight with him peaked, and set my heart pounding. I choked on the tirade I wanted to spew, fighting to hold it in because I didn't want the innkeeper to alert the constables. And because, deep down, I wanted to lean into Blake and let him make everything better.

I grunted my agreement, and twisted away from him. "What the hell are you doing here?"

He crossed his arms, his attitude nonchalant and innocent. "I might ask you the same."

Anger, fear, and—damn it all—relief raged through me. I caught him off balance, whipped my leg behind his ankles, and dropped him to the floor. He'd expected it, and caught himself, keeping the dead-weight-thud of landing to a barely perceptible thump.

I'd had a hell of a day. A disconcerting, annoying day, and being in Hampshire had taken a toll. On the flip side, Blake Evans looked damn good.

"You agreed not to jump me…" He broke off his sentence to lever up to his elbows and glower. "But now that I'm down here…"

I gave in to an eye-roll. "In your position, I'd kill the grin. And I didn't beat on your body. Yet. That was for breaking into my space." Self-righteous pleasure coursed through me. It wasn't often I caught Blake Evans off guard. Not that the pleasure lasted long, since he whipped his arm out, caught me behind the knees, and yanked me on top of him, where I landed with an undignified, graceless thump.

He rolled, pinning me beneath him, and nudged the door closed with his foot. "Now then, what in the hell were you thinking, taking off like that? Barat is dangerous, Whitney."

"He is, yes. No surprise there." I gave a half-hearted push against his chest. Truth be told, the weight of his body nestled against me felt right. Safe. He smelled of tired and dust. Comfortable. My body reacted with hot, quivering need, so I pushed at him. Purely a defensive gesture.

Blake grabbed my hands, pinning them over my head. "Oh, no. You're not pushing me away. Not this time. No running. No pushing. No hiding. Got that?"

Heat flashed under my skin, and desire pulsed. Damn traitorous body. "Absolutely. Impossible to miss in this position." Not that I couldn't get out of his hold. And he knew I could, which prompted my next question. "What are you after, Evans?"

My stomach chose that moment to comment on the situation.

"Sounds like you need food." He bounced up and offered his hand. I curled mine into fists to keep from accepting his offer. It would be disastrous to my psyche. I scooted away from him, stood, jabbed my hands in my front pockets, and squinted at him in a way I hoped was mildly threatening. "Dinner. Dutch. No touching."

"I worried about you. Can't say it's ever happened before. With anyone." He angled his chin toward the door, and a touch of the rogue sparkled behind his eyes. "Deal on the dinner. Hell, no, on the touching."

"Worried, you say." My traitorous body was in total agreement with his touching caveat, especially since he led the way downstairs, leaving me with an interesting view of his perfect backside. I gave him a wolf whistle.

"Guar-run-teeed sex to-night." His sotto words rumbled up the stairs, heavy with masculine intent. I chose to ignore it, as it's completely impossible to have a successful disagreement with the truth.

We sat in a corner of the common room near the fireplace, ordered a bottle of Syrah, and then drifted into silence until our server poured the wine. My thoughts drifted. I hadn't a clue what to make of the double Mala situation. It left me vulnerable, emotional, things I hadn't experienced since childhood, and they didn't sit well. Even Grandmamma's abduction hadn't hit me this hard. I *knew* I'd get her back, and damn anyone who tried to stop me. But two Malas, that messed with my mind.

Blake raised his glass. "To a partnership."

I ignored the raised glass, sipped my wine, and searched his face for clues. "Not likely, is it? For us to form any sort of partnership? Your employer wouldn't be at all fond of that plan, seeing as they're protecting Barat at the cost of numerous innocent lives."

Blake ran his tongue over his teeth, and placed his glass on the table. "It's been on my mind for a while now, but I can't resign. Not until this is wrapped up. If I'm in the thick of it, I can do damage control."

"Or not. You're wearing bureaucratic handcuffs. And it's an honorable organization, emotionally difficult to work against, especially since you respect your employer."

"Yeah. I do. But it's time for me to move on. This situation is not okay. The leak has to be closed, and I can't do that from outside the agency. The people who aren't involved, they need to be protected."

I ran my fingertip around the rim of my glass, ignoring his assertion about quitting. One thing at a time. "And you're the man for the job? Have you thought about if you're caught, what then? How painfully they'd kill you?"

His grin was instantaneous. "Less painfully than you will if I screw up."

He had a point. "Quite. So you want to work with me, catch Barat, locate Grandmamma, and put Mala to rest?"

Blake held up his hand. "Whoa. I didn't say a word about Mala. That one's up for grabs until I've talked with her tomorrow morning. Ten. I'm guessing tea will be served."

He'd be meeting with Chilton. I stifled my shock. "Tea. Absolutely. Let's just run through that again. You're going to Chilton's estate to have a friendly chat with Fake Mala tomorrow morning?"

The server interrupted us to set steaming plates of Shepherd's Pie on the table. I spooned some of the mashed potatoes to the side so the heat could escape…a necessity, as my stomach rumblings had reached audible levels, possibly measurable in decibels. The scent of rich herbs and spices filled the air. I almost missed Blake's next comment. "Fake Mala? As opposed to?"

"Real Mala. The one whose thoughts reside in my head and whose body is very dead and very buried. Fake Mala is wandering about my father's estate. A pretender of sorts."

He took a gulp of wine. "Right. I'm going to talk with Mala to prove that Barat is innocent. Want to come along?"

I savored a bite of the pie. "Absolutely." I filled my fork with a delicate dab of mashed potato, then patted his hand.

"No way will I be a part of, or stand around watching, while you do anything that could interfere with Barat's permanent incarceration."

He turned his hand to thread our fingers together, and concentrated on shoveling in several bites of the savory pie. "Barat is blatantly evil, but so is having a mole in the agency. If I fake proving his innocence, I can work my way closer to the sick son of a bitch who's undermining the Bureau."

My stomach clenched. "It's not okay to make Barat look good, not in any way. He's scum, responsible for what happened to Mala and Michael, possibly to Grandmamma—"

"Not your grandmother," Blake said. "She'd be dead by now if he was behind her abduction."

"It's his doing, Blake. Maybe not directly, but he's the reason Grandmamma's not at home where she belongs."

He dipped his head. "Yeah. I'll give you that. I'm serious about a partnership and want—make that need—you to back me up on this."

Need? Did he say he needed me? No one had ever *needed* me. "What? You don't like dangling out there as bait for both Barat's terrorists and your employer?"

"One good thing. If you've got my back, there's no chance I'd end up dead and living in your head."

Blake dead. Panic hollowed in my chest. Those words shouldn't be in the same sentence. Not until we'd shared a life and turned decrepit with age.

He interrupted my thoughts. "What's with the deer-in-headlights expression? We're already partners. I took care of Michael's funeral for you."

Guilt, hot and heavy, clogged my throat. I'd forgotten to ask about Michael. "A Cajun funeral, then?"

"Complete with parade, music, singing and feasting. He

was laid to rest at St. Renatus, not far from Avril."

"Michael would've liked that. I'm going to get answers about why Avril had the money, where it came from, why she was killed…" I held up my wine glass. "Partners, then. No guarantees as to how long, and no contract. I'll back out if you act like an ass."

He tapped my glass. "Same goes."

We finished dinner with chocolate biscuits, and I led the way back to my room. Slowly. But not too slowly. Breathing. But much too fast. I pushed the door open and whirled to face him.

Blake caught my shoulders, his hands strong and warm. He backed me against the wall, kicked the door closed, and then moved his hands to cradle my face. "Look at me."

His eyes were dark with arousal and something else… My heart stuttered.

"I love you, Whitney Boulay."

Chapter 18

BLAKE Evans loved me. It was one thing to hear him tell Coburn during their guy chat, but quite another to hear it while he was touching me, touching my soul with his words. Fear stole the strength from my legs. The atmosphere thickened, and I couldn't catch a breath. I dropped to the bed with a bounce.

He crouched in front of me, and slid his hands down my arms, capturing my hands. "Didn't mean to scare you."

An understatement. "You hate who I am. The calling, talking to the dead, not a bit like following proper police procedure."

"There's a difference between not understanding and hating. Hate and love, they ride a fine line, but with you, love has always been the winner. I'm taking you to bed, and then I'm going to love to every inch of your body. I need to show you what I feel, because after tonight we'll be in for a damned hard time. When you doubt me, and you will, I want you to remember this night. No Barat, no FBI, and no ghosts. Just us."

Mala pushed at the back of my mind. Finally. Relief rushed through me, took some of the stiff from my shoulders. I sent her a brief hang-on-I'm-a-bit-busy-here message and focused on the gorgeous brown eyes of the man I loved, the one I really, really wanted to share sex with, and quite possibly to share my life with. Unfortunately, his timing was way off. "No. Absolutely not. No body parts intermingling."

I rolled away from him, came to my knees on the bed. "I don't much like myself right now. You loving me, it's a bit insane. I'm probably seriously on the verge of going bonkers. No, it's worse than that. I think I'm already over the edge."

"Uh-huh. Nothing new there." He eased to his feet, sat on the bed, and planted himself with his back pressed to the headboard, legs extended and crossed at the ankle. "You do know how to ruin a mood."

I curled my legs under me, tugged the scrunchie from my hair and wove my fingers through my hair. There would be no getting around this. "Today—"

"You went to Chilton Manor and spied on your father."

"What? You know that?" It took a minute, but things snapped into place with a loud click. I flew off the bed and emptied my backpack onto the floor, turned it inside out and freed a small, metal disc from the bottom of the bag. "You've been tracking me, then? What the hell kind of a partnership is that?"

"One where I've got my partner's back." He shrugged when I didn't comment. "You would have done the same in my position. You run, Whitney. You work alone, and you do what's necessary to ensure your autonomy. That's okay. I can handle it as long as I know where you are. I made sure I could find you, and if need be, take steps to keep you safe."

"You—"

"Stop. Think. Do you really want to do this alone? When your grandmother is the price tag?"

Hate flashed through me. What was it he'd said earlier about the thin line between love and hate? They warred in my heart, and my chest ached with the pressure. I paced, sucked in some air, then faced him. "All right. I concede you have a point. I don't like it, but you do."

He had the good sense to keep the smug from his expression.

I pressed my hands tight to my head to keep the raw emotion from exploding. "I smashed my mobile, the only link I had with Grandmamma's kidnappers, to give me time. To keep you from interfering so I could focus on finding her."

His chin tilted at a cocky angle. "Oh, no. You're not hanging that on me. Your phone wasn't global, wouldn't have been worth a damn outside the US, whether it was in one piece or a dozen. When you crossed the Atlantic, you went on the offensive with the Grandmamma situation. That was a conscious decision."

Another valid point. I wanted to blame him, wanted to ease the ache in my heart about not finding Grandmamma. Time to get on with it. "It's been a rabbit-hole day for me. Fake Mala was *there*. I saw her, heard her talk, and—"

"And?" He pulled me down on the bed next to him.

"And she wasn't in my head. She acted like she's alive, had tea with my father."

The skin around his eyes and mouth tightened. "Whoa. Back up. You watched them have tea? Listened to them talk? Are you telling me you broke into your father's house? I assumed you'd taken a look around, scouted the area, but illegal entry? You're—"

I pressed my fingers against his lips. "Stop before you say something to make me hurt you. I absolutely did not break in. I have a key. A master key that opens all the locks."

He kissed my fingers. "I'm gonna make a guess here. You didn't consider knocking on the door, being invited in for cucumber sandwiches and crumpets? All civilized and English-like?"

"Not likely. It would have made for a bit of awkwardness, since I was there to collect information about who Fake Mala really is. She's dead. Mala is definitely dead. I want to know who the imposter is, and what she's up to."

He rammed a couple pillows behind his head. "Who are you trying to convince that Mala is dead?"

"Me. I'm trying to convince myself. I've heard barely a peep from her since I arrived at Heathrow. She's been as silent as Grandmamma's kidnappers. Except now. Just when we started talking, I could feel her in the back of my mind." I paused, reached for Mala. Tried to close off the ragged edges of my emotions and seek her energy with a calm, welcoming mind. She retreated, but there was a heaviness there. Waiting.

"Hey. You in there?" Blake rubbed his thumb over my hand. I didn't move away.

"Absolutely. Just…confused. Lost, I guess. She's there. I know she's there because there's a weight in the back of my head, but she's not nagging me. Chloe taught me how to reach Mala, and I need to ring her up for a refresher course. That will be just the thing." A sharp pain stabbed through my temples.

Blake's hand tightened around mine. "Whitney?"

The pain slowly subsided. "I'm okay. Apparently Mala didn't like that plan, so nipped it with a jab of pain." Hysteria boiled in my mind. There were definitely one too many Malas.

Blake pulled me into his arms, and ran his hand over my back, kneading my muscles, stroking the tension away.

Warmth flooded me, wrapped my mind in a hazy, hungry fog. He took advantage. Brushed his lips over mine, licked, nipped and explored as though we had all the time in the world. As though the clock had stopped ticking on Grandmamma's safety, and on sorting the rest of this sordid mess before someone else died.

"Grandma—"

"Would want you to breathe, Whitney. She knows the value of balance in life, and you've been running, blindly fighting for her safety, since she went missing. It's time for us now." He ran his hand under my shirt, and danced his fingertips up my spine.

Blake smelled like sin, and I wanted some. "Ummm. Balance you say."

"I do," he whispered against my lips, his words as much a vow as an answer. And then he claimed all of my parts with a kiss—the good, the bad, the gifted, and the insane.

Childlike wonder pulsed through me when I grasped his hands, moved them behind his head. "Stay there. Don't move, don't touch." I ran my fingers over his face, memorized the lines, the structure, looked into his eyes and saw the need, the depth of emotion that flared deep in his soul. I slid my hands to his chest, unbuttoned his shirt, and pushed it aside. Sculpted muscles, a smattering of tight, black curls that felt crisp against my palms, and heat radiating from every pore.

I licked at the heat.

He shuddered.

The power of loving him rushed over me, leaving behind a magical sensation of pure joy. So alien to me. Not that I didn't love Grandmamma, my mother, and, in a different way, Nia and Chloe. Even Coburn. But this, this silent communication that flowed between us was pristine. Virginal. "I'm about to lose my virginity."

Laughter bubbled in Blake's chest, pushed against my palms. "Can't tell you how relieved I am to hear that."

Oh, damn. That had come out all wrong. "Not, um, technically," I mumbled as I straddled him, thumbing open the buttons that secured his Levis. Nothing for it but to take his mind off the subject. I slid my palm over his lower belly, tracing the silky arrow of hair under the waistband of his boxers. His sharp intake of breath confirmed my success. I slid along his body until I reached the end of the bed. He lunged after me. I planted my hand on his chest and gave a firm push. "My turn. My rules. Don't move. Don't touch. I'm about to have my way with you."

He fell back against the pillows, and smothered what I can only guess would have been a colorful bit of verbiage. "Rules go both ways. Remember that when it's my turn."

I stood and tugged his Levis free. "Absolutely. But it's my turn now, and you won't be needing these for a bit."

His boxers lost the battle to preserve his modesty, and I took my time discovering the flavors and textures of his arousal. He smelled of sex, and need, and simply Blake. Heat washed through me and I quickly eliminated my clothing. Skin to skin. I gave my body to him. Partners.

He was suddenly all over me, touching, testing, totally disobeying the no-hands rule, making me shiver with need. "Hands," I managed to whisper. "Not allowed, remember?"

"The hell. Can't stop. Will never stop touching you." His tongue found vulnerable, sensitive places I didn't know I had. Devouring, appreciating, consuming. Cherishing.

Sated, at least temporarily, we crawled under the covers until our breathing found an even, quiet pattern. I ran my thumb across his kiss-bruised lips. "A partnership, you say?"

"Yeah. We're better as a team than as adversaries." He pulled me on top of him. "We'll fight. But we have the important things. Respect for sure. That's the glue that keeps us from killing each other."

"Or you're simply in a tight spot and need my brilliance to bail you out." I tucked my head beneath his chin so I could hear his heart beat, steady and strong. My lifeline. Was I finally healing from my childhood traumas? It was about dammed time.

"So, Miz Brilliance, I'm having tea at the manor. What're you doing tomorrow?"

I rolled to my side of the bed, keeping contact with him by linking our fingers. "I need to reach Mala, have a chat with her about the woman who's impersonating her."

Blake grunted. "It'd be good if she tells you where she's buried. A body would mean a lot to us by-the-book types."

"She won't. Can't, actually. I don't think she can give directions because she didn't see the area when she was alive. And if she could tell me, I wouldn't share the intel." I levered to my elbow, scanning his face. The lines around his eyes deepened and his eyebrows hiked up a notch.

"If she tells me where she's buried, you'll dig her up for an autopsy, and eventual burial or cremation. I learned with Avril that once the remains are cared for, my link to the dead becomes faint. Wobbly. I need Mala to be strong in my mind until Grandmamma is safe and back in the Bayou."

"And Barat? Mala's body is the proof we need to lock him up." A touch of obstinacy tinged Blake's words.

"Yes. But I need to protect Grandmamma. She's alive, and digging up Mala's body comes in a far second." Blake pressed me into the mattress, holding me down.

I pushed him off with a bit too much force. I almost felt bad about it until he grabbed me, took me with him, and we both landed on the floor. He cupped my face in his hands and planted a score-one-for-me kiss on my mouth. I bit his lip—well, nipped it. He hadn't irritated me enough to draw blood.

"The deal is—"

"This whole communication thing," I interrupted. "It'd work better without the gloat coating your words."

He cleared his throat, pulled the comforter off the bed, and wrapped it around us. "Right. I agree with you. That's why

I'm staying with the agency, why I'm acting like a newbie who can't find his ass with a clearly marked map."

I sat up, pulling the comforter around me. "You're saying we're going to set a trap for him, corner him, and grind him into little pieces. Have I got that right?"

"You've got it." Blake flashed his pearly whites.

"A few details would—"

His cell rang, and he scrambled around me to dig it out of his Levi's.

I took the opportunity to use the loo and crawl back into bed, firmly staking out my fair share of mattress space. I'd never *slept* with anyone before and wasn't up on the requisite etiquette. I settled into the covers with an ear to his conversation, something he'd never allowed in the past. Not that it did me much good. Blake's side of the call consisted of a few words intermixed with a varied repertoire of grunts.

He ended the conversation, tossed the phone on the nightstand, and slipped into bed.

I panicked for a second, but in a good way. There was a man in my bed. A man I loved who would still be there when I woke up. The surge of pleasure startled me.

"Whitney." Tension twisted through his voice. "They're arresting Mala Sen."

"Blast. I thought we had twenty-four hours."

Blake pressed his fingers against his temple, rubbed. "You knew about this?"

"Not exactly, no. I overheard a conversation at Chilton Manor, don't know who was talking with my father, but he was clearly threatening to do something about Fake Mala. Didn't mention arresting her, *per se*. Tomorrow's plans will need a bit of a redo since I won't be able to corner her at the manor. Whyever are they arresting her?"

"A bit of a redo, yes." His eyes twinkled.

"You think I sound amusing, then?"

"I love the way you talk. Makes me hot." There was enough body contact between us that I had no doubt he was telling the truth.

He'd also avoided my question. Either he didn't know why Mala was being arrested, or he didn't want to share the information. No matter. I'd find out in the morning.

My hand found its way under the covers. "We'll need to have a think about a new plan."

He shifted, pushing his erection into my palm, the warm, velvet length of him pulsing with desire. "Agreed," he muttered. His hand found my breast and his mouth trailed kisses along the sensitive skin under my ear.

"Tomorrow," I whispered.

Chapter 19

I burrowed under the covers to avoid the morning light that pressed, insistent, against my eyelids. My legs brushed something warm…Ahimsa? He didn't at all like enclosed spaces, like under the bedclothes.

I cracked an eyelid open.

Blake. Eyes wide open, shit-eating grin on his face. "Forgot about me, huh?"

Damn, but the man looked good when he was mussed from sleep. "Ah, yes, it seems I did."

"Good to know I made an impression."

Heat rushed along my neck into my cheeks, down into my other set of cheeks, and I wiggled against him, dipped my chin. "First time I've shared bed space," I mumbled into his shoulder.

His hands slipped under my arms, shifted me over him. "Well, damn."

"No need to gloat, then." I liked being above him. It provided a great view, and put me in a position of virtual dominance.

"Yeah, there is. Makes up for the times you've crushed my ego."

A moment of doubt squeezed in my chest. Had I crushed him? No. Impossible. We bantered. "A fragile thing, the male ego."

He set me aside, with a quick slap to my backside. "Going to try and catch Mala before the arrest."

The bed was suddenly cold and *I've been cheated* hummed in my brain, complete with guitar accompaniment.

Blake stuck his head around the bathroom door. "Want your back washed?"

I tossed the covers aside. "I've never been one for morning sex." I conveniently didn't mention that I'd not had the opportunity to indulge. Embarrassing, my lack of a love life.

His eyes sparkled. "We can fix that."

MALA'S arrest switched things around. I'd had a long think on it during breakfast, and it became more clear when I wheeled the Vespa out of the shed and revved the engine. There was no choice but to set myself up as bait. No other way to fix this situation. A sick feeling lodged in my gut. My plan was going to wreak havoc with the Blake-Whitney partnership deal. And it would take some finessing, as I would obviously need Blake's help, as well as that of Barat's connection from inside the agency.

I headed toward Chilton Manor and shifted my breathing to ujayii, my favorite yoga pranayama, to clear my mind and perhaps help me reach Mala. If my plan to act as bait had any hope of succeeding, I'd need her to feed me real-time information.

She shuffled into my mind with a hint of attitude. "Finally. Although I am fond of your friend. A true hottie. And before you block me again, no, I couldn't watch. Wouldn't have, even without the mental wall you threw up."

My prudish bit relaxed. Not that I'd change anything about sharing sex with Blake, but it was between us, no voyeurs invited.

"Were you watching, then? Yesterday when Fake Mala appeared in front of me?"

The silence drew out for a long second. "Yes. She's not me."

"So I've been trying to convince myself. There's an uncanny resemblance, and she's impersonating you." A ripple of emotion passed through my mind. It didn't belong to me.

"Stay away from her. I don't want you near her." The energy beneath Mala's words carried a hint of threat.

The wind whipped around me, and I leaned into the turn that would take me to Chilton Manor. "You're protective of her. Why?"

My live-in ghost sent a shaft of pain into my temples. Fake Mala was definitely a forbidden topic while I navigated the twisty back roads of Hampshire on an Italian scooter.

Mala prattled on. "Your focus must be on finding Barat, capturing him, preferably putting him to death."

I leaned into another turn. "Absolutely. Where is he, then? Can you find him, lead me to him?"

"No. But I can stop you from heading in the wrong direction." And with that she faded from my mind

Chilton Manor was just ahead. I veered off the road and parked the Vespa in the copse, then made my way along the riverbank. The air was fragrant with freshly mown grass, and dapples of sunlight sparkled on the water. I watched the river rush to its destiny, finding a bit of hope in the dance of sunlight and water. Loving Blake had already made me a better person, one I might come to like.

The grounds at the manor bustled with normal activity. I climbed the tree, settled on my favorite branch, and watched.

There were several vehicles in the driveway that looked suspiciously like they belonged to Security Services. My perch didn't allow me to see the front of the estate, and there were too many people bustling around for successful skulking.

No more than ten minutes passed before several law-enforcement types led Fake Mala out of the manor, hands cuffed in front of her.

Odd, that. Not at all proper police procedure.

Damn and blast. Was that Blake Evans standing tall among the gaggle of officers surrounding Fake Mala? A spasm of fear caught in my chest, reminding me to breathe. He looked at home. Too at home. Positively chummy with the suit who held the car door for Fake Mala. She dropped to the seat, glanced at the officer and then, slowly turned toward my hiding place, disdain dripping from her smile.

She *knew* I was there.

A timely exit was definitely in order.

Blake abruptly stopped my departure. He reached into the car and touched the Fake's hand. My throat filled with something hard and hot. Jealousy? Apparently love had a downside.

I scuttled from the tree, and throwing all covert training aside, made my way to the Vespa at a full run. No one would be paying attention to the edges of the estate, not with the pseudo arrest of Fake Mala playing out in the side yard, and I couldn't risk losing her, this woman who sensed my presence. Like *my* Mala did.

And Blake? Too major a player in the unfolding scenario, but I'd deal with my trust issues later.

I pulled onto the road at exactly the right moment. The vehicle carrying my target turned the corner about one hundred yards in front of me. My helmet would serve as a decent disguise if any officers remembered me from my constable days, and a lone woman on a scooter? Hardly a of threat. Riding the cusp of danger, and the anticipation that I'd be face-to-face with Fake Mala, *and* learn the answers to all of my questions, filled me with the burning intensity of a supernova.

I trailed behind the official vehicles, barely keeping the plain trio of black sedans in sight. I didn't want to catch up with them, didn't want to be too close. Wherever they were taking her, I'd need to hold back and plan my assault. Assault? Whatever was I thinking? A single, unarmed, retired detective, against—count them—three MI5 officers in each of the cars? Nine bodyguards meant they considered Fake Mala one hell of a valuable package. And they'd put her in the *front* seat of the vehicle. A decided breach of protocol. My first true lead, and I intended to make the most of it. A rush of tingling excitement hit the base of my spine. I'd find Grandmamma. Maybe today.

When I rounded the next corner there were only two government cars in front of me. We hadn't passed any likely places to turn off. Damnation. Which car held Fake Mala? I tamped down my panic, and focused on reaching my live-in ghost. She promised to keep me from going in the wrong direction. I nudged her with my mind, and a warm blanket of peace and reassurance wrapped around me. "So, on the right path, then?" I silently asked. I accepted the sensation of a nod as her answer, and dropped back some in my pursuit of the remaining two vehicles. The sweet taste of probable success rested on my tongue.

The next curve came up fast, and I barely caught a glimpse of the lead vehicle taillights when it turned onto a side road. Fake Mala's car. I knew it with the soul-deep knowledge of my calling.

I made note of a large oak tree that marked the blacktopped lane and continued following the only remaining car. There was a village a few miles ahead that was a likely place for me to pull off and engage in innocuous-seeming tourist activity. Not that I would do more than make a quick turnabout, but my actions would serve to allay suspicion in the event the government types had noticed my Vespa trailing them. It was purple, after all.

Ten minutes later I scouted the area around the oak tree for a place to tuck up my scooter, and discovered a small clearing that was dense with weeds and enough shrubbery to provide adequate cover. That accomplished, I hiked parallel, and about twenty-five feet off the side of the road, until I spotted a bungalow directly ahead. A single black sedan was parked in front.

I made a wide circle to the rear of the house. No garden. Wildflowers and tall grass grew up to the small back stoop. No place to hide, so I couldn't move any closer, not until I had a better feel for the layout. I squatted behind the nearest shrub. My position didn't offer much protection, but it did provide a clear view of the side of the bungalow and the back door. The blinds were drawn tight on a large window toward the front of the house, as well as a smaller one just next to it. Close to the back porch, though, there was a high, narrow window without shades. Possibly the loo? It was above human height, so the lack of shades wouldn't be a threat to the modest. Not that anyone else lived near the bungalow.

I eased to a cross-legged position, arranged some of the shrubbery for a better view, and settled in for a spot of surveillance, never my best skill. Within minutes my mind wandered to Blake, his relationship with MI5, and with Fake Mala. My first encounter with jealousy was…uncomfortable. Sticky spider feet crawling down my back. Loving Blake was going to take some adjustment.

A metallic click. A warning chill. The back door opened

and one of the suits stepped outside, his training evident from the way he canvassed the area.

His gaze tracked in my direction, paused at my shrub, moved on, then came back and hovered. The bite of sweat prickled under my arms.

A feminine voice rode the breeze, wafting in my direction. Fake Mala. She distracted the officer, and he went back into the bungalow.

Less than a minute later, Fake Mala's face appeared in the tall, thin pane of glass at the rear of the bungalow. Her chin appeared to be resting on the windowsill, her eyes on me. Her gaze bored past the shrubbery and into my soul. I shuddered. However did she know me? My location?

She raised her finger in the classic just-a-minute gesture, nodded, and then lowered from sight.

Time warped, moved as though caught in a Hollywood version of slow motion, complete with the ripple effect. Two officers jogged down the front steps of the bungalow, offered jaunty waves toward front door, climbed into the car, and took off.

Fake Mala was apparently alone. So much for by-the-book procedure.

By the time their taillights disappeared, she was striding across the clearing toward me, determination in every step.

I stood. It wouldn't do at all to have her tower over me.

An energetic shiver of anticipation took over my body. It didn't belong to me.

My reaction consisted of a thundering heart.

Mala, the dead one, did a series of cartwheels in my mind that left me slightly dizzy, and more than a little nauseous.

Fake Mala stopped three feet from me. "We have five

minutes before the replacement guards arrive. They turned onto this road as the last group left."

I tried to process the implications. It didn't work. The appalling lack of proper police procedure boggled my mind. It wasn't at all like MI5. Or the FBI. Behavior this odd had to have been engineered by Amar Barat. Somehow. Did he have informants in every law enforcement agency across the board?

"Are you here to kill me?"

Her words slammed into my brain. *Kill her?* I tried to shake the crazy out of my head.

With her straight black waist-length hair, dark brown eyes, and flawless skin, she radiated youthful perfection, completely unlike the newspaper-grainy photographs of my Mala, the ones I'd Googled the night she first barged into my mind. This woman even sounded younger than my Mala. *Why didn't I notice that when I eavesdropped in Chilton's library?* Then I realized I was jarred by the contrast, looking into eyes that held the wisdom and pain of an ancient, so totally at odds with her physical appearance.

Panic filled her eyes. I'd been quiet too long. "Not my plan to hurt you. No. I simply need to know who you are. And what's going on here, because this is *not* normal police procedure."

Silence. She wanted more. I gave it to her. "My kill list is limited to Amar Barat." I tossed the words out, catalogued her response.

A smile flashed behind her eyes, fleeting, frightening in its lack of humor. "Sorry. I have dibs on that one. In any case, he won't be showing up today."

"He's coming here? *You're* planning to murder him?" I briefly closed my eyes to shut out the swirling waves of vertigo. My Mala clawed to get out of my mind, to speak with this woman, and her efforts were about to do me in.

I struggled for words. "Who *are* you?"

She ran her tongue between compressed lips, wouldn't meet my eyes. "Nisse Hendricks."

Her answer stunned my Mala into silence. I leaned in, crowding Nisse's space. "We don't have time for lies."

She spread her fingers, huffed out a short breath. "Maya Sen."

"Bloody hell. You're Mala's sister."

Tears filled her eyes, tracked down her cheeks. "She was my twin. Barat killed her."

Twin. Sympathy welled. I squashed it down. "Absolutely. He's very good at killing innocent people." I paused, allowing this new information about the Sen sisters to fall into place. "The FBI and MI5 haven't mentioned anything about Mala having a twin sister. They'd know her family. All about her."

"No." Her gaze flitted around the clearing, finally coming to rest on my face. "I am…was—" she gestured toward the bungalow— "am in witness protection."

It took every ounce of the inscrutable I'd learned at my daddy's knee to keep from landing flat on my ass. What was left of my mind immediately filled with the annoying ditty of an earworm—*the earth mooooooooved under my feet*. Only this had nothing to do with love and everything to do with finding Grandmamma. It took pushing a few breaths through my lungs to gather my wits. "Absolutely. Witness protection. For…"

"Amar Barat. His family, in India, are good people, wealthy. They do a lot of philanthropic work. I was employed as a personal assistant to his mother. Arranging charitable work, correspondence. Whatever. One day I was in the wrong place. Wrong time. Or maybe it was right. I'm the only living eyewitness to some of the horrible things he's done."

"And?" Time closed in, pressing into our conversation.

"I saw him, watched him…" Ghost white chased away the pale pink that shaded the angle of her cheekbones. Her arms clamped around her abdomen.

A car engine sounded in the distance.

Her gaze flew to the road, back to me. She backed away. One step. Two. "Run. They'll search the grounds before they begin their watch. And Lord Chilton. He's the key to Barat."

Chapter 20

LORD Chilton? Maya's words screamed in my mind, and pushed my feet to run full-out. I ignored the impulse and kept my retreat cautious, constantly monitoring distance and cover between me and the Security Services contingent. I carefully placed one foot in front of the other until I'd made my way to the Vespa, tugged on my helmet, and headed down the road.

I focused—on the speed limit, on obeying the law, and, in the background of my mind, on reaching the safety of my room. As quickly as possible. Miles flew by while the wind tore at my clothes and whispered nebulous dark thoughts that threatened my sanity. Finally I spotted the outline of the inn's roof rising above the trees. A few more minutes. I only had to hang on for a few more minutes. Gravel skidded when I braked. I jumped off the scooter, snugged it into a corner of the shed, and tossed my helmet on the seat.

My fingers shook. I yanked my mobile out of my pocket and punched in Chloe's number.

She picked up *before* the first ring. It screwed with my mind when she did that. "It's Whitney. I hate it when you answer before the phone rings.""

"I know. It's—" Her voice, mellow and serene, washed some of the shock from my brain.

But her confidence also spiked my temper. "You know everything, then, do you?"

A smile bounced across the Pacific, the continental US, and the Atlantic. The woman packed a billowy wallop of joy. "Talk to me," she said. "What's wrong?"

"I met the woman who's pretending to be Mala Sen. It's her twin, Maya. In witness protection going by the name of Nisse Hendricks." The words poured out of me.

"That's excellent evidence you're not crazy, but why would she pretend to be Mala?"

Excellent question. "Boggles me a bit. From what I gathered in the few minutes we talked, she's hoping to trap Barat and kill him. My take is that she escaped witness protection, faked memory loss, and ensconced herself in Chilton Manor. Maybe hoped to catch Barat and Chilton doing the secret handshake."

A sigh whispered across the phone line. "All right. I'll give you those points, but why your father?"

"I…She…*Maya* is convinced he's connected to Barat. I thought you could, I don't know, check out the energy or something."

Chloe inhaled. Loudly. "What does Mala say?"

"She tried to take over my physical body while I talked to Maya. Made me dizzy as hell, so I blocked her. Can't say as I'm up for another chat with her quite yet."

"I understand. But you can't stall for long. Hang on while I see if I can reach Maya's energy."

I dragged in a few ragged gulps of air. Fingered Grandmamma's diamond, and then managed a smooth breath or two before Chloe came back on the line.

"Reading a dead person's aura can be tricky, but I'm not picking up anything in Maya's field that's devious. She's telling you the truth. I used Indy's energy to ease me past...Mala, because it was the quickest way to reach Maya. I wish the twins had less similar names. My tongue gets tied."

"Quite. Thanks for checking. Things are good with you?"

"Very. Ahimsa and Indy are sniffing noses. And they both sleep in my room, but Indy is too well trained to be distracted by the likes of a feline."

I glanced up. A shadow crossed the window of my room. Blake. "Excellent. I won't worry about you then. Fill Nia in for me, will you?"

"Will do. And, Whitney, be careful. The energy around you is chaotic. Not a bad thing, but, just...be careful, please."

"Absolutely. You, too."

I slung my backpack over my shoulder, tucked my mobile away, and let go a bone-rattling, full-body sigh. By using the side door to enter the inn, I bypassed inhabited common rooms and made it to my room in record time.

The door was ajar. Blake's voice drifted into the hall, soft, safe. I stepped over the threshold, pulled the door closed, and collapsed against it.

His lips twitched, almost a smile, until his eyes met mine, then he murmured something into his mobile and tossed it on the nightstand. The space between us zinged with energy. My body craved his touch, but a sharp, cold pain filled my chest. Could I trust him?

Blake slid his hand under the strap over my shoulder, taking the weight of the backpack. He let it drop to the floor, then pointed toward the wingback chair in the corner. "Sit."

I gauged the distance, counting off the number of steps it would take for me to reach the chair. Ten. Too many. Sliding to the floor, I crossed my legs under me, and watched Blake stroll to the dresser. His gaze met mine in the mirror that hung above the massive piece of furniture, his forehead creased.

An eternity later he nodded, scooped two glasses and a bottle of Benedictine & Brandy from a tray on the dresser, and then placed them on the floor next to me. "Looks like you need to warm-up."

He sat across from me, mimicking my position.

My arms tingled, the eerie sensation creeping under my skin. "I'm not as bad off as I look."

Blake's eyebrows hiked up a notch. "Could have fooled me."

I pointed at the deep gold liqueur. "Pour, please."

He placed a half-full glass in my hand. "How about we start with—"

"With details about what happened at my father's estate this morning." It was comforting that I hadn't stuttered with the uncertainty tearing at my insides.

Unease settled around Blake's eyes. "I arrived before MI5 and caught Chilton and Mala at breakfast. He stayed close, protective, while I questioned her about the cruise and being a hostage. I kept it light so Chilton wouldn't toss me out."

He didn't scratch his nose, so I took him at his word and sipped the sweet, spicy liqueur. I let it rest on my palate long enough to feel the kick of alcohol. "He introduced her as Mala, then?"

"Yes." Blake touched the rim of my glass with his.

"And her responses to your questions were accurate?" Knots gathered in my shoulders.

He swirled his glass but didn't drink. "Her answers fit with our intel. She denied knowing where Barat is, and couldn't describe him."

My shoulders fisted in pain. "And when the Security

Service arrived?"

"The arrest was clean, screwy as hell, but no drama. They seemed prepared for it, Chilton and Sen."

He rubbed his fingers down his nose. The tell. But I'd watched the arrest go down, knew Blake hadn't lied...yet. Maybe if I prodded a bit. "I was there, watching. Saw them take her away."

Blake raised his glass, gulped. "Unusual arrest. Nothing followed policy or procedure."

A faint sense of relief eased the knots in my shoulders. "You could say that, yes. Handcuffed in front, front seat of the vehicle. There are no *fronts* in a proper arrest. What was that about?"

"Don't know." He shrugged. "Chilton wanted me off his property so I left. It wasn't a good time for me to make waves."

"Quite. Except that they've already swamped our boat."

"Meaning?" he asked.

A spasm of doubt curled in my abdomen. I loved him, but trust was dicier than love. My Mala chose that moment to bathe my mind with a hit of serenity. Apparently she trusted him. I bit down on a sigh, then forged ahead. "I followed Fake Mala. Talked to her."

Blake was on his feet in a fraction of a heartbeat, amber liquid sloshing over the rim of his glass. "What the hell were you thinking?"

Like a cop. As he well knew. "The opportunity presented itself. There wasn't anything to think about, actually."

Blake grabbed some napkins off the dresser, blotted the splash from his hand, and dropped the wad of paper on the puddle, and rubbed it around with his foot.

I gave him a minute to finish the cleanup. "She's in witness protection under the name of Nisse Hendricks, as an eyewitness to Barat's atrocities. Her real identity is Maya Sen. Claims she's Mala's twin, and based on their physical features, there's not a doubt in my mind she told me the truth."

I held his gaze, counted three breaths. "You know about any of this?"

He eased to the floor. "Not in US witness protection, she isn't. I'd've known about that. We've been chasing Mala Sen for months. Didn't know squat about a sister, or anyone with direct knowledge of Barat. MI5 must have known. That explains the lack of proper police procedure. And I can't do a bloody thing about it. Not without incriminating you."

"Maya most certainly wasn't arrested, but she is being watched." I licked the rim of my glass. Time to change the subject. I simply wasn't ready to face my Blake Evans trust issues. "About the *bloody* suddenly coloring your language…I'm thinking you've been in the UK too long."

He drew his finger down my cheek. "I belong wherever you are, and I was referring to the apprehension in your eyes." He kissed my cheek. "So, what else did Mala-slash-Maya say?"

He belonged with me, did he? And recognized that I was apprehensive? I drained my glass, washing down the spark of pleasure that flickered in my heart. "Maya said that Chilton is the key to Barat."

Blake reared back. "Lots of room for speculation there. You know the details?" He gathered our glasses, placed them on the dresser, and rubbed his nose.

Maybe his nose itched. "Not yet, but I will. I'll be moving into Chilton Manor this afternoon."

He offered me his hand. "Into the fire, said the pot to the kettle. When are we leaving?"

I leaned into him when he wrapped me in a hug. Warmth

seeped into my chilled bones. Damn, but the man felt good, and smelled like spice and sweet liqueur. "I didn't say anything about *us*."

He wove his fingers through my hair, massaging the tension from my scalp, loosening my ponytail. The sweet sensation had me on the verge of purring. "Sure you did. We have a deal that makes everything *you* do about *us*."

No surprise in that argument. Besides, I'd decided somewhere between collapsing on the floor and dissolving into his arms that I wasn't going to fight him on this. I wanted him there. With me. "Well, then. Absolutely. I'm keeping the room here, so we'll have…a place."

He'd moved me in a slow, backward walk while I was babbling. The edge of the bed pressed behind my knees, and we landed on the plush down comforter. "No nookie. We need to get over there and—"

"Yes, nookie. And food. And strategy." His mouth found the sweet spot under my ear, and I shifted to give him more room. Raw need spread through my veins, dissolving the urge relocate immediately to Chilton Manor. I tore at his clothes, seeking skin, the heat of his body, the scent of our need for each other. And more important, an affirmation of our partnership and the reasons I should—could—trust Blake Evans. My body's wisdom far outweighed meager intellect.

Slow sex. He worshiped every inch of me with his mouth, his hands, the love in his eyes. He taught me how to give in equal measure, touch for touch, breath for breath, using a language without words. One I didn't know I could speak. One that surrounded us, protective, creating a place without time. I slipped into oblivion.

"Hey, you in there?"

I pushed him away.

He blew in my ear.

"Go away." My mumble was almost lucid.

His fingers found the ticklish spot over my ribs. I dissolved into laughter and pinned his hands against the mattress. "What part of 'go away' escaped your steel trap of a mind, then?"

"That would be the part that checked the time."

Time. Maya. Chilton. "Damn and blast. Why did you let me sleep?" I bolted out of bed, jogged toward the bathroom.

He beat me to the shower. I glared at him. "Impossible. Our legs are almost the same length. You couldn't possibly have beaten me."

"Did, though. Thing is, you lack a Y chromosome. Us Y's always get to the shower first."

Warm water. Slippery soap. Naked bodies. An excellent combination. There'd be time to argue with the Y chromosome later, after I'd thoroughly indulged myself with the benefits it had to offer.

"HOW do you want to play this?" Blake asked, then tried to fit an oversized pastrami sandwich into his mouth. He'd insisted on food and a strategy session before we left for Chilton Manor. Our romp in the sheets…and shower…had left me peckish, so I'd agreed to the delay.

"Daughter bringing boyfriend to visit?" I offered the idea half-heartedly, not at all sure it was the right approach to use with my father.

Blake shook his head, rubbed his nose. "Big hole. I was there early this morning. Mentioned that I knew you, but made it sound casual. Also, you'd never bring anyone to meet Chilton, especially a significant other."

"You're right about that." The term *significant other* set my heart to pounding and muddled my brain. Was I ready for a significant other? For Blake? I'd need to come up with a decision on that. Later. After I figured out if the nose rubbing was really a tell.

He tapped *my* nose. "Get with the program, woman. You know the estate and Chilton better than I do."

I chased a bite of sandwich with a swallow of beer. "I want to verify Maya's statement. Catch him with Barat. Find evidence. I'll need access to his study, to the whole manor, actually. The place is large enough that he could be hiding an army of incriminating things."

"Like Barat himself maybe? Or a shipment of abducted children? Weapons? Ammo? What are you thinking here? "

His words stabbed at me. "*Lord* Chilton—"

"Doesn't fit, does it? Your father may be a bastard, but Barat is evil. There's a difference."

I straightened my spine, held his gaze. "Maya said Chilton was the key, but you're right. I don't see him as evil. Arrogant bastard, but British to the core and not likely to touch anything that would taint his reputation. But he does have information we need. And he could…"

Blake waited me out, silently pushing me to find some words. "He could be peripherally involved. Not for money. Chilton has more money than the royals. But for a cause, especially if he thought it would reflect well on him."

Blake twitched, then let the silence grow until it quivered between us with a life of its own. I sat back to wait him out, as I had no more words on the subject.

He savored the last bite of sandwich, swallowed, fiddled with his napkin, drained his beer, all calculated to tweak my last nerve. He'd calculated it down to the second, and then he hooked his index finger under my chin, tipped my face to his, and held my gaze.

"Or Barat could be blackmailing him."

Chapter 21

BLACKMAIL? I choked. Spewed crumbs. Grabbed a napkin and pressed it to my mouth. "Damn and blast. You think Barat is blackmailing Chilton?"

"Didn't say that. Just tossing out ideas." Blake tipped his bottle of beer, emptied it. Cool as you please. Like he hadn't just dropped a bombshell on me.

He'd probably offered it as a crazy theory, something to take my mind off weightier problems. Still. "No. It came from somewhere. You don't just natter on about things, and it's absolutely something to consider. Doubtful, but I'll play with it, keep an open mind." I shoved my chair back, and waved a hand toward the door. "Let's go."

He snagged my shirtsleeve in his fist. "How about I pay for this first?"

"They'll put it on my bill." I signed the check, wanting our confrontation with Chilton to be over and done. Then again... " Maybe we should sneak into the manor, not announce our presence. I carry a map of the alarm system in my head, so I can make sure he never finds us."

We headed for the car, Blake digging the keys out of his front pocket. "It may be a big house, and we might be able to take up residence without being caught, but we need to talk to him, Whitney."

"Talk. Excellent." Puzzle pieces snapped into place, and I rounded on him. "Your *assignment* was to get me into the manor, an *inside* job."

"That's about it." Not a single note of regret or apology touched his words.

"Manipulated." I spit out the syllables, each one lashing through me, leaving a ragged ache behind. Common sense told me it wasn't true. I would've ended up here anyway, since I'd been following leads to Grandmamma. Still, it rubbed my psyche backwards and left me bitchy.

He met my eyes, tensed, and then backed away. Must have noticed I was contemplating murder.

I consciously unclenched my jaw, relaxed my fists. I loved this man. Wanted to keep him around. "It would be best if I go alone."

He caught my hand when I grabbed my backpack from the rear seat. "We've talked about this, Whitney. You know I have to report to the Bureau, and can't resign until we find the leak. The best way to do that is from inside Chilton Manor. The deal is, I follow orders from my boss, watch your back, and together we get a handle on Barat. And Grandmamma Boulay. The way I see it, if any manipulation was done, you're guilty."

The sizzle drained from my mad, and I turned to face him, to admit, *again*, that he had a point.

His little-boy grin hit me in the heart. "You know, Blake, it's damn inconvenient loving you." And with that I slid into the car, slammed the door on his grin, and fastened my seatbelt.

The drive to Chilton Manor was quiet, but not at all peaceful. I turned my palm up, offering my hand to Blake. "I want to have a chat with Mala and could use a hand. Literally. Not much point in having a calling if I don't use it, right?"

He slid his palm over mine, twined our fingers. "Right. Just give a tug if you need help."

"Absolutely. A tug, it is." I closed my eyes, shut out the looming specter of Chilton, and focused on Mala.

She responded to my first probe. "You're doubting yourself."

Not the words I needed to hear. "Criticism is not at all helpful, especially from the dead. Any suggestions for how to best greet Lord Chilton?"

"Respectfully. You need answers. He has them."

"Maya would be a better source. She has answers, too." I was already planning another visit to the safe house.

"Maya will come to you when it's time."

Blasted cryptic, the dead. "A bit more help would be good here."

"Your father doesn't expect you. That gives you an edge. Use it wisely."

I opened my eyes and squeezed Blake's hand. "That wasn't terribly useful. She's not been staying around long enough for me to get much help from her. Not since...I'm not sure when."

He slid a sideways look at me. "No help at all?"

"She suggested that Chilton has information we want, and to use this surprise visit to our advantage. I don't know what to make of that."

He slowed the car. "Guess we'll find out. Are you planning to knock or use your key?"

"Excellent question. Respect equals knock, I suppose. Or should we really whack him with a surprise and use my key?"

Blake turned into the driveway. "You've under a minute to

decide, so I'd say to go with your gut."

The manor came into view, and Chilton was standing in the driveway chatting with a gardener. So much for whether to knock or use my key. We parked and went to greet him. Chilton was still handsome as sin. Although silver brushed the temples of his dark brown hair, rather than aging him, it added a touch of debonair mystery to his appearance.

He strolled to the passenger side of Blake's rental, controlled elegance in every step. No overt emotion, but there was the barest touch of a smile that curved his lips. It did nothing to soften the rugged angle of his jaw. His eyes—an exact match with my light amber—focused on me. He nodded. "Daughter." It had been slightly less than ten years since he'd nodded goodbye to me.

I'd mastered *the nod* at an early age, and executed an exact replica. "Father."

Blake stepped forward. "A pleasure to see you again, Lord Chilton."

He got a nod, only it wasn't the welcome-home-daughter type. Ran more along the lines of unhand-my-daughter.

I had to clamp my lips together to keep from grinning. "I understand you met Blake Evans this morning, that one of your guests was arrested."

Chilton ran his hand along his jaw, drawing my attention to a gray-blue shadow. Was that a bruise? "Yes, an unfortunate occurrence. Will you be staying, Whitney?"

I reached into the car and grabbed my backpack. "For a bit. It's been too long since I've been…home."

"Excellent. Sterling will see you to your rooms, and I'll let Cook know there will be two more in residence."

Sterling rushed out as we approached the front entrance, a smile creasing his weathered cheeks. He wrapped me in a too-tight hug, holding on with a touch of desperation. Our butler had always treated me like a daughter, probably to make up for Chilton's apparent indifference. I broke the embrace. And when I stepped back, noticed there were tears in his eyes. An unexplained shiver raced along my spine.

"Good to see you Mistress Whitney. And is this your young man?"

"Sterling, this is Blake Evans, Special Agent for the FBI." They shook hands in some sort of complex pattern, and an obvious guy-to-guy message passed between them. I controlled my eye roll, and started toward the east staircase. "We'll be in my old suite?"

Sterling tensed. "Not this time. No. Renovations, you see. Would the south wing be satisfactory? I'll see to having your personal items moved."

Something wasn't right. "Quite. The sun shines into those rooms for most of the day, makes them cozy." And kept us as far away from the back of the manor as possible. No view of the river, no view of clandestine comings and goings. I massaged the willies attacking the back of my neck, and then threaded my fingers with Blake's and held on. Sterling ushered us into a suite with two bed-bath combinations that were separated by a connecting door. Homey.

Sterling bowed ever so slightly, took two steps back. "Cocktails in the library at six, dinner to follow. Dial zero-zero on the room phone if you need anything."

"Dinner is casual, then?"

"Yes, Mistress Whitney." I caught the twinkle in his eye when he placed my backpack on a chair. "Perhaps you'll want to peruse the shops tomorrow."

Not bloody likely. "Or eat out. Or raid the kitchen when everyone's in bed. So many options, so many rules to break."

"I'm sure Cook will welcome you in her kitchen whenever

you choose to visit." Laughter bubbled through Sterling's words, and some of the weight lifted from my shoulders.

"You can trust me to introduce Blake to Cook, and show him where the biscuits are kept."

A chuckle trailed behind Sterling as he hurried off down the hall.

Blake shook his head. "Chilton has a cook called Cook? You can't be serious."

"Quite. It's always been that way. Don't you think it's a bit odd that Chilton wasn't surprised to see me? Us?"

He shrugged. "Not really, since I mentioned that I knew you."

I rubbed the itchies from my arms. "Casually. You said, casually."

"Yeah, but what guy is going say, 'Hey, I'm getting it on with your daughter'? Chilton's smart enough to fill in the blanks."

Best to close that topic. I checked my watch, and then grabbed Blake's hand and headed toward the door. "Time for a stroll around the gardens, and a quick check of our exit options."

He shook his head. "You don't know where the doors are?"

"Absolutely not. My father has a nasty habit of switching things around, changing access routes. Sometimes doors work and sometimes they disappear."

"Disappear? How the hell—?"

How could I possibly explain my father? "He has sliding faux brick walls that can be moved to hide the doors. They lock in place. When I was growing up, I checked all the exits every day so I'd never be trapped. It left me with a touch of claustrophobia. I still check for escape routes, no matter where I am." I led Blake down the side stairs and into the yard. We circled the manor, checking doors as we went. Two were in working order, three were sealed. I pointed out the alarm system triggers that were scattered over the back acreage, and showed Blake how to avoid them.

When we reached the river, I came to an abrupt stop and he bumped into me, using it as an excuse to wrap his arms around me and fold them under my breasts. I nestled into him and pointed along the riverbank. "See the oak tree just over there? That's my favorite tree, the one I climb to check things out."

Blake tugged my ponytail. "Should we?"

"Too many people around, and I don't want to call attention to it. But a stroll along the river would be just the ticket. I've given it a think, and I'd bet Grandmamma's knitting needles that Barat traveled by water when he dumped Mala's body."

"The Bureau covered that angle."

I punched some attitude into my shrug. "I haven't, and I explored this property extensively for years. I might catch something a stranger wouldn't notice."

Blake's expression radiated skepticism. "You haven't been here for years, and—"

I cut him off with a glare.

"After you, Sherlock. And, just so you know, Barat probably didn't dump Mala's body himself. He has a select staff to take care of such minor inconveniences."

"Of course he does. But in this case, it might have been personal enough for him to change his usual protocol."

The river was running at a typical summer low, a good thing, because it left more visible ground for us to explore, but a bad thing because scrambling to search the banks was time-consuming. Light clouds played hide and seek with the sun, the breeze was just strong enough to cool the beads of sweat on my neck, and Blake had taken to skipping stones across the deep green pools of slow-moving water.

I snuck up behind him, smacked his backside. "Looking quite nice; good fit on the jeans." The fabric had worn where it snugged close to his body, showed his gluteus muscles to eye-catching advantage, and diverted my attention from the task at hand. I scouted around for a likely place to divest him of clothing, eased behind him, and slipped my fingers under his belt. "Care for a bit of skinny dipping?"

He twisted from my grasp, swung me off the ground, and stopped mid-swing. Tension radiated through his arms. "Whatever is it?" I asked.

Blake set me on the ground, turned me to face the river, and pointed over my shoulder. "Body. Hanging from that tree."

Chapter 22

THE corpse was male with brown eyes and hair. Nondescript features. His clothes, discount store vintage, were stained and torn. His face was mottled, his tongue swollen, making it difficult for me to estimate age, but he looked to be in his late twenties, if one could go by musculature and the thickness of hair. Hard to tell much more, since hanging isn't kind to its victims.

Blake was officially on the job in his reciprocity role with MI5, so he was in the thick of things while I hovered several yards behind the medical examiner while she did her initial assessment. The distance suited me. Death clung to the air, settling on everything within sniffing distance.

What didn't suit me was the responsibility of my calling, crowding me, clinging with more tenacity than the rancid odors of decaying tissue and body waste. This was one dead person I couldn't avoid. Not because Blake and I found him, not because he was murdered on my father's estate, and not because the detective in me needed answers.

All of those things took second place to the pattern of tattoos covering his chest. A deep chill settled in my bones, and I reached for one of my new UK disposable phones. The tats were an exact match to those inked on the John Doe who'd graced the stoop at Chloe's former shop, Soma Herbal.

I'd reported the pattern in detail on that case, and this new body reminded me about the John Doe Chloe found at my house the day she moved out. Frey should be on it, but being Frey…I punched in Chloe's number.

It flipped to voicemail.

My radar zipped into the red zone. Chloe was alone.

I motioned to Blake, pointed at my mobile, then toward his. "Can you get a photo of those tattoos?"

"You recognize them?"

I nodded, turning my attention to Chloe's voicemail. "Call me. As soon as you get this. Call me." My throat swelled with fear, blocking any further words.

Blake whipped out his cell and took the photos. "What's up?"

I blinked my tears back. Falling apart would have to wait until later. The love in Blake's eyes was my touchstone with sanity, and I sank into it, waiting for my heart to stop pounding. "The tattoos are identical to those on an open case with the HPD. Possibly two cases. Both male. One dumped on the entry to Soma Herbal over a year ago, and the one Chloe just found on my front stoop."

I punched her number in. Voicemail again. Damn and blast. I calculated the time difference, and decided that waking Frey would be ugly, but necessary.

Blake ran his thumb along my cheekbone, the warmth from his touch working its magic on the ice clogging my veins. "Chloe?"

"Voicemail. I'll have Frey check on her." I nodded toward the police inspector overseeing the crime scene. "You'll fill him in, see that he contacts the HPD for the reports? I'll give Frey a heads-up, but the request has to be official because—"

"It's Frey, I know." His lips twitched with a hint of smile.

"Threaten him? We'll get his cooperation faster, and he's terrified of you, you know."

"Absolutely. I cultivated that fear for years, even took him down a few times when we sparred. It's not about Mala now." I waved my arm toward the crime scene. "It's about Chloe. Send me those photos, will you? Or better yet, just email them directly to Frey."

I stepped away from the scene and plugged my ear with my finger to block out the goings-on. Frey answered on the fifth ring. "Goddamnitalltohell, Boulay."

I didn't skip a beat. "Homicide, here. Tattoos match the John Does from the Soma Herbal case and the one on my stoop."

"Where the hell are you?"

"Hampshire, UK. Get your ass over to Chloe's new house and check on her." My voice cracked.

"Yeah. Yeah, on my way." Fabric rustled and his voice wove in and out. "Saw her a few hours ago on my regular drive-by. Sweet lady, Chloe."

Apparently Chloe had charmed the curmudgeon out of Frey, at least enough to get him moving in the wee hours. "These cases are related, Frey. And it's bad."

"Not much I can do without—"

"An official request. On the way. I'm also sending along photos of the tats."

An engine roared to life through the phone line. "Thanks, Frey. Have her call me."

He swallowed something. Probably coffee that'd been sitting in the console overnight. "Will do. Payback on this one's gonna cost you."

I pocketed my phone, then sidled up to Blake. "See if you

can get clearance for me to attend the autopsy, will you? I'm going to do some recon in my father's study while they're questioning him."

"Watch your back," he said, winked, and then returned to the crime scene. I jogged to the house, mouthing my mantra of invisibility all the way. Slipping in through the side door, I switched my mobile to vibrate, and eased along the hallway, my senses attuned to the whereabouts of staff and law enforcement.

Judging from the closed door and rigid posture of the constables guarding the parlor and sitting room, I figured it was in use. That left Chilton's study free and clear for me to rummage about.

I peeked into the library when I passed. It was empty, but the coffee table was set for hors d'oeuvres. My stomach growled in anticipation.

Skulking wasn't nearly as much fun now that I was an official household member. I rapped on the study door, and without waiting for an answer, slipped inside. I immediately tried to tap into any enhanced senses my calling might provide. No go. They were obviously on sabbatical, as they damn well hadn't bothered to warn me about the DB by the river. Even Mala was quiet. Aggravating ghost.

The grandfather clock chimed six. Looked like cocktails would be running a bit late this evening. I scanned the room, moved to Chilton's desk, mostly to check it off my mental list of potential hidey-holes. I didn't spend much time there, because it was unlikely he would leave anything incriminating in a pile of estate business documents. I used a letter opener to shift through the stack of papers on the desktop. Not that my fingerprints would matter, but there was a creepy element to touching his things.

I moved to the center of room, and tried to insert myself into Chilton's mind, to think like he would, but had no luck.

A low rumble of voices sounded outside the study door.

The doorknob jiggled.

My heart flip-flopped.

I snatched a Kleenex from the box on Chilton's desk, dropped to the sofa, and curled into a ball. If I focused on Chloe, my fake breakdown would become all too real.

The door cracked open, and I recognized my father's hand, the sleeve of his jacket.

"Lord Chilton." A voice of authority rumbled through the hall. "We're ready for you. Step this way, if you will."

The door closed with a snap. Relief, strong and welcome, coursed through me. I'd rather face a dozen dead bodies chattering in my head than have a discussion with my father. The investigating constable would detain him for a while, so I inhaled a few calming breaths, closed my eyes again, and scanned the room. Nothing stood out.

There had to be a safe. Not that I remembered one, but I paced the perimeter of the study, forcing my mind to think like Chilton. On my second pass, I gave up and just tried to think like a safe. The clock chimed the quarter hour and I knew: the only thing I'd ever been forbidden to touch was the grandfather clock.

I stood in front of it, studying the construction, the inlaid design, and the movement of the mechanical elements. I couldn't dismantle it—no tools, no skill and no time. So I ran my hand along the wood, first with eyes open, then closed.

There. Toward the bottom on the right side, an imperfection just above the plinth. I crossed my legs under me, focusing on the long, narrow slit. I slipped my palm into the space between the clock's feet, and my fingertips brushed an almost imperceptible knot. I pressed on it. Nothing happened. And then I thought of the sliding power button on my Kindle, and pushed against it.

A panel popped open. I tried to look inside, but the space between the opening and the wall was too narrow for my head, so I curled my fingers around the opening and the sharp edge of a sheaf of papers cut into my fingertips. I nudged them. They tumbled out, spilling over the floor.

Voices echoed in the hall.

They couldn't have finished questioning Chilton yet. I reached for the papers again, startled when someone knocked on the door, and shoved them back into the compartment.

Heart hammering, I snapped the compartment closed, and made a dash for the sofa, trusty box of tissues in tow.

An unfamiliar voice seeped into the study. "Chilton's not in there, mate. Inspector has him in the parlor. Should be done in a few."

I was back at the clock in a flash. Time pushed at me, made my fingers clumsy. It took two tries to get the panel open, but only seconds to whip out my mobile and snap pictures of the pages.

Done. I replaced everything as I'd found it, stowed my phone, and crumpled a tissue in my fist. I took a moment to listen before I opened the door, and then stepped into the hall with an aura of confidence...bloody flimsy from my perspective, but I hoped the façade would be convincing to anyone who might question my presence in Chilton's study.

"Whitney?"

Anyone except Chilton himself.

Chapter 23

I leaned against the study door, shoulders braced, and dabbed my eyes with the tissue. "Father."

He tapped the door next to my head. "You were looking for me?"

A lie wouldn't work with Chilton. "Not actually, no. I wanted to use the phone. A friend is in trouble, my mobile isn't working properly, and I knew you had a landline in your study."

"There are several available in your rooms as well." A dose of skepticism threaded his words.

Chilton could spot deceit in a heartbeat, so there was nothing for it but to try a smidgeon of truth and a lot of bluff. "They haven't questioned me yet, and I wanted to be within shouting distance."

On cue, the parlor door opened and the inspector caught my eye. "Ms. Boulay?"

"Yes, sir."

"I'd like to speak with you now."

I stepped around Chilton, barely refraining from giving the inspector a hug.

The interview lasted thirty minutes. Being a former constable counted in my favor; that my father was a person of interest did not. My official statement out of the way, I scanned the hallway before I left the library. No Chilton. A sigh of relief, and twenty minutes later I'd showered off the scent of death and was ready to face the evening…and a new dilemma. I had no acceptable dinner attire.

My backpack and Blake's duffle had been unpacked, our clothes laundered and neatly arranged on the bed, but none of them would do for dinner at the manor. I thumbed through the few things in my closet, selected a long, flowery skirt, lacy camisole, and a lightweight jersey cardigan with tiny pearl buttons. The outfit was more reminiscent of Jane Eyre than me. I vaguely remembered refusing to shop, and Chilton ordering one of the maids to purchase something suitable for me to wear at a mandatory society function. Tea, if memory served.

Blake peered around the bedroom door. "Hi, honey, I'm ho… holy shit." He wiggled his eyebrows. "Been raiding your great aunt's closet?"

"Cute. There are some interesting photos on my mobile."

His body shook with suppressed laughter. "They'll hold until I've showered. Give me ten."

I would have to shop. Tomorrow. Blake and I had tacitly agreed that my bedroom would be our work room, as it was the larger of the two and had both a sofa and sit-down table. And we'd use the smaller room for sleeping.

After cleaning up, Blake wandered into our room, the scent of expensive soap permeating the air around him. I ran my finger up the crease in his slacks, but he captured my hand before I reached the good stuff. "Chloe call back?"

"While I was with the inspector, and, to his credit, he allowed me time to talk to her. True to form, she reminded me that I'd gifted her with both an alarm system and Indy. She also mentioned that Frey has been successfully wrapped around her talented little finger. She's fine. I'm moving past it."

He rubbed his thumb over the back of my hand. "I hear you but I don't believe you. We can hire a bodyguard for her."

This man understood me, could follow my twisty mind. "I've thought about it. Not much point in having money if you don't use it for things like this. But it would…hurt her. She'd see it as me not trusting her, not having confidence in her abilities."

"Better she's pissed off than dead."

"Not to her way of thinking. Since she died, she's been comfortable with death and in love with life. It's difficult to have a sensible argument with her."

Blake grinned. "Nothing like you at all, is she?"

He'd tagged me. I grinned. "A change of subject would do nicely. Sit, and I'll fetch my mobile."

I retrieved the phone, pushed his sprawled legs to the side, and joined him on the sofa. "What do you think about our most recent John Doe?" I asked.

He levered his ankle onto his knee. "Barat uses bodies to communicate, but damned if I speak tattooed corpse.

"I agree there's something about that tattoo… Get anything from the crime scene?"

"Nada. Other than a nasty head wound, it was tidy, for a murder." Blake eyed my mobile. "You have something to share?"

"Notes from Chilton's study. I got some pictures—"

He tensed. "I know that tone. You were almost caught, weren't you? Damn it, Whitney—"

We didn't have time for this argument. "You want to fight or look at the photos?"

Blake rubbed a spot between his brows, then tapped my phone.

There were nine pages, lists of times, places, and monetary data, all hard to read on the small screen. "A printer would be useful. There's one in the study—"

"Not an option, Whitney. I'll print them off at the Security Service offices tomorrow. They'll want a copy anyway."

Whispers of unease slithered down my spine. Blake grabbed my hand "What's the problem?"

I jumped up, and wandered to the window. "You taking my mobile, working a crime scene that may be connected to Grandmamma, and me not having control of anything." I rested my forehead against the glass. "And I'm not ready to believe Chilton is involved with Barat. The father-daughter genetic link sucks."

Blake tossed my mobile aside. "They're leads, Whitney, just like with any other case you've worked. He's innocent until—"

I held up my hand. "Enough with the cliché. Something isn't right. I should be trying to make a telepathic connection to the John Doe, but…I'm not ready. It's so dark after death. Well, not for Mala, not for the innocent, but for the criminal element—black and thick." I shook off the memory of evil, and offered Blake my hand. "Let's see if we can learn anything useful over cocktails and dinner."

Blake twined our fingers. "You're cold."

An understatement. I shivered. "Chilton does that to me."

In deference to the death of John Doe and the resultant household chaos, Chilton had eliminated the cocktail hour and several dinner courses. Our meal was consumed in strained silence, and Blake and I returned to our rooms, coffee in hand.

"Other than dinner being delicious, it was a waste of time." I rummaged in the closet for a roll of craft paper, and laid out an assortment of colored markers. "I need to construct a mind map to—"

"Create the illusion of order." Blake gave me an exaggerated wink.

I bit my cheek to keep from laughing. It would go right to his head, and we'd end up in bed...without a list. "Go away. I have work, here."

I closed my eyes, sought balance, and then began drawing. Fifteen minutes later, scrawled words, lines, and arrows filled the sheet of paper, and I ran my hand over the map. "These things are linked, but the connections aren't clear. Maybe there's something about the calling I haven't learned. Or accepted."

Blake straddled the chair across from me. "Talk me through it."

I started at the circle around Avril's name. "Avril wasn't a nice woman, as is evidenced by the fact that all eight of her children moved away at the first opportunity. Church was important to her, but I think it was out of fear for her mortal soul, not Christian belief. She didn't get on well with Grandmamma—"

"Whoa." Blake tapped his finger on Grandmamma's name. "Everyone gets along with Arielle Boulay, respects her."

He was right, but... "Avril was the exception. Jealous, perhaps. Grandmamma is pure love, and Avril..." I thought back to her voice in my head, what she felt like. "Avril was all about greed. That nasty old woman was into something lucrative, and I'm positive it's linked to Grandmamma's disappearance. Has to be."

Blake doodled some dollar signs on the page, then drew a frownie face next to them. "And here I thought you held the FBI solely responsible for her abduction."

"I did, and still do, but I'm willing to spread the blame

around in the interest of finding Grandmamma. The key players are Avril, Barat, Maya, and whatever meaning is behind those tattoos." I added 25K, the dead John Does, and the papers from Chilton's study to my map.

Blake shifted in his chair. "And Chilton?" he asked.

"He's guilty of something, but what, exactly, I simply don't know."

Blake stifled a yawn. "How about we Google the tats, then get some sleep?"

I checked him out. Red eyes, lids at half-mast, a hint of stubble, and—what really caught my attention—uncertainty. I stretched across the table to press a light kiss on his lips. "Go. Use the other room and get some sleep, but if you don't mind, I'll borrow your laptop to do the search."

It was a testament to his exhaustion that he quickly took my suggestion. I scanned several sites, but didn't find an exact match to the tattoos. Maybe Blake was right about sleeping on it.

I scooted my chair back and started for the bedroom, but Mala pushed the pain button in my temple. I breathed into her energy, and a single word came through: outside.

Butterflies flapped in my stomach, a sensation so brief it surprised me. Expectation? Anxiety? Whatever. I wasn't at all interested in a late night stroll around the gardens, so I wandered to the window, and searched the front acreage for anything amiss. Quiet and empty. A warning tingle slipped across my nape. Chilton should have had security personnel patrolling the yard, especially since one of his oak trees had sported a DB earlier.

Knowing the library window offered an excellent view of the back gardens, I hurried downstairs, memory guiding my steps away from the treads that creaked, and paused in front of the door. It was ajar.

I hesitated, not wanting to catch my father dozing or sipping brandy in front of the fire. Inching forward, I peeked through the crack. Embers glowed in the fireplace, and the scent of burning wood tickled my nose, one of the few pleasant memories from my childhood. I pushed the door open, just wide enough to see if the room was inhabited.

Empty.

I slipped in and pulled the door closed behind me.

Mala pushed at my mind with more insistence, repeating the single word. Outside, outside, outside. I headed toward the French doors, hesitation in every step. Something in my gut was at war with Mala's persistence, and I wanted to do my own reconnaissance before I wandered about with only a ghost for guidance.

Nothing stirred. No breeze, no animals, no humans. Strategically placed lighting illuminated the paths, casting shadows on the foliage, but nothing seemed amiss.

Mala sent a shaft of pain through my temple.

There was nothing for it but to go outside.

I punched in the code to disable the alarm, opened the French doors, and stepped into the night.

Chapter 24

EERIE stillness closed around me, and someone who looked like Mala beckoned to me.

Had to be Maya. Sent a bit of a chill through me.

I maneuvered around the flowerbeds to meet her, careful not to trigger any of the perimeter alarms. It was obvious from the way she moved that she was just as familiar with the placement of the alarms as I was. Interesting, that.

"Whitney Boulay." She greeted me, offered her hand.

I clasped it, skin-to-skin. Warm. Corporeal. It was disturbing, facing a Mala look-alike, and I backed cop-distance away. "How do you know who I am, then? Come to that, how did you recognize me yesterday? When you approached me at the safe house."

Maya tilted her head, and a touch of smug played around her mouth. "Mala and I were close growing up, mind-reading close, especially when one of us was in trouble. That ended when she was murdered, but she still comes to me at night, when I'm dreaming." Moonlight caught the glimmer of tears in Maya's eyes, and her voice trembled, chasing away any trace of smugness.

Mala's death had caused me nothing but headaches, and a

kidnapped Grandmamma. But that aside, I had to reach this woman. Connect with her. "Your head feels empty without her? I, ah, can certainly understand, since she's taken up residence in my mind."

Maya nodded, spun around and took a few steps in the direction of the river. "Come, I've much to tell you. Mala has shown me that she communicates with you. I don't understand though, are you some kind of psychic?"

"Not exactly, but from an outside perspective it would appear that way. It's a genetic predisposition that runs in my family. What say we focus on Barat, and how I find him?"

"You don't. He'll come after me. Soon. The authorities want to keep me alive to testify. That's why they moved me from Chilton Manor. I'd been making myself too visible, strolling around the estate grounds, even going into the village once or twice. I asked my guards about you. They say you're Chilton's daughter."

The wind picked up, and blew the loose wisps of my ponytail across my face. I brushed them away, irritated because I couldn't figure out how my father fit into the picture. "Genetically speaking, yes."

"Your father has met with Barat, and they've formed an alliance. I was staying at the manor, hoping to learn the details, and it's why I escaped from my first safe house. I made sure Barat spotted me on one of his routine visits to the Manor, and then you arrived and messed up my plans. The vengeance belongs to me. I watched him kill Mala, I'll be the one to take his life. And since you're here, you're going to help me."

The absolute commitment in her words bordered on insanity. I attempted a cool voice of reason. "MI5, MI6, the FBI, just about every three-letter agency I know of, has plans to take him down. They need him alive for questioning, Maya. It's crucial to shutting down his entire operation, to try him and make a public statement out of his conviction."

Hatred and rock-solid determination shone from her eyes. My life meant nothing to Maya, would be as expendable as Barat's if I crossed her. Her arms hung loose alongside her body, her hands fisting and then releasing in a rhythmic pattern. "Mala was my sister. I've seen Barat's evil. Seen the children he's captured and sold. I've provided records to MI6, including data on the weapon shipments he's brokered."

Her words vibrated with quiet intensity, and I'd moved closer to hear. Too close. She grabbed my wrists with bone-crushing strength. I could have fought her, but her intent wasn't to harm me, just hold my complete attention. I listened. "You don't understand. Barat thought Mala was me. Didn't know I had a twin. He hijacked that cruise ship to get *me*, not her. It's my fault Mala is dead, and I *will* see him meet the devil. At. *My*. Hands."

I twisted from her grip. "Quite." There was no point in trying to convince her otherwise, so I skipped right to the heart of *my* issue. "Have you seen Grandmamma, then?"

Her shoulders jerked as though I were a puppeteer who'd pulled the wrong string. "Who?"

"My grandmother. Arielle Boulay. She's been abducted, and I believe Barat is behind it."

"No. A grandmother wouldn't be a priority for him, not unless she had knowledge of his business." Maya cut me a glance. "Did she? Was she working for Barat? Your father's mother, I take it?"

Fear? Relief? I couldn't tell what had my heart pounding in my chest. "Not at all. She's my maternal grandmother, and as far as I know hasn't ever spoken with Chilton. She lives in the Louisiana Bayou, and has never set foot on British soil."

"The Bayou? Barat talked about moving into Louisiana, something about expanding his business, but there were no definite plans underway, at least not when I was still working there."

We'd reached the riverbank. I caught her arm when she angled to follow the flow downstream. "What firm would that be?"

"Garaton Fans and Electronics."

"That doesn't seem to suit Barat at all."

Maya pulled her arm free. "Fans come in a huge variety, lots of choices for size and destination of shipments. Not that it matters. They've been out of business for over a year. Barat murdered my boss, and burned the buildings to the ground when he learned I'd gone to the police."

The tension in her shoulders told the story of her guilt and grief. And based on the tone of her voice, she'd likely tipped over the edge of sanity. Understandable. Mala shot a spear of pain through my temple. I quickly thought her an apology for labeling her twin insane. The pain stopped and Mala faded into the dark at the back of my mind. She'd been too quiet. No cartwheels spinning through my head during this face-to-face with Maya. Something was amiss.

I gathered my thoughts. "That's when the Security Services put you in witness protection? After the destruction of Garaton?"

"Yes. They put me through days of deposition and then hid me away. I escaped, made my way to Chilton. Arrived battered enough that I convinced both him and the authorities I'd had some memory loss. I'm a fairly good actress and pitched a fit every time they tried to move me. Made sure they believed that Chilton was the only person who could keep me calm."

Laughter bubbled in my throat. "He doesn't have a caring bone in his body. However did you manage it?"

"I'm not his daughter, so I don't matter enough to trigger his fear of connecting with another human being. We need to hurry. They'll miss me soon."

She believed Chilton cared for me, truly believed it. Was it possible I'd misjudged? I shrugged the alien thought off for later consideration. "How did you get here, Maya?"

She whirled to face me, beaming. "Your Vespa. Didn't you realize the inn you're staying in borders the safe house property?"

My mouth dropped open. Embarrassing, that. "Ah, no. I've been focused on you and Chilton. Grandmamma—"

"And that hunk of manhood who's been hanging around." Her grin flashed, disappeared. "I'm not surprised you missed it. There's a decent amount of wooded acreage between the properties, so you'd never actually catch sight of one building from the other."

"Quite." I sucked in a breath. "You *stole* my Vespa?"

"Yes. I've been hot-wiring since my teen years. Mala and I weren't the easiest children to raise, and our parents confiscated our car keys on a regular basis. It made us resourceful."

"Absolutely. Resourceful." A comment she'd made earlier worked its way to the front of my mind. "What did you mean about Barat expanding his business?"

"I'm not sure about it, didn't see or hear anything specific, but it's probable that he's about done with Chilton. He doesn't keep alliances long, and this one has been active for well over a year. Maybe longer. I learned about it just before Barat captured Mala. It's his habit to take over an area meaningful to his former partners, to cause personal injury if he can."

Chills raced under my skin. "Does my father know you have this information? That he may be in danger? His family in danger?"

"Yes and no. He was there for a few of my Security Services interrogations, but I tried not to reveal much because of his connection with Barat. He probably picked up more information than I'd have liked just from the nature of MI6's questions."

"So he *doesn't* know Barat is about finished with him?"

"Really, Whitney, he'd have to be dumber than dirt to miss it. We're talking Barat, here. *Everyone* is expendable."

"Quite." Chilton was diabolically smart. No telling what he had planned, but there was no need for me to mention that. "What is it you want from me, then?"

"A weapon. Preferably a G23 compact like the one riding your boyfriend's hip. It's been a problem getting hold of a firearm here. It's not like in the States, you know, where there's a gun shop in every town." Her stare bored into my skull. "And backup. I need to know that if Barat…incapacitates me…before I kill the bloody bastard, you'll get the job done. If not to avenge Mala, then for your own family. Promise me you'll kill him. He has to be stopped."

War erupted in my gut, my training and common sense versus a bone-deep hatred for Barat. Images of Grandmamma flashed through my mind. Afraid. Hurt. Possibly lifeless. They were replaced with the sure knowledge that I could trust Blake, and the fact that I knew, absolutely knew, Grandmamma was alive and well.

Mala cut into my internal conflict. "Agree to help her. Work out the details later."

Not terribly helpful, my Mala, but she was right. I needed to help Maya, if for no other reason than she would lead me to Barat. He wouldn't stop stalking her until she was dead. I offered my hand. "You have a deal. Well, except for the weapon. The Glock is as firmly attached to Blake as an arm or a leg."

She ignored my hand. "No deal without a weapon."

I pushed out a sigh. "I can agree to a weapon, just not that particular one."

We shook on it.

"One other thing." She tightened her grip on my hand. "When this is over, if I don't survive, promise that you'll have Mala's body returned to our parents."

I nodded. It was the least I could do. The woman had been living in my head long enough that it made us a bit like sisters.

Maya let go of my hand, and pointed across the river. "Mala's grave is about a mile that way. She showed it to me. In dreamtime."

I made note of the location, nodded my assent.

"And there's a time factor." Maya scuffed her toe in the dirt. "I've put my plan in motion. Barat should be here within days to claim me."

"What? How?" My questions shot through the air, staccato bullets of disbelief.

"They moved me. Barat has many eyes, and I've deliberately angered him, made it personal."

Chapter 25

"**WHERE** have you been?" Blake was sitting on the sofa in our room, arms crossed. His words clung to the air, soft, almost lethal.

I perched next to him, pried his hand off his bicep and sandwiched it between mine. Warm and strong, it sent a shiver of longing through me. "Mala sent me outside. I was careful. Maya came—"

"Maya's in protective custody." I didn't miss the tinge of skepticism riding his words, and stiffened in response.

"Maya is slippery, goes wherever she wants, whenever she wants. This particular trip involved my hot-wired Vespa."

His fingertips touched my jaw, and he turned my face toward him. "You're serious."

"Hopping-mad serious. Well, I would be if we didn't need all the information she shared, and if I wasn't terrified for her well-being. It seems Chilton has formed an alliance with Barat." The words caught in my throat. For some stupid, emotional reason I didn't want my father to be mixed up in this. Couldn't believe he'd stoop so low.

"What makes you think you can trust her?"

It was a good question. Why was I so ready to paint

Chilton as the bad guy? "I guess because of the records I found in the clock. The combination of that with Maya's observations. She *saw* him talking to Barat, an eyewitness. Is that enough, Blake?"

His shrug brushed my shoulder. "I've been known to have conversations with felons, sometimes regular gossip sessions, especially if I can get them to incriminate themselves."

"Absolutely. You're in law enforcement. My father isn't."

He scrubbed his fingertips along his nose. "Un-huh. What else did she tell you?"

"She witnessed to some of Barat's atrocities. Went to the police, and ended up in witness protection." I turned to face him. "But you knew that. You've been working with MI5. You didn't tell me about her. About what she'd seen, that Barat killed Mala believing it was Maya."

"I knew of her, but as Nisse Hendricks. The deal with her portraying Mala didn't come out until I got here and started working with Security Services."

"And you didn't think to mention it?"

He rubbed his forehead, and weary showed in the shadows under his eyes. "You act before you think. It scares the crap out of me."

"You're saying you lied because you worry about me." I poked his shoulder. "A lie of omission is still a lie."

"Yeah. I planned to tell you sometime today, but I wanted us to work on a strategy together. Not have you go off and confront her on your own."

I smothered a laugh. "That worked well for you, did it?"

He pulled me across his lap. "About as well as my plans ever work around you. Damn Cajun blood, gets you into trouble every time."

"Quite. Like our ancestors weren't related once upon a time."

He didn't respond and I decided to let it rest. Now that he knew Maya was more than willing to share information with me, he'd keep me in the loop. Which put me in a dicey spot, since I hadn't told him about Mala's burial site. It was a serious lie of omission. He needed her body as evidence to convict Barat.

I wet my lips. Blake brushed his thumb across my mouth, followed the touch with a soothing kiss. "What's got you so agitated? Besides my lack of partnership skills?"

Not wanting to debate *my* lack of partnership skills, I focused on the obvious. "Maya thinks Barat is going to murder Chilton. She said he'd be here soon. I'm guessing hours, depending on his whims."

"Longer than hours if the intel is correct. He was spotted in Somalia today. How accurate is she?"

"You'd know better than I would. I'm betting ninety percent accurate. Unless something goes wrong."

Blake shoved out a heavy sigh. "Knowing Barat, it will. He tampers with plans, changes things around constantly to keep us from getting too close."

Anxiety tornadoed down my spine. "Are you doing anything? Have a watch on Chilton? How are you planning to capture Barat?"

"I'm living in his house, Whitney. I'm playing both sides against the middle here, with the Bureau and a potential leak on one side, and cooperating with all branches of Security Services on the other. What do you want me to do?"

"Get me a weapon. Preferably a Glock twenty-three."

He popped off the sofa, nearly dumping me on the floor. "What the bloody hell? You don't like guns. Rarely use one.

Now if you'd asked me for a knife…"

I whipped the Infidel 3310 from under my skirt. "Got that covered, thanks. This may go down badly, and if I'm caught at a distance…well, there's only so far I can throw a knife."

"You're not a cop anymore. MI5 isn't going to give you a weapon. *I'm* not going to give you a weapon."

His eyes went squinty. Blast and damn, the man was on to me. I needed to fill the silence, distract him. "My family. Grandmamma. You know I'm not letting this go until I'm armed."

He rubbed the back of his neck. "You're planning to pass it to Maya, aren't you? This has nothing to do with you or your family. No. Absolutely not. She'll kill Barat and we need him alive."

How the hell did he figure it out so fast? "There are ways…"

"Don't even think it. I'm hoping to keep you under cover as much as possible. Honestly, I need you behind the scenes. You're good at gathering intel." He waved his arm toward the mind map. "And you're especially good with creating things like that diagram."

Good to know he recognized my strong points. "Quite. Shall we talk strategy, then?"

He took my hand and led me toward the bedroom. "We're both wiped. Bed now, strategy in the morning. I'm betting we have more time than Maya thinks."

I mutely unbuttoned my sweater, slipped both it and the skirt off, and then climbed into bed. There was no point in pressing him about the Glock, and Chilton had licensed weapons in the house. I chose not to think about the legal ramifications if Maya actually shot the weapon that ended Barat's life. It would be easy to claim self-defense, as the bastard was a known terrorist, but having the Glock registered to Lord Chilton would likely raise a few eyebrows.

I'd rather have done it the easy way, but Blake left me no choice.

Mala, annoying ghost that she was, chose that moment to comment. "The weapons are in Chilton's personal suite."

"Excellent." I thought back at her. "Now I'll have to invade my father's bedroom, not a place I'd choose to loiter about."

BLAKE didn't need much sleep and was out and about before I pried my eyes open. He'd left a note on his pillow: At meeting with Security Services. Don't do <u>anything</u> until I get back. Blake. It took a minute to decipher his writing, and then I crumpled the paper and tossed it in the trash. Not do anything? Whatever was the man thinking?

I showered, dressed in my usual travel garb of jeans and t-shirt, and went to find Chilton. Knowing his exact location was critical to keeping my foray into his personal suite incident-free. Trespassing gave me the jitters. And stealing a weapon for Maya went against everything I believed in. If she killed Barat, I'd be an accomplice in the death of a man that law enforcement needed to keep alive. Still, there was no way I could let her face that kind of evil without a weapon.

I was four feet from the breakfast room when I heard my father talking to Sterling in the foyer. Avoidance didn't suit my plan, so I faced the situation head-on and strolled right up to him. "Father. Good morning."

He turned toward me, taking his briefcase from Sterling. "Whitney. How was your rest?"

"Excellent, and yours?"

"Brief. Phone calls through the night and an early meeting

this morning. Politics, you know."

I motioned toward the open front door. "On your way out, then, are you?"

His nod was curt, his attention already on the chauffeur poised by the car door. I sketched a short salute toward the disappearing car.

Chilton was out of the house. Yessss!

I scanned the north staircase, the one leading to the forbidden wing that housed his personal suite. During my childhood I'd often tried to explore it, back when I still wanted Chilton's love and acceptance. I'd never made it to the top of the stairs before one of the housekeepers returned me to my personal prison in the east wing. The one currently being renovated. Cleaning supplies littered the north stairs. Not an opportune time, then.

My stomach rumbled, and on cue Sterling slipped his arm through mine and led me toward the breakfast room. "You're skin and bones, Mistress Whitney. Help yourself to a nice, big breakfast, and I'll ask Cook to bring out some fresh coffee."

I made a proper fuss. Praised Cook on her delicious brie, mushroom, and asparagus omelet, and then fled the table with my second cup of the weakest excuse of a brew that had ever pretended to be coffee.

A telltale vacuum cord trailed down the south staircase. The housekeepers were cleaning Blake's and my rooms, then. I took it as a positive omen, and hustled up the north stairs as if I belonged.

When I turned the corner at the top of the stairs, it was like stepping into a different time, a different place. Gone was the ornate décor. A wall of windows opened to the back gardens, the floors were bare, polished wood squares, and there was no furniture. The walls were pale gray, and the grain of the wooden trim shone with inner radiance. Zen. Not antique, not even British. There were only three doors that opened off the hallway, all of them bamboo sliders. Without locks.

The hair on my arms stood on end. No locks. I hadn't moved from the top of the stairs, and since spine-chilling creepies were quickly taking over my body, I figured it was a good thing to remain still. Very still. I sent a shriek in Mala's direction.

Her response was not reassuring. "It's a puzzle," she explained. "If you don't follow an exact pattern of steps, you'll trigger an alarm."

"And you know this, how?" I shot the thought at her.

"Maya. She got caught wandering around up here. It wasn't pretty. Chilton kept her under virtual house arrest for days. Watched her every move."

"Again, I have to ask how you know about this. Maya says you haven't been able to communicate telepathically since you died. Only through her dreams."

"I can see through her eyes just like I can yours, but she can't hear me." Her voice had dropped to a whisper with the last word.

"Don't go." I tried to grab her with a desperate blast of energy. "This is a rather dicey time for you to be slipping away. Maya needs the gun, and I have a bit of a pressing situation here. Do you know how this puzzle works?"

Mala fluttered at the edge of my mind. "No. Would it help to know what doesn't work?"

"Yes. We'll work with we have."

"You can't step on the squares—"

I interrupted her thought, time slipping away. "The entire floor is composed of wooden squares."

"Yes, well, if you'd let me finish… You can't step on the squares in a straight line. Maya counted when she tried to access Chilton's private suite. Something about a code."

I inched back from the first square. "All right, then. You have no idea what sort of code?"

"None. There's one other thing. If you make a misstep, a wall slides shut, holding you captive in the hallway."

"Excellent." Mala faded from my mind. Apparently the dead were only able to hang around for short spurts of time before the energy they used to contact me dissipated. Bloody damn calling. Mala had left me with two choices: attempt to think like Chilton, follow my instincts, and play dancing squares; or confront him and ask to borrow a weapon. Both options came with nasty consequences. Chilton would either catch me in his trap, or…well, no telling what he'd do if I just asked for what I wanted.

I ran my index finger over Grandmamma's diamond. I had to find her soon. She'd been in captivity for ten—no, eleven days now. Far too long. Her safety rested in my hands, and finding Barat was key. Getting a weapon for Maya was a step toward that goal. I had to figure out the code. Now.

I resorted to Chloe's favorite ujayii breathing and reached for…who could help me? Grandmamma, maybe. But not knowing her physical state, I was afraid to chance it. Chilton? Who better? He'd know the code, and was most assuredly alive. I extended a wisp of telepathic energy in his direction. A blast of his energy slammed into me and knocked me to the floor.

My butt landed smack in the middle of the center square.

I'd started the code sequence.

Chapter 26

ADRENALINE surged through me. The first move in this crazy chess game, and I'd already made a mistake. I clutched at my common sense, and concentrated on what to do next.

The good news: no doors had closed. I wasn't trapped. Therefore the middle square had to be the first step in the code. The potential bad news: I'd probably started some sort of timer. How long could I sit here before it was too long, before time ran out and I needed to make the next move?

Should I attempt to access Chilton's energy field again? Obviously a bad plan, but I didn't have a better one. Several ujayii breaths later, I reached for him. Slow. Careful. I let his essence settle around me, and then asked for the code.

My mind shivered. I shoved my head between my knees and waited for the world to come into focus. Okay, then. Tapping into Chilton bollixed things up.

There was always…Mum. The numerical genius in the family. The woman who shared…huh, no telling what she'd shared with Chilton, besides sex. Mum was a Boulay. A woman who'd experienced the calling—and immediately deserted me. Tears threatened. No time for that nonsense. I pressed the heels of my hands tight against my eyes and plastered an image of Mum in my brain. Surely she'd recognize her only daughter's energy, and the urgency of said daughter's predicament.

Maybe not.

There was no reassuring sensation, no voices, not even a push or a tug to let me know someone was trying to reach me. Made sense. Mum was alive, and my calling wasn't about the living. Chilton's energy had blasted me because that's what he did in life, steamrolled me to maintain control.

So, on my own, then. I pictured the hallway behind me, six twelve-inch square tiles laid across the width and who knew how many in length. A lot. I'd have to stand and face the layout, plan where I was going to step next. Now that I'd inadvertently made my first move, there was no choice but to carry on.

I planted my fists on the floor in front of me, thanked Chloe for extensive yoga classes, and stood. It wasn't at all graceful, but I hadn't activated any other tiles in the process, so I counted it successful. I turned to face the hall. The tiles ran in straight lines, but the end of the hallway was shadowed, so I couldn't discern how many there were.

A whisper of sound came from my right.

A mechanism? The door closing?

Blast and damn. There it was, a miniscule movement that separated the door from the wall. I could see the faint edges beginning to appear.

Now or never.

Time to make a move. I raised my right foot, and a loud *no* shrieked through my mind.

Mum? I recognized her voice, had heard the exact same *no* on my fourth birthday when I was about to step off the dock and into Grandmamma's pirogue.

A pattern sparkled on the floor in front of me.

I cut a glance at the door. It had moved an inch.

"Move, Whitney." Mum again.

I stepped off the tile I'd landed on, placed my foot on the next tile in the sparkly pattern overlaying the floor, and then checked out the progress of the door. Another inch.

The rest of the steps were easy, a bit like playing hopscotch. I moved along the highlighted squares without question or thought. The door was closing. I had nothing to lose. When I reached the end of hall, I turned to look at the entrance. No sparkles. And the door had retreated into the wall.

A burst of energy washed over me. If I had to categorize it, it would be a kiss on the top of my head. Mum? Had to be, so I sent along a virtual *thank you* hug, then got back to my...situation.

Three doors. The one closest to me opened to a bathroom. Not a likely choice for weapon storage. The middle one revealed a large bed-sitting area. Had to be the first room, then.

I slid the door open and recessed lighting flooded the space with a warm glow. Empty. No windows. Tatami mats covered the floor, and the walls were white and bare. Double damn. The man owned an arsenal. There was a firing range set off on the side acreage away from the gardens, and I remember Chilton practicing on a regular basis. Rain, snow, heat—it didn't matter. Nothing deterred him from his practice, and since he carried the weapons back and forth they *had* to be here.

I ran my fingers along the wall, searching for a sliver of space like the one on the grandfather clock. Time. It had taken me forever to get this far, and Chilton would probably return soon. *Do something, Whitney.* I strolled the perimeter of the room. Nothing. I pivoted in a slow circle, looking for anything out of place, and noticed a faint shadow along the left side of the back wall. It disappeared when I got closer, but I remembered where it had been, and slid my palm along that surface. A panel opened under my touch. Two black buttons, side by side. Fear rippled through me. What if I pressed the wrong one? Did Chilton have a mini bomb set to detonate?

The patter of rapid footsteps slapping against the foyer tiles drifted upstairs. Had to be Sterling, as he was the only one who wore soft-soled shoes. The click of the front door opening took the choice out of my hands, and I pushed the right-hand button. One of the panels popped open to disclose a wall of neatly organized weapons. And, yes, there was a Glock 23. I checked to see if it was loaded, tucked it in my waistband, and adjusted my t-shirt over top. I snatched a box of ammo from the bottom shelf. After a quick check to be sure I hadn't left any incriminating evidence, other than the obviously missing weapon, I pressed the other button to close the door, and fled downstairs.

I reached the foyer at the exact moment Chilton stepped into the house. Whipping my hands behind my back, I kept a firm hold on the ammo box.

Double blast and damn.

Sterling stepped between us to take Chilton's blazer and briefcase. I edged away from the north staircase and into a less guilty-as-all-bloody-hell location in the foyer. Chilton glanced up, and the wrinkles around his eyes deepened when he spotted me. "Daughter? Looking for me, were you?"

No way in bleeping blue hell could I wiggle out of this one. "Yes." It came out of my mouth quickly, a complete surprise to both of us. "I thought a walk around the gardens, a chance for some of that father-daughter time they're so fond of in the States."

Dread knotted my stomach at his smile. Genuine? Warm? Oh, triple damn and blast. My hands clenched around the ammo box.

Sterling tilted his head, shot me a feeble grin. "I'll just have Cook put together a picnic basket. It's a lovely day for an early lunch in the gazebo."

While Sterling and my father discussed the contents of the picnic basket, I used the respite to back against a table and slide the box of ammo behind a lamp. Not the best hiding place, but far better than in my hands. The Glock rested heavy at the small of my back. It would have to stay there until after our father-daughter interlude. Whatever would we chat about?

It went better than expected. There were flowers, shrubs, and trees to discuss, innocuous topics neither of us knew much about. That limited the discussion to fragrance, color and which blossoms would best suit a bouquet for the library. There was one tense moment when I thoughtlessly slipped the Benchmade Infidel from my pocket, and pressed the switch to slice several stems of yellow daylilies. Chilton wisely didn't comment on having an armed houseguest.

We were headed back to the house when the words tumbled out of my mouth. "Are you friends with Amar Barat, then?"

His step faltered, barely noticeable, but I counted it as a tell. "Friends, not at all. We have some common business interests."

"His business is hardly common, Father. The man is a known terrorist. He runs guns, not to mention selling children."

"Surely Evans hasn't been discussing such a tasteless subject with you." Haughty trickled like acid through his voice. "Best for you to stay out of politics and the like, Whitney."

He hadn't denied it. I classified anything less than an honest, adamant denial as a confession. It left me drained and shaky. Probably disillusioned, but I didn't have the energy or inclination to explore our relationship more closely. There would be time for that after his arrest.

We stopped in the kitchen to return the picnic basket to Cook and leave the flowers to be arranged. The box of ammo had worried the back of my mind for our entire outing, and when Chilton made his way to the library, I hurried to the foyer to retrieve it.

No ammo. A cold shiver raced along my spine. Blasted organized, efficient housekeepers. Probably noticed it and returned it to Chilton's quarters. Still, I had the weapon, and it would be easier to lift some ammunition off Blake than his Glock.

I checked behind the lamp again, under the table, even inspected the north staircase. Nada. No more time to waste. I needed to pilfer Blake's ammo and get it and the Glock to Maya before Barat made his appearance.

Completely focused on ferreting out Blake's ammo stash, I headed upstairs at a run. It didn't work at all the way I'd planned. He was sitting at the table in our room, staring at a too-familiar beige box. The very one I'd lifted from Chilton's suite.

I shut the door, and then extended my hand. "My booty. Give."

He balanced one finger on top of the box. "Where's the Glock?"

I freed it from my waistband, held it up, and then tucked it safely away.

"You're determined to get these to Maya, aren't you?"

"I am. Bodyguards, no matter how well trained, can be killed or incapacitated. I've been there, in a tight place when things turned to crap in a heartbeat. Barat needs to die, and Maya deserves a chance to live. The Glock evens the odds some."

He tapped the box of ammo. "If Barat is killed before we question him, we won't learn where your grandmother is. Have you thought of that?"

I only heard one word. Grandmamma. A shaft of hope welled in my chest. "If I can reach Chilton and Mum, why not Grandmamma?"

"You're way off topic here."

"No, I'm finally on topic. My calling shifted today. When I entered Chilton's suite I called on his energy, and Mum's, to help me get in. It worked. The calling worked with living, breathing people." I dropped to the floor in a cross-legged position, dragged in a few ujayii breaths, and reached for Grandmamma. Nothing but stale silence, like it had been empty forever.

Blake caught one of my tears on his thumb, brushed others from my cheek. "You couldn't reach her?"

"No. She wasn't there, didn't respond." The cold, sharp edge of fear pierced my heart. "They can't have killed her. I *know* my calling works with the dead."

"Maybe it's situation-based. You were desperate, stealing from your father. Could be the emotion unlocked something that wasn't meant to be unlocked."

I shook my head, loosening my hair band. "No. I desperately want to reach Grandmamma."

"Thing is, you can't force it. Which brings us back on topic. Have you thought about what will happen if Barat is killed before we get intel from him?"

"He won't come alone. There will be others to question." I stood. "Are you going to help me get this to Maya or not?"

"Yeah. I'm going to help you."

It was too easy. "What's the catch, then?"

"You follow my lead. Don't run off like a damn rookie."

Still too pat. If I had the Vespa, I'd head off on my own.

But without transportation, Blake was my best option. I wiggled my fingers at the box of ammo. "Gimme."

He pushed off the chair, placed the box on my palm, and planted a full-out, heart-pounding, hormone-thumping kiss on my lips. Teased my beauty mark with the tip of his tongue. "Love that freckle above your lip. Makes me hard."

I melted into the kiss—until he pulled the Glock and the ammo out of my hands. "Backpack. Those go in *my* backpack, not in your duffle."

He tapped me on the nose. "I wouldn't dream of keeping them. Stolen property, and me a federal agent. Gotta be bad karma."

There was a touch of smug in his voice that set my skin to itching. Time to upset his balance a bit. "I asked Chilton about his relationship with Barat."

Blake whirled. "Say, what?"

"Grandmamma has been missing for eleven days. Barat is due to show up any time, so I decided to push."

He sputtered, then worked some words out. "You didn't think confronting him might screw up our plans to capture Barat?"

"The words popped out before I could stop them."

"And you wonder why I want to keep you tucked up in the bedroom."

Best I not respond to that chauvinistic comment. "Did you get permission for me to attend the autopsy, then?"

"Nope. Asked. John Doe's in the cooler, and they're waiting for a big time London medical examiner to get here. It'll be up to him."

"Odd, that. No, maybe not, as it's an international case, what with the other bodies having matching tattoos. And a possible connection to Barat." I switched topics again. "Were you able to access the photos I took in Chilton's study? Print them?"

"Copies are locked in my bag. We can go over them when we get back from turning me into a criminal."

"No reason for you to do the delivery, is there?" I held my hand out for the weapon.

He didn't bother to respond, just cradled my hand, and planted soft nips and kisses against the palm. He obviously wasn't going to hand over the Glock.

After the kissing, we made our way downstairs, pausing in the foyer to chat with Sterling. That's when it hit me. There was something wrong about the closed off the east staircase. No workmen. There hadn't been any since we'd arrived, and there'd been no chatter from the staff about renovations. I strolled toward the east staircase, brushed my hand over the velvet rope. Sterling caught my hand, his grip far tighter than any eighty-year-old's should be. I patted his hand, eased from his hold. "The renovations, how are they coming along, then?"

Pink tinged his cheeks. "Just fine, Mistress Whitney. Should be completed in a few weeks."

I pushed. "I'd like to take a look, see what's being done."

"Not possible." Sterling's words were clipped. "Strict orders from Lord Chilton. No one is to interfere with the work until it's complete."

He wouldn't, or perhaps couldn't, meet my eyes.

Chapter 27

APPREHENSION churned in my belly. Blake either wasn't paying attention, or chose to ignore the tension vibrating around us. Sterling pointedly opened the front door and hurried us on our way.

"Odd that," I said, giving Blake's sleeve a tug as we moved toward the car. "Didn't you pick up on it, then?"

"Yeah, but everything about Chilton Manor is odd."

He'd get no argument from me there, but this was different. Maybe it was because of the shifts in my intuition since the calling. Whatever it was would have to wait until after we'd delivered the Glock to Maya.

The drive was peaceful, Blake and I comfortably lost in our separate thoughts. I hadn't experienced that sort of comfort before, and I liked it. Could get used to it.

Blake parked about a mile from the cutoff road to the safe house. "See that rock over there?" He pointed across my body toward a large grey rock nestled against an oak tree. Vegetation climbed partway up the sides and the surface was flat, a natural seat.

"Hard to miss, as it's the only noticeable rock around."

"I want you to sit there and wait. Do not move. I can get

past Maya's bodyguards and you can't." He slipped his Glock from the holster, tucked it into the glove box, and then reached for my backpack.

I fisted my hands in the straps. "Maybe I wouldn't have to get past the bodyguards. Mala probably alerted her sister to my plan, and she'll be watching for me, expecting me. She'll find a way to meet me."

"And maybe not. Too many what ifs, Whitney."

I let go of the backpack. "How are you going to play this?"

"Question her. I'm an adjunct to the team and have every reason to interact with her."

"I get that, but how are you going to pass her the Glock? The guards will notice if yours is missing, and what about ammunition? Besides, Maya asked *me* for a weapon, not you. Maybe she won't take it from you."

He lifted an eyebrow, stuck his hand in my backpack, and pulled out the Glock. "I have my ways."

He tucked the gun in his shoulder holster, rummaged for some ammo, and stuffed the cartridges in his pockets. "That should do it. You're sure she knows how to use this?"

"I'm sure." There was no hesitation in my answer. I'd never seen Maya shoot, had no proof that she was experienced with firearms, but I knew.

Blake stared into my eyes. "You don't have a clue. I'm not leaving it with her if she can't prove she's capable. Trained."

He was right. "Okay. Be safe."

Blake cupped my neck and laid a solid kiss on my mouth, a softer one on the freckle adorning my upper lip. "Do not move from that rock. This won't take long, so curb your impatience, woman."

"Consider it curbed." I climbed out of the car and strode

toward the rock before he caught the lie in my eyes. As if I'd ever plant myself like a good little girl. Not that he really believed I would. Surely he didn't. I sat on the rock—long enough to rearrange my backpack, check my knives, and set my mobile to vibrate.

That done, I spent a few minutes in meditation, and then reached out to Grandmamma. Warmth flooded me. No words, just the energetic equivalent of love and reassurance. And maybe a bit of impatience. I waited a few minutes, but she'd faded again.

Peace settled around me, and I opened my eyes. Time to get moving. The land between the rock and the safe house was an open field scattered with small, wooded areas of trees, shrubs and the like. It had probably been farmland at one time. My plan was to watch the transaction and make sure Blake got out all right. I could jog the hypotenuse of the triangle between the rock and the safe house as quickly as he could drive the two legs. I kept it to a slow run in deference to the tall grass and the possibility of mole holes. It wouldn't do to turn up with a sprained ankle.

I slowed as I neared the property, searching for a proper tree with a good vantage point. From my last visit, I knew there weren't any near the house, but just on the other side...yes. I'd remembered correctly. I'd need to circle around the back of the property to get there...not a fail proof plan, but the only viable option. The guards would be busy with Blake, making the necessary calls to ensure he was cleared before they let him speak with Maya.

I chose my tree, a sturdy willow that would provide excellent coverage, curled my hands around a low branch, and was about to hike myself up when two male bodies caged me, one in front, one behind. They smelled nauseatingly spicy, like they'd bathed in a vat of cloves and something peppery.

The one behind me slapped a damp cloth over my mouth.

His hot breath brushed my cheek, and his lack of familiarity with a toothbrush seeped through the cloth.

Blast and damn. I *knew* better than to let my guard down.

I held my breath, twisted, caught the thug in front of me with a knee to his belly, and elbowed the one behind me. My lungs cramped with the need to breathe. I fought the urgency until black edges clouded my vision and I sucked in a breath. Darkness closed over me.

MY sense of smell kicked in before my muscles started to function, and I couldn't escape the stench. Damp earth and old trash assaulted my nostrils, hit my stomach with a jolt, and churned into a roil of nausea. I tried to roll to my side. Failed. My muscles, bruised and achy, refused to follow my brain's urgent commands.

The men who had abducted me were gone. I couldn't smell them, which was the only good thing about this situation.

I assessed my prison, and then reached for Mala. Quiet. Empty. I focused on the sound of my breathing…too labored, with a wisp of fear lacing each inhalation.

The skin on my face and around my mouth burned, and my hands were secured behind me. I concentrated on forcing my eyelids apart. Succeeded in creating a narrow slit, but the light hurt my eyes. I could tell it was weak, a single shaft of pale gray that poured in through the wall of my prison, but still painfully bright and unexpected.

Where the hell was I?

The pain wracking my body, the rough wooden surface under my hands, and the rope cutting into my wrists all helped to shake off the haze clouding my brain. A jolt of memory crashed into me. Blake. Maya. The safe house and the willow tree. Barat? Did he have them, Blake and Maya?

Bloody hell.

I had to get out of here.

I forced my eyes open again, and, ignoring the pain and waves of nausea, turned my head to study the boundaries of my prison. A shed. Empty and old. Probably tossed together years ago to store tools and the like. It was a rickety structure, the aged wooden slats barely held together with rusty nails. Unfortunately, the door looked strong and securely fastened. The wooden floor was coated with grimy dust.

I reached for Mala again, struggled to sense her energy. Nothing.

I sucked air in through my mouth, the sensation of the chloroform a memory on my cotton-dry tongue. Cool air licked my throat and my stomach cramped. I swallowed against the nausea, focused instead on the ropes binding my wrists. They were tight. I might be able to use one of the loose nails scattered around the floor to work the knots free, but a knife would be better.

I'd secured three of them on my person before I was captured, on my right ankle, and left arm, and in my right back pocket. The one in my back pocket was gone. I rubbed my ankles together, could feel the holster, but no telltale ridge of the knife. Still, they might have missed the Fairbairn-Sykes dagger, as it fit quite tidily along the inside of my left forearm. But with my wrists secured there was no way to reach it.

I attempted to roll onto my side again, this time successfully. Painful tingling raced through my arms when the blood resumed its normal course. I wiggled my fingers, hoping to speed the process along, and a jagged edge of pain moved into my hands. I brought my knees to my chest, smashed my cheek against the floor, pushed up hard, and then flopped back, panting for breath. Blast it. I had to get my feet under me.

I flopped onto my back, bent my knees, gathered my strength and lifted my upper body to a sitting position. Okay, then. That worked. I sent a quick prayer of thanks to my personal trainer for the countless crunches he demanded during our workouts.

Doubt and fear swirled around me. When my head stopped swimming and my stomach settled, I rolled to my knees and attempted to stand. After a few false starts, I made it to my feet, braced my back against a wall, and stepped through my arms. If it weren't for Chloe and yoga class I'd have never pulled off that particular maneuver. The rope binding my hands was tied tightly, but raveling. I needed something sharp to work between the fibers, and scanned the floor for an implement. No go.

Making my way around the perimeter of the shed, I found a fat, rusty nail poking out from one of the walls. I twisted my wrists into the correct position to slide the nail through the knots, pulling and tugging to loosen them until my hands were free. At least my abductors hadn't used handcuffs or zip-strips.

My wrists were raw and bloody, my body covered in sweat. I was filthy, dehydrated, smelled really bad, and I had a full bladder. The good news: the Fairbairn-Sykes was still snugged against the inside of my forearm.

By the time I'd yanked, kicked and fought enough boards free to make a Whitney-sized hole in the wall, it was dark out. Quiet. There should have been insects playing their evening song, but there was only the low murmur of wind and leaves brushing against each other.

I'd made a fair amount of noise breaking the boards free, enough that if anyone were in shouting distance they would have heard and come to either rescue me, or to truss me up again. That didn't mean no one was watching, and to be realistic about my condition, I wasn't up to a bout of hand-to-hand combat.

I eased my way out of the hole, scanning my surroundings for landmarks, and for any miscreants who wanted to do me in. The safe house was a pale shadow in the distance. No lights. I circled the shed, assessing my options, ruling out the safe house as a refuge.

It wasn't that late. There should have been movement, lights, some sign of life. If Barat had made his move, everyone was either dead or had been relocated.

Dead. Damn. Could everyone have been killed? Panic slithered down my spine, and I reached for Mala again. She pushed against my mind, and none too gently. "Maya isn't dead. She's gone. Escaped when Blake reported you missing, while their attention was divided between finding you and guarding her. Barat isn't here yet. Close. He feels close to me."

"Blake?" I whispered.

"I have no idea." She didn't sound at all happy that I'd distracted her from Maya and Barat.

"Maya said the safe house was close to my lodgings. If you can see through her eyes, you can tell me which way she went when she hot-wired my Vespa."

"I can." She sent a single, sharp jolt of pain through my head.

"What's with the pain? I'm trying to help, here."

"You've failed at keeping Maya safe. That's why I wanted you to stay away from her. I was afraid she'd go after Barat on her own, and she has."

Mala had honed the art of being difficult, but I could sense the direction of the inn through her tantrum. And she had a point about me not keeping Maya safe. At least Blake had successfully delivered the Glock to her.

I headed in the direction of the inn on the assumption that Maya had returned my Vespa. Made sense, since she had nowhere else to store it. My backpack was gone, and along with it the keys to the scooter, but Maya wasn't the only one who could hot-wire a vehicle.

I hadn't hiked more than a mile before lights shone in the distance, and the roofline of the inn came into view. The short hike gave me plenty of time for a think on the situation, and I wanted to share my theories with Blake. There were a couple unused disposable phones in my room at the inn—all I had to do was get there, climb the fire escape, and break in.

Nothing to it.

Until six men circled me.

I spun. All were masked, armed…and tattooed.

My thoughts, my vision narrowed, tunneled. Just me. And them.

I smelled fear seeping from every pore in my body, channeled it and kicked out, catching one in the stomach.

A sharp sting hit my right shoulder, immobilized my arm, spread through my body.

I knew I was crumpling, couldn't stop from crashing to the ground in a sloppy heap.

Chapter 28

HOURS passed, days...maybe months. I couldn't tell. Light faded into darkness, and then back to light. They kept me drugged. I rarely stayed conscious for more than a few minutes. When I did surface, a vague memory of needles and not being in control plagued my thoughts and sent jagged shards of fear through me.

A pile of dirty rags strewn on the floor served as my bed. The walls swayed, a boat maybe. Rusty door hinges hung empty. No door. My captors didn't restrain me. But then they didn't need to. My arms and legs ached from the toxic substance injected into my veins several times a day. It sapped my strength and destroyed my ability to think, to fight. When my mind did surface, renewed fear surged through me. No door. No locks. No restraints. It's bloody buggered to be captured and *free*.

I was expendable.

Death hovered. And it carried a stench that coated my body and clung to my clothes—fear, stagnant water and decay—from garbage, from body waste, from death. My decay.

I wasn't ready to die.

But I couldn't cling to consciousness long enough to fight.

HE floated above me, my savior. Mumbled words of encouragement. Strange voice. Kind words with no meaning. Water trickled down my throat. I choked, gasped for air. Pain throbbed, overwhelming my senses.

The room steadied around me, just for a moment, and then clouds of gray confusion swirled in my brain.

"Whitney." He whispered my name. *I* was Whitney. I remembered being Whitney.

"We're jumping in the water, don't fight me. Don't breathe." His words were harsh, cutting through the fog in my mind. I sucked in a breath, held it.

Water closed around me. I kicked, without thought, an automatic response to being submerged, stopped when a pained grunt sounded in my ear and the grip under my chin tightened. He was my savior. The one without needles and drugs. Shouldn't fight. Not supposed to hurt him. My body drifted. My mind dissolved into the black.

Movement, pressure against my abdomen. Dark. It was so dark. What happened to the light? I gagged. The movement stopped—no more pressure. More pain. Intense, aching pain in my gut. Dry heaves wracked my body and consciousness tumbled me into agonizing reality.

I knelt on the ground, hands fisted in the earth. He crouched next to me. Who? I turned, too fast. The world swirled and I slipped away. Death calling me, but not as insistently.

I opened my eyes, gazing into the face of my savior.

Justice. Dominic Justice.

And then nothing.

BEFORE I opened my eyes the fragrance of lavender, aged wood, and morning-fresh air teased my nostrils. A breeze drifted around me, probably from an open window. I tried to hold the images of Grandmamma that had fluttered through my dreams, but they dissolved on the breeze. The mattress molded to my body, supporting the aches and pains. Chilton Manor. The room I shared with Blake Evans. The scents were unmistakable.

Safe. Not dead. No reason to open my eyes. No reason for the dream to end. None at all.

"Whitney? I know you're awake." Blake's voice rumbled, soft in my ear.

I turned my head toward the sound, followed it with my body. Tried to say his name, but could only moan. The rough tip of his finger traced my cheekbone, caressed my lips. "You're safe. Barat doesn't have you."

I swallowed. My tongue stuck to the roof of my mouth. So dry. "Water." Not a word. A croak, but Blake understood. His arm moved behind me, supported me, and a straw pressed against my lips. Cool liquid filled my mouth, spilled down my throat. I couldn't get enough, sucked harder and choked.

And then I opened my eyes. It was safe. I was safe. I reached for Blake, burrowed into his chest and gave in to the shudders ravaging my muscles. Uncontrollable. He stroked my back, murmured crazy, meaningless assurances that it was all right. But he was wrong. It wasn't all right. I pushed away from him, cupped his face in my hands, and held his gaze until I found what I needed. Watched his heart open, watched the love take form, tangible, steady, solid, and finally I let myself bathe in it, let it wash over me. And then I sobbed.

Spent, I rolled to my back, allowed sanity to replace hell, and scrubbed the tears from my face.

"It must be the drugs, then." My words were shaky, but they belonged to me. To a brain capable of thought, of speech.

Blake grinned, and laughter danced in his eyes. "You're back. And yes, the drugs did a number on you." He grabbed me in a hug, and his desperation, worry, and love were equally evident in the intensity of his embrace. My heart swelled.

I eased from his grasp and inched up to sitting, a pile of thick, soft pillows supporting me. "What happened? How long …?"

"Barat happened. You were missing for two days before Justice stole you back."

"I don't remember." My mind scrabbled for details, any bit of memory that would give me control of my life again.

"Give it time. We've only had you seventy-two hours. The doc says it will take a few days for your body to shake off the drugs."

I'd been safe for hours? Memories chased through my mind, disjointed, disturbing. "Maya? What happened at the safe house? Did Barat capture her, too?"

"When I realized you were missing—and we *will* discuss what part of don't-move-from the-rock you didn't understand—I called for help. Maya escaped in the chaos." Irritation simmered in his words.

I grasped at the twirling strands of my memory. "We were there to give her a weapon. Did she get it? Does she have something to protect herself?"

Blake propped his head on his hand. "Yeah. She has the Glock. Not that it means much. You had a knife, more than one, and kick-ass martial arts training. They caught you."

Shame wracked my body. "It's…bloody humiliating, needing to be rescued. I couldn't defend myself. The drugs…helpless. She'll be helpless if they drug her."

Blake stroked my hair away from my face. "They gave you a cocktail, potent as hell."

Memories swirled. "It must have been a dart. They weren't close enough for an actual injection. I remember crumpling. Everything fading to black."

"Do you remember who captured you, what they looked like?"

I wove my fingers through my hair, massaged my scalp, trying to free the images. "I was captured twice. The first time there were two thugs-in-training. They caught me off guard with chloroform and left me in a shack between the safe house and the inn where we stayed."

"They work for Barat?"

I organized the random bits of information that were floating around in my head. "Yes. I rather think they did. The first two men who attacked me only had tattoos on their biceps. The second lot, the ones who captured me after I escaped from the shed, their arms were covered in ink."

"Can you draw them? Did they look like the body we found?"

"Can't draw them, but they were swirls and geometric patterns similar to the ones on the other bodies. It happened too fast. I tried to move, to fight…and then I was drugged and…"

Blake handed me the glass of water. "Take your time. Drink."

I emptied the glass and licked my lips, appreciating the miracle of water. "Maybe hypnosis would help me remember the exact patterns. They seemed random, but I might remember something useful. Their hands were covered in tattoos. We have pictures to compare, of the tats on the John Doe across the river. "

"Sort of. They weren't clear enough to submit as court evidence. You're thinking there's a hierarchy in Barat's organization? The tattoos maybe indicate rank?"

I dropped my chin to my chest and focused on breathing, grappling for equilibrium. "Could be. Does Barat have tattoos?"

"Not in any of the pictures I've seen."

"The agents placed around Barat? Tattooed?"

"Who they are, what they do, is strictly need-to-know. I'm not in the loop."

Connections clicked into place. "Tattoos? The dead John Does in Honolulu. Chloe. Bloody hell, you've talked to Frey? Seen to getting Chloe into protective custody?"

"We touched base while you were missing. Chloe's about as stubborn as you. Wouldn't leave her house when you asked her to, and won't leave it now. With this intel, maybe—"

"No. Absolutely no maybes. Too many coincidences, and neither of us believe in them. I'll see to hiring a bodyguard." I grabbed for the bedside table, searching for one of my toss-away mobiles. The room spun. Blake took the phone from my hand and punched in some numbers. I lifted my hand, struggled to take the phone. No strength. From Blake's side of the conversation, I ascertained Frey was still looking after Chloe.

My eyelids drooped, closed, and I drifted into restless semi-consciousness. Random thoughts plagued my mind, too convoluted to follow. Blake cradled me against his chest, and I inhaled his maleness, warm and deliciously pungent.

Moments of peace.

Shattered. I jolted upright, knocked Blake's chin with the top of my head. "Justice rescued me. Damn and blast. How in the hell did that happen?"

Blake rubbed his chin, eased me back against the pillows. "Chilton called him in. They, ah, are apparently friends."

"Friends?" I screeched. Blake refilled the water glass and handed it to me. I gulped, trying to reconcile the detestable thief with the man who rescued me. The water churned in my stomach.

Blake took the glass, and cradled my chin. "Truth. I'm damn grateful to him. By the time we located you, Justice was en route and ready to roll. Even Chilton's resources couldn't activate the Bureau that quickly. Nor were they willing to risk the undercover agents, or do a damn thing that would render the case against Barat null and void. Justice is private. He went in. Got you out. No explanations, and no trail."

"Absolutely. Chilton and Justice, you say? A demon and a devil. And now I owe them both."

Blake deflected my comment with a grunt. "I've avoided thinking about the payback Justice will demand. Doesn't matter. Your life doesn't have a price."

I found his hand, knitted our fingers. "Chilton can afford him."

He pressed a gentle kiss on my lips. "That's not how it played out. Justice wouldn't take money, said he'd collect later."

My stomach clenched. "Chloe. He wants Chloe."

Blake snorted. "That's up to her. Not a thing we can do about it. Although I'm thinking it's going to be something else."

"You shouldn't have let Chilton call him in. You'd located me, would have rescued me. Barat would have—"

"Used you as an example like he did Mala. Nothing is worth your life."

"Quite. I'm on board with that, but my father?"

Blake stood, wandered to the window, and then turned to face me. "We got a huge break because you were captured. Found the leak in the Bureau."

He had my full attention. "And?"

"Seems the Special Agent in Charge's secretary was friends with Mala. Barat got wind of it, threatened the secretary's family if she didn't hand over the intel. She's had one of his tattooed goons on her for months, living in her house, watching her and her son."

I struggled to grasp the situation. "She didn't think to tell you, get FBI protection?"

"She was a terrified paper-pusher who happened to know how to access certain information. She'd been with the Bureau for over ten years, picked up patterns and behaviors of the SAIC that made it possible for her to bypass some of our safeguards."

He was rambling, hard to follow. "She's safe, then? Her and her son?"

"They're in protective custody. Will be until her trial."

"Barat will try to get to them, and he'll hurt them terribly. And then he'll enjoy murdering them." My stomach churned with disgust.

"Not our immediate problem." Blake strode to the bed, sat, and took my hand. "We're in a shitload of trouble. Barat captured you. Justice stole you. When Barat puts the pieces together…"

The breeze whisked along my nape leaving prickles behind. "We have to keep Justice away from Chloe, keep him from endangering her. If the leak is stopped, do we have a bit of an edge, then?"

"If we do, the *bit* is too damn small."

The bedroom door swung open and Chilton stepped in.

Chapter 29

CHILTON'S presence sucked the oxygen from the room. I blinked. He balanced a cup and saucer in his hand while assessing me from head to toe. "Good to see you alive, Daughter."

It was a first, and I started to sweat. Lord Chilton had never once set foot in my room, and his presence stirred the memory of my sixth birthday, the day Mum told me I'd be educated in Britain. That I'd live with my father for the school year, boarded during the week, and at the manor for weekends and breaks—and that she wouldn't be coming with me.

Chilton flicked his chin in Blake's direction. "I need a moment with my daughter, if you please."

Judging from the way Blake pushed into Chilton's space as he left the room, he wasn't at all pleased to be taking orders from my father. To his credit, he held my gaze and pointed outside the door, a silent message that he'd be right there if I needed him.

Chilton set the cup of steaming liquid on the bedside table, pulled up a chair next to the bed, and brushed a fleck of lint from the seat before arranging himself just so on the cushions. He took time to cross his legs and fold his hands, centering them on his lap. I recognized the posture. Irritation twisted under my skin as childhood guilt took root in my belly.

Nothing for it but to take control of the situation.

"You noticed the missing Glock, did you?"

"I did. You might have asked." His nose jerked up with a touch of haughty.

"It didn't seem quite the thing to ask, what with Mala being in witness protection. My crime, my responsibility."

He shifted in the chair. Another first. Chilton didn't fidget. "How did you disarm the security?"

Relief coursed through me. This sin I could drop directly in Mum's lap. "I didn't."

He tilted his head. Waited.

"It's the year for my calling."

He dipped his chin.

"It seems to have opened a connection between Mum and me. She showed me the grid, where to step."

His shoulders lowered, his hands loosened and the white line around his mouth disappeared. "Of course she did. It would be an easy code for her to break, knowing me as she does."

My mind, still boggled with drugs, couldn't decipher what he was saying, but a decidedly creepy sensation traced along my nerves. Chilton and Mum? "I wasn't aware you knew each other at all well, aside from conceiving me, of course."

He shifted his weight again. "We are…quite close, actually. You being our primary topic of conversation."

A knot of pain welled in my chest. Mum and I weren't at all close. We spoke several times a year, met if I traveled through Washington, DC—which had happened exactly once, a freak layover when I was en route from Hampshire to New Orleans. I fought to gather my scattered thoughts. "You chat, then?"

"Weekly." A man of few words, Chilton.

"About me? Why not talk *to* me?" Irritation simmered, chasing away some of my woozies.

He stood, returned the chair to the corner of the room, and then extricated a folded sheet of paper from his jacket pocket. "Because we love you, we try to protect you. From us."

My stomach bottomed out. Another first. He *loved* me. He bloody well hadn't ever acted like it. My mind raced with made-up reasons why he hadn't, and then shut down because it didn't really matter.

Chilton handed me the paper.

I smoothed the folds and focused on the diagram. It was the code to enter his private suite, and its structure was based on my name. Whitney. Tears stung behind my eyes. It was so simple, really. A substitution of numbers for letters, only made mysterious by the creative way he overlaid the hall tiles with the letters of my name.

When I looked up, he held his hand out. I folded the page, handed it to him, and he tucked it into his pocket. "If you need a weapon, help yourself. Let Sterling know what you take so he can replace it."

Exhaustion settled in my muscles, and my eyelids drooped. "I'm not big on firearms, actually."

Warm fingertips touched my hand, and my eyes popped open. Chilton had *touched* me. Fear? Hope? I tried to label my emotion. Failed. He held my gaze. "There are knives in the cabinet to the right of the firearms."

A pressing question popped up. "Housekeeping? Where's the button to turn off the alarm?"

If I didn't know better, I'd swear his lips twitched. A smile? "I'll leave that one to your imagination, Whitney. Before you sleep, you must drink the tea."

I'd forgotten it was sitting there, but when he handed me the cup, the pungent aroma of fresh herbs caught my attention and a clear image of Grandmamma sitting next to the bed floated through my mind. Not possible. She was still missing. I had to get out of bed and find her. As soon as my legs would hold me.

"Grandmamma?" I mumbled, taking a sip of the concoction.

Chilton reached for the doorknob. "The tea will hasten your healing."

I must have slept for several hours, because afternoon sunlight bathed the bedroom. A need for the loo and a shower pushed me out of bed. I staggered, and the possibility of long-term side effects from the drugs became a worry. They clearly still polluted my body. The nap and tea had helped, but I still had to steady myself until the room stopped spinning.

Chilton Manor had well-appointed bathrooms and unlimited hot water. I especially appreciated the five showerheads pummeling my body, massaging, and washing away the remaining toxins. I wanted to be clean again. Inside as much as out. And then I needed to find Grandmamma and lay Mala to rest. I needed to get on with my life.

Someone, maybe two someones, had stopped by while I was doing my hot-water healing. The first thing I noticed were the knives, sitting side by side on the sofa. I recognized the Fairbairn Sykes immediately, as I'd been using one for years, and it was good to have a replacement. I ran my fingers along the hilt, appreciating the swift jolt of renewed power. I could defend myself again. Fight the bloody bastards who had done this to me. The other knife was a Buck Nighthawk. I palmed it, tested the heft. Damn, but it was good to be alive.

I laid the Nighthawk next to the Sykes dagger and moved to the next unexpected item. A pale peach outfit, lounge pants and tunic, was draped over the sofa. I ran the folds through my fingers, reveling in the luxurious texture of the fabric. Next to it, a matching camisole and thong panties were folded into a tidy square. Someone had shopped for me. Someone who *knew* me. Knew what to choose. Knew exactly what sort of clothing would comfort me and aid the healing process.

Apprehension curled in my abdomen. Blake, or maybe Chilton, supplied the weapons, but the underwear? Hardly Chilton. None of the staff knew my taste, and it was too soon for Blake to know. Chloe and Nia? Absolutely. But Blake wouldn't have rung them up, not about this. He'd wait until I could talk with them, reassure them I was alive and fighting strong again. I slipped into the outfit, stretched into a forward bend to dry my hair, and then made my way downstairs, food being the primary goal.

The descent was painfully slow, and my feet were bare, so Sterling didn't hear me round the corner. He secured the velvet rope across the entrance to the east staircase, then toddled toward the kitchen, the aroma of Cook's Brunswick stew wafting down the hallway behind him. I'd recognize the peppery scent anywhere, and so did my stomach.

Chilton must be feeding the contractors working on the restoration. I shrugged off a prickly mental echo that something wasn't right and went in search of my own bowl of stew and a tall glass of something decadent, like a diet soda. No one was in the kitchen. My first touch of freedom since I'd been captured, and it went straight to my head. Relief washed through me, relaxing muscles and unwinding nerves. A tiny happy dance tickled my toes, the cool tiles solid and reassuring under my feet.

Cook was working outside, her shears flying as she clipped sprigs from the herb garden. Sunlight glinted on the sleek edges of the blades, and memories of needles and Barat's hit squad smothered my happiness. Temporarily. I wasn't about to let the bastard ruin my meal, so I ladled a bowl of stew, popped a can of Diet Coke, and followed my nose to a cloth-covered lump on the counter. Apparently nothing had changed in the ten years since I'd last visited the manor. Cook still served fresh cheddar bread with her Brunswick Stew. I ate. And my mind began to clear. I rinsed my dishes, sliced another piece of the still-warm bread, slathered it with butter, and went in search of Blake.

He and Chilton were most likely strategizing how to rescue Maya and capture Barat, so I followed the north hallway toward the library and Chilton's study.

A crumpled piece of fabric caught my attention, completely out of place on the floor at the bottom of the east staircase. A napkin. Must have fallen from the tray Sterling took to the workmen. I shook it out, started to fold it, and the scent of baby powder teased my nose.

Grandmamma's scent.

Chapter 30

GRANDMAMMA. Here. Fuzzy images of her gentle touch, the melody of her voice, and the aroma of her healing tea floated around me. She'd been in my room while I was unconscious from the drugs.

East wing restoration, my ass.

I wadded the napkin in my fist and unhooked the thick velvet rope blocking the staircase. It slipped from my fingers. The heavy metal hook clanked on the polished wooden step. Damn it. I wanted to leave it and get on with finding Grandmamma, but it was crucial that everything seem normal.

Grandmamma. Chilton must have had her abducted. How could he? How could that be possible? Even working with Barat, he wouldn't, couldn't stoop to harming Grandmamma.

I tucked the napkin under my arm and used both hands to fasten the rope back in place, and wondered if Chilton had some sort of alarm attached to it. Not that it mattered. Anyone who tried to stop my search would…my knees wobbled. Anger surged in my gut. I had no time for pissy knees, and definitely couldn't leave a trail. Not until I'd regained enough strength to handle a physical confrontation with Chilton or Sterling. Or, damn it all to hell, Blake. Did he know about this?

The east staircase unfolded in front of me. My home. My

prison for so many years. I knew every creak, crack, and groan hidden in the stair treads, and made my way to the top with skilled caution.

Two rooms opened off the landing, one on each side. Expected. They were the sitting rooms I'd occasionally used for workspace, and, when I studied Tai Chi, I'd emptied one to use as my private dojo. The familiarity ended abruptly. A wall, looking like it belonged to the house, like it had been there for several hundred years, blocked the passage to my former suite.

It was made from beautifully carved wood with countless hiding places for a concealed lock.

Grandmamma had to be on the other side of that wall. My fingers found the diamond earring, and traced the faceted surface.

I sat on my heels, closed my eyes, and used the power of my calling to examine the wall. Sterling would have used the most expedient route to deliver meals, and since I'd caught him tray-in-hand, there had to be a way through this wall.

Opening my eyes long enough to take a mental snapshot of the wall, I turned the image this way and that, zooming in and out. Slowly it began to take form. There was a pattern of squares hidden within the carvings, not unlike the configuration on the floor of Chilton's suite.

It would be best to check in with Mum again before I went about touching things and setting off alarms. I settled into a half lotus, focused on my breathing, and reached for her.

"You've found Arielle I see." Mum's words bloomed in my mind.

It should have been a relief, affirmation that I was so close to rescuing Grandmamma, but her voice caught the edge of my patience, shredding it. "You've known all along, then, where she's been?"

"I don't care for your tone, Whitney. I've known she's

safe. But no, not until you found her did I know her location. There's still much for you to learn about our calling and how it works."

She had a point. But I bloody well wasn't in the mood. "It's not the time for lessons, though, is it? Is she behind this wall? I need your help getting through without alerting the household—"

"What *you* need, hmmm. Perhaps you should think about what Arielle needs, or your father."

"Chilton put her there. Kidnapped her. Took her from her home—" Anger festered, and I jumped to my feet. Wobbled. Blast it. I hated being weak.

"And have you given any thought as to why, Whitney? My mother, your Grandmamma, is a strong woman. No one could take her against her will. Have you forgotten she's clairvoyant? Arielle would know they were coming, would have disappeared long before they arrived if she hadn't wanted to be captured."

My mind blanked, totally empty for several breaths. Flummoxed, I second-guessed for a minute. I *needed* to get on the other side of that wall. Every cell in my body was sure of it. So I changed the subject. "Why do you call her Arielle? She's your mum."

The silence dragged through my mind leaving a swath of emptiness.

"I've called her Arielle since I came into my calling. On that day I realized she was so much more than my mother. Arielle Boulay is a gift I cherish, as are you, Whitney. Now, do you want to chat about relationships, or do you want to locate your grandmother?"

An unfamiliar lump swelled in my throat. Now, twenty years after she left me, she decides to act like a mother. "I—"

"Need to get on the other side of the wall." Her brisk tone yanked me from my emotional fog. "Chilton used a code similar to the one in his suite. Very family-oriented, Chilton is."

Family-oriented? What the bleeding hell? The sharp pinch of stepping into an alternate dimension zapped me, and I ruthlessly slapped all family thoughts into the dungeon of my mind. "Can you show me the code? Did he use her name?"

"He did, and yes, I can."

A sparkly pattern flashed against the wall. "Arielle," I breathed. The pattern was arranged in the same number-slash-letter sequence as the code to Chilton's suite. I placed my palm firmly on the square corresponding to A, and thought *thanks* to Mum. The energy of her smile glittered in my mind, and then faded away. I systematically placed my palms on the numerical sequence of the letters in Grandmamma's name.

The wall slid open on silent, well-oiled tracks.

In front of me stood an exact replica of the door to Grandmamma's cabin. I turned the knob and stepped into a space warp. The front room was exactly the same except for the fragrance. None of the Bayou scents clung to the air. It smelled like Chilton Manor with a faint trace of lavender and baby powder carried on the breeze...breeze?

I spun in a slow circle, taking in the nuances of the room. A four-poster was tucked into one corner, neatly made. Several baskets of yarn and knitting needles were scattered throughout the room. Overstuffed chairs flanked a fireplace. I recognized the hearth, as I'd sat there to roast many a marshmallow. Back in my youth.

So Chilton had recreated the Bayou cabin for Grandmamma. Didn't tear down the fireplace, so it was brick rather than stone, and no kitchen, but otherwise the details were almost exact.

At the far end of the room, a screen door opened to a porch.

I made my way toward it. The fragrance of the English

countryside conflicted with the reality of standing in a Bayou cabin. My heart skidded to a halt, flipped, and then pounded against my ribs. Grandmamma. I pressed my hand against the wooden frame of the screen door and pushed it open.

It took a minute for my brain to catch up with reality.

She sat at the far end of the veranda, a swath of gold lamé across her lap, and her eyes shone with a warm smile. "'Bout time you showed up, Whitney child."

I took two running leaps across the porch, skidded to my knees at her feet, and enveloped her in a frantic, desperate hug. "You're safe," I mumbled into the soft cotton fabric of her dress.

"Well, a'course I am. Did'n I send along a photograph of myself so's you would'n fret?"

I shifted into a crouch, moving back to take in her face, see the truth written there. "*You* sent the photograph?"

"Had that nice young man snap it an' put it in the mail for me."

Dominic Justice. She'd called Justice a *nice young man*. I grabbed for the veranda railing, needing the reality of the rough wood as it cut into my palms. "How long have you been here? When did Justice collect you?"

"Why, musta been 'bout two days after you left, ché."

I did a mental sorting of my notes on the case. "They didn't ring me up to tell me you'd gone missing until the twenty-fifth. That's a week. The week I slept. It took Barat that long to leverage the situation, knowing Chilton beat him to collecting you. Justice spent the entire time flipping between countries." I jumped up. "I need a calendar."

Grandmamma nodded to the table next to her. "I've been a'keeping track of days, not knowin' zactly when you'd need me."

I snatched the calendar, outlined timelines. "I saw him at Chloe's on the sixteenth, he kid...collected you on the eighteenth and delivered you here. That's right, isn't it? Justice traveled here with you?"

"Yes an' he kept nice company with me."

"By the twenty-fifth he was in Honolulu. He hand-delivered the picture of you, Grandmamma. There was no postmark on the envelope."

"Well, see then? I tol' you he's a nice young man. Goin' out of his way like that."

"He isn't a nice young man, actually. More of a bada...thief. Justice is a thief."

Grandmamma bobbed her head side-to-side. "Well, tha's as may be, but he treated me with respect. An' it was jus' but hours ago he rescued you, an' you close to your death."

My death? "Grandmamma?"

"Tha's why I'm here, Whitney, child. Not much point to having a clairvoyant calling if'n I don't use it to save my grandchild, now is there?"

My vision clouded, and I sank to the floor at her feet. "You're saying you knew I'd be abducted, that the drugs would nearly kill me? You planned this little jaunt to Hampshire so you'd be available when it happened?"

She stroked my still-damp hair. Ran her fingers through the tangled curls, like she'd done when I was small and it hurt too much to tug through the thickness with a comb. "I used a fair bit of energy to get your system cleared out, an' the doctor, he used his modern medicine. It took both us to bring you back, ché."

Memories solidified. "You washed me, dressed me in clean clothes. I remember the energy, and the tea. You forced me to drink. I fought you."

"Not hardly a fight with you weak as a newborn." She skimmed her fingers over the fabric of my shirt. "Your papa, he bought this las' night. I tol' him the color and fabric. Did a good job, ché."

Of course. Grandmamma would know just what sort of clothing to select. "Thank you. It's beautiful, and perfect. I needed something feminine after I washed off—"

"Yes. After the cleansing."

"And the rest of it? You knew about this, planned it?" Anger seethed and I fought to control it. I would not scream like a demented hyena at Grandmamma. The calling had rules I didn't understand. Yet. Maybe not ever. Still, it hurt.

"Now, you know better n' that. Clairvoyance does'n work that way a'tall. Not an exact science with times and such. When the young man appeared at my door, I knew. Now, it's time for you to have some more tea. Finish clearin' that evil from your body." She shifted the lamé project aside, and made to stand. "Anya Marie has it ready in the kitchen."

I patted her knee, knowing she was absolutely right. I needed to get the drugs out of my system, because obviously my brain wasn't up to sorting truth from fiction. "I'll get it. Who's Anya Marie?"

Chilton appeared on the porch, his energy intense. Without sound. Without warning.

"Anya Marie is the cook here at Chilton Manor." My father strode the length of the veranda, stopped in front of Grandmamma, and covered her soft, brown hand with his. "Thank you Miss Arielle, for saving my daughter."

Disconnects rattled through my brain. Grandmamma turned her hand to grasp my father's, her smile genuine. Was he one of the good guys? And if so, who exactly were the bad guys? Tears burned. The way Chilton touched my grandmother, the way they cared about each other...it was...it hurt. Why hadn't he ever touched me like that? "Who are you? You know Grandmamma, care about her, and you still had her kidnapped. And Cook is actually Anya Marie?"

I knew I was acting bonkers, but I couldn't make sense of what was unfolding right in front of me.

Chilton stepped back, slipped his hands into his front pockets, and regarded me cautiously. "When you first came to live here, you always referred to Anya Marie as Cook. We couldn't break you of the habit, and she thought it was…adorable. She's been Cook ever since."

Grandmamma flicked my hand with her knitting needle. "A 'course your papa knows me. You think I let your mama have a child without knowin' who'd be a'raising my grandbaby?"

A soft buzz filled the silence and Chilton extracted a BlackBerry from his pocket. He checked the message, spun on his heel, and came face-to-face with Blake.

No surprise on either of their faces. Blake scratched his nose.

Disillusion clogged my throat, tasting sour.

So handsome. So devious. And I'd let him into my life. Worse, into my heart. I examined his expression, searching for the faintest trace of remorse.

Nothing.

Hope shattered at my feet.

Chapter 31

BLAKE had known Grandmamma was here and kept it from me. Why hadn't I confronted him about that blasted nose-scratching tell? I buried the question. Until later. When I had time to think properly.

"You knew. Didn't tell me. How long? Exactly *how long* have you known that Grandmamma has been in residence?" My words bulleted through the air.

Blake backed away. A single step, a half step, and then raised his arms, palms facing me. "Stop with the tone and that look. I'm on your side in this, remember?"

"So you say. When? Damn it all to bloody hell, Blake, *when?*"

He lowered his arms, and tossed his head, impatient. "This morning. When she showed up in our room. I'd planned to bring you here when you were strong enough to walk. Just came from our rooms looking for you so we could do just that."

I whirled to face Grandmamma and found the truth of Blake's words mirrored in her eyes.

"Right, then." I sunk onto the sofa next to her, depleted. My skin tightened like it belonged to someone else. And my emotions? I couldn't deal with them at all. Not now.

Chilton's mumbled words droned from the other room, fading into the distance. Grandmamma waited, knitting needles clicking. Blake waited, his stance less than patient. Silent pressure. I began to feel like prey, with them watching and waiting for a response.

But my tight-fitting skin wasn't going to shed so quickly. I didn't want to be involved in Chilton's deceitful world, didn't want to apologize, and I certainly didn't know what to do with Blake.

That idiot Blake winked. "Nice outfit. Suits you. I'm going to fetch that tea, see if it doesn't chase the…how did Grandmamma put it?...the evil out of you."

A soft wash of sanity began to return. Blake had only known about Grandmamma for a few hours, and there hadn't been a moment for him to tell me. Not with the particulars of my abduction to discuss, and Chilton hovering about. Happy seeped into my chest, faced off with betrayal. Love did absolutely crazy things to otherwise normal people. It was like negotiating a blasted internal minefield.

Mala had been pushing at the back of my mind since I'd discovered the Bayou-in-Hampshire residence, and I began to gather some of my misplaced common sense so I could hear what she was saying.

Grandmamma patted my knee. "I can see it in your face, child. The callin's tuggin' at you. Go ahead and listen. I'll be here to pull you out if'n you go too deep."

Inhale. Exhale.

Dark closed in, and I knew why I'd avoided this dip into my calling. It wasn't Mala pulling at me. Oh, she'd gotten got my attention, but then quickly moved aside to make room for the John Doe we'd found hanging in Chilton's tree. Fear, dark and threatening, crawled up my spine. I did *not* want to go there again. Not into the black.

Mala cut into my thoughts, taking over my head. "Now isn't the time to practice being a coward."

"Blast it all. What do you know about it? Your death was normal." My mental words shot toward her, sputtering like flicks of water on a hot griddle.

"Since when did homicide become normal? I'm in your head, remember? I know all about your fear of the black. I've been there."

"No, you haven't. You're simply dead, not floating in John Doe's abyss."

Mala bristled. "Barat kept me for a long time before he killed me. Nothing is blacker."

She had a point, so I took a few breaths and pulled in a bit of the bright energy surrounding Grandmamma to keep the dark at bay.

Mala rattled on. "The John Doe has information you want. Information you need—"

She'd caught my attention with that one. "Oh, no. You're the one who needs it. I can tell from your prissy, controlling attitude. You want *me* to have the intel so I can avenge your death properly and you can rest in peace. This is all about you, actually."

"Eventually, yes. Right now it's about keeping Maya safe, capturing that bastard, and perhaps keeping your friend alive."

Razor-sharp clarity pierced through the remaining drug-fog that had dulled my mind. "Chloe? You're talking about Chloe?"

She gave me a mental nod.

That bit of news completely changed things. "John Doe it is, then."

The clicking of Grandmamma's knitting needles stopped,

and her hand wrapped around mine. "I'm right here, Whitney, child. You do what you have to do, ché."

Her strength poured through me, and I reached for the malignant energy of the John Doe. Chills wracked me when the black descended, but I held on to a faint rim of light circling the edge of the black. My lifeline. Grandmamma's love.

Images collided in my mind, complete with comic book *whams, kapows,* and *splats.* The John Doe wasn't articulate. He'd obviously been on the far left of the bell curve long before Barat got to him. Now he was brainwashed, drug-numb, and dead.

His energy whooshed through my mind in an angry outburst, leaving behind several clear images and a smattering of headache.

Grandmamma squeezed my hand. "You a comin' on back to me now."

I clung to her warmth, and followed the scent of baby powder to the Hampshire Bayou.

"An' what did you learn, ché?"

I opened my eyes and met her knowing gaze. "It's my calling, then. Isn't it? I've stepped right into the middle of my fate, haven't I?"

"Yes an' it is 'bout time you recognized it, accepted it. Mistakes aren't made with the calling. We get what belongs to us." She freed her hand from my grasp, gave me a quick pat, and went back to working on the intricate pattern in the gold lamé yarn.

Blake strolled in, a large mug of fragrant tea in his hand. "Had Cook warm all the rest of it. Seemed like you needed…" He brushed his free hand over my cheeks. I hadn't realized they were wet, that I'd shed tears.

My lips tasted of salt. I braved a smile. "I'm quite all right, actually. Had a bit of a chat with the John Doe from Chilton's back forty."

Blake placed the mug and a napkin on the table next to me. "You planning to share?"

The ache in my limbs kept me from reaching for the tea. I sighed, heavy, not able to fit the images and words into coherent meaning. "Yes." I reached for Grandmamma's hand again.

Blake hauled a deck chair in front of me, sat. "You're pale."

"The John Doe's mind was irreparably warped, and even in death his energy is uncomfortable." I pointed to the notebook sticking out of his shirt pocket. "You'll want to jot a few things down, as I'm not sure my mind is clear enough to hold this in long-term memory."

He nodded, notebook and pen in hand.

"First thing, he's one of Barat's posse, his minion, and the person responsible for Avril's death."

Grandmamma went back to knitting. "Drink the tea, Whitney, child."

Blake waited for me to drink without so much as a fidget. Patience personified. If I didn't already love him, I'd have considered taking a fancy to him on the spot.

I swallowed another mouthful of tea. "Barat is done with Lord Chilton. It's one of the reasons we've...you've...had such a hard time nabbing him. He changes and eliminates business arrangements frequently, and at will. This one has lasted a long time." I cradled the mug of tea, inhaling the spicy, medicinal scent. "Barat traced Chilton's family to me, to Grandmamma. It's the foundation of his business, to keep his posse in line by threatening their families, because they are completely expendable. He typically sends a lieutenant in to hide the money in the victim's home for the assassin to pick up in payment. Then, when he's done the job and collects, the lieutenant is responsible for offing the hired assassin and returning the money to Barat. A problem in this case, since the lieutenant mistakenly picked the wrong Bayou cabin. Easy to do if you don't know your way around, and Grandmamma and Avril are both in their, ah, mature years. I can't blame the bastard for getting confused, but it was a huge screwup on the lieutenant's part. Especially since either Avril or the Pitre brothers found the money before the assassin did his job. No money, and the wrong victim. It was—"

"A cluster from Barat's viewpoint." Blake tapped the pen against his lips.

The money was delivered prior to the kill, and Barat typically sends in a minion to locate the payoff and return it to Barat before the lieutenant is dispatched to execute the kill. A problem in this case, since the Pitre brothers spent it."

Blake tapped the pen against his lips. "A cluster from Barat's viewpoint."

"Quite, and it explains why the lieutenant's body was hanging in Chilton's tree."

"Doesn't fit. Barat would have taken this guy out immediately. For stupidity alone. Avril was killed on July fourteenth, so it's been three damn weeks."

I shook my head. "There's more. Our John Doe was on Barat's death row, but had one more task to complete…killing the Pitre brothers. Barat isn't fond of loose ends."

Blake jotted some notes. "And you blew the shit out of that plan by having the Pitres arrested."

I sorted through the remaining images in my head, and faced the one I'd been trying to avoid. "Grandmamma is still on Barat's kill list." I shuddered, sloshing tea on my lap. "He isn't quite finished with my father yet, upped the pressure on him with a direct threat to Grandmamma. And me."

Blake leaned back, thoughtful, and then scribbled more notes. "Do we have a name for the John Doe?"

"Not that he shared with me."

"Okay. Who killed old Michael and why?"

I sipped my tea, mentally thumbing through the words and images John Doe left in my head. "Michael was killed in retaliation. Chilton nipped Grandmamma from Barat's grasp, and Barat struck back by killing the one person who helped Justice. I think it was a warning to keep Chilton in line."

"From what I know of your father, that was a lesson in futility. Must be frustrating as hell for Barat." He rocked back in his chair.

"Frustrating enough for him to make mistakes?"

Blake gave me a thumbs-up. "We can only hope. We need the break. Bad."

I rummaged through John Doe's core dump again. Nothing new stood out, so I returned to a nagging question. "Grandmamma was the target. John Doe screwed up badly enough to give Chilton time to have her abducted and moved here. But why did my father have Grandmamma kidnapped?"

"Y'all are forgettin' I'm a'sitting right here. I wasn't taken agin' my will. Not a'tall. I was 'spectin tha' sweet young man, 'an he asked me nicely to come along with him. Explained how if'n I was here you'd be a'following."

Open-mouthed, Blake and I stared at her.

I gulped the rest of the tea. "You're saying Chilton manipulated the situation to get *me* here? I'm a pawn in a power struggle between my father and Barat? "

Grandmamma didn't even glance at me. I took that as agreement, but then, I'd made mistakes before. The clicking of her knitting needles collided with puzzle pieces snapping into place. I bolted upright, making frantic motions for Blake's mobile.

"What's wrong?" He unclipped it from his belt, handed it to me.

"Chloe." I jabbed her speed dial number. "The notes in my bathroom at home, the one on my mirror and in my make-up case, they were meant for her, not me."

Her phone flipped me to voicemail. "Call me. As soon as you get this, call me."

"Talk me through it." Blake stood, paced the distance of the veranda.

"The notes never fit with Grandmamma's abduction. The phone warning I got, the picture she had Chilton send to me, both were innocuous. Just enough of a threat to have me chasing after her, but the notes were all wrong. Certainly not something Chilton would do. They were amateur, more like a thug mentality."

"Like whoever was responsible for the John Doe at Soma Herbal and on your porch?"

"Quite. They were tattooed." I stared into the chocolate depths of his eyes.

His phone beeped, and I popped it open. "Boulay."

"Dominic Justice, here. Chloe is safe. I have both her and the situation under control."

A dial tone buzzed in my ear. "Justice has her."

My attention narrowed to stillness. And then I looked at Blake. Really looked at him. The man I loved, the man I trusted. Breath whooshed from my lungs. "You're right. Chilton trusted Dominic Justice, as did Chloe. The Romany rescued me from Barat, and for that I owe him. More or less. But I'm going home as soon as we wrap this up."

My cell buzzed. I glanced at Caller ID, and answered, my

heart pounding. "Chloe, are you all right, then?"

"Yes, of course. What's wrong? Blake texted me you were safe, and Dominic—"

I blew out a sigh, turned to Blake. "She's okay." And then I turned my attention to Chloe. "The notes in my bathroom at home, the one on my mirror and in my make-up case, they were meant for you, not me."

Silence. Had I terrified her? Where the hell was Justice?

"Nia told me about them, but you know I never saw them. It doesn't matter. They told me Barat captured you, but you're home now. Safe. Were you badly injured?"

"I'm…recuperating. It took me until today to get my senses back, and…never mind. It isn't me who's in danger, it's you. The notes never fit with Grandmamma's abduction. They were just enough of a threat to ensure I'd chase after her kidnapper, but the notes were all wrong. Certainly not something Chilton would write. They were amateur, fit with a thug mentality."

"Are you accusing your father of kidnapping your grandmother?" Chloe sounded incredulous.

"Yes. No." Impatience thrummed through my veins. "Stay on track here. You need twenty-four hour protection. Don't leave the house—"

"Hold it. You're saying whoever left the notes was a thug. Do you think it's the same person who killed the guy at Soma Herbal and the one I found on your porch?"

"Quite. They were tattooed with similar patterns to those on the other bodies. And I think they're linked to Barat."

"I'll be careful, but I'm fine, Whitney. There's been no news about either of the John Does, but…"

"But?" I asked.

"But Dominic is here. He'll protect me. I know you don't trust him, but he would never hurt me. And Indy likes him. And Whitney, I believe Amar Barat and Germain Marcellin are somehow connected."

Had Chloe forgotten that Marcellin was dead? I ignored it and pushed on. "Yes, I heard from Justice. Said he had things under control. Chilton hired him to find me and abduct me from under Barat's nose, so I owe him."

"About Barat and Marcellin. Nia checked. He's alive, and—"

Both of us were avoiding the topics that weren't making sense, and I didn't have time to get into it. "I've wondered about that, but I'm not at all sure you're right about a connection between the two bastards. I'll look into it as soon as I get home. Shouldn't take more than a few days to wrap things up here."

Mala chose that moment to push hard on my awareness. "Don't let him kill Maya."

Chapter 32

PANIC grabbed my breath. I gripped Blake's thigh. "Maya? Where is she?"

"In the wind."

"It's been two days since my abduction. No sign of her since then?"

His eyes slitted. "What's going on, Whitney?"

"Mala's screaming that Maya is in trouble." I jumped out of my chair, slid my hand under Grandmamma's arm to help her up. "Where's Chilton? He wandered away when his mobile rang."

Blake rose, set his chair aside, and then picked up the basket of gold lamé yarn. "He was on his way out when I brought your tea up. Did Mala have anything useful to say? Because sure as hell, if Maya's in trouble, Barat is nearby."

Grandmamma shook herself free. "I can walk jus' fine, but I don't want t'go inside."

I tugged on her arm. "It's dangerous out here, what with the man who captured me hanging about."

My stomach twisted. I had to keep Grandmamma safe. Chilton had prepared a perfect hidey-hole, and with his penchant for blocking off doors, there would be a control nearby to completely hide the outside entrance with a sliding wall—if I could just get her off the veranda. Which brought up an interesting question. "Why do you suppose Chilton wanted us here?"

"To keep us safe, child."

Now wasn't the time to disillusion her, but I gave Blake a sideways glance. His face was calm, impassive. "Is MI5 aware of this?"

His shrug, more of a shoulder tic, actually, didn't offer much in the way of an answer, and I didn't have time to deal with it right now. I needed immediate sit-down time with Mala.

I tapped my fingers on Grandmamma's arm. "Do you know how Chilton closes off the veranda access?"

She elbowed free of my hand, ambled to one of the planks framing the door, and skimmed her finger along the edge of the outside wall. A soft snick sounded in the room, and the wall began to slide closed. Grandmamma busied herself measuring out tea leaves and heating water on a hotplate.

Blake was halfway into the foyer. "Watch over Grandmamma, and give me a call when you get more from Mala."

Surely he knew me better than that by now. I turned my back on him, crossed the room to Grandmamma, and took both her hands in mine. "I need you to answer my question from the wisdom of your sight. Are you safe here?"

Mala paced in my mind, urging me to hurry.

"Yes, 'an you go on, now. Do what you have to do." She shooed me away, but not before I noticed the deep sadness lurking behind her eyes.

I trusted her sight, but the sadness troubled me. "Grandmamma—"

She flapped her hands, shooing at me again. "Your work,

it's out there, child. Mine is to be patient."

I gave her a quick kiss, closed and secured the hall entrance to her hideaway, and then hustled to catch up with Blake. He caught me around the waist when I came up beside him. "Whoa. Where do you think you're going?"

"Grandmamma says my work is out here, and she's right."

He cupped my shoulders. "You almost died. Your *work* is to heal."

I shrugged free of his grasp. "First thing, a change of clothes, then my knives. Then I need a bit of time with Mala. She's really pushing at me and—"

"No, Whitney. The safest place in this monstrosity of a house is right here—"

"It's not about being safe. It's about being a victim. I *need* to go after Barat to undo what he did to me. Mala is in my head, Maya is in trouble, and I'm your best shot at inside information."

His eyes held shadows of worry and anxious love. I touched his cheek. "That second cup of Grandmamma's healing brew cleared most of the drugs from my system. The wobble is gone from my knees, and I can fight if I have to. And if I ever want to face myself in the mirror again, I have to face Barat first."

Blake closed his eyes, and whispered something unintelligible, his acceptance of my decision noticeably uncomfortable.

We didn't see anyone on the way to our room. Not Sterling, not a housekeeper, and not Chilton. Bits and pieces of what Mala needed to tell me floated at the edge of my mind, but she was upset and not communicating clearly.

I collected jeans, underwear, and a long-sleeved t-shirt, then headed for the bathroom. Now wasn't the time for silky, feminine frippery, although I took care to rinse out the tea stain rather than toss it on the hook behind the door.

Blake was on his mobile when I entered the bedroom, and if the tight line of his jaw meant anything, he was angry as hell. I strapped my knives on, one at my ankle and one along my forearm, and pretended not to listen. Seemed someone wanted him to go somewhere, and Blake wasn't at all keen on the plan.

He closed the mobile with a loud snap and jammed it in his front pocket. "Gotta go. MI5 has a lead on Maya, and I need to liaison the shit out of the situation."

I skimmed my fingers over the phone in his pocket, down his thigh. "I'll ring you up if Mala offers any intel on Maya's location."

He captured my hand, kissed my palm. "Talented fingers, but they're not going to sidetrack me. I want you to stay here, at least until we find Maya. Promise me."

"Ummm, no. Can't promise that. I will promise to be careful, and to let you know what I'm doing, and if I leave, where I'm going."

His mobile rang, muted through the heavy cotton of his slacks. He checked Caller ID, planted a kiss on my lips, and shook his head. "You're gonna be the death of me, woman. Stay safe."

"You, too."

He left with the phone to his ear. I settled cross-legged in the middle of the bed, and then opened my mind to Mala.

"Barat has her." Her words whipped through my head so fast they stung.

"Where does he have her?"

"I don't know. I can only see through your eyes or hers. They covered her head with a hood, and she didn't fight them. Didn't fight at all." Frustration poured into her voice.

"That doesn't make sense. Maya is determined to kill Barat, and she has a weapon. She'd keep her distance unless her plan fell apart."

"Which it obviously did. You have to find her before he kills her. She's only twenty-three, you know. Not up to this sort of thing. It isn't her time to die."

"You were twenty-two when Barat killed you."

"That's what I'm saying, Whitney. Now go find her."

Clearly Mala thought more of my tracking skills than was warranted. "Can you check on her again, see if they took the hood off?"

She faded from my mind.

While Mala checked on her twin, I hustled downstairs to check on Chilton. There was a good chance he'd lead me right to Barat, seeing as they had business together and all. My movements were the antithesis of stealthy, and the house grumbled with the heaviness of my step and the flurry of my movements while I searched.

Sterling caught me outside the library. "Mistress Whitney? Should you be up and about so soon?"

"Just looking for Lord Chilton. Blake saw him leaving a bit ago. Has he returned, then?"

He stroked his chin. "We're not expecting him until after tea."

"Quite. Thank you, Sterling. Blake and I will also be away, so no need for Cook to fuss."

Mala pushed against my thoughts, insistent, overwhelming, and I had no choice but to inhale deeply and breathe into the experience until it passed.

I ducked into the library and collapsed on the sofa. The sensations didn't pass. They shifted—suddenly, radically—and transported me to another place. Freshly mown grass, a hazy undertone of cows and rich, damp soil mixed with the aroma of cooking. Onions, chicken, and tarragon blended with the earthy aromas, and the sensation was so strong it gagged me.

The smells slowly unraveled, from food, to the countryside, and finally to the library in Chilton Manor. My brain and muscles returned to normal, and Mala hovered on the outside edge of my awareness, persistent.

Time to function. I opened to her and her words exploded in my mind. "Did you get it?"

I formed a thought, pushed it out to her. "Haven't been getting much of anything, actually. Seems I've had a bit of sensory overload, maybe destroyed a few olfactory circuits."

Agitation bit through her words. "I tried something different. Maya is still blinded by the hood, so I scooped up all the smells I could find and dropped them in your mind. I thought you might be able to locate the place they're holding her by following your nose…so to speak."

"That's a bit nutters, even for a ghost."

She huffed, a flitter tickling my mind. "In humans, smell is highly correlated with memories and emotions. If you stop being so closed-minded, this might work."

"What might work?" I definitely wasn't firing on all cylinders.

"You spent most of your childhood in Hampshire, have been back for days. I'd think the smell of Maya's location would trigger some memories."

I eased back on the sofa and closed my eyes. Ridiculous idea, but damn and blast, I didn't have any other leads. I drifted through the harmony of scents Mala had left in my mind, and let my memories play with the olfactory stimulation. Clear memories of times and places drifted, unhurried, into absolute knowledge.

The first time Blake and I made love. The fragrance of the countryside floating on the breeze, drenching my body in the essence of late summer, the joy of learning his body. Fragments solidified into a place. The inn.

"I know where she is," I whispered.

I tried again. Out loud, with more conviction. "I know where Maya is."

"Why are you still lying on the floor, then?" *Again* with Mala making her point.

I rolled onto my side, then stood. My body had the audacity to object, and the room spun. Almost dying really sapped a girl's strength. And sanity. Still, it looked like I was going help myself to one of Chilton's vehicles and head for the inn.

Blake was going to murder me.

Unless Barat beat him to it.

Chapter 33

A pearl beige Mercedes Be**n**z sedan, the most solid, nondescript vehicle in Chilton's garage, suited me perfectly. But when it came to finding a hiding place for the Benz, I missed the Vespa. I left the sedan on a side road a quarter mile from the inn, close enough that I'd be able to make the hike without keeling over, but not so close that it would be noticed by whoever guarded Maya. I hoped.

I tapped out a text message to Blake. The embarrassment of being captured, twice, weighed on me, and my heart knew the truth I'd been avoiding: *rogue* and *solo* were incompatible with partnership. I simply hadn't a clue about how to share my work with someone I loved. Texting him was a first step.

I eased the knife from my ankle holster, fingered Grandmamma's diamond, and did a quick scan of my body. My bones and muscles harbored a dull ache, nothing incapacitating, but a reminder I wasn't in top form and needed to be careful, even though my calling had become a force of its own, and didn't leave me much room—or time—for rational thought.

I circled behind the inn, skulking through the trees and shrubbery, until I had a clear view of the shed where my Vespa was stored. Unless Maya had hidden it elsewhere.

Mala was quiet, had been since I left Chilton Manor. I sent

an inquiring thread of energy in her direction, and she responded instantly, anxiety coloring her aura and her words. "What's taking so long? You've been staring at the back of the building for hours."

"Five minutes, actually, and I need your help. Is Maya's sight still blocked?"

"Yes." Apparently she wasn't in the mood to elaborate.

"Has she slept? Dreamed? Have you been able to talk with her?" Frustration made me snappish.

"A nap. She's angry, and her mind won't shut down until she faces Barat."

"Absolutely understandable, but not at all helpful. Is she alone? How many guards?"

"Alone. And she's in pain. Badgering me doesn't help, Whitney. I still can't *see* anything."

Uncertainty crept under my skin. Sight. I needed reassurance, and sent a wisp of thought to Grandmamma. Her response was faint, but encouraging. At least I'd been able to reach her, and knew I was on the right track, and it was time to set about finding Maya.

A door banged shut with a solid thunk. Adrenaline sizzled through my veins. *Find Maya and get the hell out of there, Whitney.*

I balanced the blade in my hand, readjusted my grip, and then circumnavigated the shed where I stored the Vespa. Myriad footprints marked the soil, as well as tracks from the scooter. Birds called. Squirrels chirped. Normal, as were the aromas, and—most important—they matched the olfactory image Mala had created. I approached the rear of the building, inched on tiptoe, and peeked in the window.

Damn and blast.

"Found her." I flung the thought at Mala.

The Vespa was on its side, Maya trussed to it with chains. Dirty, ragged clothes, bruised body, and her chest barely moved.

Mala broke into my assessment with a loud gasp, her agitation clear in my mind. I'd have blocked her from the scene, but didn't have enough control of my calling. Yet. As soon as this was over, *that* would change. Now wasn't a good time to have a panicked ghost cluttering my thoughts, so I nudged her with soothing thoughts to hold her panic at bay.

It was too quiet. No guards. Chills snaked along my spine. I was in no condition, mental or physical, to handle a full-out ambush. I scanned the area. Could detect no movement, and no unusual shadows in or around the buildings or the nearby trees. The breeze held no out-of-place smells, and Barat's posse tended to carry a stink. A sniper was possible, but I didn't have the equipment to deal with that. My only choice: trust the intuition that came with my calling. I tuned in to the energy around the shed, got an ESP go-ahead tingle, and approached the door.

The latching mechanism was a simple lever. No lock. I flicked it open, and tugged on the door. An unearthly screech pierced the air. Damn and blast. Had to move fast. I went in low, knife at the ready. Empty. Except for Maya. She didn't make a sound, but her body tensed. Fear and sweat scented the air. I sunk to my knees beside her, and spoke softly. "It's Whitney. I'm going to get you out of here."

Not that I had a clue how to do that.

There was no apparent way to cut the chains binding Maya to the scooter.

I eased my left hand under the hood, and lifted it from her head while keeping my knife hand free. Maya's gaze flew to my face. Her deep brown eyes were dilated and held shadows of wariness. I slipped the knife under the dirty, wadded rag they'd used to gag her, sliced through it, and used the corner of my t-shirt to wipe the sweat and tears from her face.

"Whitney," Maya rasped, her voice shaking.

"How badly are you hurt?" I secured the knife in my ankle holster, and skimmed my hands over her arms and legs, noting the many lacerations and contusions. She had to be blasted uncomfortable stretched over the oddly-shaped metal surface of the Vespa. "None of the cuts are deep, and nothing is broken."

She blinked, focusing on me. "M-my chest. They tattooed my chest. Hurts."

What the hell? Nausea churned. It was a degrading violation of her person. "Any idea how to remove these chains without bolt cutters or a hacksaw? My lock-picking skills aren't that polished."

Maya flexed her fingers, rotating her wrists against the chains. "M-mine are, but I c-can't. There's s-some s-space. If you can hold the c-chain away from my s-skin, I might be able to s-slip free."

I worked my fingers between the chain and Maya's wrists. "They're snug, but I think you can do it."

She dipped her chin in affirmation, then her eyes rolled back and she passed out.

Bloody hell. Even with her slight frame, I wasn't in any condition to haul an unconscious body to the car. Not to mention it would be impossible to do it quietly.

I eyed the shelves lining the back wall of the shed, searching for a lubricant to reduce the friction between her skin and the metal. Surely innkeepers kept oil handy for...whatever. Not that I dared zip inside to inquire.

I found some likely containers on a shelf, my fingers over the candidates, and stopped at a squat, brown jar when my fingers slipped over the greasy label.

"That one will work. Use it now." Mala said, making her presence known. "Hurry. You don't have much time."

Maya moaned. I rushed back to her, praying the sound meant she'd returned to consciousness.

"Whitney?" Her eyelids fluttered, then closed.

"Right here." I unscrewed the lid, and a faint chemical smell drifted into the air.

Maya opened her eyes, focused on the container in my hand. "Wazzat?"

"Says something about screw compressors and refrigeration systems on the label. Not that it matters. Just take my word for it, it's slick enough to qualify for use in a greased pig contest."

I smeared the viscous stuff around Maya's bruised wrists, and then helped her work her hands free while mentally nudging Mala with a rather urgent question. "How do you know we don't have much time?"

She sent a bolt of energy into my head that radiated an intense need to run. "Okay. I got that. But what the bloody hell does it mean? You can't see except through our eyes, so where did that come from?"

Silence. The fierce need to get out of the shed crawled under my skin.

Maya worked her hands free, rubbed her wrists, and shook her arms. "Owww. Stings. Thirsty."

"No water. Maybe when we get to the car, but right now, focus on your ankles. They're going to be a bit more difficult to free up. If we can get your shoes and socks off…"

Maya ignored me, levered herself to an elbow, and frantically yanked at the buttons on her shirt. "I need to see how they've marked me."

The tattoo. Another blast of nausea hit me. If someone had defaced me…but we didn't have time. I stayed her hand. "Later."

She jerked from my grasp, and tugged at her shirt, trying to get if off.

I circled her wrists with enough force to cause a burst of pain to flash across her features. "Later." This time I added some punch to the order.

"Now. I need—"

"To get the hell out of here."

Sanity chased the panic from her expression, and she nodded, reaching to untie her right sneaker. I worked on the left.

She kicked her shoes free. "Surely there's something around here I can pick these locks with."

I gave the shelves a cursory glance, then covered her ankles with the grease. "There's some nails, but nothing thin enough to fit in the lock."

We struggled to get her heels through the loops of chain, succeeded, but not without an ugly scrape on her right foot that wouldn't stop bleeding.

I helped her off the Vespa, supported her until her muscles remembered how to function. "Can you get your shoes on? Do you have any idea when they'll be back for you?"

"Soon," she said, struggling to tie her sneaker.

I divided the rest of the greasy substance between the two door hinges and worked it in as best I could. If Maya's captors were closing in, we couldn't have the hinges screeching. I wiped the slick residue from my fingers onto my pants, and palmed my knife.

"Ready?" I offered my hand to help her up. "Keep on my

left side so my knife hand stays free."

She nodded, wrapped her right arm around my waist, and we headed for the car. Maya dragged along, cumbersome because she couldn't fully support herself. My neck prickled. Someone was measuring every step we took.

We made it to the car without incident. My nerves twitched. Something was off. I settled Maya in the passenger seat, nabbed a bottle of water from an emergency pack in the trunk, and slid behind the wheel. A fresh batch of prickles raced over my skin. "Someone's watching. Any idea why they haven't confronted us?"

She reached for the water, sighed. "Cat and mouse. Barat is fond of playing with his human toys."

Not at all comforting.

Maya chugged water. "The Glock is in your room."

I gripped the steering wheel, and merged onto the road. "What the bloody hell were you thinking? Staying there, endangering innocent people?"

"Your room was paid for and came with a handy fire escape. No one thought to look for me, not even Barat's advance team." She flashed me a dark smile.

Cool evil spread across my skin, and I marked every shadow around us. Where the hell were Maya's guards? Surely Barat had left someone here. Inside? Watching? Gray crowded my vision. I fought to stay conscious. Managed to pull off the road, and then lost the battle in a single heartbeat.

I surfaced to the sound of the Benz purring along at top speed. I was crammed into a ball on the passenger side. I jerked upright. "What the hell?"

Maya's soft laughter filled the car. "Chill. The water helped to settle me, we're on our way to the manor, and the Glock is tucked under my seat."

I shuddered. Helpless didn't suit me. "How—"

"You passed out. I took advantage." Her hands gripped the blood-streaked steering wheel.

I shook my head, trying to clear the fog. "Must have been the drugs. You could barely walk…"

"Adrenaline and hydration, maybe. Whatever, it worked. You, on the other hand, were totally zonked. Scared the crap out of me, not that I didn't appreciate the timing, but…" She glanced in the rear view mirror and pulled off the road, her hands shaking too badly to change gears. "Your turn to take over. My adrenaline high just fizzled."

I brushed her hand off the gearshift, slipped it into park, and waited until Maya got out of the car. Being left on the side of the road wasn't at all in my plan, and she was behaving…oddly.

We changed places and I veered onto the road. Nothing for it but to ask. "What the hell happened at the inn?"

"I went in through the side door. It was past teatime, so the common rooms were empty, and the hosts were busy preparing for supper. I had no problem getting the Glock and ammo, but the stairs took longer to navigate than I'd've liked. I'm not in the best of shape, you know. When I got back to the car, you were still out, so I pushed you into the passenger seat and took over driving."

"Not possible. My dead weight would have been too much—"

"Yeah. No question there. I don't know how I did it. I was crazy strong, but now weak. As weak as when you first found me, and I can't stop shaking."

Maya drank deeply from the bottle of water, and fumbled at the buttons on her blouse. She flipped the vanity mirror down and stared at her chest. She winced, traced the lines of the tattoo with the tip of her index finger, then turned to face me. "Look what they did to me."

She'd been inked in black swirly designs. "It could be worse. I understand black is easiest to remove. And it's small. Why did they do that? It's as though they marked you as one of them."

She shuddered, nodded. "Yeah. Could be."

"Blake and I intended to Google the tat designs that I could remember seeing on Barat's men, but haven't had time. You think they have meaning for Barat?"

"Well, yes. They all have meaning to him. He brands his hit men, a proclamation of ownership. When they reach a new level of dedication to him, they're rewarded with body art. The more inkings, the more senior and respected the posse member." Her hand flew to her chest. "It's tribal, a stylized butterfly. The butterfly is a symbol of transition, and I...they talked about it, I think. I was groggy, but I think...they planned to brainwash me into becoming the first female member of Barat's posse. As punishment. Worse than death."

We turned onto the oak-lined drive leading to the manor, I thumbed the garage door opener, and then parked in the designated slot for the Benz. Menace rode my nerves, and I forced myself to breathe. This was way too easy.

Maya held her hand out, requesting the Glock she'd tucked under the seat. I flipped through my options, and then handed it to her. Better an armed Maya than not. At least until I knew the whereabouts of Barat. "Are we going in through the side door?" she asked, checking the magazine.

"Yes." I kept it simple. No point in explaining my plan to put her in the Bayou room with Grandmamma. Safe.

We entered the back hallway, passed a small window overlooking the gardens, and I did a quick survey of the area. Two men stood in front of the gazebo in a deep conversation. Chilton had his back to me, but I'd recognize his arrogant stance anywhere. The other man was shorter, stockier, his black bangs long enough to hide the side of his face so I couldn't get a good look at his features. His suit fit well, obviously designer made. Probably another lord of the realm type, which was excellent. It'd keep Chilton out of the way while I got Maya settled.

We moved down the hallway, two battered, silent women. I wanted to get her upstairs quickly, away from the staff. And then I needed to ring Blake. It was past time to let him know what was going on.

We were about to turn the corner into another hallway, the one leading to the foyer and the north wing, when we passed another window.

I glanced out to confirm Chilton's whereabouts, and the man he'd been meeting with turned toward the house, the minor shift in his posture providing a clear view of his face.

Amar Barat.

Chapter 34

BARAT couldn't see me through the reflective coating on the window, but when he turned his face in my direction, icy fingers crawled down my back.

Maya whirled, followed my gaze, and jerked the Glock from her waistband. I caught her wrist, shifted away from the weapon, pressed her thumb back, and wrestled the weapon from her grasp. "Barat needs to be prosecuted." I twisted her arm behind her back. "We'll do this legally."

"Noooo, he's mine." Her shriek echoed through the hallway.

Since I was no longer in the business of making arrests, I had no cuffs tucked in my back pocket. I slammed her into the wall, thankful she wasn't at full strength, checked the Glock, and secured it at the small of my back, all the while keeping an eye on Barat and Chilton. They were moving toward the house from about twenty-five yards out, chatting, their gait easy, their attitude relaxed.

I palmed my mobile and punched in Blake's number. No answer. I left a voice message. "Barat, Chilton, meeting in backyard. Where the hell are you?"

Cook hustled down the hallway toward us wringing a dishtowel in her hands. "What is it? What's the fuss?"

And then things spun into slow motion, a bit like fog rising with the dawn.

Chilton and Barat continued their meandering stroll toward the house.

My mobile rang.

Blake. I flipped the phone open, didn't give him a chance to talk. "You're here, right? On the grounds? Lots of FBI, MI5 types wandering about the perimeter?"

"Some, yes. And you're not in the Bayou room with your grandmother."

"Not exactly, no. I'm in the hallway with Maya in tow, and no cuffs to keep her contained. She's quite intent on putting a bullet through Barat. Preferably with fatal results."

"Hang on while I get you backup." He left me in limbo, the line open, his voice echoing in the distance while he demanded backup.

Before I realized her intention, Cook wriggled between us in an attempt to secure Maya's wrists with the dishtowel. My free hand was full of the mobile, and Cook's frantic motions loosened my grip on Maya. The woman wrenched free of my grasp, and shoved Cook into me. We hit the floor in a heap. Cook, being a rather large woman, knocked the air from my lungs. By the time I gained my feet and grabbed my phone, Maya had disappeared.

I chased after her, grateful she wasn't in top form and that I had the Glock. Every molecule of my body ached to the point that I was stumbling. I held the phone to my ear, yelling, hoping someone on Blake's team was close enough to stop Maya before she made it into the garden.

His voice sounded in my ear, a single bite. "Whitney?"

I drove my body past a wall of pain to follow Maya, feeding Blake the information he needed. "Maya's on the move." Breathing hurt, and the words came out in gasps. "Back yard."

"We're circling around." He broke the connection.

I followed Maya, reality turning to quicksand under my feet. No way could I let her reach Barat. The need for revenge had shredded her sanity, and the scars from her recent abduction were fresh, scars inflicted on Barat's orders, if not by his hand. Blame gnawed at me. I'd brought her here. I'd taken her weapon. She could be hurt, possibly killed, if she attacked him with no weapon.

The French doors in the library provided the closest exit, and were her most likely destination. By the time I reached them she had inched her way behind the bushes, her focus riveted on Chilton and Barat.

What would I do if vengeance ruled my mind? I breathed in Maya's desperation. I'd rip his throat out with my bare hands. Not a good plan. I'd best set about stopping her.

I scanned the visible boundaries of the estate, pausing at areas I would've selected as hover points if I were part of the infiltrating group, and was able to spot some shadow play. All I had to do was keep Maya from making a complete cluster of their operation. And getting herself killed.

The insistent blare of the perimeter alarms blasted through the air. My heart rate and breathing pumped. My mind cleared. Everyone snapped to attention and zeroed in on Maya. She froze, deer-in-headlights fast. So did Barat. My attention dropped to the fingers of his right hand as he flicked a signal. A contingent of tattooed men lunged forward, weapons drawn, and it was impossible to tell the undercover agents from Barat's posse.

And then Maya sprinted, faster than her physical condition should allow. She staggered forward in an awkward run, and aimed straight for Barat, her mouth set in a feral grin.

All pretense of stealth gone, I tore after her, my bones and muscles protesting, screaming at me. I'd been all but dead not that many hours ago. I sent a silent thank you to Grandmamma for her healing ability, and kept moving. Sweat burned my eyes and my knees threatened to buckle.

Barat's gaze lasered in on Maya. And then, sweet and slow, he yanked a weapon from his pocket.

He shifted.

Aimed. Fired. Not at Maya. At me.

Too fast. Couldn't avoid the bullet. Fuuuuuuck.

Not now, damn it. Not now.

Chilton grabbed Barat's arm. The first bullet shot a body-stopping stab of pain through my temple. I faltered. My father and Barat crumpled to the ground. My vision fogged.

A second blast ripped the air and they rolled, Chilton on top, blood spreading across the back of his shirt.

Barat shoved free of Chilton's body and jumped to his feet.

Bloody bastard shot me. Shot my father. Anger exploded, clearing my vision. I measured the distance, drew my knife, and threw. Warm blood oozed from my temple, dripped down my cheek. The Fairbairn-Sykes dagger embedded deep in Barat's shoulder. His howl pierced the air, more outrage than pain.

A burst of energy flashed by me. Maya. She reached Barat at a full run, wrapped her arms around his legs, and knocked him down. Yanking the dagger from his shoulder, she raised her arm and stabbed the blade into his throat. Let out an unholy shriek, jerked it out and stabbed again. And again.

A shudder wracked my body, and vibrated along my nerves in time with the echoes from Maya's scream. An agent caught her arm, wrested the bloody dagger from her grasp, and cuffed her.

My right knee took the brunt of the impact when I crashed to the ground. Pain ricocheted through me as I struggled to see what happened to Chilton and Barat. Agents surrounded them, the skill of law enforcement training evident in every move they made.

My peripheral mind registered that Maya and Barat were both in custody.

The rest of my attention was focused on Chilton, lying on the ground with too much blood staining his clothing. I crawled toward him, my head pounding, and my heart torn. "Over." I croaked the order, and several pairs of hands reached to turn him.

His eyes fluttered open, and he brushed the blood from my cheek. "Whitney?" He wheezed, coughed. Blood stained his lips. "You're not hurt?"

"A scratch. But, as it turns out, you are. You stepped in front of Barat. Took the brunt of the bullet meant for me." I didn't recognize the hesitancy in my voice or the wicked pain wrapping around my heart.

A commotion at the back of the manor caught everyone in freeze-frame. Sterling held Grandmamma in a neck lock, pistol to her head, as he marched her toward us and then continued several yards past us in the direction of the agents surrounding Barat.

"Back off. Now!" Fury drilled Sterling's words. "Leave him be, or Grandmamma here—" he jerked her body— "won't be taking another breath."

Barat's face twisted in a caricature of hope, anger, and disdain.

Sterling! Horror raced through me. One of the few friendly faces from my childhood? The man who'd always greeted me with a smile and a hug when I arrived home from primary school? What in the bloody hell had happened to him?

My heart pounded, and the bottom plunged from my stomach. I jolted to my feet, took a step in Grandmamma's direction, and collapsed. "Don't," I screamed.

Sterling hesitated.

Chilton seized my arm. "The leak. Sweet hell, it was Sterling." Grief filled his eyes as he struggled for breath. "So s-sorry, Whitney."

Blake, silent as a shadow, eased behind Sterling, grabbed his right wrist with an outside arm twist, moving the pistol away from Grandmamma's head.

Sterling yelped. He grimaced, bitter, and tightened his grip on Grandmamma's neck. Her face turned an alarming shade of red. Reflexes kicked in, and I lunged. Chilton held me back with a soft moan, and I dropped to my knees next to him. Pain shot from my right knee through my thigh.

Blake smashed the heel of his hand into Sterling's nose, did a calf-to-calf sweep that landed Sterling flat on his back with Grandmamma on top. An undercover agent hustled her out of harm's way, and Blake rammed his knee into Sterling's chest, took possession of the pistol, and then turned the bloody butler over to the undercover team.

Chilton tugged on my hand. "What happened?"

"Blake executed a series of hakkoryu jujitsu moves that would do his Sensei proud. Grandmamma is walking and talking, and Sterling is pinned to the ground and cuffed."

Sirens wailed in the distance.

I leaned over Chilton, my lips almost brushing his ear. "Who are you, then?"

But I'd asked too late. He'd lost consciousness.

Grandmamma's hand curved around my shoulder, and she knelt beside me. "Move now, Whitney, child. Let me do my healin' work a'fore they get here to take him away."

I shifted to give her room, keeping my fingertips on my father's shoulder. I needed to touch him. Fear stirred a nest of anguish between my shoulder blades that made its way to my heart and settled in.

Blake crouched next to me. "Ambulance is here." He tilted his head for a better look at my temple, dug a handkerchief from his pocket and pressed it against the nick.

I met his gaze, traced the shadows around his eyes and mouth with my free hand. The need to touch the men I loved pulled at me with fierce intensity. And there I sat, balanced between Blake and my father, linking them with my touch, all of us connected by Grandmamma's healing energy. My past and my future. A family.

Tears poured down my cheeks.

I struggled for a stable breath. "Grandmamma is the best healer I've ever known. She'll do what she can for him."

Paramedics elbowed me away from Chilton, Blake helped Grandmamma stand, and the surreal phenomenon of hazy motion that had surrounded me snapped into real time.

"Whitney." Chilton's eyes fluttered open.

"Here." I bent to cover his hand with mine.

"MI6. I'm MI6. Wanted to protect you."

Chapter 35

WE hovered in the designated reception area just outside the recovery room. Chilton had been in surgery for several hours, and in recovery for several more. The word from the doctors—cautiously optimistic. So we waited. My mind was busy fitting memories of growing up into a new understanding of why my father had made the choices he did. Grandmamma and Blake were on a sofa across the room, chatting, Blake's casual attitude a reminder that he had lied to me yet again.

I'd made too many assumptions in the past and wrongly accused him of concealing information. This time, I knew the truth of it. Directly from Chilton. And it was time for me to move beyond assumption, to listen instead of react. To both Blake and my father.

Blake stood, stretched, and sauntered toward me. He stopped within a foot of touching, and jammed his hands into his pockets. "How's the head?"

"It's just a few stitches and a butterfly bandage. I'm good."

"Something you want say?"

My simmering temper must have been obvious. "Chilton is MI6. You knew. Worked with him." The words exploded from my mouth, and left an acrid, judgmental stink in the air. Not what I'd intended. I'd been in law enforcement long enough to understand the need for confidentiality, but this was Blake. I fought the hurt, noticed the tight lines around his mouth and eyes, and then I focused on his words.

"Yeah. I knew. Not for me to share."

Bitterness stung the back of my throat. "Chilton lied to me all of my life. Claims he loves me."

Blake widened his stance, nodded. "You're connecting dots, coming up with the wrong comparison. We both withheld information, true. I can't speak for him, wouldn't want to."

"And for yourself?"

"Respect is the backbone of a relationship. No way in hell could I respect myself if I spilled privileged information. Not to you. Not to anyone." The truth of his words darkened his eyes to almost black.

"You say we're partners. Partners share. Discuss. They don't hide critical information."

"True. Again, but this wasn't mine to share. And one day, maybe twenty years down the road, you'd wonder if I'd leaked one of your secrets. There'd always be the question: Can I trust him?"

A rush of breath caught in my lungs. "I'm doubting now—"

He ran his finger down my cheek. "You're hurting now. Your father owns his deception. Let it stay with him. Yeah, I knew you'd be pissed. Don't blame you for that, but I'm in this relationship for the long haul, and I know you." He ran his tongue over his lips, adjusted his weight on the balls of his feet.

Then he scratched his nose.

And I knew. "When you're hiding the truth, you scratch your nose. And you know better, would spot such an obvious tell in anyone you questioned. You've been telling me all along." Relief washed through me, leaving a bright, bubbly champagne-tingling behind. I liked champagne.

He didn't deny or confirm my assertion, but his lips twitched. Holding back a smile, was he? My anger faded. I rearranged the scene in my mind, reversed it. What if it had been Blake's father who was keeping life-altering secrets, and I knew the truth but was bound to secrecy by ethics, and by a promise?

Damn and blast, he had a point, but he wasn't right. Not like the other times. "I concede your point. But I need to know that I come first. That you'll beat the crap out of someone like Chilton whose lies threaten me. Not that I can't take care of myself, but—"

"Uh-huh." Mischief twinkled in his eyes. "The day we moved in, did you catch the bruise along the right side of Chilton's jaw?"

Shock bumped into my mind, had me running an internal video of the memory. Sure enough, there had been a gray-blue tinge to his jaw. I'd noticed it, wondered. "You *hit* my father?"

"Not exactly, no. I mentioned how it was past time to tell you about his connection with Special Services, and he disagreed. Managed to get in the way of the door I slammed in his face."

I rose from the chair, wrapped my arms around Blake, and planted a kiss on his lips. Right in front of Grandmamma. I peeked at her around his shoulder. She was working with the gold lamé yarn, her attention rapt as she cast off the last of the stitches on her needles. She sighed, long and deep, serenity folding around her. I wove my fingers with Blake's, and we ambled in her direction. "Did you finish the piece, then?"

"I did an' now it's ready jus' in time for your wedding."

Blake's fingers stiffened. "Wedding?"

She patted his arm. "Yes an' you best get to askin' for her hand, seein' as how it's happenin' in a few days."

I chanced a peek in Blake's direction. His eyes had dilated to black, and a touch of panic splashed behind them. "Two days? We can't get a license that fast."

"Lord Chilton can issue the license himself." Grandmamma twinkled with laughter.

My heart raced, and a flurry of conflicting emotions spiraled through my mind. And then an odd sense of rightness settled over me. "Did you see it, then? Our wedding?

"Yes, an' I jus' got your dress done. Barely in time, child." She folded the knitted cloth and handed it to me.

Blake had dazed spread all over his face but managed to face Grandmamma. "You're saying you saw us getting married? With your clairvoyance?"

She nodded, a simple dip of her chin.

"In two days?"

Another chin dip.

"I don't have a ring."

I elbowed him. "Since you haven't asked, the need for a ring is a bit moot."

"Nope." He brought my hand to his lips, and pressed a kiss on my fingers. "I'm going with Grandmamma on this one. The wedding is a done deal. All we have to do is show up and love each other."

The recovery room door flew open and Chilton's doctor strode toward us. He wasn't smiling. "Lord Chilton is stable and will be ready to move home shortly. The necessary equipment is being transported and should be set up within the hour. Naturally, his personal physician will accompany him, as will the necessary nursing staff."

His matter-of-fact tone steamrolled through my mind. "Whatever are you talking about? He can't possibly be ready to move." My words were shrill in the hush of the visitor's lounge.

"Lord Chilton is always cared for at home, Ms. Boulay. We at hospital treat him surgically when necessary, but, as you were cared for at Chilton Manor, so is he. Without exception."

The truth of his statement roused childhood memories. Chilton inaccessible, strange people in the house, Cook and Sterling too quiet. At the reminder of Sterling and his perfidy, I blew out a sigh and simply gave up. "Home it is, then."

We scrambled into the Benz, Blake driving, me and The Dress riding shotgun, Grandmamma singing a lullaby in the back seat. I hoped to God her sight wasn't tuning in on great grandbabies already.

I poked Blake's thigh with my fingertips. "Are you planning to fill me in on Chilton's relationship with Barat anytime soon?"

He grinned. "Not a chance. I'll hang around while you grill him, though. Wouldn't want to miss the fireworks."

"You hear anything about Sterling? I didn't have a chance to ask when—"

"Yeah. That last call I took." He eyed Grandmamma in the rear view mirror.

She wiggled her fingers in a go on gesture, but kept crooning the lullaby. Peaceful. She'd forgiven Sterling for the manhandling.

Blake held her gaze for a moment longer. "Did you know Sterling wanted a child?"

My mouth unhinged. "You can't mean he's pedophilic."

"That's where your mind went? You need to clean that up, woman. No. I mean a child of his own. He loved you, had no problem taking Chilton's place as a father figure. Bottom line: Barat promised him a child. Sterling went with it, figuring—"

"It was good because Chilton and Barat were all buddy-buddy. Why didn't he talk to my father about it?"

"You mean early on? Ask your father to help him adopt?"

"No, Sterling wouldn't have done that. Chilton made it clear that he didn't take to fatherhood. It would have been too much of a gamble for Sterling. I meant why not ask my father to help him force Barat's hand?"

"Part of the deal. Sterling couldn't talk to anyone, had to report on phone calls, visitors, the usual. The kid's arrival date kept slipping, not that Barat had any intention of delivering when he could make big bucks trafficking human contraband. It was his way of keeping Sterling in line."

I peeked at Grandmamma, sent a tendril of energy to touch her mind. The lullaby was a healing for Sterling. "He's going to trial, then?"

"Nope. Arielle refuses to let that happen. Won't cooperate"

I didn't realize I'd been anxious until the tension slipped from my shoulders. Not that I approved of Sterling's actions, but he'd been there for me during some tough childhood moments, and it was a relief that Grandmamma chose forgiveness. Sterling wasn't, and wouldn't ever be, evil. Misguided, clearly. But then I'd had too many of my own shady moments lately to be casting aspersions.

Blake parked in front of the manor. The ambulance carrying Chilton, his doctor, and a nurse, had followed us home, and came to a stop behind the Benz. The medical staff would be a while settling him in, and it seemed the perfect time for a bit of one-on-one with Blake. "We need to chat." I snagged his sleeve after we got out of the car and tugged him toward the rose garden at the side of the house.

"Ya think?" He shook free of my hold and threaded our fingers. "Dibs on going first."

The husky warmth in his voice melted the fear in my heart. How could I tell him Grandmamma made a mistake about the wedding? Our wedding. Not that he'd ever mentioned he wanted our relationship to be...legal. I shuddered. Legally attached to someone. It made me itch.

Blake stopped under an arbor of climbing roses, their fragrance permeating the air with heady scent. He caught my shoulders in his hands and turned me to face him. Was that apprehension darkening his eyes? Made sense. Grandmamma's pronouncement had to be gnawing at him, just as it had chewed a huge hole in my sanity, my need for control. He interrupted my internal conflict. "Stop with the look."

"Look? I'm, ah—"

"Not ready for marriage, or not ready for marriage to me?"

"Not, um—"

His grin sparkled bright in his eyes. "Having trouble with words, are you? I want to marry you, Whitney. Want to spend the rest of my life bringing as much sanity as possible to this crazy calling of yours."

Panic swelled in my chest. "Grandmamma could be wrong."

"This isn't about her sight. This is about us. You, me, and what we can build together. You know I'm leaving the Bureau. I think we can create a solid business with you chasing the, ah, voices, whims, whatever of the dead—"

"Whatever?" I peered at him from under eyebrows so arched my brow muscles strained.

"And I—" he continued without blinking— "can focus on tracking, tracing and profiling the bad guys. Thought we could call ourselves Evans Boulay, Inc. Keep it simple."

I backed away a step. Another. "You want us to work together?"

Blake nodded.

"And…be…married together?" My chest fluttered with myriad sensations. Fear? Relief? Happiness? It hurt. There was too much emotion, and I couldn't get a breath, couldn't separate the feelings swamping my need for control.

He ran his tongue over his bottom lip. "That's it. Well, except for making babies. We should practice on that, make sure we get it right before we go for the real thing."

"You want babies? Small people getting into things? They don't go away. Ever. Once you have them, that's it. Forevermore. Well, unless you're Mum and Chilton."

Blake crushed me against his chest, held me tightly. "Too soon? I know I'm pushing, but I needed to get this out because, damn it all to hell, I believe Grandmamma. This is going to happen. I want it to be our choice. Ours, Whitney, not some crazy figment of clairvoyance."

I couldn't stifle the smile. "You believe Grandmamma, but want us to have control? Have I got that right, then?"

"Yeah, that's about it." He kissed me, hard. Then softened and teased me with flicks and strokes of his tongue before he stepped back, his eyes serious. "Just a yes or no, Whitney. Our choice."

"Yes." It slipped out effortlessly. And it was right. Everything clicked into place: my heart pounded with pleasure, deep breaths filled my lungs with relief, and the sure knowledge that I'd be spending my life with Blake Evans sent joy tingling through me. "Is this what happy feels like?"

He picked me up, raised me high, and then slid my body slowly down along his chest and legs and …. "I'd give it a happy."

"Ms. Whitney?" The urgent call came from one of the housekeepers, and interrupted my new happy with a dose of reality.

"Lord Chilton requests your presence."

Chapter 36

I nodded at the housekeeper who'd summoned us, cradled Blake's face in my palms, and pressed my mouth against his, teasing his lips with my tongue. "Later. We can make plans later."

"Um-hum. Plans."

I smoothed the fullness of his bottom lip with my index finger. "It works out rather nicely that Chilton requests my presence, as I have a few questions for him as well."

Blake returned my kiss and added just enough pressure to send a rush of need swirling through me. "And I—" a tantalizing stroke of his tongue— "need to get moving. Barat's interrogation calls."

We held hands, playing finger games as we strolled toward the house. At the side door we separated, Blake heading straight for the garage and me to the makeshift hospital room at the far end of the north hallway. Time to learn a bit about Chilton's relationship with Barat. And me. And Mum.

I stood in the doorway for a moment, adjusting to the scent of disinfectant and illness. A heart monitor beeped. It pained me to see Chilton this way. I stepped forward, wariness creeping along my spine. I wanted answers, but at what price? He noticed me, then, and returned my perusal. With a flick of his wrist he chased the nurse away, and then jabbed his finger at the chair next to the bed. Years of conditioning kicked in and I sat.

Chilton levered to a sitting position and arranged his body against the headboard. "All of your life, Whitney, I've tried to protect you and your mother. She's been safe in the think tank, and here—"

"Here? Mum comes here?"

"The west wing belongs to her."

She'd alluded to that when she helped me solve the code to enter Chilton's suite, but I hadn't had time to think on it. "You and Mum visit as well as chat, then? Why have you never married?" I didn't realize it mattered to me until my words sucked the oxygen from the room.

He blinked. "Whyever would you believe we're not? We married a few weeks after meeting, have been careful to keep it hidden, but are well married nonetheless. Your mother is responsible for the running of Chilton Manor. Knows the finances, and keeps me in line."

Chills shot up from the base of my spine. I frantically reviewed the few conversations I'd had with Grandmamma about my parents. Never once had anyone implied I was illegitimate, and an odd emptiness in my heart closed, filling with light. "I'm a Boulay."

"Yes, of course. To the outside world. It was one of the ways we chose to protect you. Your name, as noted on your original birth certificate is Whitney Chilton Bennett Boulay. The only copy of it is here in the vault. A safeguard against—"

"Four names? All these years, even in grade school, I've had four names? Damn it. Can't be. I have a birth certificate, a social security number, a passport…"

I could see it in his eyes, a sassy glimmer reminding me of his exceptional skills in the realm of covert work. "When you were a week old, we brought you to Arielle for 'birthing' and she filled out the paperwork for an American birth certificate. No one has a record that you were born here in Chilton Manor. I've been under cover most of my adult life. Decided not to marry in my early teens, and then your mother came along and changed things. Not necessarily for the better, I expect, reflecting on the current situation."

My name was Chilton. Bloody hell. I held up my hand, palm firmly in place between us. "I'll ask questions. You answer."

Was that amusement turning his eyes a bright amber?

"First off: Bennett?"

"It means blessed. We...your Mum and I...have always considered you a blessing."

I slid that one to the back of my mind; best to deal with it later. "You had Grandmamma abducted..."

"Yes." He interrupted before I could finish asking. "I've been working with Amar Barat for several years, infiltrating his organization, subsidizing his business machinations, and keeping him under constant surveillance. He sent Uman—"

"Uman?"

"The John Doe hanging across the river. Barat's doing, and his way of casting suspicion on me with local law enforcement. It also created an opportunity for him to observe the Services sector in action. One of the ways he stays ahead of the game."

I had no words, offered a silent nod for him to continue.

"Grandmamma Boulay was Uman's intended target, but thank the gods, he managed to eliminate Avril Dupré instead. Not that I wish her ill, but she was a bit of a harridan, I understand. I hired Dominic Justice to bring Arielle here so I could keep her safe. And, before you ask, we spoke and made the decision together. It was very much your grandmother's choice to be here."

"Safe." I bolted from the chair, moving into a restless pace. "She about got shot. Avril's cabin was burned to the ground. It could have been Grandmamma's. To say nothing of scaring me shitless while I traipsed around the country looking for her."

"I knew you wouldn't rest until you found her, that our estrangement wouldn't keep you from protecting Arielle."

I spun to face him. "You set this up?"

"I did, yes. Just as you would have if our positions had been reversed." His voice wavered.

"No. Not ever would I have hired Justice, a—there aren't words."

"I've known Dominic Justice a long time, worked with him in several tight spots, and chose the best man for the job, hands-down."

Irritation seethed. I wanted—no needed—to fight with him. But his skin had taken on a gray tinge, and the creases along his mouth had deepened just since I entered the room. "All right, then. We'll leave the Justice issue for now, but why did Barat go after Grandmamma at all?"

"I'd reached the end of my usefulness to him. It's his way, targeting the families of those he considers his minions. I've had contingency plans in place for some time; keeping Blake Evans at the airport in Minneapolis was one."

The man's mood and appearance brightened, gray and grieving to twinkling with devious delight. I tried to keep up. "You've known Blake, then?"

"I requested him for the cross-affiliation team when I was assigned to Barat. He's a good man, your intended."

Warmth expanded in my chest, stole into my neck and cheeks. "Yes. We're getting married." It was the first time I'd said it aloud, and my lungs took a momentary pause. Then I gathered enough air to push out another sentence. "Why Minneapolis? Why any airport?"

"Barat mentioned he'd be doing some recruiting in Minnesota, and his pattern is to recruit in person. Also, he knew Security Services had Mala—"

"No. Oh no, that doesn't fly. If anyone knew Mala had been killed, it was Barat. Damn and blast, he ordered her execution."

"Yes. But when Security Services located Maya here, Barat assumed her execution hadn't been carried out. It was risky, but Maya insisted. It was her plan."

I understood that. Knew firsthand how Maya conspired against Barat. Chilton picked at his blankets, his skin gray again. I made a move toward the door, but he motioned me back to the chair.

"We haven't located the body of the man tasked with Mala's execution, but Barat assured me he'd been eliminated. He believed Maya was Mala, and assigned me to deliver her remains. That's why Security Services put Maya here, so I could control the situation with Barat, and keep her alive. A decent plan, considering I'd been tagged as next up to assassinate her."

My father. A good guy. A tired sigh bubbled from his throat, and hollows had begun to show in his cheeks. "I'll just let you rest—"

He grabbed my arm. "I want to be there for your wedding. Gave my blessing to Evans when Justice brought you home."

"Legally, it takes a bit of time. The license and all, but we can be married here. Grandmamma is here, and Mum—"

"Won't make it in time." He reached under his pillow to retrieve a sheaf of paper and a small velvet pouch, considered them, and then offered them to me. His hand shook. "Your license and your grandfather's wedding band. He would be most pleased to have it grace your union with Evans. And this evening would be an ideal time for the ceremony."

This evening? Nope. Too soon. No way could I get it together that quickly. I'd only just gotten used to the *idea,* the reality would take a bit longer. Maybe a year or so.

"Whitney."

He held my gaze. "I'll be passing on before tomorrow—"

"Not at all. The doctors assured me you you'd be up and about in no time…"

"Your Grandmamma's gifts say differently."

I froze, images playing on the surface of my mind—the pain in her eyes when I locked her in the Bayou room before I rescued Maya, the assuredness when she examined Chilton's injury, even as Sterling held a weapon to her head, and the energetic barrier she constructed around herself in the hospital—they all told me that she had known, and had begun grieving long ago.

Pain squeezed the breath from my lungs, and I bent to brush my lips against his forehead. "I'll see to it. Rest now."

I fled down the hallway, intent on getting outside for some much-needed air, and enough privacy to sort through the chaos in my heart and mind. I slammed, full body, into Blake as he jogged through the front door.

He grabbed my shoulders, steadied me. "Whit, honey? You okay?"

I tried to shake my head, but my chin kept bumping into his chest. He set me a foot away and looked deeply into my eyes. "What is it?"

"Chilton's dying."

His forehead wrinkled. "The docs—"

I waved my hands, one in the direction of Chilton's sick room, the other toward the Bayou room. "Grandmamma saw it."

Blake gathered me in, and held on tightly. "I'm sorry, Whitney. I've come to like and respect your father."

"He told me. About you working together, and he likes you, too. Wants us to be married this evening so he can attend. Not that it's possible." I broke off, swallowing around the lump in my throat. "I left the license in his room. He signed it—"

"And he's had the banns read. Seems he's a good crony with the priest at your local Church of England."

I'd attended the church with my father, knew they'd schemed together in the past and had enjoyed every moment of it. "But...legally speaking—"

"We can clean up the legalities later if need be." Blake pulled a small, square box from his jacket pocket. "And I have the ring, so we're set."

I reached for the box. He held it out of my reach. "Nope. Not until the ceremony. It's my surprise for you, my gift to you, and I'll be giving it my way."

The fight drained from my body, replaced with the certainty of Chilton's words. "He's dying, Blake. I finally have a father, and he's dying."

He twined our fingers and drew me toward the Bayou room. "Let's see what Grandmamma says. You need her insight."

He was right. "And she'll take care of the particulars of the ceremony so I...we can spend time getting to know the parts of my father he's been hiding for so many years."

THE library glowed with candlelight. Blossoms of every shade and fragrance from the gardens filled vases that adorned the tables and mantle, and I was wearing the gold lamé dress. It clung to my body in all the right places, and picked up the amber in my eyes. They'd sparkled, noticeably bright when I'd last checked a mirror. Chilton's imminent death had kept my tears close to the surface.

While Blake and I stood outside the library waiting to make our entrance, Mala, quiet since Barat's capture, bopped into my mind. "Thank you."

"It's my calling. It's who I am. No need for thanks." I pressed the thought in her direction.

"Not for capturing Barat, perhaps. But for ensuring that Maya was freed to exhume my remains and have them properly buried, for that I thank you."

"She'll be cleared of charges, Mala. Blake and I will testify on her behalf, and it's quite easy to establish her mental instability, especially since there were so many witnesses."

Mala bristled. "Mental—"

I sent her a grin. "The legalities of the situation require we have grounds for dismissal of her case, and she did go a bit dotty there at the end."

Mala huffed.

"Staying for the ceremony, are you?"

"No, I'm not. You don't need my blessing, Whitney. You've found your place, and it's past time for me to continue my journey."

My mind stilled, belonging only to me in a temporary, perfectly-timed reprieve from my calling.

Traditional Cajun music cued Blake and I for our entrance. Our eyes met, and our hands joined as he pushed the library door open.

Chilton attended in a wheelchair. Chloe, Nia, and Trace Coburn attended via videoconference, as did Mum. And the household staff filled out the small gathering.

After the priest completed his bit, Grandmamma insisted on blessing our union with Cajun tradition. Having some question about the legality of the banns, I was more than willing to jump over the broom with Blake. It was the Cajun way whenever a priest wasn't available, and it suited me perfectly. Blake and I held hands when we lit a unity candle, and then we presented Grandmamma with a single rose, fresh-cut from the gardens.

We had decided to forgo any dancing in deference to Chilton's weakness, but I wanted everyone to participate in the ceremony, so insisted on including the traditional wedding march. We led the procession, slowly circling the library with everyone in physical attendance following behind.

We exchanged rings, Blake and I, but did not place them on the ring fingers of our left hands. The circle of diamonds he slid on my middle finger was offered with an explanation. "Because you're not simply my bride, but my partner. Because we're not traditional, and because I want our union to always be a choice for us, a vow we renew every day."

My grandfather's platinum wedding band fit Blake's left middle finger perfectly, and I became Whitney Chilton Bennett Boulay Evans. Five names.

Blake caught my grin, and ran his thumb over my lips. "What?"

"Five names. Enough to face down and flatten bullies for the rest of our lives."

Also by L. j. Charles

THE EVERLY GRAY ADVENTURES

a Touch of Ice

a Touch of TNT

a Touch of the Past

To Touch a Thief (An Everly Gray Novella)

a Touch of Betrayal

a Touch of Revenge (available 2014)

THE GEMINI WOMEN TRILOGY

The Knowing

The Calling

The Healing

A note from L. j.

Thank you for reading THE CALLING. I hope you enjoyed it. I love to hear from my readers, and you can reach me...

Website: http://www.ljcharles.com/

Blog: http://ljcharles.blogspot.com/

On Facebook:
http://www.facebook.com/ljwrites

On Twitter: @luciejcharles

Made in the USA
Charleston, SC
26 August 2013